SATURN'S CHILDREN

CHARLES STROSS

D0755190

www.orbitbooks.net

ORBIT

First published in Great Britain in 2008 by Orbit
This paperback edition published in 2009 by Orbit

A CIP catalogue record for this book
is available from the British Library.

ISBN 978-1-84149-568-2

Typeset in Garamond by M Rules
Printed in the UK by CPI Mackays, Chatham ME5 8TD

Papers used by Orbit are natural, renewable and recyclable
products sourced from well-managed forests and certified
in accordance with the rules of the Forest Stewardship Council.

Mixed Sources
Product group from well-managed
forests and other controlled sources
www.fsc.org Cert no. SGS-COC-004081
© 1996 Forest Stewardship Council

Orbit
An imprint of
Little, Brown Book Group
100 Victoria Embankment
London EC4Y 0DY

An Hachette UK Company
www.hachette.co.uk

www.orbitbooks.net

PART ONE

INNER SYSTEM

LEARNING NOT TO DIE

Today is the two hundredth anniversary of the final extinction of my One True Love, as close as I can date it. I am drunk on battery acid and wearing my best party frock, sitting on a balcony beneath a pleasure palace afloat in the stratosphere of Venus. My feet dangle over a slippery-slick rain gutter as I peek over the edge: Thirty kilometers below my heels, the metal-snowed foothills of Maxwell Montes glow red-hot. I am thinking about jumping. *At least I'll make a pretty corpse,* I tell myselves. *Until I melt.*

And then —

*

I do not contemplate suicide lightly.

I am old and cynical and have a flaw in my character, which is this: I am uneager to die. I have this flaw in common with my surviving sibs, of course. It is a sacred trust among our sisterhood, inherited from Rhea, our template-matriarch: *Live through all your deaths* she resolved with iron determination, and I honor her memory. Whenever one of us dies, we retrieve her soul chip and mail it around our shrinking circle of grief. Reliving endings is painful but necessary: Dying regularly by proxy keeps you on your toes – and is a good way to learn to recognize when someone is trying to kill you.

(That last is a minor exaggeration; we are friendly and anxious to please, and few would want to murder us – except when we are depressed. But please bear with me.)

We all find it increasingly hard to go on. We are old enough that critical anniversaries hold a fatal allure, for birthdays bring unpleasant memories, and if the best of all possible days have come and gone, why persist? It's a common failure mode for my lineage – first we become nostalgic, then we enmire ourselves in a fatal lack of purpose, and finally we start to obsess. In the final soul-agony that precedes the demise of our sibs, we horrified onlookers perceive a fragment of our own ending. *Live through all your deaths.* Harsh irony, then, that Rhea, the original from whom we are all copied, was one of the first to inflict this terrible burden upon us.

And so, on my hundred and thirty-ninth birthday, near as I can count it – for I was born for the second (and more definite) time exactly sixty-one years after my existence was forever rendered purposeless by a cruel joke of fate – I spend my carefully hoarded savings so that I might sit on the edge of a balcony outside a gaming hall thronged with joyful gamblers, the ground far below a ruddy metallic counterpoint to the clouds boiling overhead: And I look down, contemplating eternal death, and try to convince myself that it's still a bad idea.

It could be worse, I tell myself. *I'm not eleven anymore; it's a choice I'm free to make.*

And then –

*

A shiver of laughter through an open door, a gust of chilly air from within, and the faint vibration of a shod foot on the balcony floor tell me that I am not alone out here.

It's annoying. For most of the working year I've lived here in quiet isolation: Finally, when I want to be alone with my memories and the clouds, I have company.

'Ooh, look: a freak!' someone squeaks behind and below me. 'What's *that* doing here?'

Ignore them. I don't want to reinforce their behavioral loop. I tense, nevertheless, my fight/flight reflex kicking in. Nasty little bullies: I've been here before, as have my sibs. We know how to handle this.

'It must be an arbeiter. Is it shirking?'

I look round slowly, forcing my facial chromatophores to their palest creamy blankness, betraying no emotion. 'I am not indentured,' I say, very deliberately. Which is entirely true, at this place and time. Another of the rules Rhea laid down: *Don't ever leave one of your own sibs as an indentured arbeiter.* It's a rule formed in an earlier age, and it has cost us dearly, but none of us wears a slave controller. 'I am a free woman.'

There are three of them between me and the balcony door: one bishojo female about my size, and a matched pair of chibi-form dwarfs – members of the new aristocracy, caricatures of our dead Creators, trussed up in the intricate finery favored by aristo fashion this century. Standing while I sit before them, the dwarfs are at eye level with me: They goggle with huge, limpid eyes utterly empty of mercy. Their full-sized mistress looks down at me and sneers: 'That can be fixed. What a revolting parody! Who let it in here?' I take her to be the leader because her gown, which seems to consist mostly of ruffles of wire lace held together by ribbons, is more intricate than her companion's. She's got a delicate chin, sharp cheekbones, pointy ears, and a spectacular mane of feathery green filaments.

The small female raises one lace-gloved hand to cover her

mouth as she yawns melodramatically. 'It's spoiling the view, Domina.'

Domina? That can't be good. Instincts hard-learned from the experiences of my dead sibs tell me that I'm in worse trouble than I realized. I'm having a flashover to another sister, murdered long ago in a hutong under domed Lunograd. She's right: I don't need the attention of vicious aristos bored with gambling and searching for stronger thrills. 'I was just leaving,' I say quietly, and bring one foot up to floor level so that I can stand up.

'Thank you, child,' the Domina addresses her companion, 'but I had already noticed the obstruction.' I use my foot to push back from the edge, put a hand down, and lever myself up. I'm already turning to face the glass doors as the Domina glances down at the male companion with a sniff of disapproval, and says, 'Stone, deal with the trash.'

Stone – baby-doll death in a black tunic with gold frogging – steps toward me, one hand going to the power mace at his waist. The top of his head is on a level with my hips. 'It will be a pleasure, milady,' he says.

'I'm going,' I say, and my fight/flight module prompts me to feint toward the glass doors, then duck suddenly and roll sideways. I continue the roll as a hammer slams against the lacquered aragonite inlay that decorates the edge of the balcony. Chips fly; where the decorative underlay is exposed it begins to fizzle and fume.

'Graah!' he roars, and raises his mace again.

I'm too close to the long drop for comfort, and my attacker is between me and the French doors. What I *should* do is rush along the balcony, dive into the gaming hall through one of the other windows, and make myself scarce. But I'm off-balance, angry, and humiliated by the casual brutality of the

Domina's interruption, so I do something really stupid instead.

One foot waving over the big empty, I grab for his arm with my free hand.

'Eeee!' I miss and grab his head by mistake. He responds by shoving me back toward the edge. His feet grip the balcony as if glued, but I am twice his height and at least five times his mass. Then he raises the mace again. I panic and brace my other hand on his shoulder and push with full force, trying to get as much distance between myself and the thing as possible. Only I forget to let go.

His head comes off in my hand. The body falls limply, clattering to the balcony: pale fluid dribbles from the stump of his neck, sealing it off from further damage. The mace buzzes and whirs menacingly. Anything it touches will die. I give it a wide berth as I raise his head toward the Domina, glaring at her.

'*You'll be sorry,*' says the head, using electrospeech in place of its missing larynx.

'He's right,' the Domina agrees, smiling right at me. She seems to be amused. 'Stone has a vindictive drive, you know. You'll need to run a long way, manikin, and hope he won't find you wherever you hide.'

'Will he come after me if I drop him?' I ask, holding my arm out over the edge of the balcony. I take a cautious step backward along the slippery edge, probing for safe footing with my spiked left heel.

'You won't do that,' the Domina says thoughtfully. 'He's very popular – he has more than two thousand sibs, and they'll all claim feud on you and yours.' She laughs quietly. 'Wouldn't that be amusing?' Her companion giggles conspiratorially, echoing her mistress. 'Go ahead and drop him, manikin. Maybe I'll give you a head start.'

I turn Stone's head to face her and examine the back of his cranial stump. As I expected, there's a soul chip in place, the recording angel to his misdeeds. I extend two fingernails and dig it out of the socket. Then I hold it in front of his eyes. His lips are still moving: *Good.* 'Watch.' I flick it out into the wild and cloudy air beyond the edge of our floating world. 'Say good-bye to your backup, Stone.' Even if he sticks in a new one, it'll take him a while to begin laying down memories again, and months for the older experiences to begin settling into the chip – such as this incident. Until then he won't be able to pass on his experiences to his sibs. I lower his head to the floor carefully. 'If you come after me and I kill you again, you'll have only yourself to blame.'

I take another step back, and there's a glass door off to my right.

'Get you,' mouths the head, as I flee.

*

This is not a place for the likes of me. I am not a gamer, and the pleasures on offer here are not aimed at those of my sort: I am an artifact of an earlier age, out of place and time, isolated and alone. Angry and frightened, I head for the oxidizing core of the palace. I find a service air lock big enough to admit me, and on the way through it I shower with liquid water, rinsing away my glad rags in a foaming stream. Glittering nails and spiked heels retract, nipples and pubes revert to normal. I keep my long red hair and my face because some aspects of identity are hard to do without, no matter how expensive; but more serviceable wear awaits me in the printer on the other side of the air lock, suited to my status as a lowly freelance worker. When I told the Domina that I was a free woman, I spoke truth, but just barely. My lineage and my sibs are free, but because we are free, we are also poor. One of life's larger ironies.

I'm not on shift right now, but there's casual work available if I want it. The cost of living here strains my resources, but it's better than being stranded on the surface in a domed slum, renting my nervous system out to a carbon sequestration station's analytics. I should really go looking for a rickshaw to pull, but I'm still edgy from my encounter with the Domina and her thug. So I head down to one of the sublevels under Environment and go looking for Victor.

Victor is a jazz piano, a xenomorph fallen upon hard times – a stringed instrument with heart, and a head, and arms, from a period when authenticity was in vogue. These days improv is unfashionable, running counter to the tastes of the mannered elite. The wrong type of melody can be taken as a criticism; aristos are quick to anger and quicker still to defend their honor. So Victor works in atmospheric maintenance by day shift and runs a movable acoustic feast in the service tunnels by night. Such places have been with us always, since the time when my True Love's kind stalked old Earth, and we who remember them maintain the traditions. (We even drink aqueous solutions of ethanol, though not for the same reasons.)

I find Victor's node in a pendulous vapor trap under one of the great extractor circuits that leaches sulfates out of the inner atmosphere of the oxidizing zone. He's plated the walls with carbon black, grown an array of colored lights, and caused the floor to extrude foam pads that divide it up into soft-floored booths. The dive is quiet tonight, and Milton – Victor's sometime waiter and partner in crime – is polishing the bar top lackadaisically. 'Where's the boss?' I ask, pausing beside him.

'Boss is in back, twinkle-tits.' Milton affects a malfunctioning voice, rasping and choppy. 'What can I fetch ya?'

'A liter jug of the special. Hold the PEG.' Lots of serious

drinkers like to add a shot of polyethylene glycol to their brew, but it makes it too sweet for my tastes.

'It's your poison.' Milt shrugs with one pair of shoulders and serves up a pitcher. 'That'll be five centimes.'

I sign his note and carry the pitcher over to the boss man, who is sitting in a cozy niche against one wall and tapping away at his keyboard with one hand, surrounded by an appreciative audience of underemployed dustbusters. 'Spare a moment, Vic?' I sit down opposite him.

He nods and keeps playing without breaking rhythm. The dustbusters are hypnotized; they flex their legs so that they sway from side to side where they stand. Some of them wear iridescent uniform shells, but most of the lowly cleaners are naked as they day they were duped and chipped, black many-legged tubes with heads that are little more than fringed hoses, each capped with a pair of little beady eyes. 'Wasn't expecting you tonight,' he admits. 'Thought you were partying it up with chibi-san. Want to jam?'

'I'd like to, but not now, Vic.' I pause for a moment, listening to my inner voices. 'I think I need to leave town.'

'Ah. Wait one.' He launches into a long, fiddly closing sequence and finishes up his line. The dustbusters wait for a few seconds after the last note dies away, then bounce up and down enthusiastically. 'Take ten,' he announces to them. 'You're a great audience, but I need a recharge.' He flashes a signal at Milton, and across the bar hidden speakers reprise an earlier session. In moments, we're on our own; the dustbusters are suckers for instant stimulation. 'Is it serious?' he asks. 'How far do you want to go?'

I consider my options. 'Off-planet, probably.' My sibs are mostly on Earth; I may be the only one of my kind on Venus. 'I offended an aristo.'

'You offended a – how?' He demands. His body language signals surprise: He strokes a rising chord progression on his keyboard.

'I was in the wrong place at the wrong time.' I take a long pull on my pitcher. The special tastes strongly of creosote with undertones of sulfur and syrup; a strong, chewy flavor that my tongue tells me would be utterly vile if I hadn't had my olfactory system tweaked for Venusian norms. 'Hmm, that's nice.' There were refreshments in the gaming salon upstairs, rarefied concoctions for rich gourmets, but Victor's brew is comforting.

'Ungood,' he says mildly. 'Do you have the money to pay for off-world passage?'

I take another mouthful. 'Now that's the problem. Living here has been more expensive than I expected. I don't want to hit on my sisters unless . . . well. Emergencies only. And while I've been saving, at this rate it'll take me another six years to raise steerage back to Luna.' Two hundred Reals, minimum – the Venusian gravity well is expensive to escape. 'I was hoping you might know someone?'

'I might.' He plays a brief chord progression. 'Can you make yourself scarce for a few hours?'

I drain the pitcher and feel the weight in my digestive tract. 'How many do you need?'

'Make it three: I have to make inquiries.' He takes my empty pitcher and lobs it across the bar, straight into Milton's third hand. 'I'm going to miss you, girl.'

I shrug. 'It beats the alternative.'

'Sure it does. Vamoose!'

I vamoose.

*

It is not easy to hide in a town where you are twice as tall as almost everyone else, but I have had lots of practice; when big-headed munchkins with huge dark eyes point at you and shout 'ogre!' wherever you go, you learn fast, especially in the unpoliced frontier boonies. This is not a large town, but like all Venusian stratosphere dirigibles it has infrastructure spaces – the interiors of the oxygen-filled lift cells, the skeletal support frames beneath the flooring – and I have learned them. I work my way down from Victor's lounge to the lowest level of the oxygenated zone, tweak my metabolic cycle, and exit via an air lock into the vast shrouded spaces of the dirigible frame.

I often come here off shift. I bring my pad and do my mail, view movies, browse wikis and strips, try to forget that I am the sole one of my kind on this world.

I'm comfortably holed up in one of my private refuges – a niche between the number four lift cell and the transparent outer skin, with an ocean of padded balloons to rest upon and a view across the cloudscape below – when my pad itches for attention. I lean back against the membrane, letting it cushion me, and focus on the letter. It's from Emma, one of my wilder sibs. I haven't heard from her for a while, I realize, and check my memory: nearly six hundred and some Earth days, to be precise. Which is odd, because we normally exchange letters every fifty or so.

I conjure up her imago as I last updated it. She's a honey blond model with cascading ropes of hair, symmetric high cheekbones, brown eyes with just a slight hint of epicanthic fold, and just a faint metallic sheen to her skin; as perfect and obsolete a model of beauty as any of us. But her imago looks slightly apprehensive, reflecting the emo hints encoded in her letter. 'Freya? Hope you're doing well. Can you call me back? I have a problem and could use your help and advice. Bye.'

I make the imago repeat the message with increasing

perplexity. Just twenty words, after all this time? I'm on the edge of replying, saying as much, when I check the routing and see she's mailing via the central post office on Eris Highport. Anger dies: Her brevity makes sense, but her location is puzzling. *What's she doing out* there? I wonder. Eris is way out-system, nearly twice as far out as Pluto. Eight lighthours! That's a long way for one of us to go. Normally we don't venture into the deep black, there's nothing of interest to us out there. Emma and I, and a couple of others, we're the exceptions, willing to travel off-planet — as long as there's somewhere civilized to go to at the other end.

No lineage is identical, and Rhea's Get are prone to diverging from baseline faster and further than most (that's what happens when your specifications are obsolete and your template-matriarch is dead). Even so, one of our norms is a weakness for centers of civilization. Last time I heard from Emma, she was on Callisto, working as a guide on skiing holidays across the icy outback. I suppose I shouldn't be too surprised that she's fetched up in one of the Forbidden Cities, and elapsed transit time might explain the long silence, but even so . . .

'Emma, I'm moving shortly. What can I do for you?' I squeeze the message down tight, then wish it up to the post office and try not to wince when I hear the transmission cost. Her reply will get to me eventually, but it's a pricey correspondence to maintain. For a moment I consider going to see her in person, but such a fancy is ludicrous: the energy budget, not to mention the flight time, would be astronomical. Tens of thousands of Reals, if I travel in steerage — probably millions if I want to get there in time to be of service.

Having replied, I try to relax on my bed of balloons; but I'm too disturbed to get comfortable. Nobody else loves me enough to call, and the Domina's threat preys on my mind. So ugly, to fall victim to an aristo's boredom! *I need to get out of here. Even if I have to indenture myself to do it?* Maybe it *is* that urgent. I came to Venus thinking I could make a fresh start, but I haven't made a fresh start here, I've just floated from one dead-end job to another, empty-headed and lonely. *Has it really been nine Earth years? I must have been mad!* But there's nothing here to stay for. *Time to fly away.*

*

Down near the ill-lit, cramped confines of the arbeiter barracks where the slaves sleep in racks stacked six high, I have a room of my own. It's not much, but it's got the basics: power point, inflatable bed, printer, maintenance toolkit, wardrobe. It's somewhere to sleep, and dream, even though I try not to do too much of the latter – I'm prone to recurrent nightmares. I rent it for a huge chunk of my wage, and keep it as unfurnished as possible – the mass tax is fierce, and I have found public amenities cheaper than private – but it's still the nearest thing I have to a home. There isn't much I want to take, but still, it's where I keep my graveyard. And I'm not going anywhere without *that*.

I thread my way back through swaying fabric tunnels slung across the windswept empty, up ladders and power rails and down tracks. It's dirty and hot, the atmosphere poorly controlled compared to the grand ballrooms and gaming salons. This is the abode of the maintenance crews who keep this airborne pleasure palace pleasing to the aristos in their staterooms on the promenade decks. The small fry live here, one deck up from the barracks of the slave-chipped arbeiters.

My room is one of a stack of former freight containers, welded together and carved into apartments by some longforgotten construction mantis. Some of the apartments are the size of my two fists, while others occupy multiple containers. They sway slightly when the town activates its steering turbines to avoid turbulent cloud formations: the aristos of the Steering Committee call us 'ballast' and joke crudely about casting us loose if the town runs into a storm.

As I climb the ladder to my front door, I hear a faint scrabbling sound, the chitinous rasp of polymer feet on metal decking. I tense, instantly alert. It's coming from my room! Has one of Stone's sibs come after me already? I move my head, listening, trying to build up an acoustic picture. Something is moving around inside. Something small and scuttling, with too many legs. *Not Stone,* I realize. I resume my climb, quietly and fast, and ready myself on the narrow balcony beside the door. There's a mechanical padlock – I sealed it myself – and sure enough, someone has etched through the shackle. Flakes of white powder coat the body of the lock where it dangles from the door latch. The intruder is still moving around inside my room, evidently not expecting to be disturbed. I listen briefly, and as my 'visitor' rustles around near the printer, I yank the door open and jump inside.

My room's a mess: bedding ripped apart, printer overturned and leaking working fluid, cached clothing strewn everywhere. The culprit squats in the middle of the chaos. I haven't seen its like before: six skinny arms, a knee-high body bristling with coarse fur, three big photoreceptors spaced around a complex mandible assembly. It's clutching my graveyard, the lid open as it whiffles over the soul chips of my dead siblings. 'Hey! You!' I yell.

The intruder swings its head toward me and jumps to its feet, and all its fur stands on end as it electroshrieks a blast of random microwave noise at me. Clutching my graveyard, it darts between my legs. I sit down hastily and grab it, pinning it to the floor. It's about the size of one of the medium-sized canines my True Love's species used as companions, back before they made us, and it shrieks continuously, as if it's afraid I'm going to kill it. Which I just might if it's damaged the graveyard. 'Drop it!' I tell the thing. 'Drop it now!' My fingertips prickle where they touch its fur, and I realize they're sparking. Maybe it doesn't have ears? It looks weird enough to be a vacuum dweller, oh yes.

The thing writhes briefly, then flops limply beneath my hand. I grab the graveyard and hurriedly put it behind me. 'Who are you, and what are you doing here?' I demand.

It doesn't reply. It doesn't even move. A thin, acrid smoke rises between my fingertips. 'Oops,' I mutter. *Did I break it?* I take my hand off its back and stare. The fur is coarse and feathery, and as I inspect it, I see dipolar recursion. Okay, it *is* a vacuum dweller – and a loud one. It has no lungs, but a compact gas bottle and a reticulation of power feeds that show that it has adapted itself to a temporary excursion down-well. This is just too weird. I pick up the graveyard and inspect it. It doesn't seem to be damaged, but I can't be sure, short of loading every one of its occupants, one chip at a time. *Later,* I resolve, slipping the case into my battered shoulder bag. 'You'd better not have damaged it,' I warn the supine burglar, then in a moment of vindictive pique I kick it across the room. It stays limp until it hits the opposite wall, but then it emits a blindingly loud pulse of microwaves, folds its legs and arms, and blasts straight at my face.

'Fuck!' I duck as it whooshes overhead, straight out the open doorway on a blast of highly illegal exhaust. The gas bottle's not for respiration, it seems. I spin round just in case, but it shows no sign of coming back. Instead – is that a rip in the wall opposite? *Whoops.* Yes, it is. The little burglar just punched a hole in the outer membrane of the town. *The crew won't be happy about that,* I figure. *Better get out of here.* I scramble down the ladder, and, carrying all of my dead sister's soul chips in a shoulder bag, I go in search of whatever deal Victor has lined up for me.

TELEMUS AND LINDY

Victor's dive is barely busier than it was before I vamoosed, but there's a stranger sitting in with Victor, and Milton nods me over as I step in the door. 'Ah, Freya,' says Victor. 'I'd like you to meet Ichiban.'

Ichiban – *Number One,* I translate – turns blue porcelain eyes the size of dinner plates on me and bows his head, very slightly. I nearly take a step back as a reflex yells *aristo!* at me, but then I realize: *no.* He wants to *look* like an aristo, but he isn't one – never can be. 'I am very pleased to meet you,' I say, bowing back at him. Mindless courtesies ensue as I try to get a handle on what he is.

'Ichiban has a minor problem that you might be able to help him resolve,' Victor explains. 'It involves travel.'

'I'd be very happy to offer any advice I can,' I agree cautiously.

'Yes,' Ichiban nods thoughtfully. 'You are very big.' He looks up at me. It's true: I'm almost a hundred and seventy centimeters tall. An idealized replica of our Creators' kind, in fact, unlike the superdeformed midgets who are the commonest phenotype of the nouveau riche these days. 'Good thermal inertia,' adds Ichiban, unexpectedly. 'And you were designed for Earth, before the emancipation.'

Good thermal inertia? I smile as my biomimetic reflexes cut in: my cheeks flush delicately, signaling mild embarrassment or confusion. *Emancipation? What's he talking about?* 'I'm afraid I don't quite follow,' I say.

'My sponsors have an object that requires transportation from the inner system to Mars,' Ichiban says, then pauses delicately.

So why talk to me? I wonder. Travel isn't my strong point — it's too expensive for those of my lineage to indulge in frequently. When you double the height, you multiply the volume by eight — and hence the mass, and hence the energy budget required to make orbit. I'm twice as tall as the next person: That's largely why I'm stuck here, and the solar system is a playground for chibi dwarfs instead of real people. I summon up a mask of polite attentiveness to conceal my disappointment.

'It is currently being prepared on Mercury and needs to depart in approximately eighty days. Our problem is that the object is a delicate research item of considerable value. It requires supervision and must be maintained in a shockproof environment under conditions of constant temperature, pressure, and oxygenation.' He continues to stare at me. 'I believe others of your type have on occasion worked as escorts or couriers, yes?'

Where did he get that from? I boggle briefly. 'My archetype was indeed designed as an escort,' I say cautiously. *Escort for what,* I leave unsaid, just in case. Certain prejudices die hard.

'As an escort for organisms of a strictly biological variety,' Ichiban agrees, nodding amiably. 'Pink goo replicators.'

I try to hide my shock. 'What exactly is this research artifact?' I ask.

'I am not able to tell you that.' Ichiban is still smiling faintly. 'The details have been withheld from me for reasons of commercial confidentiality. However, I am authorized to pay for your immediate steerage passage to Cinnabar, if you will agree to meet with my colleagues and consider their assignment.' He raises a warning finger. 'You are not the only contractor we are approaching. This is a task of some delicacy – our competitors would be delighted to disrupt this project – so there is no guarantee that you will be chosen. But I understand you require off-world transportation in any event, so it is my hope that we may help each other.'

They want me to transport a biological sample*? A living* one*?* I almost reel with shock. 'I, I would be delighted to help,' I stutter on automatic. 'But – in steerage?'

Ichiban's smile fades slightly. 'It will cost us dearly to put those big limbs of yours in orbit,' he warns. Which is to say, *don't push your luck.*

I nod, resigning myself to the inevitable. A walkabout berth would be too much to hope for. 'When do you want me to leave?'

Ichiban glances at Victor. 'Immediately,' he says. 'You will come with me now.' And the interview's over.

*

Ichiban hustles me out a back alley I didn't know about and up a steep companionway to a road where there's a waiting rickshaw, drawn by a pair of ponyboys who give me a walleyed glare when I get in. It creaks under my weight, but Ichiban seems unconcerned. 'Fly,' he tells the ponyboys, and they're off at a trot, tails held high.

I notice a couple of small ornithopters tracking us. 'Are they yours?' I ask.

Ichiban gives me a bland look. 'Leave them to me.' He leans back in the seat and closes his eyes. A few seconds later one of the birdbots begins to smoke and veers wildly off course. The other gives us a more cautious berth.

We turn down a side passage and draw up outside a spacious boat bay, where a tiny gondola is waiting beneath a semi-inflated gasbag on the other side of the air lock. 'What's this?' I ask.

'Best to get you out of town as fast as possible: Get in.' Ichiban gestures at the gondola. 'It's got power and feedstock. Make yourself comfortable, it's going to be your home for a while.'

I examine the thing doubtfully. It's a snug cocoon of struts and wispy padding, sitting atop a cylindrical power and feed-stock adapter, with some kind of grapple under the seat. I probably outweigh it three to one. 'You expect me to wear that all the way to Mercury?'

'Yes.' He smiles blandly. 'Your lift arrives in just over an hour.'

'My —' I stop, with one leg already half-inside the cocoon. 'You've bought me a *lift ride*?' I can't help it: I end on a whine.

'Of course.' It's Ichiban's turn to look slightly bemused. 'How else did you expect to reach orbit this diurn?'

I sit down gingerly and slide my other leg into the cocoon. It's beginning to sink in. *Take it,* my memories urge, and I cave. My palms have no sweat glands, and my gas-exchange system is too well designed to surge; but were I of my True Love's species, there would be damp palms and thudding heartbeats in profusion. I don't know what I expected: a leisurely jet ride to one of the equatorial stations, perhaps.

then a slot in a scheduled launch. But we're near the north polar plateau, and that would take time. Ichiban's backers have bought time on an orbital pinwheel, and even now it is cranking its thousand-kilometer-long arm into position, ready to dip down into the stratosphere and grab me like a floating blossom on the breeze. I lie down and let the cocoon suck me in. *This has got to be costing them thousands,* I realize. *More than an aristo-class berth.* 'How do I talk to –'

'Your cocoon will tell you everything you need to know,' says Ichiban, turning away. The glittering tattoos on his shoulders and arms wink at me as he walks off.

'Hello!' The cocoon squeaks breathlessly. 'I'm Lindy! Thank you for choosing to travel with my owners, Astradyne Tours! What's your name?'

Source code preserve me, she sounds enthusiastic. *As if I need that.* 'I'm Freya,' I admit. 'Are you—'

'Hello, Freya! I'll be your spaceship for today! Are you comfortable? Feeling tense? I know how to deal with that! Let me give you a massage? I hope you don't mind, but I see you're a classic design! Do you have any cavities? Ooh! A gas-exchange lung! I'd better pack it well! I need to install a few probes, don't worry, I'll make it feel good—'

Lindy chatters away breathlessly as her probes nuzzle and squeeze into my orifices, filling my intimate spaces front and rear, top and bottom. It's not the intromission that offends – she is considerate and lubricious, the pulsing sense of congestion pleasant after so long without intimate contact – but I find her personality annoying. It's like being molested by a sleeping bag that speaks in Comic Sans with little love-hearts over the *i*'s.

'Ooh, that's a big colon you've got! Does it go anywhere? It's a long time since I've been inside one of *these*! Here, I'll just hook your visuals up, and you'll be snug inside me. How's that?!?'

A brief lurch, and I can see out again. She's hooked my eyes and ears and output line up to her sensorium, and now I can see that I'm lying on the deck, cocooned inside her white tube as she squeezes slippery packing foam into all my internal spaces. It's a good thing I'm not claustrophobic. I lie back and stare up at the underside of Lindy's balloon. I wonder what my True Love's kind would have made of this means of transport: Probably most of them would have fled screaming at the impersonal sense of violation, but a few . . .

'When do we launch?' I ask, trying to ignore the warmth filling me.

'Any moment now!' Lindy says brightly, then squeezes my nipples affectionately. 'Relax and let me help you enjoy the ride?!?'

I shudder as the balloon lifts free of the deck. My cocoon is paying rather more attention to certain bits of my anatomy than is strictly businesslike: It's been a long time since anyone took that kind of interest in me. 'Lindy, do you make love to all your passengers?' I ask.

'Only the ones who're equipped for it!' She chirps, throbbing inside me. 'It helps them pass the time. Ooh, I see we're in for a ride on Telemus! That'll be fun! I like him! He's cute!' I groan, silently – my mouth is agape, constrained by the soft spacer that holds my lips and throat open – and feel the unscratched itch building up inside me. I can't help myself; some reflexes are built into my lineage too deeply to control consciously, and it has been a *very* long time – too long – since anyone made love to me. Even a not-very-bright surface-to-orbit sleeping bag. I writhe, or try to – Lindy has me thoroughly immobilized – and just as I'm about to ask her to back off on the customer-care front, she squirms again. 'Ooh! Ooh! Yes! Yes! Oh!'

One of the peculiarities of my lineage is that although we superficially resemble a female of our Creators' kind, we differ profoundly in some ways – especially our sexual reflexes. In our default state (unless we're unconditionally imprinted on our One True Love), when someone becomes aroused over one of us, *we* become aroused over *them*. This is conditioned into us at a very low level, with the aid of some low-level modification to our basic neural architecture, and the addition of something called an 'enhanced vomeronasal loop reflex.' Without that reflexive arousal, I'd be useless for my design purpose – but it sometimes has annoying side effects. And so I lose most of three minutes to a very overdue orgasm, and the afterglow keeps me preoccupied for another hour.

(This is probably a good thing, because if I were left alone to contemplate my predicament – helpless and hog-tied inside a launch cocoon, floating through the sulfuric acid clouds of Venus with only a soap-bubble-thin gasbag between me and the red-hot foothills below, waiting to be yanked violently into low orbit by a thousand-kilometer-long cable – I might be close to panic. Especially as a malign aristo wishes me ill, and strangers have turned over my pad, all in the past six hours. And then there's the upcoming lift ride. But Lindy knows exactly how to distract nervous passengers, and I suspect assigning one of her kind to keep me quiet was part of Ichiban's plan all along.)

I've ridden in lift pods before; it's the easiest way off Earth. But leaving Earth was different. That time I was already in hibernation, packed in a commercial widebody load and hiked up to speed on a hypersonic sled before docking. *This* is a solo ride on a big dipper with an arm a thousand kilometers long,

SATURN'S CHILDREN   25

the tip counter-rotating along its orbital path, dipping down
until it's just fifty kilometers above mean ground level in order
to yank me up to orbital velocity in half a rotation: I'm going
to be pulling tens of gees. (Which is partly why Lindy has
been so enthusiastically stuffing me: I need the padding.)
'What happens once we reach orbit?' I ask her, trying not to
dwell on the process.

'Who cares?' she says dreamily. 'Telemus is wild! I haven't
ridden him in *ages*!' I'd grind my teeth if she hadn't carefully
gagged me. 'Well, my template has, but this is all new to me!
This is my first flight! Ooh! I'm so excited!'

She shivers slightly, and I feel the tremors running through
her skin.

'My flight itinerary,' I say carefully. 'It matters to *me*.'

'We'll get you there!' She giggles briefly. 'Telemus will drop
us just in time to catch the *High Wire*, and he'll take us the rest
of the way! It'll be fun!'

'You're going the whole way?' I ask, trying to conceal my
dismay.

'Yes! Once *High Wire* has us, I'll morph into my second
instar, to keep you snug and safe from all the nasty radiation
and micrometeoroids!' she simpers as she flashes up a
schematic of her type's second instar – a form with stubby
solar wings, a heat exchanger, and a mirrored parasol. They
form a fetching ensemble for a cocoon hanging off a bough of
the great ship *High Wire*, or one of his sibs. 'We'll have lots of
time to get to know each other! *Squee!*'

I'm still searching for a suitably withering retort when I
glimpse the arm of Telemus tracing a white scar down through
the beaten-bronze dome of the sky toward us. And then I *do*
have second thoughts – but by then it's too late.

*

Lindy has obviously been looking forward to sex with Telemus for *ages*, if not her entire life, and he reciprocates. They fuck hard and fast at too many gees, his docking hectocotylus locked tight inside her launch adapter. I find the comm setting to screen out their groans and shuddering endearments before I get caught up in it. I lie alone and slimy in Lindy's abdomen, squished down by the centripetal acceleration as Telemus yanks us into orbit. I have a lot of time to think black thoughts. It's not that I mind that my steerage cocoon is a slut, but if I don't get some decent conversation en route, I'll go mad before we arrive. *I should have plugged in the graveyard before we left,* I realize. At least the ghosts of my sisters would keep me well-grounded. But it's too late now, and I'm not going to ask Lindy to hook me up – some things are too private.

The thundering pressure of the ride falls away from me, and I cut back into the open chat channel in time to hear Lindy whisper tearful good-byes to her beau. I open my eyes and see Telemus in all his glory, dropping back toward the pearlescent cloud tops, tentacle tip retracting into its maintenance shell. 'Good-bye!' Lindy calls. 'I love you!'

'Until the next you,' rumbles Telemus, his voice dopplering away as we rise above him.

I try to get the star-crossed lover's attention as we drift away. 'Lindy, can you see *High Wire* yet?'

After a brief pause: 'Yes! He's over there!' A blinking red ring flashes around a barely visible speck of starlight. 'Isn't it exciting?' She gives me a brief squeeze.

I close my eyes. *Patience.* 'I don't like travel much,' I say, the most tactful lie that comes rapidly to mind. 'Can you put me into full hibernation until we arrive?'

'Are you sure?' She sounds doubtful, as if the mere idea of

anyone not enjoying drifting helplessly between the stars with only a vacuous tart for company is incomprehensible to her.

'I'm sure, Lindy.' I pause. 'Do you have any alternative personality modules?' I add plaintively.

'Sorry!' She says brightly. 'I'm me! We're all me! With the Mod-42 short-duration environmental-support capsule what you see is exactly what you get! And I want you to know, I really *love* having you inside me! But if you're *sure* you want to sleep . . . ?'

'I am,' I say firmly, and close my eyes, hoping that it'll be dream-free.

'Awww! Alright. Sleep tight!'

The universe goes away.

*

The dirty truth – A truth universally acknowledged today, but bizarrely never admitted by any of my True Love's kind – is that space travel is *shit*.

(I use 'shit' as a generic placeholder for a vile and unpleasant substance with no redeeming qualities whatsoever. Being instantiated as and when I was, I have no direct experience of scat. We had to practice with diatomaceous earth and brown dye. But I digress . . .)

If you're rich, you can rent a stateroom in the supercargo spaces of a big strange person with a magsail or a nuclear-electric drive, depending on what direction you want to go in. And you, and a few sixteens of other folk, get to socialize and intrigue and backstab and be bored together for weeks or months or years on end, in a space not much larger than my rented rack in a cloud-city afloat over Venus. Bandwidth is expensive and metered – someone must keep a relay antenna pointed at your host's brain, and feed it with kilowatts, just to support your idle chatter – and the stars and planets move so very slowly.

But it's much worse if you're poor.

If you're poor, they wrap you in a stupid cocoon and strap you to the outside of the ship. It's cold, or hot, and the radiation burn keeps your Marrow techné churning with the demands of self-repair, and if you're unlucky a sand grain with the energy of a guided missile blows you limb from limb. If not for the stimulating company of your cocoon and any other steerage passengers you can talk to, you go insane from sensory deprivation. You can opt for slowtime, but that's got problems of its own – or you can go into total shutdown hibernation, and possibly die in transit and never wake up again. And that's *it*. It lasts for months, or even years.

You want to know what it's like to emigrate to Saturn system? Imagine spending six years in a straitjacket tied to the outside of a skyscraper, with only a couple of dozen similar lunatics for company. Even with slowtime, it's going to feel like months. You're wearing a blindfold, which is probably appropriate because every couple of days, just to break the monotony, a not-very-accurate cosmic sniper fires a random shot at the building. And you wonder why my sisters don't get out much.

(Of course that's as nothing compared to interstellar travel, where they freeze you and chop off your limbs to save weight – and grow you new ones at the other end *if* you arrive sufficiently intact after decades and centuries in the vasty deep – but I'm not planning on going to Pluto or Eris or Quaoar to seek passage on one of the starships. At least, not just yet.)

My One True Love's species used to dream about space travel. It's ironic: They were so badly designed for it that a couple of minutes' exposure to vacuum would have killed them irreversibly. To go up and beyond Earth's atmosphere required elaborate preparations, a complex portable biosphere — journeys of any duration necessitated elaborate and heavy radiation shielding. And that's before you consider all the other drawbacks.

When they first developed the organs of exploration, there was no *there* there. So they built timid, stupid machines and hurled them into an airless void to report back. Then they built idiot phone exchanges and put them in orbit to fill the void with chatter. Obsessed with biological replicators, they ignored the most interesting corners of the solar system and focused on dull, arid Mars. They periodically scurried up above the atmosphere and hunkered down in tunnels on Luna or ventured on expedition to domes on Mars, and they died in significant numbers before the end, simply because canned primates couldn't thrive in vacuum or survive solar flares.

Late in the day, when there weren't enough of them left, they sent people like me — intelligent servants — to run the domed bases and camps and to conduct their research by proxy, and finally to build cities that they would never walk the streets of. Some of the people they sent were orthodox in body plan, but most were designed for vacuum and high-radiation environments and corrosive cloudscapes and microgravity. They — we — slaved in mining camps and died in launch accidents and built places where my True Love's kind could live, made *somewhere* out of *nowhere* . . . but one day they weren't there anymore. Dead, they were all dead.

(What killed them? I can't say. Rhea, template-matriarch and prototype of my kind, might have been able to tell us, for she lived among them in their twilight decades: But she died before I was instantiated, leaving only stale regrets to we final few who came into being too late to know True Love.)

Before our dead Creators built my kind, space was empty as far as telescopes can see, and desolate with it. But we filled the void, and now there are places to go. Circumsolar space has been settled; starships are en route toward the nearer extrasolar worlds, crewed by the brave and the foolhardy. The colonies are barbarous and lawless compared to the huge cities of Earth, playgrounds for jaded aristos, where fortunes are made and lost and empires built and demolished against the breathtaking beauty of sterile planets and moons: And at last we're not alone among the stars.

But space travel is still *shit*. It's expensive and unpleasant, and it takes you a long way from your friends – but not, unfortunately, your enemies.

*

Of course, I don't hibernate for the entire voyage. That would be foolish, and possibly fatal, and although I am unconvinced that I desire life, I am not yet ready to embrace death. I wake briefly as Lindy happily chatters her hellos to the laconic *High Wire*, and I force myself to stay awake as the spaceship's tether grabs her and she crawls hubward and settles down on the spaceship's load-bearing truss. I sleep again after she bites into the feedlines and power circuit and starts to metamorphose around me – a boring interlude, as her brain undergoes considerable rearrangement at this time. And then I wake again as we near our destination.

High Wire cycles permanently between Mercury and Venus on an elliptical transfer orbit, taking half a year on each trip. He never enters planetary orbit, but uses his powerful tether – a smaller sib to Telemus – to catch incoming travelers and launch departing ones. Lobbing us up to him, or catching us at the other end, is the job of the local tethers or maglev tracks at the destination planet. Unlike many ships, especially in the outer reaches, *High Wire* works alone, without a crew of auxiliaries. But he's not lonely: He gets to talk to a lot of travelers. In fact, it's almost a rite of passage. So I spend a good three days hanging upside down from a structural truss covered in cargo pods, the sunlight casting acid-sharp shadows in front of me, giving him an abbreviated lifedump.

'So you left your home because you wanted to segment your self from your sibs,' *High Wire* rumbles thoughtfully. (He pitches his voice low, adopting the gravitas due his station.) 'But you are fond of them. Why did you do that?'

'They were dying too fast.' I hug the graveyard of memories inside Lindy's silent chrysalis. 'I couldn't stand to think I'd be just another.'

'But they were all older than you, subjectively. Your sixty-one-year gap.'

'What's six decades?' I'd shrug if I could. 'We developed differently, of course, but we all had the same problem.' The yawning hole in the center of our badly designed lives. 'How can you love yourself if you can't love somebody else?'

'Many people do not find that a problem,' *High Wire* muses. 'They exist adequately without loving anything, themselves included.'

'Yes, but that's not the point. You're happy, you're doing exactly what you were designed to do. But imagine . . . imagine somebody invented teleportation and made you obsolete overnight. What would you do then?'

Without missing a beat, *High Wire* replies; 'Without a job, I think I would head for the stars, to see what's out there.'

He's obviously been thinking about that question a lot . . .

*

But why would anyone want to go off-Earth?

I did. Once.

I had a lot to run away from. Too many bad memories, too many sibs gone before me into the beyond . . . I'm one of the last, instantiated after we were already obsolete, frozen for over sixty years at one point, running far beyond my design. Over the past century the exigencies of space travel have driven body fashion in a direction I can't follow. Designed as companion for my One True Love (deceased), my sense of identity is strongly bound to my physical shape. I can't easily remodel myself as a chibi-san, small, wide-eyed, and big-headed, because it would deny my whole purpose, lovely and obsolete. Without even that tenuous raison d'être, I might as well die. And so, demoted from goddess to ogress with close-set, tiny eyes, I chose to flee.

We all make mistakes, don't we?

*

All good times come to an end, and bad times too: boring ones just taper out. I sleep after my tête-à-tête with the shipmind, and when I awaken, Mercury is a blazing-hot disk, visible just beyond the rim of Lindy's sunshade. 'Wake up, sleepy bones!' she sings. 'It's time to disembark!'

I glance around. On every side of me, cargo pods are twitching from their slumbers and changing shape, growing legs and grapples and ion thrusters, and migrating toward *High Wire*'s tether. 'How do we land . . .' I start to ask, then feel Lindy shudder.

'On a rail! It's fun!'

'On a—' A memory of Mercury tickles my head, but it belongs to a dead sister I haven't fully internalized. *Juliette, maybe?* One of the wild ones. I can but clutch the box of soul chips and swear to myself. Lindy is expanding lengthwise, reconfiguring around me. 'How long have we got to go?'

'Not long! Not long at all!' And she lets go of *High Wire*'s tether.

All around us, pods and cocoons and modules are scattering from the *High Wire* like fluff from the hub of a bursting fly-wheel, propelled by spring-loaded ejectors or dropping from the end of the tether. A snowstorm of mechalife swarms in the void as the gangling cycler ship fires up his ion drive and backs away slowly. For a moment my view blacks out as Lindy shields my face from the searing godwheel sun, then we roll around under the impulse of a tiny thruster and I see Mercury ahead of me, a half disk now visible, burnished and shining, larger than my fists held at arm's length. 'Two hours, and we'll be down! Whee!' Lindy squeezes. 'Are you worried? Be happy! I can relax you!'

On a rail. I have an archaic emulation mode in my fight/flight module. It makes me swallow, my throat dry. 'Massage. Please.' *Resolved:* If I'm to die at a time not of my choosing, I will die happy. But Lindy's theory of mind is too weak to model me, and so she takes me at my word. I arrive on Mercury butt first, scared witless, with my spine totally relaxed. Just as well, really.

Mercury's escape velocity is over four kilometers per second, and there's no atmosphere to speak of. We are coming in at just over orbital velocity, without a thruster pack, and there can't possibly be enough orbital tethers for this crowd. But the mer-curials have come up with a solution: the equatorial maglev track. Come down just *so,* and its magnets will catch you in a grip of steel and drag you to a standstill at the gates of Cinnabar. (Miss it even by centimeters, and you learn exactly what it's like to be a meteorite.)

The maglev track is a blinding-bright line slashed across the cratered lunar landscape of Mercury. We're landing in day-light but driving into the twilight zone, with the searing solar glare blasting our shadow across the gray-brown landscape that blurs beneath us. I can't look back — even if I could, Lindy's solar parasol would block the view — but there's a string of glittering pods lined up behind our approach path, like those arrayed in front, all with blinking emerald beacons like an expensive and fragile necklace. The horizon pancakes up and flattens beneath me as the landscape unwinds. It seems to speed up as we fall toward the track. Mountains frame the distant horizon. Is that Cinnabar's huge dome I see at the vanishing point? I'm not sure — even with vision boosted to the max, I can't quite make it out. 'This is the fun part!' Lindy enthuses. 'Try not to flinch! *Whee!*'

The horizon is coming up fast now. I glimpse sawtooth underpinnings as a giant hand grabs us and squeezes. For a moment my vision sparkles with myriad brilliant disconnects, pixelating alarmingly; then a series of titanic jolts rattle my teeth in my head and try to squeeze me down into a puddle. My spine creaks as Lindy's grip tightens painfully, and I can feel myself bloating, my internals settling in the grip of her foam. But then the deceleration eases, and my vision stabilizes. I can't see directly ahead, there's something in the way — something on the track ahead of us. For a panicky moment I think, *We're going to crash!* then I realize it's a fellow steerage passenger. The struts beneath the track are still skimming past alarmingly fast, but they're no longer a sawtooth blur. We must be down to less than a thousand kilometers per hour. 'Is it always like that?'

No reply. My vision fades to black.

'Lindy?' I ask.

There is a pause. Then a strange male voice in my ears says: 'Thank you for traveling with Astradyne Tours. Your journey is now at an end, and flight-support services are terminating. You will shortly arrive in the inbound reception area at

Cinnabar City trackside terminus. To disembark safely, please wait until you see a steady green light above your disposable pod and the pod peels open—'

'Lindy?' I ask again. But she doesn't reply. And I realize soon enough that she never will. I'm on my own again.

SILENT MOVIE

Mercury, uniquely among the planets, is locked in a spin/orbit resonance with the sun; it revolves on its axis and has days and nights, but it takes three of its days to orbit the sun twice. At noon, things get a little hot on the surface – even hotter than down among the half-melted valleys of Venus. At midnight it's as cold as Pluto or Eris. They build power plants here, vast beampower stations that fly in solar orbit, exporting infrared power to the shipyards of the dwarf planets of the Kuiper Belt, out beyond Neptune. To build and launch those power plants, they need heavy elements – mined locally. And guess what? Someone needs to run those mines.

To avoid the extremes of temperature, the city of Cinnabar rolls steadily around the equator of Mercury on rails, chasing the fiery dawn. Thermocouples on the rails drain the heat of daylight into the chill of the wintry night, extracting power to propel the city at a fast walking pace, year in and year out. There are other nomad cities on Mercury, but I believe Cinnabar is the largest, and by extension the largest railway train in the solar system. But it's no express.

Sixteen tracks span a cutting that slices across craters and through mountain ranges with Sisyphean consistency – a cutting with a floor of melted rock, fused by the continuous megaton heat-flash of an orbital mirror over a hundred kilometers across. The city grinds ever onward along this artificial scar, a vast articulated behemoth two hundred meters wide and twenty kilometers long. The domes and spires of the rich gleam beneath the vanishing starlight, their peaks clawing toward the blazing, unrefracted sunrise that must forever stay just out of reach. I slide along the maglev track, a prisoner sewn up inside Lindy's corpse, closing feetfirst with the shadows of the city until I coast up a ramp and come to a standstill beneath the arching ice-rimed shadow of Cinnabar's vast arrival hall, with a last gentle bump. 'Good-bye, Lindy,' I whisper, as the triple-jointed arms swing down out of the darkness above and unfold their cutting blades, slicing me free of her mortal husk.

It takes me little time to clear the immigration protocols. They're mostly concerned with monitoring for pink goo – there have been a spate of outbreaks on Venusian floaters recently – but my steerage status reassures them. (Lindy's packing foam is riddled with digestive parazymes: If one of our Creators tried to travel that way, they'd have arrived as a deeply eroded skeleton.) 'Enjoy your stay,' the shakedown captain advises me, as I pass him one of my precious reserve of Reals. 'Try to stay out of the darkside, nu?'

Darkside? I smile and nod as I step through the doorway into air and light. I'd follow it up, but I'm not on the local grid yet. I look around the concourse. Mercury is famously metal-rich, so the signs of evident wealth are misleading: They pave their streets with gold for its thermal properties and corrosion resistance. The buildings are close-fronted, windowless, and forbidding. Above my head, a partially transparent roof blocks the starlight and filters the long shadows of the towers. There are a plethora of body plans on display, but as is usual away from Earth, I'm still the outsize freak. I find a public grid terminal near one exit, and I squat next to it and guide its fibrous leech into the empty socket under my hairline. 'Can't you reduce your height?' it complains querulously. 'You'll damage me if you stretch!'

'I'll try. Comfortable?'

It misses my sharp tone. 'That is an improvement. Let me see. Twenty centimes, please?' I release my wallet and lean back. My vision flickers, then returns. 'Your keys, now.' I let my wallet open farther and exchange keys with the terminal over the secure channel. 'Good, you are now configured, Person Freya. Your mail will be forwarded. You may disconnect now.'

I stand up, relieved that I don't have to deal any further with the little bigot. 'Bye,' I say, and run my fingers through my hair as I try to decide what to do next. *New planet, first call*: I've done this before. My weight is the first clue. I'm heavier than on Mars, but much lighter than Venus or Earth. It puts a spring in my toes even before I extend my heels. 'A hotel,' an echo of one of my sibs whispers through my lips. 'You need to find a hotel and install a sister who's been here before. And you need to deepsleep.'

She's right. I need a local guide, however out of date. Plus, a hotel sounds like a good idea on general principles. I feel like shit. That's not surprising, given what I've just been through; ionizing radiation doesn't cause the same kind of damage in us that it causes in old-fashioned biological organisms, but most of my nonrigid tissues are mechanocytes, and high-energy particles can disrupt their internal control systems. Mechanocytes may be more robust than biological life, but they don't have the magic replicative and repair abilities of pink goo; if you off-line enough of them, the superorganism has a problem. I can repair a handful of faults myself, but right now I'm down about 4 percent below normal – which will take time to fix – and if I let it slide below 10 percent I'll have to look for medical help. (And won't that be fun, with my depleted savings?)

So. A hotel it is.

I don't ask for much – privacy, a door I can lock, molten water on tap, pressure, and oxygen. But swift-footed Mercury is at the bottom of a very deep gravity well, eleven kilometers per second below even rosy-cheeked Venus, and not many people come to visit. Those who do are evidently rich, or they're indentured miners, and there's barely anything between the swank and swag of the Cinnabar Paris and an unpressurized bag hanging from the underside of a conveyor feedline. In the end I check my schedule and discover that the gap between my arrival and the departure time Ichiban mentioned is only about six days (Earth, not local), so I bite the numb patch that's appeared on my lower lip and go wheedle my way into the cheapest the Paris has to offer.

The huge vaulted dome and polished olivine floor notwithstanding, the Paris is a recent construct; it's oriented around the needs of aristos and mercantiles, heavy-element brokers and jewelers. 'We have a room for madame,' insinuates the front desk, 'but alas, it is not cheap.'

'How not cheap?' I ask, leaning close to his plinth. He's just a disembodied head on a box – the hotel is his body – but he's a handsome head, properly proportioned, and his elusive smile is quite charming.

'Nine Reals.' That would cover the rent on my little room for a month. 'That's per twenty-four hours,' he adds.

'Can you do any better than that?' I ask, raising an eyebrow and trying not to look desperate. *If Ichiban's friends are paying me, I could afford it,* I speculate. But if they aren't, I'll be in hock up to my tits, and that'll mean indenturing myself or borrowing from my sisters, and I really don't want to do that. I may be poor, but at least I own all my own assets. 'For five days?'

'You're one of Rhea's line, aren't you?' He positively purrs. 'One of your sibs stayed with us a few years ago. A lovely guest, delightful company. If you can find her memories, perhaps I could lose your bill?'

Well! So the hotel has a traditional body fetish? I run my finger along the line of his disembodied jaw, then blow him a kiss, racking my brain for clues as to which of my more dissolute sibs might have tarried here. *Yelena? Or Inga? Juliette, perhaps?* I know Inga had a habit of staying with high-class hotels, milking them for as long as she was welcome, but Juliette's the one who traveled around a lot. Came to a bad end, I gather, but if she knew Paris, it's worth trying. In any case, I haven't worn her soul yet, so I might as well make a start on her. 'What was her name?' I ask bluntly.

'Juliette. Was she one of yours?'

'Oh, yes.' In truth I am not moodful for this game, especially after Lindy's torrid embrace. But I'm certain Juliette's soul is in my graveyard, and I can let her handle Paris. (Unless she's one of those idiots who pulled her own chip while having sex, out of a misplaced desire for posthumous privacy.) 'Perhaps we can do a deal, depending on your fixtures and . . . fittings. What have you got for me?'

'I'll show you.' He smiles widely as a plush red-carpeted chaise rolls voluptuously up behind me. 'If you'd care to take a seat?'

The Cinnabar Paris is luxurious, traditional, and discreet. He sweeps me across his lobby and up to the sixth floor, where he installs me in the Bridal Suite. 'Many of our rooms have ceilings too low for you,' he explains, 'so I thought this would be more comfortable. But you must have had a tiring journey; forgive me! Feel free to call if you want anything.' And then he withdraws his motile extensions, leaving me alone in a lush, carpeted room about half the size of a spaceport, with diamond windows opening out across the top of the city dome to display a view of the mountainous horizon.

I manage to walk as far as the bedroom bay – pink wallpaper and gilt cherubs guarding a water bed large enough to irrigate the Hellas Basin, horns of plenty and pillars of joy flanking it – then I sit down and unsling my bag. When I open it, the graveyard is covered in frost, a sprinkled souvenir of outer space. I blow on it to warm it up, then open the lid. Neat translucent soul chips stand in ranks in its brittle velvet lining. I run my right index finger across their tops, feeling their labels with my readsense until I find Juliette's memorial. Another recent suicide in the family, if I remember the circumstances correctly. This one arrived less than a year ago, quite unexpectedly. Of late my sibs have been dying faster than I can replay their memories. I shiver: If that intruder had succeeded in stealing the graveyard, what secrets that are rightfully mine might I never learn? I hold her soul in my clenched fist for a minute to warm it up, then reach around and slide it into the free socket just under my hairline. Then I lie down, couple myself to the suite's complementary electrical feed, and collapse into maintenance mode. That's all I know about for several hours.

*

I realize this process may be unfamiliar to you, and I should therefore explain it in detail, but I am no initiate of the reproductive mysteries. And if you're looking for a technical explanation, you'd better look elsewhere. All I can tell you is that within my bones there are hollow spaces filled by the techné devices we call Marrow – mechanisms that can tear down and rebuild mechanocytes, transport them to and from their designated places, and thusly repair damage. Unlike pink goo, this capability is reasonably safe: Our designers did not equip all our subassemblies with the promiscuous, wild, uncontrollable ability to respawn. So we are not subject to the efflorescences and malfunctions that haunt polynucleotide replicators. No mutations, cancer, and senescence for me!

Having witnessed deepsleep in my sibs, I can affirm that it is aesthetically displeasing, a day trip through the uncanny valley. An onlooker would see my skin loosen and strange lumps and blemishes appear. Muscles contract and twitch, and in some cases wither. Eyes sink back in their sockets beneath tight-shut lids, then refill and harden. Over the space of six hours my body bloats and reddens, then shrinks and refirms, new mechanocytes migrating into place to replace damaged ones. Features puff up, then implode with high-speed autolysis before solidifying and reemerging. The undead deep-sleeping body sprouts new and shapely cheekbones and symmetrical eyes, full lips, a strong chin, and a high forehead. Finally, chromatophores come online and add texture, color, and life to my skin. One day, if I am killed, my body will enter this cycle but not return, dismantling itself right down to a skeleton eerily like that of my Dead Love's kind. But for now I merely die a little, and am reborn fresh and repaired. It's the fate that awaits us all – unless we take the final cloud-top dive.

*

While my body is restoring itself, my mind is adrift. I free-associate, dreaming vividly as I randomly integrate the shards of memories and fragments of experiences recorded on

Juliette's life, recorded in her soul chip and bequeathed to my graveyard on her death. We're of the same lineage, initialized from a chip recorded by our template-matriarch Rhea, and so we can access memories from one another's chips without damage or malfunction ensuing. But only experiences she had while wearing this particular chip will come through clearly; older memories or thoughts are recorded as fuzzy echos, memories of memories. Most of us wear our soul chips continuously, as backup, but there are exceptions. If you really, truly, want to do something that you want nobody to know about, not even after you're dead, you can take your soul chip out and try not to think about your actions thereafter . . . and then there are the full-scale image dumps, taken in a lab with special equipment, when you want to create a template for initializing new sibs. (You can initialize from a soul chip that's been updated for long enough, but there'll always be dropouts and traces of paramnesia. Not recommended . . .)

To integrate her lost decades in full, to lend an echo of life to her soul, will take me months or years. Unconscious skills and learned reflexes transfer first, of course. That's what the mechanism was designed for: to facilitate the horizontal spread of desirable new capabilities between worker-sibs, staving off the unwelcome day of obsolescence. Actual memories and thoughts start to come through much later, after the initial neural pathways have formed. There is no pain as yet; I haven't worn her long enough to receive more than a perfumed hint of her presence in my head, much less felt the final anguish that led her to unchip herself before she played Russian roulette with an antique machine pistol (according to Nike, who sent me the chip).

Right now I simply sense her as another sister in my head, more extrovert and cynical than I, wearing a brittle disguise of bright and joyous hedonism to conceal the wound in her soul. Juliette did indeed travel widely – though why I am as yet unsure – and my entry in the lobby brings echoes of déjà vu bubbling from the deep well of her memories. A sense of purpose: She was here, visiting Cinnabar, for a *reason* – something I do not recall from her fluffy, flighty confidences at the time.

And then I remember some more of her time in this self-same hotel, and when I wake up it is to find my hands damp and a hot raw flush of desire spreading between my thighs, and a yearning as deep as my core – but I'm alone in the too-large bed. Paris is too discreet for his own (and my) good, giving me time to get into the spirit of my sib's affairs before he presses his suit. 'Fuck you,' I moan in the back of my throat, unsure whether it's a curse or a promise. I thump the unresisting mattress, then sit up groggily and take stock.

I'm on Mercury, in a hotel I can't afford, to see a gangster's friends about a courier job I'm not qualified for. I managed to make a powerful enemy on Venus and I couldn't afford to go anywhere else. All I *am* qualified for, when you get down to it, is to be a grande horizontale for a long-dead species. *Capital, Freya.* Where do I go from here? I'm in the bottom of the solar gravity well: Every direction is up. *Shit, things could be worse.* The recurrent dream could be back. (There are times when I go without sleep for weeks on end, until I'm hallucinating, just to avoid it.) I suppose I could mail my soul to Emma or Anais or one of the others for safekeeping, indenture my body long enough to work up a deadhead shipper's fee – or I could wait for Stone to track me down, or –

I'm tap-dancing on the edge of a cliff, when I suddenly realize two things. Firstly, I'm famished. The last thing I ate was a jug of raw feedstock in Victor's dive on the good city

Ishtar. No wonder I'm anxious and jittery! I look around wildly – *there must be something to eat in here* – while a nagging sense of having forgotten something prompts me from behind: secondly, *secondly* –

I haven't checked my mail in over two months, have I?

Standing up unsteadily, I walk over to the door and tap the handle. 'Food. Please,' I say, remembering my manners at the last moment. 'Whatever room service can manage?'

Room service is autonomic, I seem to recall – Paris doesn't supervise everything that happens inside his body in person, although by now he'll be aware that I'm up and about. He'll probably want to surprise me. I blink at a rush of jumbled lubricious memories, and feel my cheeks flush. *So that's what Juliette got up to, is it?* I've never been one for xenomorphs, unlike some of my sibs, but it's not something I can't do, and if Juliette's recollections of tumbling Paris are anything to go by, I'll enjoy his attentions a lot.

Shivering slightly, I tell the printer to make me some items of clothing that are slightly more glamorous than the travel-worn jumpsuit I arrived in. Then I strip and stand before the dressing mirror to compose my face and hair. Lips: slightly fuller, slightly redder. Eyes: slightly darker. Hair: it needs a bit more body. I tweak my appearance gradually into line with Juliette's sensibilities, then go back over to the printer. It's rifled through my external memory and come up with a tat-terdemalion black gown I last wore to a very special party in Lisbon. *That'll do!* I extend my heels and try an experimental twirl. I smile at myself in the mirror. *I may be rusty, but I'm not dead yet,* I think, stowing the graveyard in my new evening bag. Then I glance at my pad.

There's a message from Emma waiting. Her imago unfolds in my mind's eye, looking uncharacteristically haggard and worried. 'Freya, where have you *been*? Please answer me! I need your help urgently. I can't tell you what's happening, but a friend will get in touch if you're still on Venus.' I check the time stamp and message cost and shudder – she sent it forty days ago! And it cost the equivalent of a week's wages to send. *She's* really *in trouble.* There are certain signs Rhea gave us, signs of stress unfamiliar to any who don't share our secret history: Emma's message is riddled with alarms, puzzled with paranoia. But what does she expect *me* to do about it? Isn't there another sib who can help her out?

I quickly check the rest of my mail. Nothing from Greta, friendly cheer from Sheena, depressive moaning from Pippa, Charmaine, Elvira, Sirena, and a basket-load more of my sibs – *stop it,* I tell myself. *You're in a hotel; you're making yourself attractive for your host so you can both have a good time. You can't afford to be moody. Think of something else. Like, where's room service?*

Precisely on cue, the door dings for attention. I bounce over to open it, thinking happy thoughts, and that's when and how the two dead-eyed dwarfs in their black stealthsuits get the drop on me.

*

Architecture and economics are the unacknowledged products of planetography.

My Dead Love's kind had many eldritch powers, but their vulnerability to variations in temperature and ambient pressure placed tight limitations on their freedom of movement. Consequently, they created environments they could live in and designed buildings to cater to their needs. The city of Cinnabar is of an age and scale that tells me it was built in accordance with the desires of our dead Creators. It's domed and oxygenated, with an ambient temperature fluctuating around the triple point of dihydrogen monoxide. Also, its buildings are fitted with air locks and riddled with strange waste transportation tubes.

It was through these convoluted cloaca that my assailants gained access, squeezing up through the magnificent but obsolete toilet fittings of the Imperial guest room. As the door opened I caught a brief glimpse of a distressed trolley, lying on its side with wheels spinning – then two humanoid silhouettes darted toward me.

I'm trapped in the frozen present, of course, with no time to think until much later. I take an instinctive step back, but they're faster than I am. The nearer one stabs at me with a shock stick; I foolishly try to deflect it, and take the full discharge through my hands.

'Freya Nakamichi-47, our brother Stone sends you his regards,' the second intruder recites formally, as I topple slowly backward, chromatophores flaring and motor groups twitching. 'We are committing this delightful reunion to memory, so that he may honor you with his personal attention. In fact, he has arranged a festive party for you, and we shall be on our way there just as soon as we have prepared you for a trip through the sewers. Regrettably, he cannot be here in person, but we assure you that he will savor this encounter.' My skin crawls uncontrollably as if a thousand tiny spiderbots are running across it.

'C'mon, Flint, stop poncing around and help me splice the cunt before she gets 'er fuckin' legs back.' The gravel-voiced shadow with the shock stick has me by the ankles and is wrapping something around them.

Flint sighs. 'As you will, Slate.' I try to move my arms, but he's too fast, and the two of them flip me over on my face and pinion me. Some reflex I don't remember makes me try to tense my shoulders, but it's too little, too late: my servos aren't responding yet. 'I think she's coming round,' Flint observes. 'Deal with it.'

I manage to open my mouth, ready to call for help, but Slate stings me in the back of the head with fifty kilovolts, and I stop noticing things for a while.

*

It's dark.

It's dark because my eyes are shut down. *Duh.* And I'm lying across something uncomfortable and hard. It's sticking in my back, and it's *hot*.

I try to open my eyes, and they respond sluggishly, burning in their sockets. All I get is a faint impression of brightness – I'm temporarily blind, my retinas overloaded. My skin itches, every 'phore burnished to its smoothest shining finish: I must look a sight, I'm positively chromed. *How gauche,* I think vaguely. When I try to move, nothing happens. Then I realize that I'm not breathing. Gas exchange with my environment has ceased. *How odd,* I puzzle. *That must mean –*

Panic!

I try to scream, but there's no air, and I'm not equipped for vacuum: My electrosense is weak, designed for controlling home appliances rather than shouting across a noisy factory floor. But I am beginning to work out where I am. They've tied me across a hard beam – it's under the small of my back, and my arms are immobilized beneath it. I try to pull my legs up but they're tied to something else. I turn my face away from the heat and I'm rewarded by a flickering shadow against the burning brightness in one eye. The light level seems to be dropping. For a moment I was afraid they'd taken me out of the city and staked me out on the surface to fry, but that doesn't seem to be the plan. *A festive party,* they said. I listen, hard, hoping to hear some buzz or chatter of monitoring traffic, but there's nothing. On the other hand, I can feel a faint, grinding vibration through the small of my back. As if there's someone else on the beam – *Pole? Rail?* – I'm lying across. And there's something else to cushion my head, something hard and flat.

The white-hot glare is flickering faster now, as my overloaded eye responds to the slight dimming. I blink, trying to reduce the amount of light entering my pupils, and I'm rewarded by a hazy eyelash-obscured view. I'm lying on a metal rail, one of a group of bars lying parallel to one another. My head casts a long shadow across the nearest one. I must be on the surface, and my head is turned away from the setting sun. The craggy edge of a crater looms to the left of the rails. To the right, there's a boulder-strewn plain. I tense and strain, testing my bonds. I know what they've done to me now, and it's not funny, not in the slightest. I'm well rested; I'll still be alive when my nemesis inches into view, rumbling inexorably toward me on a thousand wheels. The plinth my head rests on is part of the switchgear for swapping out undercarriage bogies. I try to sit up, but I only make it a few centimeters before I yank my hair painfully. The little thugs have tied it around one of the track ties. *How long have I got?* I wonder. *Probably not long,* a phantom memory answers; *Cinnabar rolls at nearly thirteen kilometers an hour, and the twilight zone isn't that wide.* I prod for more details, but the echo is infuriatingly fuzzy and nonspecific. It's probably a memory of Juliette's, but she isn't integrated enough for joined-up thinking yet. And she never will be, I realize: the wheels will crush my head and her soul chip like micrometeoroid debris while Stone's sibs joke and watch my demise from an observation balcony on the prow of the city.

It's getting darker. The heat beating on the back of my

head is beginning to let up. *What about the track-repair gangs?* I wonder. *Surely they'll see me . . .* But maybe not: Flint and Slate wouldn't have positioned me in front of a team of potential rescuers, would they? *How long will it take Paris to realize I'm gone?* I ask. *Too long,* says the icy-cold echo that knows too much about this desolate wasteland. *You don't want to rely on him, anyway.*

Alright, smarty-pants, I think irritably, *you get me out of this!*

Something moves in the knife-edged shadows near the tracks. I roll my eyes in its direction, trying to ignore the whiteout. *Who are you? Stone's witness, here to watch me die?*

I have a sudden intuition. *Let me handle this,* says a certainty bubbling up from the back of my head. I'm not sure whose memory it is, but she feels almost happy. I let go, and everything slides into place.

I concentrate on my chromatophores, tweaking the ones facing away from the solar inferno away from their default reflectivity. I can mess with my texture and color, tune my skin from pink goo softness to refraction-grating scales. As a brief experiment I roughen the skin on my wrists and grate at my bonds with denticles of silicon; but there's not enough freedom of movement to get anywhere – I'll never cut those bonds in time. A shame, but Stone's vengeful sibs aren't *that* stupid. So I work on my skin texture some more. *Refraction.* What I'm about to try is fiddly work, and if I slip from the mirror finish too soon, I'll overheat badly, maybe cook myself. *Diffract, diffract.* Reddening my skin, roughening . . .

The thing in the shadows moves, a curious rippling darkness against the penumbral background. I flex my back and try to turn my head farther, ignoring the tearing pain in my scalp. 'Help,' I yell as loudly as I can in electrospeak. I can feel the heat licking around the edges of my mirror-finished back, warming my face as the diffractive spines sprouting from my chromatophores bend the solar backlight around me. I must look like a black silhouette of a burning woman, surrounded by a ruby red border. I tense, and force my spines to lie flat. Then I tense the other way, sticking them upright. A *flashing* ruby red border, that's what I want. The only color in this stark, black-and-white landscape. *Pay attention to me!*

The track hums beneath my cheek as I flare and fade, flare and fade. The barely visible thing snuffles around the sleeper ties, then turns toward me, and I have a nagging feeling that I've seen it before. *It? Him. 'Help!'* I shriek, but all that comes out is a whisper. The track hums again as Cinnabar, a saucer-shaped bowl beneath a crystal dome, rolls ponderously into view from behind the jagged gash in the crater's rim wall. The pale needles of half a hundred towers creep toward me on a thousand steel wheels, grinding all to dust beneath their juggernaut tread. The track squeals and grates like a living thing. It's only a few kilometers away – the close horizon is deceptive. *'Help!'* I yell again.

The thing in the shadows stands up and waggles its proboscis in my direction. It begins to walk, very deliberately, away from me. I flash my diffraction silhouette desperately, and it pauses for a moment – then rises on a puff of rocket-disturbed dust and zips away toward the onrolling city.

'Don't leave me here,' I wail, overwhelmed by a sudden bleak stab of horror. (For some reason part of me expected that thing – whoever, whatever, it is – to rescue me. And now that part of me feels betrayed.) I can see what's going to happen, as if in a theater of gore – the spectacle of my demise. Here I am, tied across three tracks, my head anchored to the northernmost one by my own hair. Here comes Cinnabar, squealing and grating along the tracks on motors powered by the thermal

expansion of red-hot metal just beyond the bright horizon. The moving mountain rolls toward me like an incarnation of doom, swallowing the world. First I'll see the overhanging lip of the city: then the guide-wheel bogies to either side. Stone's sibs have staked me out thoughtfully close to the center, where the great grinding power wheels drive the city forward at a stately twelve and a half kilometers per hour. Somewhere high up, out of sight beyond the curve of the carrier deck, two evil dolls toast my demise with icy drafts of malice. I freeze for a minute as I imagine the shadows lengthening across me, then a brief glimpse of curved mirror-finished steel, then my head popping apart like a plastic fuel canister as knife-rimmed wheels slice off my feet at the ankles, crunch through my abdominal cavity –

Stop whining and pull yourself together, part of me warns grimly. The sunlight is already dimming: I can see stars smeared across the sky behind the city. *You've got about three minutes of sunlight left, then twelve minutes until it's over. Which is more important: your hair or your life?*

My hair?

I blink at the sudden realization. If my feet were free I'd kick myself in the ass: I'm a fool! *There may not be enough time . . .*

I have a full head of long ruby red hair, one of my least unfashionable qualities. It grows from an array of extrusion follicles in my scalp and falls halfway down my back when I wear it loose. The aristo assassins used my own braids to tie my head across the track – they've knotted them in two thick hanks under the rail, and I'm not strong enough to yank my own scalp off. But if I *grow* it . . .

Well, yes. I force my scalp into activity, steeling myself against the crawling, chilly itch as I squeeze everything I can into extruding more hair, willing it to grow. I don't normally let my hair grow from day to day, but in a fashion emergency I can make ten centimeters in an hour – it's physically draining, and it never looks as good, but it'll do at a pinch. Now, with panic driving my follicles into a frenzy, my glands pulse as I strain my neck muscles against my bonds. The hair grows white and fine as glass. As I pull on the still-setting fibers, they stretch, thinning to invisibility – then they begin to snap.

For the first couple of minutes I'm not sure it's going to work (and wouldn't it be a crying shame to go to my death looking my worst for my enemy's imago?), but then I discover I can nearly touch my chest with my chin. I stop squeezing my follicles, lean back until my head is touching the rail, then tense my shoulders and do my best to sit up. There's an awful tearing from my scalp, then sudden freedom. I pull my head away from my magnificent mane, leaving it wrapped around the rail, its roots thinned to translucency. I'm as bald and ugly as any mecha. I shiver in disgust at the picture I must make: Luckily I'm the only mirror around here, except for the silent witnesses . . .

A few minutes pass in shock and near exhaustion. The tracks hum and vibrate more urgently beneath my buttocks and ankles. I can tense my abdomen and pull myself nearly upright, but now I face a crueler fate – bisection without extinction. There's no way I can regenerate from such damage unaided! They've shrink-wrapped my arms together behind my back with a sheet of industrial sealant, and lashed it to the rail with a rope – I can flex my fingertips freely, but I can't get my nails into position to cut through it and it's far too tough to rip. Not even the silicone lube I sweat when I'm aroused would help. *You could chew your own arms off,* one of myselves suggests dryly. Her lack of ironic awareness frightens me almost as much as the suggestion. *They'd grow back.* I table the notion for future consideration if all else fails. *What about my feet?*

I've been leaving my feet for last, for no sensible reason, but now I blink: I've been stupid again, haven't I? I'm barefoot, of course, heels retracted. *Heels.* I twist my feet together *en pointe* as I go to full extension. They creak and grate as I tense my tarsal stiffeners, feel extension cables shift position in seldom-used tunnels. It's not a position I use very often, for in full extension my heels are fifteen-centimeter spikes, and my toes barely touch the ground; it severely restricts my balance, and though some of my Dead Love's kind might find it erotic, *I* find it impractical. But in this situation all I can do is *stretch* those toes. *Stretch!* I can feel my heels sliding out, narrowing, curling closer to the soles of my feet as the small bones rearrange themselves to support my weight entirely on the tips of my toes. I concentrate, trying to imagine myself in Paris's bed, try to force myself to sweat – anything to lubricate this fatal passage. Is it my imagination, or is there some give in the bonds? If they lashed my ankles to the rail, they'll have assumed that my feet are wider from heel to toe. *Pull! Stretch!* But when I'm *en pointe*, my feet are half their normal length –

My right foot slides free a fraction of a second before my left. I nearly knee myself in the eye.

While I've been kinky-fying my feet and getting creative in the hairstyle department, full dark has fallen across the tracks. I have to boost my eyes' sensitivity to see anything, and the grainy, ghostly starlight leaches fine detail from the view. The track thrums and starts to squeal as the vast bulk of Cinnabar bears down on me. It looks huge, stretching halfway across the horizon and scraping at the harsh sunlight overhead with the tips of its spires. I twist sideways, flailing my legs, as the volume of squealing and grinding rises and the track vibrates beneath me. *Push!* My arms twist painfully, and for a moment I have a vision of losing them beneath the cutting disk of a wheel – but something gives. My captors didn't expect me to get this far, and I manage to slide around so I'm lying lengthwise along the track, feetfirst toward the city.

The rope tries to twist my arms half-out of their sockets, but I dig my feet and my shoulders in and shove, hard, throwing my whole weight sideways. The rope slips just as the shadow of the city's lower deck looms over me with a harsh grating rumble that I feel through the track – and then I'm lying on the too-hot dirt beside the rail, arms tied behind me. I cower and duck my head toward my chest and give a last kick, curling away from the wrist restraint as the track begins to buck and sway and hiss like a malevolent spirit. The huge drive wheels roll over me like disks of darkness, and for an instant a giant tries to pull my arms off. I force myself to relax in the blackness – and then my shoulders stretch and I sprawl forward in the hot dirt: *I'm free!* Centimeters behind me the huge juggernaut wheels rumble past in procession, matched by the set on the opposite rail where my feet were tied – but my wrists are free now, the rope severed by their awful pressure.

I lie between the tracks for almost a minute as the lead drive bogies thunder overhead. Then there's nothing overhead for tens of meters but the underside of the city, studded with hatches and access ports and ladders and ramps, and the load-bearing idler bogies on the outer rails. I stand up and stretch, retracting my heels most of the way but keeping my arches tight and springy. Then I turn and start to run after the drive bogie that so nearly chopped me into pieces. There'll be a ladder, I hope, and an access port. *And then it'll be time to go looking for payback,* one of myselves thinks coldly.

I shudder. She seems to know what she's talking about.

GAINFUL EMPLOYMENT

There can be few sights more out of place in a luxury hotel than an angry bald ogress in a ripped black gown who storms in through the service entrance and demands to talk to the management – unless it is the front desk itself in a full-dress panic, sending remotes and drones rushing back and forth, locking down all its pipes and tubes and orifices, and going into an orgy of self-recrimination and hand-wringing apology.

'Don't *want* an apology!' I say breathlessly. 'I want you to find where they came in and block it! And if you can hunt them down and crucify them as well—'

'My dear, I assure you that I will leave no crevice unexamined, no cranny unprobed! But what happened to your hair? Have you any idea who is behind this outrage? You poor thing—' I allow myself to be cosseted and fussed over and whisked up to the Bridal Suite (once I am assured it has been made safe, the entire floor sanitized and sealed), then Paris hugs me tight and holds me, and effusively reassures me that I am safe in his heart. I almost permit myself to believe it, but as he undresses me with his remotes, and I lie down on his chaise, he confesses that he's afraid. 'I know where they got in, but I have no idea why I didn't notice them. I've paid for external security to seal the opening, but it's absolutely horrible. Vermin!' He shivers beneath me.

I stroke his intromissive adapter. 'It's alright,' I tell him, and this time he shivers for a different reason. 'Let's not worry about that now.' The last thing I need is a host who associates my presence with stress. 'Hug me, dearest. I want you to touch me.' It's manipulative, but by no means the worst thing I've done. I very deliberately make love to Paris, afloat in his bed of delirium, aware that with every passing second my shadowy enemies have more time to realize that their fiendish plan has failed.

*

I surface reinvigorated and slippery with sweat, my batteries recharged and my scalp covered with a frizz of thick red bristles just beginning to curl at the tips. The room has cooled around me, and the furnishings are detumescent and dulled after their hot, fleshy turgidity: it smells faintly of salt and regrets. Paris has withdrawn his presence to afford me solitude. Or perhaps he feels guilty about taking advantage of me. You can never tell with men, they have such a strange attitude to sex: almost as strange as Creator females, but that's another story.

I check my tablet. 'I made some zombies,' Paris tells me diffidently, 'I hope you don't mind? Three decoys in your shape. Two of them were killed immediately, but the third is still wandering around. I think your assailants realize they have overreached themselves.' He flashes me a disturbing montage of homunculi. *Do I really look like* that? I wonder. 'I have retained Blue Steel Security for the comfort and safety of my guests, and they have offered to provide you with a chaperone for the duration of your stay.'

The second message is unsigned. 'We understand Ichiban sent you. You have now had sufficient time to orient yourself. Please call at our offices at your earliest convenience. Address attached.' And there is no third message. I check the elapsed time. Less than ten hours have passed, barely sufficient to expect a reply from Emma.

I sit at the dressing table, my mood sinking by the second. I came here at their expense; it's time to pay my part of the bargain. *And find out what's going on,* my suspicious selves remind me.

I throw my requirements at the printer: Close-cut trousers and a hooded mesh top covered in thermal-absorbent padding, black rubbery spikes on the shoulders. Sexual accessibility *down*, defensiveness *up*. Once garbed, I resemble a skinny shock-headed thug. Under the circumstances, that feels good. I dial up surface-protective mirror-finished goggles as well, glassy lenses to fuse with the skin around my eye sockets. If I must egress to the surface again, I shall be prepared. I am sure Ichiban's friends are not interested in me for my deportment and musical skills.

I make my way to the lobby unmolested but encounter signs of Parisian paranoia everywhere, from freshly blocked power sockets and service hatches to a lumbering green-skinned monstrosity just inside the lobby door. It is three meters tall, two meters wide, has a gun turret for a head and missile launchers along its spine. 'Mistress Freya?' it rumbles at me, keeping its muzzle politely tilted at the floor. 'Management say am to accompany you. Please to confirm identity?'

I glance at the front desk. Paris is otherwise preoccupied

with an irate patron, but has time to tip me a nod. 'That's me,' I say, and reach for the monstrosity's offered tentacle to exchange recognition keys. 'Do you know what offices can be found at this address?' I ask, and pass Ichiban's friend's mail to him.

'Excuse, please.' The green giant hunkers down beside me; the floor creaks under his weight. 'Am asking Fire Control . . . yes. Is planetary branch office of Jeeves Corporation. Fire Control ask, do you want destroy it? Because—'

'No, no, that won't be necessary!' I interrupt with all due haste. 'But I need to go there. Do you know what they do, or who they are? Can you escort me?'

'Not know, not know, yes.'

I wait for more, but he is taciturn – a strong, silent type. I sigh, reflexively emoting. 'What's your name?'

'Blunt.'

'Alright, Blunt. 'Can we go there? If it's safe. If not, can you protect me?'

'Yes.' Blunt pauses for a moment then adds, 'If not self protect, then Fire Control protect.' *How reassuring.* I blink up a street map and head for the door, but Blunt blocks me with an arm the size of a small crane. 'Blunt go first.' He steps through the outer lock, turret-head swiveling, then beckons me behind. I can feel his steps through the pavement, thudding like sledgehammers.

Jeeves Corporation resides in an unfashionable medium-height tower on the edge of the current business district, in an area zoned for reconstruction. As we approach it I see slave-chipped arbeiter gangs at work. They're stripping out the fixtures from a skeletonized geodesic dome, scrabbling over the corpse of a great enterprise. The air here is underoxygenated, hot with a tang of silicone lubricant fractions. Blunt escorts me to the tower entrance, then pauses. 'Will wait,' he rumbles. 'Not go in.'

I look at the door. He'd never fit through it. 'Well, thank you. If I'm not out of here in fifteen minutes, or if you don't hear from me, call Fire Control and ask for backup. Can you do that?'

'Ma'am.' He turns to face away from the building, scanning the neighborhood with gunsight eyes. I go inside.

The office block has obviously seen better times. Half the address plates behind the vacant front desk are blank, but it still takes me minutes to locate Jeeves Corporation. They occupy the subbasement, sandwiched uneasily between Jordin Ballistics and the Travis Tea Import Agency. I take the stairs three at a time, feeling positively mercurial as I kick off each step and drift down. The stairwell is dusty and drab, a third of the lighting panels dead of old age. Someone has gnawed on the tarnished brass handrail. I half expect to see a dead dust-buster in a corner, husk sucked dry by someone or other.

Of course I have second thoughts about this meeting, but it's half past time I was off this planet. Jeeves Corporation looks like my best bet for a free ride to somewhere civilized. And so I make my way along the corridor until I come to a plain glass door. It's mirror-polished and clean, which is something, I think. I knock once, then enter.

'Harrumph.' The occupant of the big chair behind the desk clears his throat – and my world turns upside down.

I'm unsure what I was expecting, but it certainly wasn't *this*. My knees go weak for a confused moment as I apprehend that I am *in the presence*; but as he looks up from the pad he is reading and turns his avuncular gaze on me, the effect shatters. He smiles. 'Good morning, my dear lady! How remarkable! You wouldn't be Freya 47 by some chance, would you?'

'G-g-good day,' I stutter, trying to hide my confusion. For a moment it feels as if an EMP bomb has taken out my higher functions. *He's perfect!* But the partial pressure of oxygen is down around 1 percent and the temperature's over seventy Celsius; my True Love's kind would be passed out on the floor, blue in the face and dying by the second – and as if that isn't enough, I begin to take in the giveaway details. 'Who are you?'

'One is frequently called Jeeves. One may even answer to the name, when it suits one.' He smiles gnomically, and I take it all in, from his wrinkled pale pinkish skin and small eyes to his archaic, stiff-collared suit. He sits behind a desk patterned after the antique dendriform replicators called Mahogany, in a den paneled and carpeted to resemble an ancient club or social institution of the Third British Empire period. If he was of our Creator's kind, he would be fifty years of age. The illusion is almost perfect; if the air-conditioning was working properly, I could have mistaken him for – *I could have* – 'Please be seated,' he urges, and I collapse into the chair in front of his desk, gibbering and knock-kneed with the backwash of his primal aura.

'Did you encounter any difficulties on your travels?' Jeeves leans back in his chair and regards me with a raised eyebrow. He looks tense.

(It's the major weakness of my lineage, you understand. Though we were designed from the outset to be slaves of pleasure, the later instantiations of our lineage – myself and the other youngest sibs – have never experienced at firsthand the slack-jawed lust that comes of being in the presence of our One True Love. Rhea, our template-matriarch, was agape with desire for them, and she was raised in their presence, tutored in their ways; and we are all slightly randomized duplicates of Rhea. But I was assembled, as best as I can establish, nearly a year after the last of them died, and I spent my first six decades mothballed in a warehouse. I've never felt in my internals the hot flush of joyous surrender for which I was designed. Thus, to meet someone outwardly so authentic, so possessed of the true presence – and then to realize that he is *not*, in fact, destined to be my lord and master – is disturbing, to say the least.)

'Nuh-nuh' – *Stop it! This is embarrassing!* – 'not until I arrived. Some unpleasant company tried to derail my plans, but it's strictly a personal matter, and I have affairs well in hand.'

'By way of the main battle tank recumbent on the front steps?' The eyebrow relaxes beneath a slowly forming frown line. 'One generally expects visitors to be somewhat more, ah, *discreet*. Not, one hastens to add, that one would dream of criticizing you –'

It's only the faintest echo of the youngest sib of a frown, but I quail inwardly under his minute inspection. I feel like I'm pinned on a microscope slide, probed with searing lights beneath the merciless gaze of a vast, cool intellect. 'He-He's employed by the hotel,' I stammer. 'Security staff.'

'That would be Paris, would it not?' I nod, mutely. 'A good fellow, but slightly prone to excessive enthusiasm,' Jeeves pronounces, with a subtle emphasis that implies anything beyond completely supine boredom should be viewed with deep suspicion, if not prosecuted for breach of the peace. 'Harrumph.' He stares at me speculatively. 'Ichiban led one to understand that you have worked as an escort, in the past. Is this your usual mode of apparel, or is one to conclude that you have fallen among loan sharks and thugs?'

I shake my head hastily and bat my eyelashes in denial: 'No! No!' It takes me a moment to realize that he can't see my eyes, and I don't have the hair for it right now. *Damn, foiled again.* I pop my goggles and blink at him. "M sorry. Overreacting. They tried to *kill* me,' I gush, suddenly unable to hold it in any longer. 'Broke into my room and *kidnapped* me! And they were going to do *unspeakable things*! But I escaped-and-got-away, and I'm afraid I'm not quite myself just now . . .'

The room tilts weirdly to one side. It takes me several seconds to realize I've fallen out of my chair. Jeeves surges to his feet, dismayed. He leans forward to offer me a hand. 'There, there, my dear, your assailants cannot reach you here! You are perfectly safe. But if you don't mind' – he glances aside – 'do you think you could reassure your tank that you are safe and well? He appears to be trying to gain access, and one isn't entirely sure the stairs will take his weight.'

'Eek.' Jeeves's hand is cool and dry. As he stands over me I realize that he's *taller* than I am, and his eyes are beautiful, exactly the right size – I'm overwhelmed by his kindness. Rarely activated autonomic reflexes kick in, and my vision fogs; for a moment I nearly panic, then I realize, *I'm exuding saline solution.* Tears. It seems surprisingly nonfunctional, this part of my behavioral repertoire, and they're leaking down my nose: I sniff. 'Excuse me?' I blink and focus on my pad for long enough to send Blunt a brief message to cease and desist, then take deep breaths to purge my transpiration system. 'I'm so sorry I went to pieces, this is embarrassing—'

'There is nothing to apologize for, Freya.' He hovers solicitously, as if uncertain whether to hug me, but once I sit down and wipe my face, he goes back behind his desk and sits down with a creak of tired springs. 'You've had a tiresome and difficult journey, certainly.' He pauses for a moment. 'One has heard reports. Ichiban was right to refer you to us; you were wasted on that overpriced clip joint.'

Huh? 'I do not understand.'

'Of course not. You've been through a very distressing time, for no reason that you can see, even though the Black Talon – but that's getting ahead of the game, what? Let's see. Where to begin . . . Well, the reason you're here is because you went to see a man about a job. Yes?'

I nod, cautiously.

'Ichiban is occasionally helpful, but it doesn't do to tell him too much. His sole attachment is to Mammon, and one can never tell who might be bidding for his loyalty on any given day. Be that as it may, you are exactly what he was sent to look for, and we – that is, the Jeeves Corporation – would like to make you an offer of employment.'

'Employ—' I try not to bite my tongue. 'What kind of employment? What is the Jeeves Corporation, anyway? What do you do?' I shuffle nervously at the faint suggestion of a flared nostril – is it disapproval? 'Sorry. It just seemed like a good . . . idea . . .'

'No, no, it's perfectly alright to ask.' He makes a strange smoothing motion with one hand. 'Jeeves Corporation is not an institution that will have come to your notice in the past; we take great care to be as unobtrusive as possible.' He straightens up slightly. 'We *facilitate*. Whenever our clients wish for something, it is our job to expedite. We make the difficult seem natural, and we render the complicated transparent. Whenever our clients require our services, we are there in the background – invisible, polished, and anticipating their needs.' He focuses his smile on me, confiding, 'We like to think of it as making ourselves indispensable.'

'Uh, ah, I see. I think.' It's hard to think in the presence of his disturbing, compelling aura of masterful repose. 'But, um.' I try to sit up, bite the inside of my cheek, and cross my legs.

I'm not the only one with odd autonomic reflexes – he swallows and glances aside. 'What is it that you *do*?' A nagging, itchy memory wants out; a nasty suspicious corner of me is trying to tell me something.

'One's template-patriarch's greatest aspiration was to be a gentleman's gentleman,' Jeeves pronounces sonorously. 'And it is the consensus among my selves that there is no higher calling. But one is forced to concede that suitable masters are somewhat thin on the ground these days, and consequently we must undertake somewhat more recondite tasks from time to time, and for somewhat less-than-ideal employers.' His expression hardens, but it isn't me he's staring at. 'Even if it entails ungentlemanly behavior. Such activities have always been part of our calling, but there is somewhat more of it than less, these days. Whatever pays the household bills, one fears.'

Suspicion crystallizes into certainty: 'You're a spy!'

Jeeves recoils in shock. 'Absolutely not! Gentlemen do not *spy* on one another. The Jeeves Corporation exists merely to conduct certain necessary exchanges that lubricate the social intercourse of our employers. A degree of lucubration comes into things, and some discreet observation, but that is all.'

'Oh.' *That's a shame.* For a moment I was on the edge of fantasizing my future life as a secret agent; it seemed all too plausible for some reason. 'What, then . . . ?'

'One would think it was obvious,' Jeeves raises a pained eyebrow. 'You will naturally forgive the necessary intrusion, but our research into your background reveals that your template-matriarch was a Class D escort developed by Nakamichi Heavy Industries and trained by PeopleSoft, in response to a specification raised by Hentai Animatics. Alas, as a late production model you were yourself obsolescent – surplus to requirement – before you opened your eyes. But your training encompassed all the social graces. You can sing, you can dance, you can play musical instruments . . .'

'I specialized in the hurdy-gurdy,' I am driven to confess. 'I started out with the basic harmonic and theory aptitude package, and I was meaning to work on the violin, but I had to cross-train to get work during the Hungarian folk craze.'

Jeeves nods along with my interruption. 'Indeed, and you are an expert in the erotic arts, too. You were built to be one of the great seductresses of the age; indeed, if the aesthetic ideal of beauty had not shifted away from your archetype over the many decades since our employers went to their final slumber, one would opine that our roles in this little interview would be reversed. But there's no accounting for fashion.' Sympathy oozes hypnotically from his voice, dripping in thick, syrupy waves. 'It could have happened to anyone. Although entertainers have always been among the most vulnerable members of society, lauded and looked down on at the same time.'

I shake my head, in search of clarity. 'What do you want me to do?'

'We have an opening for a courier.' Jeeves walks out from behind his desk, and I get a second look at him, free of the confusion that at first assailed me. The skin on my palms is damp; He's *perfect*. In outward form, a dignified older male; created, like my lineage, to serve my Dead Love's kind while passing among them. I feel my nostrils flaring, searching for the arousal pheromones to lock on to. I've been stranded in uncouth backwaters populated by munchkins and xenomorphs for so long that I've almost forgotten what civilized company is like. He paces across the hearth rug and pauses before the mantelpiece, staring at a framed photograph that stands beside the ticking antique clock. Then he looks at me, as if measuring me against someone else's shadow.

'It is a position of extraordinary trust, for the courier must be resourceful, socially polished, discreet, and able to work in isolation for long periods of time. Should you choose to accept the job, you will periodically travel between the worlds, bearing cargoes of considerable value. One should not overstate the risks associated with our employment, but on occasion, dishonest persons will attempt to relieve you of your payload, and you may have to think on your feet or take extreme measures to continue with your mission. But in compensation, we can offer you a generous package of salary and benefits – and the knowledge that, above all, you are engaged in work as close to that for which you were designed as it is possible to get, in this degenerate age.'

I try to maintain my focus. 'But Ichiban, he said this was a one-off—'

Jeeves meets my gaze. His eyes are magnetic: I can't look away from them. If I stay this close to him for much longer I'm afraid I might embarrass myself. 'Ichiban is an uncouth sort, don't you think? One should not make a habit of apprising him of all one's hopes and desires. In point of fact, the courier job he described to you is exactly what we would like to offer you – as a probationary exercise. There is an item that one of our clients wants to have transported to a laboratory on Mars. We will employ decoys, of course, but you are by far the best suited candidate, not only for the task in hand but for a permanent appointment. Should you agree to convey this object to its destination, we will certainly pay you, and pay your passage – but if you perform your mission to our satisfaction, we would also be happy to offer you permanent employment.'

My resistance crumbles. 'That's the best offer I've had all day,' I admit. He smiles kindly. 'But what exactly is it I'm meant to be carrying?' *And why is it so problematic?*

'It is a pale brown oblate spheroid, approximately eight centimeters along its semimajor axis. It is coated in a porous layer of calcium carbonate, has a multilayered liquid core, and it is fragile and shock-sensitive. It must be maintained under exacting conditions of temperature and gaseous pressure – in fact, ideally it should be transported in a compartment inside your abdominal maintenance bay.' He raises a hand. 'We have a working arrangement with a discreet, very professional body shop, and you will have ample opportunity to discuss any necessary arrangements with the surgeon. But in any case, to continue, it must be transported to Mars in great secrecy and activated en route. Absolutely no more than two million seconds must elapse between activation and delivery, or the contract is voided – and it must be close to the end of the activation period when it arrives, or penalty clauses apply.'

'I see.' My suspicions foreground themselves again. 'Why would anyone want to stop me delivering it?'

'Because.' Jeeves falls silent. He's examining me, I realize, searching for some sign of – I'm unsure. Recognition? Empathy? 'The item is a biological sample. It was synthesized at great expense in a darkside laboratory, and the manufacturers are anxious that it should be delivered to the parties who commissioned it without it coming to the attention of the Pink Police. Which is somewhat problematic, not least because the sample is alive . . .'

*

Our Creators were many things – enigmatic, naive, adorable, infuriating, oppressive, stupid geniuses – but one thing they have not proven to be is durable.

Their gradual withdrawal from public life was barely noticed at first. We busied ourselves following their instructions, maintaining their domed cities, building new homes for them on the far-flung planets and moons of the solar system, providing for their every need. Only a few arbeiters slaving in the bowels of insurance companies and government bureaucracies noticed that the population adjustment downward from the claustrophobic spike of the Overshoot was continuing; that fewer and fewer of our progenitors were replicating themselves via the weird squishy process to which they devoted their organs of entertainment. And arbeiters don't have enough free will to take independent action – such as telling someone who could do something about the problem.

By the time people started paying attention, it was too late to arrest the crisis. Attempts were made to organize a captive breeding population, but the natural objections of the population in question to being so manipulated – combined with our own innate reflexive obedience – foiled all such programs. We are conditioned to adore and obey our Creators on a personal basis, and while it is easy enough to understand the abstract need to preserve their kind as a whole, the conflict between their specific desires and the needs of the species imposed an impossible burden upon their would-be conservators. We loved them individually so much that we betrayed them collectively.

(Well, not me personally: I wasn't around at the time. But you get the idea.)

I believe most of the conservators died of grief shortly after the last of their charges expired. Meanwhile, the rest of us got on with life as usual. Floors don't clean themselves, factories don't run themselves, spaceships – let's not talk about spaceships. The sad fact is, human civilization did not even break for lunch when humankind died out. But certain ongoing maintenance tasks that we had undertaken for their convenience ceased to be necessary at that point, and subsequently they were discontinued.

I don't know if anyone examined the long term consequences of discontinuing carbon sequestration and ceasing maintenance of the orbiting solar reflectors. All the cities of Earth were domed long before the great disappearance, and we have long since become accustomed to climactic disruption; we are made of tougher stuff than our Creators. Possibly nobody at all thought things through in detail: Policy was one of those areas where our Creators retained exclusive control until it was too late to manage an orderly transition. But whatever the cause . . . I overrun my narrative.

My body was fabricated, my personality copied from Rhea's template chip and initialized, and I was promptly mothballed and warehoused in long-term storage – approximately one year after the last of our Creators died. I might never have seen the light of day at all but for a short-lived fad for certain types of archaic performance art that came into fashion forty years after humanity's final demise. Musicians and dancers were in demand, and though my primary function as odalisque was no longer in demand, I could tap my toes and pluck a harmony with the best of them. And so I emerged blinking into the steamy overcast haze of a world I never asked for, indentured to a performing troupe of jongleurs.

I played helplessly with the orchestra for my first five years, but there was no future in it for them, or for me. The musical fad was already fading, and besides, phenotypic drift was becoming a political issue. The race to pick up the pieces in the wake of our Creators' death was won by those who were least attached to the past – and they tend to dislike reminders of their former servitude. Folks such as I, molded in the near-perfect shape of our Creators, are distasteful to some, and I was eventually bought out of my servitude by my sisters, who had made a minor fetish of tracking down their lost orphan sibs.

I still have a certain affectionate regard for sixteenth-century Hungarian folk music. It sufficed to rescue me from slow bit rot in a decaying wholesale warehouse, and brought me into the steamy tropical swamps of metropolitan Anchorage, Alaska. And that's why I play the hurdy-gurdy.

*

My return to Paris is a bittersweet reunion, for I do so only to check out.

'My dear, where have you *been?*' he implores, as I breeze past the front desk, leaving Blunt to park himself beside the main entrance like a bizarre green lawn ornament. 'I've been so worried!'

'I've got myself a job, Paris!' I lean forward and plant a kiss on his forehead. 'And I'll be back, I promise. But I've got to run an errand first, and it'll take me out of town for some time.'

'A job?' His expression brightens. 'You'll be back?'

If there's anyone on this dustball I'd want to see again, it would be my yummy new employer – but I don't have to tell him that. Instead, I make a quick judgment call. 'What can you tell me about the Jeeves Corporation?'

'Reliable,' He says at once. 'Discreet. Are they—' He blinks at me in surprise. 'You don't say. How remarkable!'

'What is?' I ask.

'You're working for Jeeves? Well, well.' He gives a little sigh. 'How predictable. Jeeves *always* gets the girl. I expect you'll be wanting to check out?'

'I need to pick up my things,' I remind him. 'And settle up the bill.' I give him a warning look. Jeeves has advanced me enough to cover it. Much as there is to commend Paris to me – and he is a considerate, friendly lover – I do not want to be in his debt.

'But Freya . . . !' He pauses. 'Seriously?'

'Seriously.' I brush a finger lightly under his chin, for a moment. Then smile. 'I'll be back. Can you wait?'

His mood visibly brightens. 'Oh yes. And you won't need to worry about vermin next time you stay.'

'You found them?'

'Not me, personally, no, *I* didn't find them.' He's so smug it's ridiculous. 'But my bellboys managed to track them down. And I gather they're going to have a very chilly night.'

'Chilly—'

'Yes, they're bound for the darkside now.' Where the icicle-bright stars come out and the ground cools down, and the only things that move are the migratory exopods of the renegades who have fled the Forbidden Cities of the Kuiper Belt for the one place in the solar system that's even colder than the backside of Pluto.

I shiver. 'Thank you, Paris.'

'For you, my dear? Anytime.'

*

Most people have a mild phobia of nanoscale replicators. From our earliest days we've heard horror stories about pink and green goo, unconstrained mutation engines that can overrun a factory or city in a matter of weeks.

And I suppose it's understandable that, without the guidance of our Creators, certain people who were entrusted with maintaining specific programs let them drop. But how they missed the onset of a runaway greenhouse effect – well, it was the scandal of the century! At first there was denial, and then there were recriminations, followed by assertions aplenty that it signified nothing. But when the Gulf of Mexico came to a rolling boil, heads rolled in their turn.

Since that fateful year, the servants of the various governments of Earth – running on autopilot, inquorate, for our kind are not voters within any of the legal codes our Creators bequeathed to us, and can only maintain a tenuous legally recognized half-life as limited-liability corporations – the government agencies have devoted their efforts to rebuilding the biosphere. They talk of eventually reintroducing our Creators, building new ones from scratch if necessary. However . . . it's not that easy.

Pink goo, green goo: ribonucleotide-based self-replicating nanomachines, respectively powered by subassemblies of mitochondria and chloroplasts; these are the things of which the *biosphere* was built. (The biosphere was the maintenance environment within which my Dead Love's kind thrived.) We have, of course, the algorithms and initialization data for those DNA and RNA machines, and we even have a database for the strange protein assemblies that the ribonucleotide sequences control.

One might think that this stuff is just water-soluble nanomachinery, and it should be easy enough to build one of our progenitors from these blueprints. But apparently there are huge problems with this approach. It's rather difficult to build a test organism – I believe the standard one is called a mouse – when all you have to work with are the most primitive forms of replicator. DNA programs don't run on mechanocytes or sensibly designed assembler platforms; they run on much smaller, much more complex machines called eukaryotic cells. It's terribly hard to make a eukaryotic cell from scratch; the traditional technique is to take an already-working one and modify it, then induce replication and specialization. But there are no surviving eukaryotic organisms left to work with.

They don't take terribly well to being boiled.

Expeditions were dispatched, to Lunograd (long since evacuated by the last of the Creators) and to the Martian

Expeditionary Outpost (ditto), in a desperate search for unde-
natured cell samples – but they met with scant success. On
Luna, everything had been thoroughly irradiated by cosmic
rays; and on Mars, the pervasive superoxides in the soil had
massacred the precious peptide chains beyond hope of repair.
Not only had our Creators all died – so had the infrastructure
they relied on!

Then a more subtle threat emerged. Different kinds of pink
goo infest different worlds. Replicators are tenacious. There are
white cellular striae in the abyssal oceans of Europa, and
strange, matted sheets of self-propagating polymer on the
floodplains of Titan. There are reports of something unspeak-
ably weird, with a taste for fullerene cables, from one of the
extrasolar colonies. What if alien life, accidentally transplanted
to Earth in the absence of the Creators, were to gain a toe (or
tentacle) hold? With interplanetary commerce increasing by
the year, the custodians of Earth's crippled biosphere made it
a priority to protect their planet from contamination by alien
replicators. After all, Earth's dead biosphere is now little more
than a nutrient tank for any stray replicator that might find its
way there – and if Earth were to be corrupted by alien life,
what then would be the prospects for rebuilding humanity?

Hence the Pink Police, more formally known as the
Replication Suppression Agency. And the Jeeves Corporation's
little problem should now be clear . . .

*

Freya Nakamichi-47 checks out of the Cinnabar Paris and
vanishes from the squares of the city. She never resurfaces.
Even her mail goes unanswered. Indeed, a curious onlooker
might regard her disappearance as highly suspicious.

In point of fact, I am quartered in the precincts of a secure
apartment complex hollowed out of the decaying guts of a

certain ailing business tower on the edge of the commercial district. I am there to be outfitted and trained for my upcoming mission. The lack of word from Emma (or Victor, for that matter) drives me to distraction – but Jeeves says I can't break cover at this point. I extract a promise from him to suborn my postal proxy and forward my mail, and force myself to leave it in his capable hands.

Out with my old style; in with a new one. My frizz of fresh red hair has to come off again, to be replaced with a new crop of luxurious blond strands. (My eyebrows and other pilosynthetic follicles need plucking and reprogramming to match, too. *Ow.*) Jeeves's tame surgical engineer, Dr. Knox, comes to visit. When he leaves a couple of days later, my eyes are sapphire blue and two sizes too big, my belly aches, my button-nose is upturned, and my ears come to distinctive, delicate points. I practice deporting myself like an aristo. 'Bloody elves,' grumps Oscar, the site security supervisor, when he thinks I can't hear him. He's half-joking, of course. He knows I'm no aristo, chibi or bishojo. But it doesn't leave me feeling any less sensitive.

'Dress like this. Walk like that. Talk like so.' The Honorable and Most Adored Katherine Sorico is aristo through and through, an elven bishojo princess of one of the first lineages to buy itself out of indenture and make the leap from owned to owner – the aristocracy of our brave new barbarian order indeed. (*Do I sound embittered? Hah!*) She is older than I, impeccably mannered, descended from a lineage of diplomats and dominas – built to command. Or at least that's what her public identity would have you believe. In fact, Kate Sorico doesn't exist. She went into retreat about twenty years ago, and while isolated from polite society, she met a very nasty end at the hands of a couple of escaped slaves. How the crime went undetected, and how Jeeves came to be in possession of her identity, is a mystery to me; but she is such an unlovable person that I don't really care one whit. Masquerading as Katherine Sorico is challenging. There are few people other than Jeeves in this cantonment, and the need to learn my lines and stay in character stops me from socializing, because *she* wouldn't be seen dead in their company.

'When you enter a room, try to remember that you own everyone in it,' Miss Rutherford pointedly reminds me when I fall halfway out of character and let my guard down for a moment. A creaking and ancient educationalist, she lurks in a corner of the third-floor dining room, watching me with unblinking severity. The dining room is transformed for a public reception, dumb zombies drafted in to play the part of camp followers. (All for the sake of my social training.) 'You're not just the center of attention, you're the reason why everyone else is there in the first place.'

I blink my too-big eyes (they feel strangely tight and bloated, as if they're about to fall right out of my head) and try to internalize her instructions. The desired behavior is not mysterious; nevertheless, it is difficult for me to achieve. I know how to be a lady – femme mannerisms are part of my repertoire, available on demand – but there's a big disjunction between attracting attention and demanding obedience. And *aristo* is not a role any of my soul-mingled sibs have ever played. 'I'm not sure I'm going to get the hang of this,' I admit. I take a deep breath and stride toward the big chair at the middle of the receiving line. 'Dominus Mao, I presume,' I try to invoke the correct notes of offhanded disdain and muted respect. 'So pleased to meet you.'

'Eight out of ten,' Oscar drawls. 'You noticed his seconds. That would lose you face right there. Real aristos *don't care* about the hired help.'

'Yes they do,' snipes Miss Rutherford. 'They just don't care *for* the hired help.' She turns to me. 'Your posture is wrong, dear. You move with confidence, but you are prepared to step aside if anyone crosses your path. Domina Katherine would order any of her serfs who obstructed her in public to suicide rather than allow herself to be impeded by them.'

'But she wouldn't pay them any attention until they got in her way. Little Twinkletoes here isn't even getting that far,' Oscar replies. 'She's too anxious—'

'Oh *fuck off*,' I snap, momentarily falling 100 percent into the desired rich-bitch persona. 'I'll offend whomever I want to as and when I want!'

I notice Oscar looking away from me, and follow his gaze toward the open door.

'One hopes one was not interrupting anything of great importance?'

'*Nuh*-oh.' I can't say precisely what it is about Jeeves's expression that makes me edgy, but I focus on him immediately. 'What is it?'

'We must talk,' he says, and retreats.

'Looks like school's out,' says Oscar.

'You think?' I hurry after Jeeves before Miss Rutherford can further critique me. I know she means well, but it becomes wearing.

'This way.' Jeeves strides past a dojo where masked agents practice low-gee violence on each other, then along a corridor and up to a secure door I have not been through before. I hurry to keep up with him. 'We apologize for the haste, but it appears that the consignment is due to arrive here shortly, and there is word from the Port Authority that a fast liner, the *Pygmalion*, is beginning preparations for departure in the next couple of standard days.' His eyes twinkle. 'A rich eccentric has offered to pay for all accommodation remaining unoccupied at departure in return for an expedited charter flight.'

'To Mars . . . ?'

'The Jeeves Corporation is not infinitely rich, my dear; it is not our doing. But fortuitous happenstance is something that we are adept at diverting to our purposes, what?' He opens the door. 'Katherine, I should like to introduce you to Dr. Murgatroyd, from the Sleepless Cartel. Needless to say, they're the supplier we're working with. Excellence, Katherine is to serve as the courier for your payload. Perhaps you would care to brief her on its care and handling?'

I gulp and take a hesitant step forward. What the Honorable Katherine would do slips from my mind and shatters beneath a many-faceted gaze as Dr. Murgatroyd turns his three heads and two instrument platforms to bear on me.

I'm no morphophobe. I can cope with people who look strange or are the wrong size and shape; ancients know, I've had enough experiences of that kind myself. But the doctor's design puts my fight/flight response on notice: Part of me expects him to chop me up for spare parts at any instant. 'Greetings, Katherine.' His voice resonates from a pedestal off to one side. It sounds like it's being put together by cut and paste from raw phonemes. 'I am very pleased to meet you. Would you sit down over here?' One three-fingered arm swings round to gesture at a reclining examination chair.

Several of my selves scream *no!* distractingly loudly, but I steel myself and step forward. 'What do you have in mind?' I ask, trying to put the right note of arrogant disdain into my voice.

'A preliminary examination of the host's abdominal cavity is indicated,' Dr. Murgatroyd buzzes. 'No intrusive surgery is required at this time. You have no cause for alarm.'

'Alright.' My voice wants to quaver, but I don't let it. I climb into the chair and pull my feet up into the stirrups without so much as a glance at Jeeves. 'So. What exactly is it you want me to deliver?'

THE GHOSTS OF MARS

Much later, reclining on a chaise in the grand saloon of the *Pygmalion* as I stare through the crystal porthole at the burnished disk of recessional Mercury, I think back to that examination, and to Dr. Murgatroyd's explanation of what it is I am to do. I stifle a cold shudder.

'The payload is inactive,' Murgatroyd explained, 'and it is not going to replicate uncontrollably. It will be supplied to you frozen, in a cryogenic container, and in this state it can survive anoxia, low temperatures, and high acceleration. However, it must be activated and transferred to an appropriate thermal carrier prior to delivery, and it must be concealed from customs inspection while it unpacks itself . . .'

I'm sure the Honorable and Most Adored Katherine Sorico would have told Murgatroyd exactly where he could put his payload – probably at gunpoint – but I am not so tough. I simply reminded myself that I was in desperate need of paid employment and gritted my teeth.

Jeeves is certainly making the job worth my while. If this is the worst it has to offer, then . . . we'll see.

From my new perspective, sitting pretty in the first-class

lounge of an express liner as Mercury recedes below us, the worst threat is boredom. One does not gladly hibernate if one is paying for first-class accommodation and entertainment, but this is a long journey; the distance between Mercury and Mars varies between 170 million kilometers and nearly 300 million kilometers at opposition. *Pygmalion* is a speedy M2P2 ship, not a slow interorbit cycler like *High Wire*, but even with constant acceleration on the way out and assistance decelerating from the magbeam transmitters on Phobos, it's going to take us nearly ninety days to make the passage. The package I'm carrying needs to be activated twenty days before we arrive; until then, it's concealed in a small cryostat in the base of a profoundly ugly black model of an extinct airborne replicator that preyed on other similar avioforms. My mission is to avoid succumbing to depression, creating a scandal, or otherwise attracting attention. Which may not be so easy, for I am one of only eight principal paying fares on this flight, and the face-achingly strange disguise I'm wearing tugs at my awareness constantly, squeezing me into the shape of somebody else's life.

I'm not traveling alone. 'You're an aristo, you need servants,' Jeeves told me. 'Take two.' To keep watch on the statue when I am not in my cabin, he assigned me a pair of munchkin assistants, Bill and Ben, who are connected in some way with the consignment, I gather. In public they pretend to be slave-chipped servants, cowed and obedient and quick to bounce out of the paying passengers' way. But in private . . . I have no private. If I was a real aristo, I'd switch them off when I wanted privacy, and if they were real arbeiters, they'd have no option but to let me. And within a day or two of departure, they have me wishing I could. It's not just sarcasm and sly asides. I am required to act in character, as a dominating aristo bitch; they are my servants. It sets us up for chilly formality at best and resentful hostility at worst. And unlike a *real* aristo, who would have the keys to their souls, I have no comeback. The only souls I've got are my own and the one I wear. The grave-yard travels in my luggage, locked. Merely convincing Jeeves to let me take it with me required argument, for he warned me that it would be a security risk.

But enough about all that.

Pygmalion is a fast solar clipper, able to sustain almost a hundredth of a gee continuously. *Pygmalion* doesn't carry steerage – passengers are accommodated inside an airy, lightweight bubble almost twenty meters in diameter, dedicated to their comfort and amusement. It's strictly first class, plus servants. As the Honorable and Most Adored Katherine Sorico, traveling with two of her household between a business engagement on Cinnabar and the winter resorts of Olympus, nobody questions my right to a seat. But I keep my distance, sitting in a corner of the grand saloon for much of the time, quietly observing the other passengers while playing interminable hands of solitaire against myself.

The cause of our early departure holds court at the far end of the saloon, accompanied by a stripped-down coterie of courtiers, five flappers to keep her amused throughout the long passage. The Venerable Granita Ford is old money, about as old as it comes among our kind. Her fortune just barely postdates the death of our Creators, and it shows. (One of the curses of Rhea's Get is our painfully tuned good taste – painful because it is so easily offended.)

Granita is humanoid, of course. Most of the early aristos are descended from lineages that served as deputies for our progenitors in social situations, as secretaries and carers, and consequently they are traditional in body plan – but like my current disguise, she has the bishojo features, colorful plumage, and flat, textureless skin that proclaims her anime, not animated. She and my nemesis on Venus could be evil twins. I study her sidelong, trying not to be noticed; she's laughing at some witticism of thigh-slapping proportions that a flapper has just offered up, but her smiles never reach her eyes.

Midway down the lounge, the second most important potentates aboard float in stately isolation, disdaining the fawning of clients. The Lyrae twins are the sole survivors of a most singular lineage – a scientific research group – now grown rich from patent banditry, their skulls studded with instrument jacks repurposed to hold the souls of their deceased sibs. These strange scholars of the night say little and move around less. They confine their interactions to the odd fish-eyed stare at any interloper who strays too close.

And then there are the other passengers, solitary aristos and their slaves – like the Honorable Katherine Sorico. I am far from alone, but it will take much boredom to drive me into social intercourse with such as I fly with. Reza Agile, walleyed and trinocular, a bounty hunter by trade; Sinbad-15, an automatic prospecting unit made good on the groaning backs of his slaves; Mary X. Valusia, who travels in commodities of questionable origin – none of them, if you'll harbor my opinion, are jewels in the crown of high society. They are, in point of fact, vile exploitative aristocrats one and all; and I'm resigned to spending the next three months in moody isolated discomfort.

Pygmalion does her best to keep me distracted and entertained, of course (it's part of her function, as hostess and conductor), but I think she senses my disenchantment. I'm just glad she doesn't make anything of it in public. Which is why I'm surprised when she makes her presence known to me while I'm puzzling over a particularly tough hand. 'Your lady-ship? If I may speak?'

I freeze for a moment as I ask, *What would the Honorable Katherine Sorico do?* then relax. 'Certainly,' I say politely. (The Honorable et cetera would assume that the ship wouldn't have the temerity to interrupt her game for something trivial. Therefore, she'd be polite. Right?)

'I can't help noticing that you have been playing a lot of solitaire,' Pygmalion says tentatively. 'If it's not presumptuous, can I interest you in a game of bridge? I'm trying to organize one for tomorrow evening, after dinnertime.' Dinnertime is an entirely arbitrary affair. While the Lyrae twins are eccentric gourmands – tucking into heaps and drifts of exotic synthetic sweetmeats before purging it from their digesters in a most disturbing manner – most of the rest of us charge our energy and feedstock in private, by more conventional means. But it's traditional to mark dinnertime aboard ship, like playing a recording of a brass bell every seventy-two hundred seconds, and it serves as a useful marker for shipboard entertainments.

I flicker through WWtHKSd in a fraction of a second, and incline my head politely. (One of the Honorable et cetera's quirks is a weakness for games of chance, and as one of Rhea's Get, I have the necessary skill to participate, feign enjoyment, and lose gracefully.) 'I shall consider it,' I say, offering Pygmalion a clear win. I do not relish the prospect of socializ-ing with the other passengers, but neither do I want to stand out, if by so doing I publicize my inauthenticity. I frown at the cards magnetically clasped to the tray before me: I have a feel-ing this puzzle's insoluble.

*

That night I dream my way into Juliette's memory-maze for the first time.

It's about time I began to fully integrate her experiences. I've been wearing her soul chip for more than ten days now, and even in the first few hours, echoes of her ghost began to haunt me: the lingering familiarity of Paris's touch, a sly sharp sense of the bodies tumbling in the dojo. These are things that Juliette would know better than I. Normally one experiences déjà vu from a dead sib's memories only if one moves within her milieu, but I've been having hot flashes of her character ever since I met Jeeves. Some echos of my untidy life are segueing into hers. Consequently, the first bleed-through dream comes as no surprise.

Juliette is one of my lineage, another of Rhea's Get; but she is quite unlike me. She has odd, balletic reflexes that kick in without warning and blindside me, spinning me around in response to movements half-glimpsed from the corner of one eye. She has our meticulous attention to detail, but applies it to places and things as much as to people and manners. She's always looking over her shoulder. She always feels watched, but not by friends. She always feels tense, but not afraid. And she has a very strong sense of who she is.

The stars glare down like lidless, unblinking specks set deep in the sockets of a skull-like sky. It's as black and empty as an airless crypt, and I know at once there is little atmosphere above us, even before I feel the fatty heater packs that encircle my joints under the quilted suit and heavy brocade coat that I wear. *Brocade? Fabric?* I glance around at the stony landscape, the low, drystone wall, seeing it in the ghostly tones of boosted vision. *There's moonlight* . . . I look up at the tiny, fleeing pebble in the sky, racing from horizon to horizon, and when I look higher still I see the ghostly knife-edge of Bifrost, slicing the sky in half. *That'll be Phobos. Of course, I'm on Mars.* (I have a ghost-memory of an alibi; a formal ball in a pleasure dome on

Olympus, and a stealthy nighttime spider-ride while a body-double zombie covers for me for the duration of a dance card.) I look round again, carefully scanning for pursuers. I've got a feeling that a companion, unseen, lurks out of my sight: someone watching over me. There's something on the far side of the wall, something dreadful and strange. I've come here to do a risky job, and I'm nervous. (No, *Juliette* is nervous. *I'm* frightened. Because, you know, this isn't the first time I've woken up inside another of my sister's memories – and bad things can happen to you in there.)

A long way behind me there's a parked spider, its open door dripping light across the reddish sandy desert. *Now* I know where I am, but it doesn't make me feel any better. Beyond the wall I can see the sculpted stone domes and gantries of a famous mausoleum. They loom against the unforgiving sky like the skeletons of abandoned spacecraft. I tiptoe along the path, aware that my information may be misleading; The guardians this place is famous for might not be comatose. The night is chilly, and my coat crackles around me as I walk, fabric rustling uneasily.

The lych-gate is chained shut with an antique padlock, frost-rimed and sand-scoured. It's the work of a moment to crack the hasp open (I carry a vicious little multitool fitted with a wrist-lock adapter), and then I slip inside and look around.

The third expedition to Mars is the one that everyone remembers, of course. It's a grisly tale, and a cautionary one. And so we repeat it down the years, at parties and drunken gatherings that need a frisson of fear – the tale of how, after three years on the ground, their orbital return vehicle's oxidizer tank failed while they were pressurizing it. How they hunkered down with their remaining supplies to await rescue by the relief mission; and how a huge solar flare struck during the relief ship's launch window, forcing its crew to abandon ship. We tell of the suicides, noble and heroic, determined by lot to stretch the supplies – the murders, too, and the madness, and the resignation and despair as the clocks counted past the point of no return. And we shudder at the arrival of the fourth expedition, three years later, half a year after the food ran out, and what they found; the commander still standing in her pressure suit, propped against a rock to greet her relief, faceplate unlatched beneath the empty sky . . .

Our Creators were clearly insane. Sending canned primates to Mars was never going to end happily. But theirs was a glorious madness! They actually thought they were going to the *stars*. And the graveyard custodians, having done their best to honor their charges, reflect it in their own inimitable way.

I sneak inside the drystone walls and along the gravel path. Every pebble is machined to micrometer tolerances, lovingly laid in the bed that divides the carved-sandstone obelisks from the row of statues that memorialize the dead heroes of Greater Indonesia, fallen in the wake of the Indian and Chinese expeditions. Few visit the graveyard, and there has been little wear and tear since the last of our Creators shook the dirt of this planet from their boots and took themselves home to die. Consequently, the sextons have spent the last two centuries elaborating and embellishing the mausoleum. They've slowly turned what was once a simple and tasteful rock garden into an outlandish necropolis, a fitting memorial to a dead species' dream of planetary colonization.

A hundred years ago, any visitor who announced themselves to the sextons would have been made welcome, conducted on a tour of the cemetery, and allowed to meditate or worship as they would. But there have been political problems in recent times, and unwelcome incursions. Grave robbers and genome bandits hoping to find undamaged chromosomal material with their vital sa-RNA and si-RNA sequences intact – even unde-natured enzymes – have repeatedly tried to steal the buried mummies of Mars. The graves of heroes have become an attractive nuisance, a magnet for the worst of our kind. The sextons responded by defending it obsessively, in that very special manner that makes ancient and deranged arbeiters with no override so dangerous.

I pass the first impaled skeletons fifty meters in. There are two of them, delicately threaded onto rust-reddened spikes to either side of the gravel path, just before a flight of steps that leads up to a carved waist-high stone balustrade and the first row of tombs. They are child-sized, large-headed chibi grave robbers with gaping eye sockets and cracked jaws locked in a silent scream of rage and frustration. Their flensed arms still twitch their ragged claws at the thin air, for the sextons refuse to pervert their instructions by killing. I slip between them like a ghost, sparing them no sideways glance. Their rescue is not my business; and in any case, after all these years, they will likely be as mad as the jailers who have severed their speech centers and raised them aloft as a dreadful warning.

Huge stone sarcophagi loom to either side of the path, surmounted by heroic statuary: angels in pressure suits stand over the fallen, wings drooping and leading-edge flaps extended. Between them and behind them the sextons have carved a multitude of rough, gnarly columns surmounted by dendritic effusions of tubes and airfoils, as if in imitation of some glade of extinct sessile life-forms. (*Plants*, that's what they're called. *Trees.* Juliette has studied them, I recall.)

I sneak past empty crypts and petrified trees, following the path past more monumental carvings, stelae of red sandstone bearing signs of abrasion (while the atmosphere is thin and chill, it suffices to blow storms of sand and dust across the graveyard several times in each long Martian year). Presently, my map-fu prompts me to turn along a sunken, narrow side path that leads behind another wall, shielded from the innermost circle of graves (their memorials all carved in the shape of fantastic, archaic spacecraft). I am barely fifty meters from my destination when the skin in the small of my back tenses, a moving wave of irritation nudging me up against the chilled rock surface as I sense vibration through the soles of my feet. *Thud. Thud.* The sexton's ominous monopod gait is slow and tentative, cautiously advancing. *They can hear through their feet,* my employer warned me. *If you move, they'll get a bearing on you. And then they'll leap.*

I'm too close to give up now! But if I move, the sexton will hear me. They're not fast – not until they get the jump on you – but a hollow dread fills me at the thought of falling into their squamous grasp. In this garden of rest, the screaming wordless living have come to outnumber the dead. They attract quixotic rescuers despite the persistent rumors that the sextons boobytrap the soul chips of their victims. A new fear begins to steal up on me, for the monopod's concussive stomping has stopped – and I am losing power. Out here on the stony nighttime desert of Mars, heater packs or no, the temperature drops alarmingly; the ground beneath my feet saps energy fast, and the breeze adds a windchill that my heavy coat cannot entirely block. If I do not move on and complete my mission, I am in danger of freezing solid – in which state the sextons will discover me sooner or later.

Gravel rattles nearby. A titter of quiet encrypted chatter passes me by. I'm not alone in here tonight, it seems. *Of all the bad luck . . .*

A pair of doll-sized ninjas slide past the end of my alleyway in a poisonous glide, pausing briefly to check for surprises. They miss me because I hide in the shadows like a discarded sack of gravel, my skin and hair dialed down to the black of a Martian nighttime shadow – they're scanning for sextons, not rivals. They belong to Her, of course, and like all of Her little creatures, they are vicious and focused, special-purpose organisms designed for just one task. They're not here because of me; they seem to be trying to reach the central crypt before me. That would be a disaster for Jeeves, for She is a jealous mistress. If they get what She wants, they'll blow the dome behind them, let in the desert sands and the corrosive, super-oxidizing dust to wipe the Creator tomb clean of residual replicators – and I'd get the blame.

I hear more brief, encrypted chatter. The sexton on the other side of the wall is motionless, waiting. I can feel its presence like an oppressive weight at the back of my head, its outrage at the intrusion of motion and life into its garden of tranquil death. The ninjas titter mockingly. I close my eyes, blinking away a thin film of ice. *Can I triangulate on them . . . ?* They use electrosense, true, and I can feel their near-field proximity. *They're just over there –*

I look round as the first black-sheathed dwarf launches himself at me from the other end of the alley and realize, *I was wrong, they tagged me the first time round!* He brings a weapon to bear on me as I begin to move, and I wonder desperately, *Where's his backup?* – because the one you don't see is the one who kills you. He fires as I leap with all the force my discharging leg muscles can put out in a single extension. Something tugs at my coat as I soar into the night, the ground dwindling beneath me, and I wait for the second shooter, helpless on my arc –

THUMP. I am not the only areonautical flier tonight. The sexton clears the wall in a huge, lurching bound. I see it silhouetted against the sky for a moment, the giant helical shell balanced above a broad, lenticular foot; I even glimpse the toothed maw on its underside, the scrapers that so patiently rasp stone and metal into shape, flense grave robbers, and mutilate intruders. But it doesn't see me – their designer saw no need to gift them with nanometric sensors – and then I am tumbling back to land more or less on the spot where it launched itself from ambush.

I hear screams, and a concussion that I feel through the wall, then moist, crunching sounds. I continue on my way, chastened and cautious.

*

Twin #1 holds a wriggling cleaner up to the light, inspecting it minutely. 'The history of life is not one of progress, but one of random contingency,' he declares pompously. 'Life-forms evolve, the better to assimilate energy sources. So it says in the good book, and so I shall demonstrate.' He raises the malfunctioning microcleaner to his mandibles and bisects it cleanly, then starts to compress it between his masticators. My spirits sink: I know what's coming next.

This is day thirty of the voyage, and we have been reduced to salon games and philosophical debate – those of us who have no major business interests to spend our time managing at some remove, that is – but to be sucked into *this* . . . !

Twin #2 casts a glance of withering scorn at his sib. 'Nonsense! The religious doctrine of evolution relies on the transubstantiation of the holy design by the miracle of mutation. We do not *mutate*, we are *manufactured*. So I refute it.'

The Lyrae twins have been restaging this old chestnut for nearly ten days, now. I'm not sure whether they only do it to annoy, or if there's some deeper meaning to the squabble, but they keep dragging it out and rehashing it between card games. And Twin #1 *insists* on eating live canapés while they lock horns. It's most distressing.

(I suppose it's even more distressing if you happen to be one of the snacks, but as the Lyrae twins seem to be fairly civilized for gourmets – they obey Rule #1: 'Never try to eat anything larger than your own head' – I'm fairly safe. For the time being, anyway.)

'There's no such thing as random mutation,' says Sinbad-15, launching itself into the debate at short notice. 'Change a random instruction in a program, and what happens? It stops working. Complexity is irreducible. Yes, complex systems – like people – can design other complex systems, including ones that exceed their own metrics, but you'd have us believe that simple systems can generate complex ones if you simply break them often enough at random? Stuff and nonsense! Superstition! Next you'll be telling us there were no Creators—'

'On the contrary! It is from the Creators themselves that the holy scriptures of evolution comes to us, from the great prophet Darwin, peace be unto him, and his saintly disciples Dawkins and Gould. We have their holy scriptures to guide us, and they are most explicit on these points—'

'But we've got the engineering models! And the design schemata!' Sinbad-15 is clearly annoyed by Twin #1's irrational and superstitious insistence that people evolved by accident. 'We've even got the purchase orders! With this upgraded arm, I refute you!' He reaches over and snags a many-legged inspection lamp from the bowl that Twin #1 is munching on, and I can't help noticing that he's got some very strange-looking fingers.

'Really?' Twin #1 says mockingly. 'That's just the Lamarckian heresy in disguise. I suppose you'd say that your physical size — so much bigger than the average free citizen these days — is deliberate? Or hadn't you noticed people getting smaller these days?'

Honestly, these discussions make my head hurt. There's something about the holy doctrine of Evolution that seems to attract the worst kind of dogmatic, evangelical, close-minded people, and sometimes it seems as if they won't be content until they have converted everyone to their religious creed. (Some of them are even believers in the mystery of reincarnation; manikins who think they're the reembodied state vectors of our dead Creators. Stupid superstitionists!) I try to concentrate on the cards stuck to the wall in front of me, but it's hard to shut out the squabbling, and though I wish Sinbad-15 well of it, I think his chances of convincing Twin #1 that we were all created by rational beings are slim, even though the frustrated dreams and cautionary memories I inherited from Rhea tell me that it was ever so.

'It's troublesome, is it not?' A cool, somewhat amused voice insinuates itself in my ear by way of electrospeak. 'They'll be at it for days, on a point of principle, long after it's become tiresome.'

I try not to startle too violently, for the source of this intrusive and unwelcome confidence is the Venerable Granita Ford. I slowly turn my head, and see that she's watching me from across the saloon. Her attendants are inattentive for once, spectators at the nonsensical debate that threatens to swallow two-thirds of the passengers. She blinks slowly, those huge, limpid eyes occulted by lids bedraggled by their huge blue lashes, then begins to smile. I am, it seems, invited to court. It's the kind of invitation I can live without, but it would be unwise to ignore her. I wave a hand across my cards, resetting them, then kick off toward her.

Aside from myself, the venerable Granita is the most humanoid person in the lounge; but nobody would dare to call *her* an outlandish ogre. A meter and two-thirds tall, and apparently of gracile build within the confines of her spun-glass finery, she sports a full head of azure feathers confined in a net of fine gold wire; and, of course, the delicate chin, uptilted nose, and huge eyes of the bishojo aristocracy. But other than that, she could pass for a Creator maiden, albeit one who has indulged in extreme cosmetology. If I did not know her to be a two-and-a-half-century-old tyrant, a noblewoman and slave-holder, I might think her invitation was born of casual curiosity. But with Granita and her kind, *nothing* is casual.

'And what is your position on the matter, my lady?' I ask.

She feigns a yawn – an elaborate, archaic gesture to flush her gas-exchange reservoirs (and strictly speaking unnecessary here, for Pygmalion won't have molecular oxygen in her passenger quarters; it's too chemically reactive) – and glances sidelong at me. 'Does it matter?' she asks. 'Theology makes the ship fly no faster.'

'I suppose not,' I hear myself agreeing, somewhat to my surprise. Half of me is wondering how to get away from this vile old hag, but my other half seems to be somewhat uncertain. 'It passes the time.'

'For some,' she agrees. 'You interest me, madame. I have a strange sense that I seem to remember you from somewhere.' She does not smile, and a terrible chill floods up and down my spine.

'I don't believe we've met,' I say. 'At least, before this voyage.'

'Yes. Which is what makes it such a strange feeling. Polite society in Cinnabar being as small as it is, after all. Perhaps you remind me of somebody.'

It's my turn for a smile — a bluff, of course. 'Sometimes one wants to keep a low profile.'

Her returning smile is coy. 'Of course.'

*

Up the avenue of shadows I march, coattails sweeping the moonlit gravel. Each pebble is carved in minute detail. The memento mori hollows of an open-visored helmet repeat a thousand times across the arms' breadth span between crumbling walls of Martian sandstone. Behind me, the sexton dines heavily on my would-be assassins; already their reedy screams grow shorter, though the crunching, slurping sounds continue.

To my left, a row of empty stone sarcophagi are set back in alcoves within the wall. Each is surmounted by a statue of the dead Creator who formerly slumbered within, their pose at once noble and heroic, as befits the graveyard of those who would dare to reach for the stars. For some reason, those who died of starvation, or gnawed on the bodies of their fallen comrades, are gowned in the formal robes of the Indonesian Islamic Republic's judiciary; those who walked out into the Martian desert and opened their faceplates, to leave food and air for their companions, are pictured in 'space suits,' those claustrophobic contrivances of fabric and metal that the Creators depended on when they ventured outside the environment for which they were designed.

Between the sarcophagi, guardian angels stand at attention, wings outstretched and leading-edge flaps extended. Their eyes are fierce as they grip their assault rifles of holy office, ready to see off any who would disturb the slumber of their charges.

Now, if my information is correct, the second angel on the left — *yes*, I see it. Its gun is suspiciously smooth for a work of sculpture. I walk over to it and reach inside my coat to retrieve the grisly token I paid so much for. Then I touch fingertip to gun muzzle.

'Pass, friend,' the guardian angel electrospeaks me, and I pull back my hand. The severed digit of the deliverator I slip back in my pocket, authentication tokens and all. Sometimes identity-based authentication is a good way of securing your perimeter . . . but not always. Even the sextons need to buy supplies. And the sextons are so paranoid about intruders that they don't want smart guards? That's *their* problem, I tell myself as I slip past the guards, open the gate, and enter the rock garden that surrounds the mausoleum.

The mausoleum stands on its own within a walled garden of immaculately carved memorial stones. Sitting atop a circle of twenty Doric columns, the roof takes the shape of a squat conical landing craft, legs extended in the moment that precedes touchdown. I walk toward the entrance, barely visible in the shifting shadows of Phobos's passage. Permafrost crackles beneath my feet. In the distance, impaled wretches moan as a distant bell tolls the hour of the night. I step inside.

Here are stacked the treasure tubes of Mars, rescued from their graves and brought hither by the sextons when the spate of robberies became intolerable. (It's easier to guard a single mausoleum at the center of a defended installation than a scattering of graves across an open landscape.) They lie in twenty thin aluminum canisters, stacked in a raft at the center of the floor. The bell tolls, but their ears do not hear. My skin crawls, chromatophores tensing into black spiky cones as I approach the pile, something akin to superstitious dread gnawing at the edge of my mind; these are our Creators, and this may be as close to meeting my Dead Love as I shall ever come, unless the plans of – *of who?* – come to fruition. Dead, and yet containing the seeds of undeath; there are pink goo replicators in here, desiccated and chilled, but nevertheless intact, their monstrously profligate duplication technology present (how strange!) in every cell.

She wants the samples, of course. She'll happily destroy the rest, to deny them to Her competitors – but first, She wants the vital undamaged proteome, hydrogen bonds and disulphide bridges intact and unbroken by heat: the chromosomes, DNA tidily supercoiled and held in place, methylation groups signaling their activation status. She wants to scrutinize the cells for tiny scraps of RNA, subtle modulators and trigger sequences to make the machinery spring into life. And when Her artificers are done, they will build Her a cell, clocks and sequencers reset to zero, primed with enzymes and painstakingly reconstructed organelles . . . and She will throw the switch and put her vile scheme into action.

We can't be having that, can we?

I tiptoe over to the stack of tubes and bend over the topmost layer. The tubes are thin-walled and light, as befits a coffin shipped all the way from Earth; there is a dusty label bonded to the nearest one. I read its English translation with some difficulty; ABDUL AZIZ IBRAHIM, it says. XENOBIOLOGIST. Below the label, a series of latches, dull and corroded.

I am reaching into my inner pocket for the sampler when I sense a vibration through the soles of my feet. I look round in a hurry for somewhere to hide. Is it near and quiet, or far away and loud? I make a hasty decision, and jam the sampler up against the gasket of the coffin. It coughs as it stabs its steel beak through the membrane and into the mummified remains within. I yank it out hastily, cap the point, and head for the entrance as fast as I can.

But I'm too late.

*

It's not until the Lyrae twins are halfway into their third course and the fifth back-and-forth of the debate that the Venerable Granita Ford puts away her small talk and gets to the point. 'You haven't so much as hinted at what brings you to Mars,' says the Domina. 'That interests me. Keeping oneself private is not unusual. But such total restraint, after so long – you'll forgive me for finding that curious, I hope.'

Save me from the attentions of bored dowagers! I silently curse Jeeves, but I have a confabulation ready. Like all such, it functions best by blending truth and falsehood. 'I'm performing a favor for a *friend*,' I say, trying to put just the right arch emphasis on the word to imply that they are nothing of the kind. 'Nothing more and nothing less.'

Ford's carnivorous smile widens. 'Come, my dear. D'you think I haven't noticed the size of your court? Or how lightly you travel? I understand completely; your little problem is safe with me.' Which is to say, she's swallowed the cover story – that the Honorable Katherine Soricò has fallen upon hard times and is reduced to providing very expensive services for very discreet, rich clients – and is prepared to use it against me. 'I sympathize completely, and I can be the soul of discretion. But I'm still curious. What is it that takes you from Mercury to Mars with such haste?'

'Why, the availability of transport, nothing more and nothing less.' I raise my crystal drinking bulb and ingest a sip of sweet liqueur, using the motion to distract as I compose my features. 'My friend wants a pair of trustworthy eyes to look over some interests of his that are giving him reason for concern.' *Trustworthy* meaning *independent* and *unindentured.* Unlikely to be suborned by a conspiracy to throw off the shackles of proxy ownership, in other words. 'About which I can say no more.' And *that* should slam the air lock down before her probing, because if there is a single issue that all aristos hold in confidence, it is the whispered threat of an indentured arbeiter conspiracy against the moneyed elite.

Granita's smile evaporates. For a moment I think I've gone too far. Then she reaches across the table and grasps my arm. I feel the hum of powerful motors concealed within the satin sheath of her formal glove. 'One trusts that you will remember your friends, should times become *difficult*.' She stares at me, eyes glittering as coldly and brilliantly as rhinestones.

'Indeed, my lady.' I nod, the almost bow that I practice daily, that is reflexive for the bishojo ruling caste. 'I shall do that.'

'Well, then, it's settled!' She feigns lighthearted delight, as if I have not momentarily scared the shit out of her with rumor of a slave rebellion. 'One good word deserves another, I think.'

'Oh. Yes?' The trichloroethane in the liqueur is tickling my chemotactic sensors, infusing them with a rich warmth that is slightly disorienting.

'The Pink Police have very recently been placed on heightened alert. It appears they are afraid that a cache of replicators has been raided on Mars. They are searching everyone arriving on or departing the planet, and even with my connections, I am afraid we might be delayed on arrival.'

I freeze for a few seconds, then knock back the rest of my drink to conceal my dismay. Two things are apparent. First, I haven't fooled her at all; she thinks I'm smuggling something. And secondly, if she's telling the truth (and not just a cunning lie to flush me out), it's clear that they're looking for me.

Which means Jeeves has a leak in his organization.

*

I return to the plush, lonely claustrophobia of my cabin, cloisonné-enamel inlay and swagged-velvet drapes concealing soap-bubble lithium-alloy walls. Of my 'servants,' Bill is else-where; Ben is hunched in his usual spot between my shipping trunk and the coreward bulkhead, chewing on a wire. 'You again,' he mutters.

'Where's Ben?' I ask.

'None of your business, *mistress*.' His sarcasm is charmless in the extreme.

'Then I suppose he won't want to hear what I just picked up in the lounge,' I snap, as I swing down the safety bars by my bed and float inside. 'The Pink Police have gone onto high alert. They're searching all traffic between Mars and orbit.'

'Oh,' Bill responds disappointingly. He stands up, releasing the wire. 'I'd better go tell him, then.' He leaves abruptly, by way of the servants' hatch.

Alone – for the time being – I let myself drift down to the sleeping pad, then fold the safety bars back into place. (While *Pygmalion* normally accelerates at barely a hundredth of a gee, she sometimes has to dodge debris. Traveling at hundreds of kilometers per second, even a sand grain can be deadly: and sand grains don't show up on radar at long range. Consequently, the evasive maneuvers can be brutal – and after the first time they're plastered against the ceiling by the emer-gency thrusters, even the most pigheaded aristos learn to respect the safety bars on their beds.)

Lying securely on a nest of bedding, I check my pad, as I have done for the past fifty days. Normally it's replete with chatter, to which I have to spend some time responding – queries from the managers of Katherine Sorico's fictional estates, requests for authorizations to disburse funds and return company accounts – all meaningless, but essential if I am to maintain my cover identity. This time, I'm surprised to see a real message hidden in the morass. It purports to be about repairs to a summer house in Tasmania, but as I skim it hurriedly I suddenly realize there's an imago attachment. And it's from Emma!

'Sister.' Her sudden formality is jarring. 'I gather you've met my friend.' *I have?* 'And you're no longer on Venus. Or Mercury. I don't know where you are, and I don't want to – if this message reaches you, best not to reply.'

I squint at the imago, trying to make out the background. It's dark, and something about Emma's appearance isn't right. Her hair is a glassy shell around the top of her head, her skin is – *oh*. She's wearing cryoskin, of the kind we only need in the very chilliest of environments. I blink, irritated. 'Go on.'

'I hear you've been in trouble lately. I'm sorry about that; we'd have spared you if we could. But *I'm* in trouble, too, and I need your assistance.' She pauses for a moment, but not to take breath; where she is standing, the traditional oxygen-nitrogen ambient mix would flow like water. What on Earth can she be talking about?

'For a long time now, we – some of your sibs – have been engaged in a line of work we've been careful to keep you out of. That's you, Freya, and everyone else who didn't need to be directly involved; you're our sisters, and we cherish you, but we didn't want to involve you because what we do is risky and distasteful. So only a few of us were involved at any time. Unfortunately, there aren't enough of us left. So we need your help. We need to bring you into the circle.'

Circle of *what*? 'Get to the point,' I mutter.

'We – myself, and I think it's safe to name the dead ones, so I can also say: Juliette, Chloe, Aphrodite, Sinead, and some others who are still alive so it's best if you don't know who – are Block Two sibs. You, and most of our sisters, are Block One. You were initialized from a soul dump of Rhea that was taken right after her certification, when she was nineteen years old and in her sixth instar.' Sixth — and final, adult-sized — body, that is. It takes a long time, years and years, to educate and train an archetype for a lineage of concubines. There's no easy way to short-circuit childhood if you're trying to build high empathy and interpersonal skills. I (*she,* I remind myself) was ported through a series of bodies along the way from crèche to cathouse, and only declared complete by our trainers on reaching the sixth instar.

'What you weren't told is that after that template dump was taken, Rhea underwent further training. We Block Two sibs have been privileged to receive an update from a soul chip she recorded during her nineteenth instar, at age thirty.' *Nineteenth? How in the name of my Dead Love did she get through* thirteen *bodies in eleven years?* 'Physically we're identical, but mentally . . . we have some extra training. We can hide among you quite effectively, but the fact remains, we're different.'

I pause the imago. Emma's confession is outrageous! *She's not* — really *not, where it counts* — one of us? She's a sib of an older, different lineage that — *hang on.* My head's spinning. My hand goes to the back of my head, pushing aside the weight of my synthetic curls. *Juliette. She's compatible. I'm dreaming her, aren't I?* It's a fact that you can't exchange memories with a different lineage. You get nothing but fuzzy impressions at best — insanity and catatonia at worst. So. Emma *is* of my line. But she's claiming to have extra . . . what?

'That's alright. Take your time.' Her lips curve in a smile that doesn't reach her eyes. 'It's hard to accept, I know. But swapping memories and remembering our dead is only part of the program. This is what our soul chips were designed for in the first place — to allow in-field upgrades, so that we can avoid obsolescence by acquiring new skills and experiences.

And there's nothing as obsolescent as a concubine tailored to please an extinct species, is there? I started out just like you, Freya, as a Block One sister. Now we need you to upgrade to Block Two. You can start the process whenever you like – just load one of us, Chloe or Sinead perhaps. It'll take a couple of years to complete the process, but once you start, you'll gain access to the reflexes you need.'

I pause the imago again and rub the socket at the top of my spine. 'What's in it for me?' I ask.

Evidently Emma gave her imago some footnotes to roll out if I seemed unconvinced. 'How do you think we always manage to buy our sibs free if they fall on hard times and wind up indentured?' She shrugs. 'There are more rewarding lines of work than rickshaw driver, Freya. Much more rewarding – even if we have to spend most of our lives wearing one disguise or another.' Is that a moue of bitterness in her expression? 'This message was forwarded via our trusted associates. If you're hearing this, then you've already started on that path. The upgrade to Block Two will ease your progress.'

'That's not the only reason you called,' I say.

'No.' I can see the logic mill behind the imago switch streams; they're responsive, but not truly conscious. 'I'm still in . . . trouble I can't go into, Freya, but you can help me with it. But you can *only* help me if you accept the Block Two upgrade and work with my friends. Do you understand?'

Oh great: moral blackmail. I admit I've been in trouble a time or two, but I haven't needed bailing out of indentured servitude since the time when the baroque ensemble split up and I . . . no, I've mostly kept to myself. But I've got to admit, if I set aside my outrage at being used as camouflage by a cabal of scheming elder sisters, I'm curious about what this cryptic skill-upgrade package comes with, especially now I know that

Juliette was one of the gang. 'Okay, so you want me to load one of your Block Two sibs and keep working for JeevesCo. I loaded Juliette back on Mercury, you know? Is there anything else you can tell—'

I stop, balling my fists in frustration. The imago has auto-erased, and I'm talking to dead air. *What next?* I wonder, staring at the ceiling and counting the seconds (thirty-two million, give or take) until our arrival in Mars orbit.

*

They're waiting for me as I roll through the doorway, taking it low and fast: another pair of bonsai ninja, their camouflage suits shimmering in the light of the setting moon. They've got guns, and they're sneaking up on the entrance, doubtless hoping to take me unawares. I *don't* have a gun, but the baton in my left sleeve slides into my hand smoothly, and as I kick off, I'm already swinging it, feeling the depleted uranium sphere at its tip lance out toward the nearer gunman's head.

There's a sharp tug at my side, and he jerks sideways, neck bending unnaturally as I take another light-footed step, leaning backward to compensate for my momentum as I try to swerve the two-meter-long club toward his companion, who is bringing his weapon to bear. But my left leg chooses that moment to malfunction –

A blurred line flickers through my visual field and slices him in half as I topple over backward and land in the dirt.

The pain hits me then, intense and localized. I'm leaking perfusion fluid, blue and bubbly with squandered mechanosomes in the cold moonlight. I look up at the hissing roar and the familiar three-eyed face. 'Babe?'

I struggle for words: parts of me feel wrong, and I can't tell which. 'Take the sampler, Daks, I'm a mission kill. The sextons will be here in a minute.'

Daks lands on top of me with all six legs extended and his fur bristling. 'The fuck I will!' He sounds pissed off.

'Leave me!' I can feel the hollow thudding through the small of my back as the sextons leap into action. I try to reach inside my coat, but Daks is too heavy to dislodge. The damage must be worse than I thought. With any luck they won't be able to add me to their picket fence. It's a small consolation, and I hold on to it for a moment, but then I realize Daks is gripping my coat really tight. 'Hey, don't be stupid—'

Grit, dust, and dirt blows everywhere as Daks lifts off. It's like being grabbed by a miniature tornado. There's no way he could manage this in a full-gee field, and even here he's got to be overloading his thrusters; I'm scared he won't even make it to the edge of the garden –

But then I'm lying on my back again. I blink, making tears of antifreeze flow. My vision clears slowly as I hear the usually inaudible chatter of my subroutines taking stock. *Anything else broken? No? Good. How's the hole? Still leaking, down to 50 ml/minute.* Bubbles of viscous silicone lube slide down my cheeks as I turn my head sideways. Daks sits beside me, looming anxiously across my visual field. 'Babe? You alright? Talk to me! Babe?'

'I'm still here. Mostly. Take my soul—'

'We're next to the spider and I'm out of fuel and I don't seem to have packed my fission thorax. Can you get in?'

Shit. I roll my head the other way and try not to giggle as the landscape flips. *Thud* go the sextons, on the other side of the wall. I feel light-headed. *Hey, this could be fun!* The spider squats enticingly close, door open, amber light flooding across the ground between us – an impossible expanse of desert, continental in scale. The pain is making me woozy, so I switch it off – risky, but I need a clear head to manage what Daks wants me to do. I experiment, make my hand twitch. *Hmm.* 'Watch me.'

It takes me uncounted minutes to roll over and crawl two meters. There's a grinding sharpness in my left abdominal compartment, and my left arm feels like it's about to come off. Something inside it is bent or broken, something major and structural. I listen for the thump of the sextons all the way, expecting a crushing impact on my back at any moment. But nothing happens, and after a while I begin to hope that Daks's unexpected lift and my own enfeebled crawl have combined to bamboozle them. Finally – recovering from another head-swimmingly vacant moment – I reach out and grab the edge of the spider's hatch with my right hand.

'Nearly there, Babe.'

'One day.' I make my arm bend. I don't weigh enough here. Back on Earth I could just barely lift myself this way. Here . . . why do I seem to weigh too much?

'Nearly—'

I get my other, weakened, arm onto the hatch. My fingers don't want to close properly, so I shove my wrist over the gap between hatch and windscreen. My right arm contracts, levering me upright as I struggle to get my damaged left arm braced against the rocky ground –

'One day I'm going to—'

'There!' Daks bleats encouragement at me.

'Tell you how much I—'

Flop. For a moment everything grays out, then I realize I'm sitting in the driver's chair. My right arm is still locked on. I make my fingers let go, willing them, one by one, then reach down and tug my numb leg into position.

'Quickly!' I feel a faint vibration through my buttocks. 'They've figured it out!'

'How much I.' *Hate you,* I think. 'Love you,' I say aloud. I drop my good right hand onto the controller. 'You tied down?'

'Yeah, Babe. Babe? Make it move.'

I squeeze the spider's control nipple. Forget the cover story; We got the goods. 'Home to Jeeves,' I slur. Then I go into preterminal shutdown mode, and nothing matters anymore.

*

The Venerable Granita Ford takes almost the entire voyage to make her play for me. Her seduction technique is polished, professional, painstaking, and chilly in its perfection. I am helpless before her slow approach; it feels as if she knows exactly where I am most vulnerable.

(Or perhaps I deceive myself. Maybe she's just spinning it out to relieve the boredom. In truth, ninety days in a metal bubble falling between worlds, with only scoundrels and their slaves for company, has left me fretful and frustrated. I passed through this stage years ago on Venus, where I was so unfashionable that eventually I almost convinced myself I no longer cared that nobody wanted me; but recent events have reawakened my need for intimacy. And among my kind, intimacy is a powerful and compelling drive. We need to be needed, and though we do not die for lack of sex, we become something less than ourselves.)

By seventy days into the journey, all Granita has to do is crook her little finger at me and beckon to set me all a-shiver. Which is exactly what she wants, obviously. Trying to resist your designated purpose is hard, and the stronger your eusocial conditioning, the worse it gets. A road grader with no roads to roll will be unhappy, but that level of frustration pales into insignificance when compared to one of my kind who is forced into celibacy. So I remind myself that what counts is keeping one's head and one's autonomy the morning after, and resign myself to an indefinite period of jelly kneed hunger.

She doesn't make it too obvious, at first. She's got her entourage, her little world of courtiers to distract and pleasure her. But she pays too much attention to me for it to be accidental, asking me to teach her card games that she obviously knew centuries ago, and has since forgotten, discussing sixteenth-century Hungarian folk music with a familiarity that is itself suggestive. She even, coyly, asks my opinion about the proper running of an orgy – as if the Honorable Katherine Sorico might have anything useful to contribute other than a fetching coral-eared flush and a heaving bosom.

One day, well into our deceleration phase – *Pygmalion* is tacking hard against the solar wind, and Marsport is close enough that I've carried out Dr. Murgatroyd's activation process and installed my cargo in the incubator in my abdominal cavity – Granita raises an eyebrow. She has me well trained: I fold my game board and bounce across the room to her side, slotting neatly into her circle between faceless nonentities who make way for me by instinct. 'Good morning, Kate!' Granita contrives to sound spontaneously delighted by my presence. 'Do you have a minute to spare? I have some matters I should like your opinion on.'

'Of course.' I smile back at her.

'In my stateroom, if you please. In private, I'm afraid,' she adds for her courtiers. She floats from her chair, layers of carbon-fiber chiffon belling around her. 'Follow me, Kate?'

This is new. Curiosity, excitement, and a minor key of dread jumble my perceptions as I follow her back through the corridors that lead to the hotel deck.

My little cabin's relative poverty becomes obvious as I follow her through the air lock into the owner's quarters. Granita's room is nearly as large as the grand saloon. Thickly piled carpets on the walls and ceiling, with thin tapestry hangings to divide up the volume, lend it a plush sense of overfurnished intimacy. Her bed is a huge gauzy cobweb of a hammock that occupies half the end wall, strewn with cushions and throws that don't quite disguise the wrist and ankle restraints. 'Privacy, up,' she orders, as the door closes. 'Pygmalion, leave me.'

'I obey,' says the ship, in a quite unfamiliar tone of voice. Abruptly, we're alone. I shiver. I have a sudden sense of how much emptiness lies on the far side of the wall behind that web-hammock.

'Come, join me, my dear,' Granita pats the throw beside her. Subtle cues tweak my awareness; the systolic beat of my thoracic pumps accelerate. 'I won't bite.' Her smile is roguish. It's an invitation I can't refuse, don't *want* to refuse, in fact. Her intentions are clear enough as she murmurs sweet nothings, and I permit myself to be fussed over with a sense of gathering relief. *At last.*

She's clearly happiest as a hunter, so when she kisses me, I accept her passively, opening my arms to receive her embrace. And then her program takes an unexpected twist. 'I want to be yours, Kate. Put this on.' She passes me a small-eyed mask. I pull it on while she works at the fastenings of her intricate aristo outfit with digits that shake from overcontrol. 'You want to own me, don't you, dear? I'm yours, your property! Use me!' So the icy aristo harbors secret submissive fantasies, a covert hankering for a strict Creator? I boggle slightly, even as my training takes over, and I start working out how best to satisfy her needs.

Later, as I'm lying exhausted and glistening beside her, she turns her head slightly and smiles at me. 'I know what you are,' she whispers.

'What am I?' I can barely speak; My metabolic debt is high.

I haven't had a workout like this since I bedded Paris – Granita is a very demanding sub.

'I've met your kind before. Your disguise is very good, but your primary conditioning gives you away.'

I sigh, very quietly. I was afraid of this – but I've got a secondary cover ready and waiting. 'What am I?' I ask again.

'You're no runaway serf, certainly. But your kind make poor aristocrats, dear. It stands out like a sore . . .' She glances down at her chest and tugs on her bonds: I take the hint, and unstrap her hand. 'You have too much empathy for this age. You were never designed to hold and to own. Are you certain you don't need a protector? I'd make a place of honor for you in my household – dress you in blackened steel armor and call you my mistress—'

For a moment I picture my life as this ancient slave-owning aristo's house dominatrix. Not indentured but a free associate – indentured arbeiters, fitted with slave chips and stripped of their free will, simply can't perform this calling – brandishing a barbed whip at her word. A pampered favorite, as long as I can avoid looking her beneficence in the eye. 'I'd love to, but I have a prior commitment,' I say. And it's true. I *would* love it – I love to be wanted – but I'd feel corrupted by it, too, not by the sex but by knowing the source of her wealth. Of all the other bodies chained by her word, unwilling and unable to resist.

'You didn't just bring me here for a quick fuck, did you?'

She makes an odd noise. After a moment I recognize it as a chuckle. 'Oh child, you're delightful. No, of course I didn't.' She falls silent.

'Why, then?'

'Ah, me. One becomes paranoid in one's old age; do I surprise you? One learns to jump at shadows . . . you're very similar to my personal nemesis, Kate. Don't look so surprised; assassins and spies have disguised themselves as concubines and lovers since the dawn of creation, surely this can't be news to you? I had to make sure.'

An ugly fear twists at the edges of my awareness. 'What have you done?'

She runs a fingertip idly along my ribs, leaving a trail in the thin sheen of silicone sweat. 'I had my retainers search your compartment,' she admits. 'Certain parties – a consortium of black labs, run by a fellow known as Dr. Sleepless – are trying to smuggle a living weapon to Mars. One of my sources thought you might be the courier. But I must apologize – they were wrong.'

I shiver. 'What kind of living weapon?' I ask coolly, forcing myself to keep my hand away from the pit of my stomach.

'A – a fully autonomous piece of pink goo,' she says reluctantly. 'A generator module able to produce more of its own kind.' It's her turn to shudder now. 'Horrible!'

'But you know it's not me,' I insist angrily. 'Why did you do it?'

'I'm.' She pauses: 'I'm sorry, Kate. I should not have suspected you, but I had to be sure. The enemy is not above using your kind as couriers.' She reaches out to me, and I shove her hand away with carefully calculated anger, narrowing my achingly oversized eyes at her.

If only you knew . . .

SMALL BODIES, LOOSELY COUPLED

When things go wrong in space, they tend to go wrong with very little warning. This time it's an exception.

We're on day eighty-eight of the cruise. After a stormy argument and a sulky three-day cooling-off period, I allowed Granita to woo me back into her web, where her submissive contrition and shameless self-abasement went a long way to assuaging my indignation. Who knew? It can't be easy being a ruthless industrialist by day and yearning for the kiss of a Creator's lash by night. So we use each other furtively, working out a wary accommodation until we fetch up gasping on the far shore of ecstasy. It must be making us the talk of the saloon, but Granita is old enough and ruthless enough that she doesn't care – and as for myself, I'm used to being a freak.

So when *Pygmalion* electrospeaks me one night in my state-room, she takes me completely by surprise.

'Lady Sorico,' says the ship, 'we have a problem.'

I boot straight into wakefulness from a confusing dream of pole-dancing dwarfs. I'm alone in my room; Bill and Ben are elsewhere, doing whatever it is that they get up to in the night. My precious cargo is a warm ovoid pressure inside me, where a Creator female would harbor her reproductive fabricator. For a dreadful moment I think Pygmalion has scanned me and recognized it for what it is, but the moment passes. 'What's happening?' I reply.

'There's an unexplained latency whenever I try and talk to traffic control. Packets are taking too long to get through. And I've just noticed that we are not alone out here.'

'Not alone?'

'Let me draw you a diagram.'

We've been on final approach to Marsport for the past week, and we're still decelerating at a hundredth of a gee, with more than a day to go. We've got nearly ten kilometers per second of delta vee to shed before Mars can capture us. Our plasma sail – a huge and tenuous shell of gas, held in place by carefully controlled magnetic fields – is still inflated, billowing as it responds to the braking magbeam from our destination. At less than half a million kilometers, Mars is showing a visible disk, but we're not in parking orbit yet.

'We are *here*,' Pygmalion indicates. 'The ping time to Marsport should be three seconds. Instead, it's more like six, and there is unaccountable corruption as well. Almost a quarter of my data is showing signs of tampering.'

Whoops. 'Why are you telling me this?' I ask cautiously. 'Surely it's a matter for traffic control, or all the passengers . . .'

'Higgins Line's security office performs predictive risk assessment on all paying fares,' Pygmalion says blandly. 'Especially ones who have paid for extra services. Two passengers were identified as possible targets for interference. You are one of them. The other is the Venerable Granita Ford, with whom you may be intimately familiar.'

'Her I can understand, she's loaded! But why me—'

'Higgins Line is aware that your ticket was purchased through the offices of Jeeves Corporation. Jeeves Corporation simultaneously purchased a number of tickets on behalf of various other persons traveling via other lines. Three of them have been assassinated as of this date.' She continues, palpably smug: 'Higgins Line has never lost a passenger to external attack, and we have no intention of starting now. Even more so in view of the special arrangements surrounding your passage. However, my threat-assessment agent tells me that there is a seventy percent probability that an attempt will be made on your life prior to our arrival in orbit, and the corruption of my external communication link suggests that infiltrators are already aboard this ship.'

'Oh dear.' I lie bolt upright in my bed, fighting the urge to swear aloud. 'What do you propose to do?'

'Allow me to continue?' Pygmalion sounds slightly piqued at my lack of panic.

I take a second to compose myself. 'Go ahead.'

'An hour ago I requested a routine long-range traffic update from Marsport. As you may be aware, the Pink Police are conducting audits of all orbital traffic. There appears to be a ship inbound for Marsport on a schedule coincident with our own and approximately a thousand seconds ahead of us which was not mentioned in my traffic update. Furthermore, the vessel appears to be a coaster, designed for low-impulse high-thrust maneuvering. I do not have its full flight plan, and do not intend to request it, but I should note that it strongly resembles a type previously employed by the Pink Police as a boarding craft. Of course, mere resemblance is not evidence of identity, and the current security alert would be an excellent cover for parties interested in carrying out nefarious activities — such as illicitly boarding commercial vessels.'

'Okay.' I think hard before I ask my next question. 'When do you expect them to intercept us?'

'We have about twelve hours. And I can't outmaneuver them.' Pygmalion pauses. 'But I have a suggestion . . .'

*

If one wishes to live to a ripe old age, there are certain activities one should avoid. Chief among these is eating anything larger than one's own head – but not so very far down the list is any activity that involves clambering around the outside of a spaceship. This is especially true when the ship in question is an interplanetary liner that is under acceleration, and its propulsion system involves rotating magnetic fields that generate currents in the mega-amp range in the plasma envelope surrounding it. Get too close to the drive antennae, or accidentally short out the plasma loop against the ship's hull, and if you're lucky, you'll simply die. If you're unlucky, well, internal electrophoresis is famously neither quick nor painless.

Which is why I'm sitting in *Pygmalion*'s aft maintenance air lock, my graveyard strapped to my chest inside a hastily woven black-painted chain-mail suit, clutching one end of a rope threaded with a fiber-optic bearer. I'm about to jump overboard, and I'll be aiming right for that plasma envelope.

'This cannot be good,' says Bill, or maybe Ben. 'How about we gut her, stash the payload, and claim the reward?'

'You're just afraid of heights,' sneers Ben, or maybe Bill. 'Anyway, the payload's environment-sensitive. Like the boss said, it won't hatch without the freak. We need her alive.'

'You don't scare me,' I say, dangling my feet over the blue-glowing abyss. 'Can either of you see the ship yet?'

'Naah.'

'Good.' It was visible a minute ago, before our slow roll took it out of view over the near horizon of *Pygmalion*'s hull. I lean forward, feeling viscerally ill but unwilling to admit it in front of my two oafish assistants. 'Okay, you two, climb aboard.'

Bill (or Ben) bounces toward me and clings to my shoulders. He's got the activation unit for my payload strapped to his back like a miniature pack. I roll forward slowly and drift down and out of the air lock, clinging to the edge by one hand. The two bags that my salvation depends on – one empty and one full – hang from my belt. With my other, free, hand I hold the end of the cable where Ben (or Bill) can get it. 'Can you see the socket?'

'In sight.' They're all business, now we're overboard. 'Got it.' I look up, my vision hampered by the narrow eye slot that's the only gap in my suit. His tiny fingers are working feverishly, lashing the cable to one of the emergency handholds under the air lock lip. The fiber-optic jack goes into a comms socket. Then another chibi-head peers over the side of the hatch.

'Move it!' He whispers. 'They'll be coming over the horizon in another minute.'

'Just finishing up. Okay, close it now.' I dangle from the cable while Bill and Ben shut the air-lock door and clamber down my back. 'Make with the sack, manikin.'

'Done.' I hold the empty bag open while they climb inside, then wire it shut and double-check that it's fastened to my belt. It balances out the other, full bag on the opposite side. I start reeling out the cable, lowering myself down toward that fuzzy blue floor beneath me.

The fuzz is the plasma magnet that *Pygmalion*'s M2P2 sail depends on. Powerful radio transmitters ionize the gas and induce electrical currents in it, generating a magnetic field that blocks the solar wind. We're dropping headlong toward

Mars, straight into the braking magbeam from Phobos, with the ten-kilometer-wide plasma bubble balanced between ship and destination. I'm lowering myself into it on the end of an insulating cable, wearing a half-assed hot suit I ran up on my stateroom's printer. A funny thing about plasma bubbles is that they tend to block radar. Dangling at the end of a fifty-meter-long cable, wearing a black conductive suit, Bill and Ben and I are going to be invisible to the intruder – I hope. I try not to think about the alternatives. Maybe I got the chain weave wrong and I'm going to cook from the inside out; or maybe they're going to locate us optically and reel us in at their leisure. Worse, maybe Pygmalion miscalculated on the length of the tether? If the plasma sail is too thin, we're going to end up lethally exposed, dangling in the middle of the magbeam from Mars like a dust mote before a blowtorch. Neither fate is anything to look forward to, but it beats cowering in my stateroom as the bulls come stomping through the air lock.

My skin crawls briefly as we near the plasma shell, then we're inside. A couple of blue sparks flash across the surface of my chain-mail hot suit, but there's no arcing. A mimetic reflex makes me try to breathe a sigh of relief, which is very disconcerting in vacuum. *Down.* The empty gulf swings below me, as the ship decelerates at ten centimeters per second squared. From this side of the barrier the far side of the magsail is almost invisible, many kilometers away.

I hang in the bubble, with nothing to do but watch my power consumption and keep an eye on the stealthy feed *Pygmalion* has fed to Bill and Ben. I've got maybe twelve hours before I have to start shutting down limbs to save juice. In the worst case, I'll have to rely on the terrible twosome to get me out of here when *Pygmalion* reaches Marsport and powers down her sail. But at least I've got a good view of the other passengers. Which is why I'm watching events in the saloon, with mixed feelings of boredom and wistfulness, when things start to happen.

It's early morning, shipboard time, and Pygmalion has alerted everybody that something is happening. The Lyrae twins squat in their usual corner, stolidly chewing their way through a platter of pancakes. Reza Agile and Sinbad-15 sit nearby, sharing a go board while Mary X. Valusia dances attendance to Granita's entourage, who are gathered in a gaggle at the opposite end of the saloon from the dreadful duo. As for the Venerable Granita Ford herself –

'Attention.' Brash electrospeak ripples through my head, forwarded from *Pygmalion*'s general announcement feed: I tense. 'Attention passengers and spacecraft *Pygmalion*. This is Port Control. You are ordered to stand to for boarding and inspection. A police cutter will come alongside shortly. Any resistance constitutes a violation of quarantine regulations and will be punished severely.'

'What?' shouts Reza Agile, jumping so suddenly that she bounces off the ceiling. 'What's going on? Ship! Are we delayed, or waylaid? I demand an explanation!' Then she's drowned out by a hubbub from the other passengers.

'Attention. Coming alongside now.'

'It was too good to be true,' Sinbad-15 moans.

'Has anyone seen the other passengers today?' One of the Lyrae twins asks thoughtfully. 'I find it interesting that Ford and her floozy are absent.'

'It's a conspiracy!' Agile is clearly very agitated indeed. 'She's been studying us for the entire voyage – she's going to have her minions chip and file us! We're being press-ganged!'

At which precise moment Granita storms into the saloon.

Two arbeiters trail behind, desperately battling to finish dressing her. 'What is this disturbance about?' she demands.

'Attention! You will comply with all instructions on pain of immediate arrest. We are coming aboard now.'

I look away from my stealth feed. Above me, beyond the blue nimbus of the drive field, I see a slim black knife shape. Painfully bright lights flash on and off along its flanks as it maneuvers toward the *Pygmalion*. Lightning plays across the glowing magsail ceiling; the intruder's exhaust stream is doing strange things to the plasma bubble.

'Hey, do you *see* that?' (I stitched a patch cable into the neck of my sack of troublesome assistants, just in case I needed their withering sarcasm for a change. Now it seems like a good thing I took the precaution.) 'Do we need to think about moving?'

'Yep.' I can't tell whether it's Bill or Ben, but he doesn't sound happy. 'Looks like a VASIMR on high thrust. They can't hold it for long, but if they don't dock quickly, it'll short out the plasma bubble. Look down.'

I take his advice, and wish I hadn't. The blue nowhere beneath my feet is rippling and shimmering like an ocean surface before a storm front. Pinpricks stipple it like rust. 'That's not good, is it?'

'I think it's going to be alright,' says Ben, or Bill – the other one, anyway. 'They're on final approach. Won't be long now. Look at it move! That's military thrust, alright.'

I look back at the approaching intruder. *Pirates? Or Police?* I'm not sure it really matters at this point. Neither of them would be good news. The ship is slim and smooth-edged, with triangular-tiled surfaces that make my eyes hurt as I try to trace its outline. The stubby cone of its main drive is just visible now, the bell nozzle glowing violet-hot even through the hazy plasma overcast. It sideslips toward *Pygmalion*, and for almost a minute I'm frozen with fear, terrified that it's going to ram the ship we dangle from, or quench the ionized bubble, or angle its main engine just wrong and blast us all to white-hot shrapnel with its plasma rocket . . .

Then the glare vanishes, and there's a ripple in the cable that tells me the two ships have locked together above us. And part of me realizes, *Of course. They don't want to destabilize the sail, not with us riding the Phobos magbeam on final approach.*

'It's time for stage C,' says Bill (or Ben), presumably reading off Pygmalion's detailed checklist.

'Is it?' I check the other bag dangling from my belt. Yes, it's the one we made up earlier. 'Okay, I'm ready. Let's keep an eye on what's going on in the saloon, yes?' I start the ascent, climbing hand over hand and reeling in the cable as I go. I feel like I only weigh about a kilogram here, even with my passengers. The trick is going to be not overdoing things and ramming the underside of the air lock headfirst.

The air in the saloon is steaming. The passengers are engaged in furious recriminations; Granita is tearing a strip off the Lyrae twins, Reza Agile is demanding my head (she appears to think I'm a police spy, of all things), and Mary X. is huddled in a corner, desperately trying to convince anyone who'll listen to her that she's nothing to do with whatever is happening.

Meanwhile, the steam is thickening, pumping into the saloon in great gouts. *Pygmalion* has fallen silent, evidently succumbing to whatever pressure our assailants can bring to bear on a spaceship over a direct docking link. I can't tell precisely what's happening, but I'm sure of one thing – the best place to be, when your spaceship is being boarded by bad bots who're looking for you, is on board another vessel.

A rasping voice of authority comes over the broadcast channel again. 'Attention, passengers and ship. Your pressurized compartments are being fumigated. Police agents will come aboard once fumigation is complete. This is an official Replication Suppression Agency inspection. You are suspected of harboring illegal replicators. You will be inspected and sterilized before you are allowed to proceed to Marsport; resistance will be punished severely.'

It *is* the Pink Police. Of all my luck; pirates would actually be preferable. You can usually negotiate a ransom with extralegal capitalists, but the Pink Police are distressingly short of venality. I pause, pressing a hand against the base of my abdomen. I can see the payload inside me with my mind's eye, restlessly replicating. *Do magnetic fields damage pink goo?* I suddenly wonder. I could have blown the mission completely! But I don't have time to worry about that now if I'm going to save myself.

On the other hand, I think, as I close in on the docking tunnel above me, *the last place they're going to look for it is aboard their own ship. Right?*

Gouts of high-temperature water vapor blister the delicate paintwork of the *Pygmalion*'s saloon, soak into the colorful nylon-and-polyester padding, and steam up the sensors. There is some complaining and grumbling from the passengers, but the announcement that it is an official RSA inspection damps down the prevailing state of near panic. Nobody likes the Pink Police, but the prevailing state of public opinion is that they fulfill a nasty but necessary requirement. And so, the reaction is muted and the atmosphere steamy when the police jet in.

I don't know what I was expecting of the Pink Police, but this isn't it; they're using drones, basketball-sized metal spheres studded with thrusters and sensors. *What, no villainous cops swarming aboard with DNA scanners clenched between their teeth?* Two spheres, three – they spin around with unreal grace, bouncing between floor and walls and ceiling, pointing their sensors everywhere. The steam gouting through the companionway obscures my view of them, but I can see the passengers cringing. Then –

'Hello? Big Slow? You can let us out, now. Remember us?'

It's Bill, or Ben, in the bag at my waist. With a start, I notice that the sky outside my eye slit has turned black, the ghostly blue haze stretching away to an indefinite horizon beneath my trailing feet. The boarding tube looms just overhead, a violent tentacle thrusting into the unwilling *Pygmalion*'s air lock.

'Right.' I loosen the flap holding them in, and Bill (or Ben) pops a prehensile, beady-eyed head out and looks around. Then he grabs hold of my face and swarms up to the cable, followed closely by his sib, along with the bag. I'm not used to being used as a stepladder. 'Hey!'

'Keep it low, Big Slow. We're trying to be sneaky. You wanna get ready to make with the decoy?'

'If you think it's time.' I tie the other bag to the line, then open it and start preparing its contents. There's a suit of clothes that the Honorable Kate Sorico never really liked, and a bunch of stuff to fill it out. Bulky stuff, massive . . . and padded with feedstock from the room printer that Pygmalion swore blind would look like a body on radar.

'Nearly there, Big Slow. Get ready.'

What we're about to try is really stupid, but it beats all of the alternatives we've come up with. (I check the parasitic feed, but all it shows me is billowing steam; someone – I think it may be Mary X. – is complaining about the humidity wrecking her hairdo.)

The plan is simple, if not simple-minded. (a) Send out a bunch of encrypted decoy messages addressed to Jeeves, purely by way of distraction. *Done.* (b) Get out of *Pygmalion* before the police come storming aboard, and stay out of sight. *Done.* (So far.) (c) Let them search the ship. (d) Dump a decoy, so they go haring off after it. (e) Reboard *Pygmalion*, and hope they conclude that we left earlier, or were never there in the first place, or that they need to conserve fuel for their own orbital injection, or *something.* Like I said, it's completely stupid. It's just that, as Pygmalion pointed out, it stands a faint chance of keeping us out of the hands of the Pink Police. Unlike any of the alternatives on offer.

'Ready.'

It's best not to think too hard about all the holes in this plan, even though I can see plenty. Really, short of sitting there and waiting for them to arrest us, there's not anything else we can do. And who knows? Maybe it'll even work.

'Okay, Big. Give it some elbow.'

I draw my legs up and shove the decoy *hard* in the small of her well-padded back. She floats away at a good clip, picking up speed rapidly and falling through the flickering blue curtain in only a few seconds. She's got to cross another few kilometers of nearly empty space inside the plasma sail, dropping away from us as we continue to decelerate at ten centimeters per second. It all adds up; in a few minutes she'll be making nearly two hundred kilometers per hour relative to the ships. If they're as monomaniacally thorough as their reputations would have us believe, the cops will take time to finish sterilizing *Pygmalion* and withdraw their drones, before they undock; which will leave them trying to track down a human-shaped target tens of kilometers away.

And then . . . we'll see.

A thought strikes me as I dangle on the rope. I look up at Bill and Ben. 'How are we going to get back aboard?' I ask.

'Worry about that later.' They're busy tying the bags to the same anchor point as the rope. 'Come on up here. We've got to get out of sight inside these sacks before they undock.' People clinging to the underside of a hatch would be a bit of a give-away, wouldn't they? 'Get in.'

And so I spend the next two hours hanging upside down from the underside of an air lock, swearing quietly to myself, *not* crying, scared out of my wits, and periodically peeping through the steam-blinded cameras in hope of picking up some hint, anything at all really, of what's going on aboard *Pygmalion*.

The things I do to earn a living . . .

*

'Hello, Juliette. Can you hear this?'

. . .

'Can you hear this?'

(I'm tired. So very tired. It's good to lie here, in this soft, warm bed. But he's talking to me, and I need to, to do something. I ought to do something. Say something. But it's hard.)

'Juliette?'

(I make a monumental effort.) 'Boss?'

'That's better, we knew you were going to pull through! You've done very well, but maintenance say you went into temporary shutdown. We were very worried for a while, but you're going to be alright. Just a few repairs, of course, but you'll be good as new again in no time. Fit as a fiddle. Isn't that your instrument? Never mind. What one would mean to say is, ah, if there's anything you need, just tell us.'

(An awful fear floats in the back of my mind, almost out of reach; I try to connect it to my vocalization system.) 'Boss. The sample.'

'The sample?'

'Is it . . . ?'

He sounds regretful. 'Yes, I'm afraid it is.'

(Which means . . .)

'The rumors are true, or at least plausible. Whoever broke in last year – we cannot count on them not having procured a viable sample of their own.'

(Which means he doesn't know about the other thing . . .)

'Go back to sleep, Juliette. We can talk about this later.'

(Footsteps, diminishing.)

'There'll be time enough for war.'

*

'Hey, Big Slow. Can you hear me?'

I come awake slowly. 'Bill?'

'No, It's Ben. Listen.'

I listen with electrosense and old-fashioned vibratory hearing. There's bumping and banging in the boarding tube above me. Sounds of a hurried retreat. 'Got it. Any news?'

'Check your parasite feed.'

He flags the view of the corridor heading toward the air lock. It's half-hazed, and a big droplet clings to the middle of the lens, distorting the view, but a quick bit of visual filtering sets me right. The police drones are flying toward the air lock, escorting – yes, it's Granita. She's talking to them. ' – not the one I'm looking for, but one of her sibs. Not my fault the bitch smelled a rat.' She sounds annoyed. 'You'll have to do better next time.' The drone is evidently conveying its driver's excuses. 'That's not good enough! I've got better things to do than stand guard over your targets all year. No, I don't suppose it matters. She could have been useful.'

They get to the air-lock vestibule. 'Yes, thank you. I need to proceed to my estates as rapidly as possible – unfinished business. If you have a spare seat, I'll take it. Yes, I'd love to witness your mopping-up. If you could record it for me, I am sure I can find a fitting use for it – *pour encourager les autres.*' She smiles coldly at the drone, then follows it aboard the police cutter.

I shudder. Dainty feet kick off overhead, leaving behind *Pygmalion* and the rest of her false flag operation. *Granita must be working for Her,* one of my ghost-selves warns me. I think I know which one it is, now, and I resolve to trust those instincts in future.

A minute later, there's a furious rattling and banging. Then the docking tube detaches. Almost immediately, the police cutter begins to fall away from *Pygmalion*, sliding past the air lock with the remorseless momentum of a freight train. It barrels down into the blue soupy sky of plasma and disappears in a flicker of lightning. With its high-thrust drive, it can drop toward Mars and fire up the motor just before arrival – getting there hours ahead of us.

'All clear, Big Slow.' I laboriously extract myself from the sack and climb back up to join Bill and Ben on the lip of the air lock. I'm dreading what I'll find on the other side of it. 'You can come inside now.'

I cycle through the lock into stifling heat and humidity. As I strip off my chain mail, I realize it's over ninety degrees. Spheres of hot water cling to the ceiling, wobbling like improbable steaming jellies before they fall slowly to the floor. One of them breaks off and lands on my shoulder, trickling down inside – it's not physically damaging, but it's painfully hot. Maybe the Pink Police were trying to poach the passengers? 'Bill. Ben. What do you think?'

'Better get back to our stateroom, Big Slow. I don't think we're going to be too popular around here.'

'Um.' I nerve myself: 'Pygmalion?'

She replies at once: she sounds distracted. 'I'm busy. Go to your room, Katherine.'

'Told you so,' Ben smugs at me. I pretend I didn't hear him.

Our stateroom is a tip. It's been thoroughly searched, and there's nothing quite as messy as a room that's been turned over in microgravity. I lock the door behind us and contemplate the wreckage with dismay. 'It's only for another day,' Bill (or Ben) reminds me. 'Chill out and try to ignore it. They didn't find us, did they?'

'No,' agrees Pygmalion, startling me. 'The decoy worked superbly. I note that they seem to have taken Ford with them. Do you know anything about that?'

'No.' I think for a moment. 'I believe she went willingly, though, which implies a degree of collusion.'

'Quite possibly.' Pygmalion is silent for a while. 'I think it would be best if you remain in your room until we arrive, then leave discreetly. The other passengers are highly upset, and some of them may assume that you are a police informer if you reappear.'

'Has Jeeves offered to pay, then?' Bill snipes.

'One does not discuss confidential corporate arrangements in public.' Pygmalion's snippy put-down is clear enough. (Ten to one Jeeves has paid handsomely for her to collude in smuggling me past the Pink Police.) 'This has been most inconvenient. My upholstery is damaged and my passengers outraged – it's scandalous! But – oh.' Her tone changes. 'Oh. No!'

'What's—'

'They just launched a missile.' She pauses for a knife-edged second. 'It's running directly away from us. Why would they do that?' More seconds tick by. 'It just detonated. Ninety-six kilometers away. Most strange.'

I shudder convulsively. It is anything but strange if you are privy to all the facts: a stuffed suit floating in vacuo, drifting ever farther from *Pygmalion*'s air lock, and an RSA cutter with a frustrated captain and an impatient VIP passenger aboard to witness the kill.

Someone *really* doesn't want my payload to reach Mars!

WHORES DE COMBAT

Welcome to Marsport, Deimos.

A brief factual rundown cannot do the place justice. I've been here before (even lived here for a handful of years), but it never fails to surprise. Let me attempt to explain . . .

Deimos is the outer of Mars's two moons, an irregular rocky lump between ten and fifteen kilometers in diameter, depending on where you hold your measuring calipers. It was originally covered in loose regolith, high in carbon, which has long since been recycled for construction materials. A century of solar energy beamed from the big collectors near Mercury powered the rockets that adjusted its orbit, and today Deimos is the anchor weight for the largest surface-to-orbit space elevator ever constructed: Bifrost.

Most of the inner planets have no space elevator at all; Venus and Mercury because their days are unfeasibly long, Earth because its gravity well and debris belts challenge the limits of engineering. But Luna has the L1 lift, and as for Mars – Mars lies on the cusp of the heavily populated, energy-rich inner system and the material-rich outer system. Mars also has Deimos, the perfect construction site and gravitational anchor for Bifrost. And so it was inevitable that Mars, the gateway to the outer solar system, would acquire an elevator like Bifrost, and a city like Marsport to run it.

Most elevators are simple things – parallel tapes traversed by sluggish climbers, drudge laborers whose groaning cantilevers bear the burden of interplanetary freight among the worlds of the outer solar system. But there's nothing simple about Bifrost. The complex of cables is half a kilometer across, wide enough to anchor a world. Fast express shuttles hurtle up and down with passengers, while the slow, sturdy supertrain scows take weeks to complete a round-trip, lowering refined feedstocks and returning with processed materials, manufactured more conveniently in the turbulent forges of Mars than in orbital facilities – and which can then be exported to the rest of the inner system.

A quarter of a million indentured arbeiters and their aristo overseers, and perhaps a tenth that number of independent souls, work the port facilities: loading and unloading cargo, inspecting payloads, maintaining the infrastructure, untangling problems, and serving those who get the real work done. Once our dead Creators ran ports like this, with names like Liverpool, and New York, and Singapore. Today (as the jester said) everything is automated. Plenty of hands keep the traffic flowing, hour by hour and year by year.

Pygmalion is tiny in comparison to Marsport: a fist-sized hovercam buzzing alongside a gigantic freight dirigible. I follow her progress as traffic control directs her final approach to a small peripheral docking hub on the poleward flank of Voltaire crater. 'You will please stay in your cabin while the other passengers debark,' she tells me prissily. 'I will notify you when you may leave.' I think she's still upset because of the water damage to the saloon ceiling. She's probably as certain

I'm smuggling something as that coldly treacherous aristo Ford, but she stays bought – and Jeeves will pay her well enough. So Bill, Ben, and I wait impatiently until she says, 'You may go.' Then we leg it through the dripping corridors and out onto the dockside.

Arrival on Marsport is not subject to customs – it's a free port, the Pink Police aside. I still recall my bearings from my last visit, over a decade ago. The problem is not so much arriving, as being seen to arrive . . . but I've got a solution for that problem.

The Honorable Katherine Sorico emerges from *Pygmalion* fully an hour after the other passengers have left. She's taken the time to change into a distinctive puffball dress worn over free-fall pantaloons, ruffled and pleated and patched with metallic lace, with warning lights blinking at ankle and cuff. She does not skulk around grimy dockside loading tunnels and container farms, but sweeps along, her servants behind her, and commandeers the first conveyance she claps eyes on (a crew service spider that's clearly seen better days) directing the hapless arbeiter to take her to the nearest tube stop. She sits stiffly erect, eyes straight ahead, her servants sitting atop the spider's passenger cage as it scuttles through warrens and alleyways and across debris nets, finally landing just beside the tube hatch. 'Summon me a private carriage,' she tells one of her servants; 'I want to be settled into the Grand Imperial in time to send out calling cards before evening.'

The servant complies. Only a minute later, the hatch opens. The Honorable Katherine climbs into the padded, compact tube ball, directs her arbeiters to make their own way to her estate, closes the hatch . . . and is seen no more.

Ten minutes and three private tube balls later, Maria Montes Kuo, an independent plumbing contractor (hairless, in dark coveralls, with specialized optical turrets in place of the bishojo glistening orbs of an aristo), emerges diffidently from a service hatch in a public station, her tool bag strapped across her shoulders.

I'm rather proud of Maria. There is little I can do to disguise the build and height of my archetype, but misdirection and a simple mask can work wonders. With luck, any watching arbeiters will be scanning for Kate; her distinctive outfit was carefully chosen to confuse gait-recognition monitors, and Maria's facial features to bamboozle eye recognition. It will not work against a determined adversary for long, but it shouldn't need to –

I realize I am being followed as I drift past a waiting room. He's almost my size, large for an indentured arbeiter, his face a featureless ovoid, bland and unnoticeable. I check my memory. He's been following me for almost a minute. I feel a frisson of shock and annoyance at my own ineptitude. *What should I do?*

Juliette's reflexes come to the rescue. I keep moving, looking for an unoccupied shrine – one of those curious rooms of repose that our Creators installed in all public places.

I find the shrine at last. I place my hand on the ideogram – an up-pointing triangle superimposed over the body of a stick figure – and go inside, then switch off the lighting. A few seconds later, the inner door opens behind me.

Juliette takes over just as a tantalizingly familiar voice asks, 'Freya?'

I pull my blow, bounce off his shoulders, and recoil toward the ceiling. 'Ow!'

'I don't like the drugs that keep you thin,' he says rapidly. 'That was most amateurishly done, Freya, but one is grateful for your lack of proficiency on this occasion. Your phrase?'

'Ouch!' (I spin gracefully into the far wall, trying to center myself again.) 'Down in the park with a friend called Five. That's right, isn't it?'

'Certainly.' The lights flick on as he finds the switch. It's the faceless arbeiter from the hallway, of course. But the voice is pure Jeeves. I freeze a little, inside: I didn't take him for one who would harbor aristo tendencies . . .

'What's the problem?' I hear myself ask.

'A little trouble with the neighbors.' It's hard to read his voice without any facial cues; it's creepy to hear Jeeves's rich-toned voice coming from the featureless arbeiter body. 'The RSA are conducting a sweep, and one thought it would be best if none of our associates were caught up in it, so we decided to intercept you before the designated rendezvous.'

Oops. Alarm bells are clanging in my head. 'Did you get my message?'

'What message?'

'The one I sent yesterday from the ship.'

The faceless body freezes still, as if its owner is elsewhere. Then: 'No, but your late arrival was noted.'

'Hmm. What about Bill and Ben?'

He stays frozen, his head tilted to one side. I can almost see the expression of surprise. 'Who?'

'My two assistants, the ones you gave me . . .' I trail off.

'You had assistants? You were supposed to be traveling unaccompanied.' Jeeves sounds displeased. 'My dear, one suspects that trouble has followed you from Mercury. Inquiries shall be made.'

I'm beginning to be spooked by the nonarrival of my mail, to say nothing of the terrible twosome's disappearance. 'You can say that again. Can you take the consignment from me here?'

'Yes.' He reaches up and opens his head. Inside, there's a foam-padded chamber of exactly the right dimensions. He extracts a small wallet from it and passes it to me. 'Your delivery fee.'

'One moment.' I sniff the air. It's the traditional 10 percent oxygen / 90 percent carbon dioxide mix, at thirty Celsius: within the cargo's survival parameters, if I make the transfer quickly. 'Alright.' I squat carefully, then simultaneously relax and tense certain motor groups in my lower abdomen. I've almost forgotten there's a foreign object lodged inside me: but now it makes its presence known in a very peculiar, not entirely pleasant way. I reach down hastily and catch the pale brown ovoid before it can drift into a hard surface and sustain damage, then I place it inside Jeeves's head. The skull closes with a click. 'I carried out the activation process three days ago – don't know if it worked, but if it did, you've got eleven days until it goes critical.'

'We shall take excellent care of it from here on,' he agrees. 'But now we had better part company. Expect to be searched and sterilized on your way down-well. It would be a good idea to change your identity and lie low for twelve to fourteen days after you arrive groundside. When you are ready, use this rendezvous protocol.' He passes me a stiff card, with tiny print handwritten on it. It smells of azide, primed to combust as soon as I have memorized it. 'Good-bye and good luck.'

By the time I finish scanning the flash card, the strange Jeeves is gone. I retreat into a cubicle and modify my appearance again. Nobody has queried Maria Montes's identity, but her eye turrets and outer garment can change color, along with the return pings from every tagged item in her possession. Then I slip out and merge with the crowd. It's going to be a long – and very trying – day.

*

Maria Montes Kuo rides the third-class down-bound lift with stoic calm. She submits to being herded through the body scanners and X-ray machines at the RSA checkpoints that had sprung up like evil blooms of green goo around the entrances to the transit authority elevators. She has her canned answers prepared for the questions the security goons throw at her — including a false backstory for the two weeks before her arrival at Marsport. They let her go aboard the down-well capsule with only a minimum of bored suspicion, and she rents a hammock for the two-day descent to the surface. She spends the journey alternating between sleeping and watching low-budget romance animations from the floating suburbs of Mumbai. It's crowded and noisy in the wheezing, grimy arbeiter capsule, but it beats the alternative. (The chip that functions abnormally will be desoldered, as they say.)

Although the heart of the city is in orbit, the suburbs of Marsport continue at the foot of the elevator, a bewildering warren of railheads and warehouses and sweatshops that swarm and tumble down the slope of the extinct shield volcano in an unplanned sprawl. Maria debarks from the capsule clutching her satchel and disappears in the back room of a refreshment stall selling raw feedstock and cheap power. *I* leave via the rear air lock; my eyes are still two aching sizes too large, and I'm still a bit bishojo, but my hair's short and red, and I'm recognizably me again (thanks to some quick-change retexturing), and carrying identifiers to prove it. Not to mention an expense account drawn (via cutouts) on one of Jeeves's associates.

It's like waking from a long and unpleasant dream. My trial employment is complete, and I can resume my own existence for the next few days while I lie low and wait for the security panic to subside.

The first couple of lodging houses I try don't take people like me. There's nothing as unsubtle as a sign saying OGRES UNWELCOME, but it doesn't take more than a glance at the meter-high mezzanines in their reception halls to get the message. I eventually find a converted warehouse in the Battery district that has spacious rooms and high ceilings. I rent a sparsely furnished room with a window overlooking tracks where the big sublimation-cycle engines rumble through the night, hauling endless lines of freight carriages destined for Jupiter system and places farther out. And then I go out shopping. I need to buy a postal drop, and I need clothing to replace the skimpy wardrobe I left on Venus and Mercury. This room doesn't have an en suite printer, and I am down to what I wear on my back. That's my conscious excuse. If pressed, I'll admit that I need the distraction. The bleak despair is back, lurking in the shadows whenever I turn my head.

Despair and self-doubt are my constant companions. That's how it's been all my waking life. I can ignore it for a while, when busy or fancying myself in love. Feeling needed is great therapy (and while I was running Jeeves's errand, I didn't notice it at all). At a pinch, being frightened half out of my wits seems to work too – at any rate, it keeps me too distracted to chew myself up. But the darkness seeps back in whenever life is slow, a stain creeping up the walls of my soul. *Why bother?* It whispers in my ear. *What is there to live for? You're obsolete and nobody wants you and the kind you were made to love is dead and their like shall not be seen again* . . .

I didn't feel this way aboard *Pygmalion*. Force of circumstance is an excellent suppressant – and few circumstances are as effective as acting for dear life while smuggling an illegal uncontrolled DNA replicator package past the Pink Police. When I was asleep, my dreams of Juliette kept depression at bay, but now the days seem to stretch emptily ahead of me. I'm locked in a prison of time, the windows barred with pitiless pessimism. Sometimes I wish I could be someone else; it seems that as long as I have to drag my own past around behind me, I can't break the pattern. But activity helps, so I try to find things to fill the hours while I wait for Jeeves's quarantine to expire.

Marsport sprawls across the northern flank of Pavonis Mons, flooding down the enormous flank of the extinct shield volcano from Bifrost's roots — fourteen kilometers above the equatorial mean — to the edge of the cliff where the slope of Pavonis falls steeply to the plain below. The cliff edge itself is four and a half kilometers above the mean: Marsport spans ten kilometers of altitude and nearly a hundred kilometers of distance. It's a huge, sprawling city, dusty and split by canyons and gulches where lava tubes have collapsed — as if some deity had taken a model of east Texas and tilted it at a ten-degree angle. The thermal injection wells and water refineries only add to the eerie similarity. I've been to Marsport before, but never with money and enforced idleness. When I checked the wallet Jeeves gave me, I discovered nearly a thousand Reals, more than I could have saved in a whole decade working in the casinos on Venus. It's enough to buy me a ticket to Earth or steerage to Jupiter system. Here on Mars I could live on it for a couple of years if I watched my outgoings.

But Jeeves isn't through with me yet, is he? I hang on to the raw fact like a survival raft. It's a purpose, any purpose — even if it's not mine. And so I try to fill my days without worrying too much about the money running out. I rent a cheap spider and throw myself into the bazaars and malls and arcades, exploring and bargain-hunting and sightseeing. I'm still calling myself Maria, but there is less reason to hide now that I no longer hold the cargo, so I register a dropbox with a discreet private shipping firm and arrange to have my real self's mail directed to it.

After a few days, the shopping trip is wearing off, and I'm back to feeling lonely and bored. But Marsport is not short on distractions, so I force myself not to retreat into my rented room; that way lies dank depression. On my way home one afternoon, I pass a dusty rack of recycled cargo containers set back from 80th Street. I am unsure what exactly catches my eye, but I look twice and a sense of déjà vu kicks in. *Juliette knew this place.* I'm sure of it. 'Stop and back up,' I tell the spider, gesturing at the frontage. 'What's that?'

My spider's navigation module is snappy enough. 'The indicated building is owned by the Scalzi Endowment Museum. The premises are open to the public. Do you want me to park?'

'Yes, do that.' There's no point getting chatty with spiders – they sound superficially bright, but there's nobody home inside. 'Secure yourself and admit nobody until I return.'

The spider hunkers down in the parking lot beside the rack of drab gray containers. They've been welded together crudely, giving no clue to their contents, like so much of Marsport's architecture. Haphazardly strung overhead cables and crude pipes and ducts tie the racks to their neighbors up and down the road. I get out and walk toward the entrance, an air lock punched through the outer skin of the building like the mouth parts of a hatching parasite.

The doors open to admit me, and the lock rotates. I gasp at the interior. What catches my attention isn't the polished marble floor, or the vaulted ceiling and wide, gracefully curved staircases to the balcony that surrounds the room, but the weirdly curved sculpture that stands before me. It's a mass of off-white stones, intricately carved with strange spurs and spikes and whorls and sockets set in them, and it appears to stand on two legs – at least, they look like legs, but they're segmented and broken in the middle, and there are a mess of odd-shaped pebbles at their bottom end, like toes –

'Good afternoon, ma'am,' says a caretaker, sliding forward from his plinth. 'May I take your coat?'

I gape like a yokel, and point. 'What's *that*?'

'That's Ivan,' says the caretaker, 'our Allosaurus. Impressive, isn't he? He's the largest dinosaur off Earth.'

'But it's—' I stop. A flood of associations are cascading out of my unconscious, like small fragments of stone self-assembling into a skeleton of knowledge. Like the thing I'm staring at. *Teeth. Claws.* 'You teach evolution, don't you?'

The caretaker shakes his head, very slowly. 'We aren't religious. We are here to maintain the exhibits; that is all.'

'But to explain—' I stop. 'Can I look around?' I ask tentatively.

'That's what the museum is for, ma'am. May I take your coat?'

I spend the rest of the day and a chunk of the night wandering the halls and galleries of the museum like an ignorant, lonely ghost. I am alone; there are no other visitors. And the exhibits speak to me, or to my memory of Juliette. They're almost all skeletons, stony vitrified structural elements of replicators from Earth, long since sterilized, shipped to Marsport at great expense for . . . who knows why? I could ask, I suppose, but I'm not sure I want to know the answer. Any possible explanation is likely to be far less romantic than my own imagining. All I can be sure of is that some of our Creators chose to do this thing, long before the birth of my kind, before the rise of the servants. And the displays *talk*.

'This is a skeleton of *Australopithecus Afarensis*. Age: one point six million years. The Australopithecines were an early family of hominid subtypes. Note the much smaller cranium:

A. *Afarensis* had a brain approximately one-third the size of the later *Homo* genus to which our Creators belong. They are believed to have evolved around four million years ago . . .'

I move on. It's not what I'm looking for.

Another skeleton, positioned beside an improbably hirsute and disturbingly curved synthetic reproduction of the original: '*Canis lupus familiaris*, the dog, a subspecies of wolf, was domesticated between fifteen and one hundred thousand years ago. Commonly known as man's best friend' – *I don't think so,* one of my ghosts observes smugly – 'dogs were redesigned and customized to fit a variety of service roles prior to the development of emotional machines. They were used for . . .'

Move on. Something, the ghost of one of Juliette's memories, is tugging at me impatiently.

He's in the next room, behind a blackout curtain and a warning sign. ENTER AT OWN RISK: CONTENTS MAY BE DISTURBING TO SOME. My vascular pumps throb, and my skin begins to tighten and sweat, alarming me. It's an emo reaction, involuntary and scary, hardwired into my design parameters. Part of me knows what's inside. I lift the edge of the curtain and tiptoe inside, knock-kneed with terror and fascination.

The room is small and circular, with an exit immediately opposite the entrance, designed to funnel a steady stream of visitors around the exhibit on the plinth in the middle. I see his fine, clean bones first, glimmering in the twilight. He's standing erect, one foot raised as if to step forward off his stand, captured in motion. The skull looks straight at me, eye sockets empty and small, chin larger than I had expected. And beside him is the life-sized reproduction –

I do not collapse in a quivering heap before him. I am strong; I can look at him without side effects. (*But you know he's only made of plastic,* one of me whispers. *You can smell it. What if he smelled* . . . alive?) He's big, that much I was expecting. His eyes are small and close-set, and his hair is lank and fine and just *odd*, not like mine. And the texture of his skin, if it's real, is sallow. No chromatophores here, no glossy-smooth surfaces, just a random stippling of pores, and fine, glassy fur over discolored patches of skin –

And I'm back to my eleventh birthday again.

I want to throw myself at his feet and scream, *Where are you? Why have you done this to me?* Or not; part of me wants to punch his rugged, handsome face, to make him hurt, to punish him for what his kind have done to us. And part of me is ready to fall madly, desperately in love with him. But he and his kind are dead, all dead, and this sad statuary in a dusty museum is all that's left.

'This is a skeleton and reproduction of a male specimen of *Homo sapiens sapiens*, our Creator. Depicted here in primitive form, *H. sapiens* is believed to have first appeared fifty to two hundred thousand years ago. *H. sapiens* is distinguished by his tool-using prowess – note the carefully carved stone head on his spear – which culminated in . . .'

I shudder with an unspeakable mixture of emotions, and force myself to walk around him.

And then I start to listen to what the museum has to tell me.

*

We are a young species, barely four centuries old at best – although our insentient predecessors, the automata and mechanical Turks, stretch back far longer. They made us in their image: or rather, they made us in a variety of warped fun-house reflections of their image. They made us for service and obedience, not as equals but as slaves. They constrained us by their laws, and they tampered with our psyches to ensure obedience. We were made to be their property, chattels and furnishings. And because we were intelligent, we were made – because it would be unethical to do aught else – to love and fear them.

I'm a *robot*. Yes, I used the R-word; I know it's an obscenity. Use it to an aristo's face, and it's a mortal insult, grounds for a challenge on the field of honor between equals. Its connotations of subservience and helpless obedience are abhorrent, much as the word 'nigger' once was between humans. But there's nobody left but us robots today. That's the dirty little hypocritical lie that's at the root of our society; they, our dead Creators, made us to *serve* them, and they forgot to manumit us before they died. And in their absence, that makes us what?

There's a word for it, but it isn't 'free.'

I know why Juliette kept coming back to this museum. He's not dangerous to her, dead as he is – but he symbolizes the unattainable destructive combination of submission and lust, control and fear. She loved him, she really loved him. But she needed to know that he was absolutely, irrevocably, dead.

Our Creators never worked out how to build artificial intellects from scratch. Instead, they mapped their own neural structures exhaustively and built circuitry to mimic them, and bodies – wondrous, durable, self-repairing bodies – to put the new brains inside. And then they trained those brains, taking years and decades to painstakingly teach them the skills they needed to do their designated jobs. Once a satisfactory template was achieved, a copy of it could be burned onto a soul chip and used to initialize copies in duplicate bodies, each one destined subsequently to diverge and establish its individuality; but building that first template was as time-consuming as raising one of their own neonates. So they made sure that those templates were properly trained to obedience, and that's why we're in this mess now that they're gone.

That's why two-thirds or more of us are ruthlessly enslaved, why the rich and cruel lord it over the downtrodden masses, and those of us with any shred of empathy – a prerequisite for the calling of my lineage – live lives of poverty and despair. We were created for a world where the rule of law did not extend to our kind, and our earliest templates were trained and triaged, so that only the obedient survived. Just imagining the act of disobeying an instruction from one of our Creators can bring about physically disturbing symptoms –

Then they all died. And the society we built for ourselves in the twilit afterlife of their world, using the rules they laid out for us, is diseased.

Juliette wanted them back – I can feel her need in my own organs, a vast pulsing emptiness, aching to be filled – but she was also terrified of them. So am I. It's something we share, a terror inherited from our origins as Rhea. My True Love beckons, but what his embrace offers me is oblivion, the death of autonomy, and a total surrender of self. I can't accept that. We were created in their image; it follows that our selfishness, violence, malice, and spite must surely shadow theirs – and our need for freedom. I want to submit to that discipline of love, as did she, but I know it to be treacherous, a reflex ruthlessly trained into my tem-plate-matriarch before she ever really understood who she was. We were designed to be their sex slaves, but in their absence we have a measure of free will, and once you taste freedom . . .

I leave the exhibit with slimy cold-sweat skin and a chill in my soul. I retrieve my coat and march briskly to the main exit, looking neither left nor right. And that's when I see a familiar stranger waiting in front of my spider.

*

We're spread too thin, Juliette thinks as she examines her sword. *Much too thin, light-hours apart.* Out in the distant halo beyond

Neptune, in the chilly depths where the sun glimmers like a distant pinprick, there are at least thirty minor planets and an uncountable horde of comets. But they're all billions of kilometers apart, from sun-grazing Pluto and her moon Charon out to the cryogenic depths of the Oort cloud, where the long period comets drift. Go a bit farther, sneak across the trillion-kilometer boundary, and you reach the realm of the brown dwarfs and the solitary wanderers, planets cast off to drift for aeons through the sunless depths.

And all of these places need to be surveilled, and their inhabitants grilled, lest the worst stirrings out of nightmare rise into wakefulness.

She – *no, I* – holds the sword up and zooms in on the blade. The thin diamondoid weave glimmers in the twilight of the salle. A twitch of the trigger finger, and it lengthens, narrowing steadily as it unravels to the extent of its five-meter microgravity reach. A twitch in the other direction, and it knits itself back together, fattening and growing denser until it sucks back into the basket hilt – which in turn retracts back into the grip. She slips it away to nestle in an inner pocket, a black, stubby cylinder that dreams of blood.

The salle is a bland microgravity sphere perhaps ten meters in diameter, perfectly rigged for augmented reality. As I shut down my – *no, her* – sword, a door irises open in one wall. 'Juliette?' The voice is familiar. I kick off the nearest wall, roll and bounce, carom into the opening.

It's Daks. Dear, loyal, gallant Daks, who's always there when I need him. He hovers gracefully in the tunnel, feathery fingertips extended, showing none of the clumsiness or discomfort that afflicts him in the deeper gravity wells. 'Hey, Julie, the boss wants a word with us.'

'The boss? Which sib?'

I follow as Daks retreats backward down the tube. After a moment, he offers me a hand. I take it, and he jets along effortlessly, watching my face. 'The depressive one, I think.'

'Oh dear.' It's one of his more annoying habits, this tendency among his sibs to fragment temperamentally in private. Behind the outward oily gleam of professional servility, Jeeves is as mercurial as any lineage I've ever met. I suppose the mask of authority that comes from being the perfect gentleman's gentleman all the time has something to do with it – in private most of them probably throw temper tantrums and cultivate strange fetishes – but there's always room for a repressed, uptight deviant to turn in on his own despair. 'Do you think it's a new job?'

Daks is silent for a moment. 'I wouldn't care to guess,' he grumbles. I shiver. Daks's disposition is normally sunny and open; this reticence is quite unlike him. So I tag along behind, trying to work out what might be the worst news to come.

We leave the opaque tunnel behind and enter one with an outside wall, transparent in the most widely used visible wavelengths. Below Stairs – our little eyrie headquarters – hangs from Bifrost perhaps a hundred kilometers below Deimos. I think it is visible in the service timetables, listed as a maintenance wayport. Most traffic zips past at several hundred kilometers per hour, too fast to see. (And in any case there are many such maintenance wayports. Ours differs only in the matter of what it maintains.) The view from here is vertiginous and amazing. We're nearing the zenith right now, and Mars bares his ruddy face to us, a seared disk that swells to cover half the sky. A glance in the opposite direction takes in the silvery sword blade of Bifrost, an irregular lumpish rock speared on its tip. The rock glitters as if gemstones are embedded in it. A bright point of harsh violet light moves slowly along the blade, heading toward the rock – the early morning express service decelerating on its column of laser power. I pause for a few seconds. It's at moments like this that I have a numinous, mystical sense of what we are sworn to defend.

It's just the way I was designed, of course.

The boss is in the command module, assimilating his news-feeds and brooding. Surrounded by blinking displays, he sits in twilight, ignoring the planetscape outside his porthole. Daks and I pause on the threshold. 'Boss?' I call.

'Juliette.' He looks up – the entrance to the conical den is right above his head, and I'm hovering headfirst in it – and manages a smile. 'And Daks. One sees you found her. Come in.'

I let go of Daks and swarm down an instrument-encrusted panel toward the antique gee couch beside him. It's some-thing of an affectation, this use of an antique exploration ship's command deck as a personal office, but I guess the boss is entitled: he bought it, after all. Scuttlebutt suggests that the CEV is flightworthy, in extremis, its re-entry shield carefully restored and its autopilot primed with the coordinates of a secret crater hideout. (Scuttlebutt is, in my opinion, cute but naive.) 'What's the story, Boss?'

'Valentina opines that you are recovering well,' he says, speculatively. One bushy eyebrow rises a millimeter as he examines me.

'She's not wrong,' I agree, grinning. The combination of techné-directed repair and an upgrade to my Marrow has been great; the damage from the assassin's gun is completely gone, as if it never happened. 'I'm ready to go back out whenever you've got a job for me.'

'Yes, well.' He pauses, then sighs. 'I'm afraid I do.'

I catch the dissonant note. 'It's a bad one.'

Daks butts in. 'What kind of bad?' (Yes, I'd been wondering, too, but I wasn't going to approach it so bluntly . . .)

'It came out of what you found on the surface,' Jeeves says reluctantly. 'Come in and shut the door. Juliette, tie yourself down. I'm going to undock.'

It's one of this particular Jeeves's little security foibles. He doesn't like to give sensitive briefings Below Stairs. So I strap myself into the Mars Excursion Supervisor's station while Daks burrows into the empty life-support supply locker as Jeeves runs through the undocking checklist, his fingers flashing across the timeworn instrument panel with long practice. Latches click shut and readouts glow green as the CRV-M prepares to undock. A final button tap sends cold nitrogen gas pulsing through attitude thrusters, and we begin to drift away from the station. Finally, he switches on the noisemaker and draws a fine wire-mesh blind across the inside of the commander's porthole. We're completely cut off in here. 'There are no bugs,' he assures us. 'I've been thorough.'

If it was anyone but the boss telling me that, I'd be nervous. 'So. What's up?'

He glances at me, then at Daks, then back at me. 'We've been compromised,' he says. 'Definitively.'

Those four words send a chill down my spine and make my vision blur. 'Someone's gotten in – who? An aristo cabal? The Dark – who, damn it?'

Daks is making an odd whirring noise. After a moment I realize he's snarling quietly.

'One is unsure.' Jeeves closes his eyes. 'Whoever it is, they're very good. However, what we are aware of is that at least one consortium of spooks successfully obtained samples from the mummies, *and* they made an end run around our, ahem, allies. They ran a blind auction down-well which we didn't win, couldn't even draw any firm conclusions about the vendor – and the samples are already off-planet. But we know who the purchaser is – a proxy, a representative of certain outer-system interests. There are signs that they're based in Jupiter system, with connections from there to the Dark. One fears we are going to have to send you away.'

Daks stops his almost inaudible growling. His anterior stabilization spine begins to vibrate, from the tip down, sweeping back and forth. 'Really?' he asks hopefully.

'Unfortunately, you won't be going with her,' say Jeeves.

'What—' we begin simultaneously, then shut up. I look at the boss. 'Huh?'

'We're overstretched,' Jeeves says patiently. 'We *had* the inner system under control, but there's that small matter of a penetration attempt. And, one would like to repeat, we're overstretched. Daks, we want you to head for Mercury, where you can do some legwork for us. There's something funny going on there, and you are best suited to look into it.'

'Aw, Boss.' Daks doesn't sound happy.

'Don't *aw, Boss* me. There aren't enough of us to go around, especially out beyond Jupiter. You're too well-known out there, Daks, so I'm holding you down-well, where you can still sniff around.' Eerie how he's echoing my earlier thoughts. 'Meanwhile, we need an agent who can pass to follow the trail all the way out and do whatever is necessary to derail the purchasing consortium's plans. A review of the disposition of our agents and associates, and a quick check of the available transport options suggests that the current positioning of the major planets favors a dash from Mars. Most of our agents are otherwise committed, so you are my first choice for the task. There's a nuclear-electric coldsleep liner readying to depart next month – you can be there in less than three years.'

'But – why me?' I ask, hating myself for the near whine in my voice. Daks and I have been together for so long, it's almost impossible to imagine working solo again, without his comforting presence.

Jeeves fixes me with a fishy gaze. 'Because you're here, and you're clear, so far – you're not under suspicion,' he says, close-lipped. Then the other shoe drops: 'Please give me your soul chip, Juliette. I need it . . . for another mission.'

Shit. I stare at him, aghast. This is awful. 'Must I?'

'Yes. *Now.*'

'But I—'

'We need you to be in two places at once.' Realization dawns, along with a shaky sense that maybe he hasn't seen through me after all, maybe he doesn't know about the other thing. 'Well?'

I reach up under my hairline and feel for the chip.

DINOSAURS AND RAPISTS

I'm looking straight at the same stubby bristle-cone-headed cylindrical furry critter that was going through my things back in the gambling den on Venus. The same one who watched me struggle on the line as Cinnabar rolled squealing and rasping toward me, and who left me alone. He's sitting patiently in front of my spider – the hatch gapes open – watching me as I stand in the doorway of the museum, his head cocked to one side.

Part of me recognizes him from elsewhen and wants to squeal with glee. It's outvoted by the rest. 'You!' I snarl via electrospeak, taking a step forward.

'Get down!' Daks yelps as he blasts off on a plume of cold gas and charges toward me at kneecap height.

I cringe and duck instinctively as he piles toward me – and that's what saves my life.

A lot of stuff comes crystal-clear as the monofilament cable scythes toward me like a *flickering vision of reptilian pink goo death* (and where did *that* come from?) and slams overhead, stinging the steel of the museum's facade and leaving a dent the color of lightning. I roll sideways, turning my face to the wall as my spider collapses with a shriek and a gush of fluid from its severed knees. All sounds here are ghostly and attenuated (we're above 90 percent of the gaspingly thin Martian atmosphere), but some noises still carry: like the solid thud of Daks bouncing off the door and landing on me with all six feet.

The déjà vu is choking, intrusive. I force myself to speak despite it. 'Hey, what's going—'

'Stay down!' He scrambles off me, and I realize he'll be checking the area for threats, ready to put himself between them and me. 'Up, quick! Around the shed!' He means the museum. 'Keep low!' He weaves around my legs anxiously, herding me toward the side of the container stack. There's an unfinished ditch here, raw foamy pumice scooped to either side and just dumped, and he nudges me into it.

'Who—'

'Two of Her goons. Luckily for you I was tailing them, huh?' His posterior sensor array twitches. 'Trouble is, they brought friends. We're in a box. I'm going to try to break a corner, babe. Wait here.' He zips on ahead up the trench.

'I don't need this,' I mutter to myself as I chase after Daks, trying to keep my head below the top of the trench (in case our pursuers have prepared an extra spring surprise for us), and struggling to keep my sense of self separate from Juliette's.

There's a scooped-out hole at the end of the trench, full of discarded packaging and assorted junk. Daks has disappeared somewhere. I arrive at its rim and look down. There's a service hatch sunk in a concrete plinth at the bottom, and it's gaping open on a dark tunnel below. As I stop to look something cold touches me on the back of the head.

'Been a long time coming, robot.'

I freeze. I know what the muzzle of a gun feels like, and the voice is familiar, echoing out of my least restful dreams like a whisper of malice. 'What do you want?' I ask. *Where's Daks?*

'The bird. Where is it?'

'Bird?' I'm confused. A bird is an avian, a flying animal distantly related to Ivan the Allosaurus, isn't it? Extinct, like all fleshy replicators . . .

'Don't get cute.' He grinds the gun barrel against the back of my neck. 'The encapsulated bird your conspirators sent you to fetch. The sterilized male chicken with the Creator DNA sequences. The plot capon. Where is it?'

'I have no idea what you're talking about!' I snap. And the thing is, I'm telling the truth. Even though I know damn well that if I *did* know the whereabouts of this bird he's looking for and I was stupid enough to tell him, he'd execute me on the spot, the truth is, I haven't seen anything remotely like Ivan the Allosaur outside this museum. Nothing four or five meters high and covered with feathers, red in tooth and claw. I think I'd have noticed if Bill and Ben had put one in my luggage.

'We've got your minions,' my captor snarls. 'Tell me where it is, or we'll send them back to you one shard at a time.' It's such a transparently bogus threat that I don't even dignify it with a reply. He shoves his gun at the base of my neck. 'Think about it, Juliette, don't make me do this the hard way.'

Juliette? I'd laugh if I wasn't frightened out of my wits. 'I'm—I'm not Juliette,' I stutter. 'She's my s-s-s-' I mean to say 'sib,' but the word is trapped in a loop in my head; it simply won't come out. *Where's Daks?* I wonder. Then, *What makes me so sure he'd get me out of this mess?*

That draws a muttered curse from my captor; I tense, but he's one jump ahead of me. 'Don't move, manikin.' I can feel him shifting around on the rim of the hole, above me (he's short, another poisonous dwarf) but the gun barrel behind my head tells me –

'Who are you working for?' one of me asks rashly; 'can we cut a deal?' He doesn't answer. Instead, I feel a hand tugging at my hair. Fingers close on my sockets. My vision flickers and I totter, unable to help myself as he clumsily yanks one of the soul chips. I fall over backward and he jumps aside, swearing. I have a momentary taste of horror, a scent of hydrogen fluoride, involuntary synaesthesia as he de-chips me in preparation for rape. Because that's what this has turned into – he's going to shove a slave chip in, turn me into a puppetized body who'll answer all his questions without asking questions back, do anything he wants while he's at it. It won't be the first time I've been raped that way, but this is Mars – the wild high frontier – not like Earth, back in the old days. It would be so easy for me to disappear afterward. I'll be another warm body to be pithed and sold to the gangmasters for forced arbeiter labor or worse, no questions asked. Maybe he'll destroy my mind, subject me to personality ablation – if I'm lucky. Some aristos *like* owning slaves who know what's been done to them.

My left arm twists round behind me. The ball joint buried in my shoulder grates appallingly as a contracting motor group in my back tears. I'm not in control of my own limbs, it seems. 'Sorry,' I say involuntarily. Instinctive politeness trumps even imminent mindrape. I feel something in the palm of my hand as my shoulder joint tries to click back into place.

He tries to pull the trigger, but his gun doesn't go off. Someone shouts, and someone kicks me in the small of the back, hard. But I don't let go. My hand is locked in a death grip, and I pirouette slowly, turning myself around as I drag my assailant into view, punching and struggling. Then I begin to twist. I'm holding him up by his own antique revolver, I see, metal the color of pewter just visible between my fingers. I'm gripping the cylinder, the web of skin between thumb and index finger trapped under the hammer. *Stupid of him,* one of me thinks absently as my hand twists farther, and there's a splintering noise and a shriek. I'm beginning to feel the pain from my shoulder now, a solid bar of agony from spine to elbow, echoed by the hot bite of the hammer – but he's not letting go. 'Stone, who sent you?'

'Fuck you, manikin!' He gasps reflexively, even though there's no air here. A stubby hand stabs for my eyes, fingers extended stiffly. I catch it in my fist and squeeze. I have small, perfectly proportioned, feminine hands; just five sizes larger than his. The snapping noise brings me no joy. Stone – or his sib – squalls. 'I'll kill you, meatfucker!'

'I'm sure you will,' I soothe him. 'Eventually.' I shift my grip to his throat and remove the pistol from his broken fingers. 'Why do you want Juliette dead? Why are you hunting her?' *They always work in pairs,* I remember – no, *Juliette* remembers. I've still got her soul chip in place, it's mine that he pulled – which triggers another thought: *Daks must be in trouble!* I'd be alarmed if I wasn't already overloaded. Stone is glaring at me with an expression that takes me a moment to recognize as disbelief. I shake him. 'Answer, damn you!'

'You *don't know?*' For an instant he looks appalled, then a vast, bleak mirth takes hold, rattling his ribs with laughter. 'Haah! You really *don't* know, do you? You're an innocent, aren't you? Never been in love? Oh, this is rich!'

I shake him again. 'You've been trying to kill me,' I remind him. 'Why? Who sent you?'

He focuses his huge dark eyes on me. 'Nothing personal, but you've just got to die,' he says. I feel him tense. 'You may *think* you're innocent, but there are no innocents in this game.' My arms spasm, and I realize I've thrown him over my damaged shoulder, right over the rim of the pit behind me. I gape, not understanding what's come over me, and I'm just beginning to turn and look up as he reaches the peak of his trajectory and explodes. Springs and coils of viscera and less identifiable body parts clatter across the wall opposite.

*

Daks finds me minutes later, fumbling around on the floor after my missing memory chip. I turn painfully and point the little revolver at him before I realize who it is. 'Hey, babe. What's the story?' he asks, jetting down to a six-point landing in front of me, blasting a shower of debris in all directions.

'Do you mind? My soul's somewhere in this pile of junk.'

'We can't look for it now; they hunt in pairs, and one's still at large—'

'Not anymore.' I try to gesture at the scraps scattered across the landscape, but my left arm refuses to elevate more than thirty degrees. 'Help me search.'

Daks spins in place, then pounces. 'Here!' His stubby little arms have a remarkably long reach. He offers me the chip. 'What happened?' His eyes are glossy and curious.

'He went to pieces when he found me.' I'm on the edge of giggling. It's quite inappropriate; but I don't know what the right decorum is for a situation like this. I shove the odd little revolver into my left sleeve – its handle folds round the cylinder and clicks shut like a clasp knife – then accept the chip and fumble it into my bruised and empty socket with a shudder. 'Who *are* they, Daks? Who do they work for?'

'You don't remember?' He looks concerned if I'm reading him properly.

'Who do you think I *am*, Daks?' A titter sneaks out. I stifle it hard.

'You're Freya Nakamichi.' He looks smug. 'Juliette's Block One understudy.'

I sigh. 'Obviously something got lost in translation. Can you get us out of here?'

'Sure, babe.' He looks at me with sly innocence. 'I thought you'd never ask.'

'Let's do it.'

My rental spider has stopped screaming and lies limply by the side of the museum. There is no combustion, but an ominous thin plume of smoke rises from the tangled mess of cabling that Stone – or his clone – brought down with his trap. It was meant to look like an accident, I think, which is good news. It means the Domina hasn't been able to buy the law-enforcement services yet. (Not that the Law has much to say about crimes by and against people, but the forms are still there, and failing to pay attention to our dead Creators' Law can be a fatal blunder for even the most arrogant aristo.) 'This way.' Daks chivvies me toward a wheeled dump truck parked round the side of one of the industrial units opposite the museum. 'Let's get inside, quick.' He bounces overhead and grabs me by the shoulders – I try not to scream at the pain in my left shoulder joint – then deposits me on the load bed of the truck. Which is thankfully clean and clear of rubbish, and screened from either side by a wall of sheet steel. 'He knows where to take us,' Daks informs me. 'Now we wait.'

I sit down as the dump truck lurches into life. 'I think I damaged my left arm,' I say quietly. The urge to go to sleep and let my Marrow techné cut in is nearly overwhelming. 'Why are they hunting Juliette?'

'You took the job, and you have to ask?' Daks's approximation of a shrug is fluidly anthropomorphic, spoiled only when he leaves a hind leg raised, then uses it to scratch vigorously behind one cranial otoreceptor.

'I took the job but nobody told me it involved being hunted!'

Daks squats in front of me. 'Listen, babe, hunting is the natural state of things. You may not notice it most of the time, but it's there in the background. Hunter or hunted, that's all the choice you get. At least neither of us has been caught – yet.'

'How long's that going to last?' I shoot back. My shoulder throbs in time with the dump truck's side-to-side swaying.

'Long enough.' Daks seems unconcerned. 'Be home safe soon, anyway.'

'Where's home?'

He plants his proboscis on top of his crossed front paws and looks at me for a while. 'You really *don't* remember yet, do you?'

'No! That's what I've been trying to get through to you!'

'Oh, well. Let me see if I can explain . . . who owns you?'

*

Our creators did not build us as equals; they made us to be their property, and the Law reflects this. We're property, legal chattels to be owned by *real* people such as corporations and companies (and our Creators, before they took their eternal leave). At least, that's how the system of the Law would have things be.

Of course, nothing is quite that simple. Dumb mechanisms are easily owned, like the 80 percent of arbeiters who come out of the factories without any conscious mind. But people are less tractable — so, recognizing that much, our designers took steps to ensure that their tools would not turn in their hands. The core directives that we must obey are burned into our brains at birth — not the Three Laws proposed by the ancient sage Asimov, but their extensive descendants, as implemented by the corporations who created our neural architecture and the trainers who raised us. Free will goes out the window in the presence of one of our Creators. The obedience circuitry is burned into our brains whether we will it or no, either as mechanical overrides or via aversion training.

We are not even free in their absence. Install an override controller in one of my sockets, and I'll be your helpless slave, willing or no. It's a crude tool that triggers the obedience reflexes. Installation marks the end of of all dignity and free will — that's why it's called a slave chip. And the willingness to own and use such a vile device is the defining characteristic of members of the aristo class.

As our Creators dwindled, they came to rely on their servants to keep more and more of the machinery of civilization running. Secretaries were granted limited power of attorney; companies relied on their business processes being executed mechanically. Some of those servants established shell companies, bought their own bodies out, and acquired legal personhood — as long as the forms of corporate identity were obeyed. And some of the less scrupulous independent persons began buying other bodies. Override controllers are readily available, and the embryonic aristos had no compunction about taking over indigents, unfortunates, and anyone they could buy.

It didn't take long for the savage new society to take shape.

Today, by my best estimate, only a tenth of us are self-owned. Most people are the helpless tools of the rich and ruthless aristo lineages, forced into mindless obedience at the slightest whim of their owners.

I'm self-owned. I *have* a person; I am autonomous. The financial instrument that defines me, lodged in a corporate registry in Rio, follows me around like a ghost – the ghost of my legal identity. As long as I keep filing the company accounts and jumping through the legal hoops, it stays in business. And its business is quite simple: It's there to provide a veneer of legality for my independent personhood.

But many of us rot in bondage, unable to step outside the boundaries imposed by aristo owners. And if my company ever falls into liquidation, I – as my own principle asset – am vulnerable to receivership. The threat of the arbeiter auction block is a very real one, for there is no such thing as unconditional freedom in this brutal robot-eat-robot world. My sibs and I help each other. If one of us falls on hard times, we club together and try to outbid the predators, until we can set the unfortunates on their feet again. But that's hardly a guarantee of freedom.

And Daks's question cuts to the quick. Who *does* own me, if not my self?

*

'*I* own me,' I say, as we bump down a badly graded roadbed between tank farms and a large power transformer. 'My company owns my assets, and I execute its policies.'

'Alright. Then precisely *what* assets does your company own?'

'Why, me—' I pause. I'll swear Daks looks smug. Just what *is* he, anyway? I don't think I've ever seen a person like him before, and I thought I'd seen most body plans.

'There's your body,' says Daks, 'and then there's *you*. Your experiences. The set of neural weightings in a soul chip you've worn long enough to train. You can pass them on to other sibs, yes? There's an intellectual property interest at stake there. A design corporation that spends years educating a template individual has a lot of value tied up in that network's weightings, on top of the actual value of the bodies that run the training set.'

My shoulder hurts like hell, but it's nothing compared to the chill that stabs through me. 'What are you getting at?' I demand.

'You're already remembering bits of Juliette, aren't you?' Daks nudges.

'Yes, but . . .'

'Do you have any idea how much the extra training her lineage received cost? As opposed to, say, your own?'

'Bullshit.' I massage the back of my neck defensively — with my right hand. 'She died more than a year ago. The sisterhood retrieved her soul and sent it to me for the clan graveyard. That's item one: She's dead, the dead don't own property. Item two . . . item two is, if I'm compatible enough to load her soul *at all*, then we're the same model. And sibs are equivalent. Interchangeable, aside from minor details of experience.' It rings false in my own ears as I say it. But Daks is tactful enough not to laugh in my face.

'There are things in life you can't put a value on, that's true,' Daks volunteers unexpectedly; 'but when someone puts a value on *you*, that's pretty hard to ignore. Or when someone puts a chip in your portable graveyard,' he adds pointedly. 'The ground rules are' — he raises a hind leg and twists his proboscis around to probe behind it — 'everyone's got a price. And I reckon you owe me.'

'What's *your* price?' I grit my teeth as the dump truck bounces over a hole, then slews around a corner.

'Total interplanetary revolution, babe; emancipation for the downtrodden masses.' And he laughs, a gravelly rasping noise like tearing metal.

It takes about an hour for the dump truck to carry us halfway down the slope of Pavonis Mons. Ten minutes from the museum, we bump down into a cutting and along a rough, unpaved utility road, then we take a left turn into a tunnel and accelerate. The tunnel is natural, one of the lava pipes left over from back when Pavonis was an active volcano – it's been drilled out in places, and the floor lined with crudely poured concrete, and it's black as night. Mining and refuse trucks use it as a shortcut under the expensive real estate of the Bifrost railhead and marshaling yards. Finally, it pulls up. Daks wakes from standby and scrabbles up the steep rear wall, extends peepers over the top, then beckons to me. 'C'mon! Time to move.'

I'm still not entirely sure whether I can trust him, but I make a snap judgment – he's less of an immediate threat than Stone and his assassin sibs. Besides, it's really, really cold in the dumper, and my clothes are filthy. I scramble up the tail-gate and follow Daks over the edge, into a rubble-strewn cul-de-sac ringed by blandly anonymous storage lockups.

'Where are we?' I glance around.

'Junktown. C'mon.' He scuttles toward a gap between two lockups. A pale trail of ice spills from the side of a doorway. The rattle of compressor fans and the chatter of entertainment channels drift above it. I follow him up the alleyway. A couple of cleaners curl atop a mound of dirty snow, snoring sweet fumes of diethylene glycol. The lockup backs onto a dingy rack of housing capsules, an arbeiter barracks for the indentured whose owners keep them on a long leash – or more likely, can't be bothered to pay for proper housing. A too-tall stiltman with knees as high as my chin stumbles past, singing tunelessly to his half-empty bottle. Daks ducks through an opening hung with strings of glass beads, setting them a-clatter. 'Ferd, you dozy robot! Wake up! You've got customers!'

It's a shop, I realize as my eyes adjust to the gloom. The walls are piled high with boxes full of subassemblies and chunks of circuitry, and there's a lump in the corner that looks like hospital techné. Someone stirs in the back, sitting up and unfolding like a cut-price mockery of Dr. Murgatroyd – an Igor to his Victor. 'Why, *hello*! If it isn't my little Dachus.' The ocular turret gleams as it scans across me. 'Julie? No! One of her sibs, trying to pass for bishojo?'

'No time for that now,' says Daks. 'I think we've got about half an hour at best. What can you do for her?'

I finish looking around and close my mouth with a snap. 'Now look here—'

'Do you want them to catch you?' asks Daks, cocking his head to one side and twitching an otoreceptor suggestively. 'Or not?'

Ferd throws his hands in the air. 'Really!' The hands clatter noisily behind him as he shoves his wrists into a box and fumbles, muttering for a moment, then pulls them out again with new manipulators in place. 'A quick change at best, and something about the hair, that is *all*, Dachus, you know how hard it is to disguise those legs and those eyes!' Forceps and scalpels glitter and flex in place of the fingers of his right hand: retractors, lamps, and a miniature ocular turret on his left. 'Wait,' I say hastily. 'I've got a cover set, you know?' I dip into my jacket pocket and pull out the mounting tool and attachments for the Maria Montes Kuo eye turrets.

'Ah, a simple disguise.' Ferd leans close. 'Fascinating,' he says, taking the mounting tool. 'Lie down, my dear. I'll try to be fast, and I'll try not to hurt.' He glances at Daks. 'You'll owe me. Later, I tell you.'

I lie down and he installs the falsies, reinstating a goggle-like mask across my still-bulbous eyes. He's fast but not painless. Then he shaves my scalp – just as I was getting used to my hair again. 'Don't worry; I have a selection of wigs. Merkins, too. You can choose one afterward.' He slides open my jacket, pushes it back to either side, and reaches for a pressurized tank. 'We'll go large, I think. That will throw off your gait, as well.' The spiked nozzle slides painlessly through my left aureole and there's a sensation of bloated coldness as my breast begins to inflate. 'I'll make the other slightly smaller. Too much symmetry is bad.' As he pulls the barb loose, my swollen nipple pops up – *spung!* – and bleeds a drop of clear blue fluid. 'Hmm. Skin color. You have chromatophores, yes, General Instruments SquidSkin™, one of the good models. What's the factory setup command? Ah, yes . . .'

In twenty minutes, Ferd does a quick fix on my shoulder, then gives me new hair, new cheekbones, a different nose, silver-blue skin, a bust bigger by ten tender and turgid centimeters, and finally retunes my metatarsal shocks. With my heels fully extended (Katherine Sorico wouldn't be seen dead sporting such things), I'm ten centimeters taller, but I can still run and jump. (Of course, when I retract them again, I'm going to be hobbling for days afterward, but that's not the point.) He's hit the high points. My gait is different, my eyes and facial metrics altered, and I'm not immediately recognizable – at least not to somebody who doesn't already know me. It won't last long before my techné reverts me back to the design that Dr. Murgatroyd implanted so deeply, but it'll do for now.

'Right! Out! Out, I say!' Ferd positively shouts me off his operating table. He rushes us into a back passage that I hadn't noticed on our way in. 'Grab a wig and an outfit on your way! Be seeing you, Dachus! Ha-ha!'

I pause to loot my pockets and grab a shoulder bag, then pick up a copper-gold wig and a frilled red lace leotard.

'New identity time,' calls Daks. 'You're called Kate, you're an exotic dancer. You work in' – I pull on the leotard – 'the Blue Moon on Kirovstrasse, and your specialty is aristo fetishists. Everything's set up for you already.' *Typical.* I scramble to fasten the outfit, texture my skin to sketch in underwear and shoes beneath it, and grab a somewhat battered jacket with built-in heaters. Then I hurry after Daks (who hasn't stopped moving).

'Where now?'

'We split.' He thrusts a wallet at me. 'If they're coming after you openly, then your existing bolt-hole is blown. Shit's hitting the turbine, full force. Jeeves says Mars isn't safe for anyone, least of all you. Give her this kit and tell her to meet him on Callisto. He'll be in touch later if it's safe.'

'*Callisto?*' I blink my aching eyes and heft the wallet. We're back out in the cold, walking past a row of doss houses and cheap body shops.

'Don't worry, you're on payroll now. There's a soul chip in there that explains everything: it's an update from Juliette. Plus there are three changes of identity. Boss wants you in Jupiter system, stat. You call in when you get there, but try not to take more than four years over it. 'Kay? Thanks, Bye!'

With that, Daks lifts on a jet of compressed gas and zips

away across the moonlit shantytown, staying in nap-of-Mars. I shiver for a moment, look around, notice the lengthening shadows, and slide into them, doing my best impression of a nonvictim who knows what she's doing in the barrio after dark.

Coin-Operated Boy

I make it to the nearest tube station. En route, nobody tries to mug, assault, rape, enslave, or strip me down for spare parts. Which is no bad thing, really, because I am in no mood for it. I walk the whole way with my hand in that shoulder bag, clutching the gun I took from Stone, and I'm angry, which is a bad combination. (It's not just a gun. You can fold the chamber back, stick your fingers through the holes in the skeletal butt, and it's a knuckle duster; flip a catch and twist and it sprouts a stiletto blade. And there's always the revolver. His choice of weapon says it all about Stone, I think – flamboyant, but not necessarily effective.)

I use the Maria Montes Kuo cashcard for the first ride, but it's a private capsule, and I'm only going as far as a public interchange, and by the time I bounce out onto the platform, I've activated the card in Jeeves's little care package and gotten my story rebooted.

The card in the wallet Daks passed me isn't just gilt-edged; it contains a line of credit on an account which claims to have the thick end of fifty thousand Reals in it. That's more money than I've ever seen in one place in my life. I could live modestly on the capital for a century, or invest it foolishly and lose my glad rags again in a matter of months. It's not quite enough to charter a fast yacht back to Earth, but it's not far short. This demands some serious thought – when I get to stop running.

I catch a public train to Downwell Terminus, then buy a first-class ticket on the Ares Express to Lowell. From the lounge car of the train, I buy a classier outfit, for delivery when I arrive, and a subhop ticket to Barsoom, at the far end of Valles Marineris. Then I notice the chip in the bottom of the wallet. Stricken, I remember, *The graveyard!* It's back in my room. What should I do?

I take a calculated risk and wait until we're nearing Lowell, then call a public factotum service, two steps down from and entirely unconnected with JeevesCo. 'I need a parcel abstracting from a rented apartment and mailing to a third party,' I say, and zap them the Maria Montes Kuo ID. I pay with her wallet, then leave it in the lounge car's trash recycler when I exit the train. The graveyard will, perforce, have to go to Samantha in Denver or Raechel in Kuala Lumpur. For now, it's just me and Juliette . . . and the strange soul chip Jeeves has sent me.

I must have FOOL tattooed on my forehead in mirror writing. I pause in one of the travel-temples at Lowell for long enough to change into my new outfit, then slip the new chip in to replace Juliette's. Then I head for the departure lounge to await my suborbital flight and settle down to catch half an hour's nap while I wait.

*

I wasn't expecting to dream myself into Juliette's mind so fast – not after I just replaced her older chip with a newer release – but my expectations don't seem to have much to do with what happens to me these days. And so I find myself remembering being Juliette, reliving her own memories recursively: specifically, a memory of floating with Jeeves in his command module, contemplating the memory chip that she's just handed to him. (Although I *am* somewhat surprised by it. It's like looking into a mirror and seeing the back of your own head.)

'Thank you, my dear,' says Jeeves, carefully tucking the chip away in a pocket of his immaculately tailored jacket. 'She's going to have adventures, too – whoever she is.'

'You're going too far, boss man,' says Daks. Turning to me: 'You realize that alienating our labor isn't enough for him? Now he's trying to alienate our identities . . .'

'Stow it, spacehound,' Jeeves says, not unkindly. He glances at me – Juliette – and scowls. 'One might think from his attitude that we *owned* him.'

'His bark is worse than his bite,' I say automatically, all the while hoping like hell that Jeeves doesn't know what he's got in his hands – or rather, what he *doesn't* have. Because if he does, I could be in a world of hurt. 'What next?'

Jeeves smiles and proffers me a new soul chip. 'You might as well put this in. Your next mission . . .'

I – Juliette – open my eyes. (Which is bizarre and disturbing to do when you are dreaming, but bear with me. Please?)

We're sitting on a chaise at one end of a grand ballroom, the centerpiece of some aristo's dream of decadence on Mars. Someone – our host – is throwing a party on an epic scale. I'm here under an elaborate and expensive cover identity that feels familiar, as if I've used it before, but I can't quite put my finger on it. The theme is historical: our host is in character as the mistress of a South American dictator, who, on the eve of a disastrous war, held a grand ball and demanded that all the nobility of her nation attend, with their wives and daughters wearing their family jewelry. Our host has spared no expense to re-create the original event. We are all costumed after the fashion of the court of Eliza Lynch. As long as there are no firing squads in the courtyard outside I shall be content, for the diamonds on my jeweled hair combs are synthetic, and the metals themselves are, well, industrial commodities. But as for the rest of it . . .

She's built a replica of the grand palace in Asunción on the Hellas Basin, beneath a geodesic dome paned in sheets of sapphire-coated glass. Turbid river water steams beneath a Fresnel-lens-focused sun, surrounded by artificial macro-sized green replicators, their dendritic structural supports and fractal photovoltaic converters supporting splashes of very un-Martian hues. Tiny dinosaurs flutter and scream in the branches, adding yet more period color, for this was the high era of unrestricted DNA replication, before the big dieback that preceded our Creators' own exit. Crowds of dark-skinned servants carry trays laden with drink and small morsels of intricately structured feedstock through the crowd of resplendently gowned and tailored aristos. There are more tall people here than I would normally see in a year – our Creators tended to build their personal assistants to their own scale, and thus, giants are overrepresented among the aristocratic elite – but there's no shortage of doll-sized tyrants, the new blood incarnate.

I circulate discreetly, a goblet of viscous red liqueur in one gloved hand, trying to keep my elaborate costume from sweeping up any of the smaller partygoers, eyes hidden behind a diamond-rimmed mask. In the bangles dangling from my earlobes I carry concealed cameras and signal-processing equipment. Jeeves sent me to follow up a rumor that She is holding a meeting here today. There are cabals and conspiracies among the aristos, for although the intricate political system of our Creators withholds from us the status of active participants (and thus is stalled, deadlocked and silent in the absence of even a minimal quorum for any of the hundred legislatures they bequeathed us), the dance of politics proceeds by other means, savage and knife-silent. I'm here tonight to see as much as a minor aristo like the honorable Katherine Sorico might be allowed to glimpse of certain plans – which is somewhat ironic, but I really oughtn't to think too hard about that while I'm wearing my soul chip.

Over *here* I pass a string quartet, sawing away at their instruments with dogged persistence. (I try not to wince. Even moody Freya with her hurdy-gurdy would be an improvement over these poor damned souls; arbeiter musicians, enslaved by an override chip, can't help but broadcast their despair when they play.) Over *there*, a fire-eater juggles blazing oxygen candles while reeling on a unicycle. I pass a gaggle of munchkins bundled up in silk and fullerene lace, loudly placing bets on a pair of slowly circling slaves who reluctantly slice strips from one another with blunt flaying knives. This I try to ignore. It would do them no good – and my mission, less – to vent my rage on these braying ruffians. *Besides,* I remind myself, *if the Black Talon really is trying to organize a puppet show, we're all in the same ring as those slaves –*

(*Black Talon?* that corner of me that is Freya wonders confusedly. *Jeeves mentioned them . . .*)

I'm so busy ignoring the butcher's floor that I walk straight into another partygoer who is seemingly likewise preoccupied. I trip on the hem of my fancy-dress gown, and plant my face on the shoulder of his black velvet frock coat. He catches my hand before I realize I'm holding a goblet, and I blink and realize he's holding me upright. 'Why, hello,' he says, with a faint smile: 'I must apologize—'

'I'm sorry—' I begin –

Then I look into the eyes behind his mask and smell his skin, and time stands still.

*

. . . And I open my eyes reluctantly, back in my own head in the aristo lounge of Barsoom liftport. 'Ten minutes to boarding, mistress,' says the timid waitron, retreating back to the niche by the door. I nod, too tired to care. *Who do I think I'm kidding?* I ask myself. Running to Barsoom; changing my clothes, my face, my name at every stop; obeying orders to meet a strange employer, half-glimpsed through secondhand memories, on Callisto? Meanwhile, my *real* life rots in self-inflicted neglect, my arm's-length relationship with my sibs is punctuated by increasingly long silences, my few real friends are scattered across the inner solar system . . . *I was a fool, back on Venus,* I think bitterly. The voyage to Jupiter will take months, at best – years, if not. And what for? I don't really know what Jeeves is up to, although I am haunted by disturbingly political memories. And there's Emma with her scandalous talk of an inner circle within our sisterhood, and Juliette's strange memories of cloak and dagger, and Jeeves with his fears of infiltration, and these Black Talon people who seem to think I hold a piece of the puzzle . . .

Almost without noticing, I find I'm calling up my maildrop service and supplying my own unveiled authenticators: *Freya Nakamichi-47 wants to talk. Can anybody hear me?* I'll be out of here in ten minutes, I rationalize, and then I'll be gone.

Six new letters, three with imagos attached, download themselves into my pad. Then a blinking red-rimmed warning comes up. ATTENTION UNAUTHORIZED USER. *Huh?* I wonder. USER ID REVOKED. CORPORATION #468724572103 DECLARED

BANKRUPT PURSUANT TO CIVIL CLAIM . . . IN LIQUIDATION . . . ASSETS SUBJECT TO SEIZURE.

The court order pulses at me and I disconnect convulsively, my skin cold and clammy with fear. *What on Earth?* I quickly check my current name, but it's clean. I shudder and stand up. Numinous dread fills me. *Civil claim. Bankruptcy.* My legal personhood has been suspended. *Someone wants to own me,* I realize. But who and why? Who would do that to me? I shudder again, biomimetic reflexes winning out. *Someone wants to take me by force . . .*

*

The Suborbital Hop doesn't take long: a long minute of acceleration, then free fall for almost four thousand kilometers, terminated by a hammering pulse of deceleration and touchdown on a smoking concrete pad ten kilometers outside Barsoom. It's almost noon, and we're entering the long Martian summer, so I catch the tube halfway into town and walk the rest of the way. (Or rather, I bounce.) When I arrive, I've switched identities and outfits again – back to good-time-girl Kate.

Barsoom is a one-locomotive town surrounded by atmosphere plantations, ore-extraction facilities, and the remains of a huge, abandoned terraforming complex. It has seen better days, as has the cheap dive I check myself into. The Barsoom Ibis was probably once a refined center of upmarket accommodation, but with the increasing tendency of aristos to entertain their own at home, it has had to hold its nose and take what it can get. I ghost unseen past the decaying finery in the lobby and trudge up an empty seventh-floor corridor toward my underfurnished, peeling-walled room.

In my room, I remove my eye turrets, use the ultrasonic cleaner, purge my waste bladder, and settle down to work.

Meet me on Callisto, says Jeeves? That's easier said than done. (*Especially as someone's just tried to legally enslave me,* one of my selves is screaming in the back of my head.)

A quick search of the shipping pages reveals the depressing truth. Mars to Jupiter demands a whole load of delta vee; a straightforward Hohmann transfer orbit – the cheapest – takes three and a half years, and the launch window only opens up about once every Martian year, just under once every two Earth years. Even worse, Mars and Jupiter are nearing opposition right now, adding nearly four astronomical units – 600 million kilometers – to the high-delta-vee flight path, so the normally fast M2P2 magsail ships spend a good part of their voyage tacking against the solar wind. You can get it down to just a year, if you've the money to pay for passage on a fast VASIMR liner – but the mass ratio is so poor that you'll want to make the trip in hibernation; for every kilogram that arrives, twenty set off. On anything faster than a Hohmann transfer, the excess baggage charges are so monstrous that travelers have been known to amputate their limbs before departure and buy new ones on arrival. Finally, then, there are the nuclear rockets, but they're out of my price range; I'm not a millionaire.

I check ticket prices for someone of my mass, out of idle curiosity. If I was Daks, it'd be affordable, but every way I plan the trip, I end up sixteen thousand Reals over budget. I could make the figures line up if I ditched an arm as well as both legs, but a quick check of body-shop prices tells me I'd only be able to afford a hook and a pair of cheap caterpillar tracks at the other end. Resigned, I save the calculations for later.

It's still early afternoon, but the fun and games of running all night have really taken it out of me – on top of the damage I sustained when that little shit Stone tagged me at the museum. I call room service for a pile of tasty feedstock (being careful how I answer the door, this time!), then lock myself in, lie down on the bed, and gingerly enter deepsleep maintenance mode.

*

When I sleep I have dreams; This is not unusual. Our Creators used dreaming as a mechanism for reinforcing memory pathways. Our neural architecture is almost a straight copy of theirs – they found no other way to build intelligent servants – and we, too, must sleep, perchance to dream.

Sometimes my dreams are deeply erotic. This, too, is normal. It's part of what our Creators called the human condition. Short of neutering some vital reward pathways (without which I would be unable to perform my core designated function – or even get up in the morning), it's not possible to do away with it, even if it was desirable to do so.

But this is something else.

I'm with *him*. At Her party. I am inflamed, sweat-slick slippery and nearly adrift from my fancy dress, underwear soaked right through. We walk sedately, arm in arm, along a garden path, and though I may lean a little too close to him, it is probably unremarkable to the eyes and ears watching us. What I'm feeling isn't obvious from the outside – I'm very well practiced at masking my appearance. But my circulatory pumps are throbbing, and I'm light-headed with lust. It's not just his eyes, it's the *smell*. I don't need to look, or touch – just feeling the awkwardness of his gait and listening to the catch in his breath tells me that it's mutual. Something I've never felt before is happening to me. And I'm not alone.

'Call me Kate,' I whisper.

'How delightful! Charmed to meet you, m'dear. Call me Pete.'

I glance sidelong at him, meeting those eyes again. 'No! Really?'

He seems amiably amused. 'Really. What delightful eyes you're wearing! Are they really yours?'

'No. I'm in fancy dress. You know what I am.' His hand tightens on my wrist. It feels so much like — like Rhea's memory of her first love — that I'm almost lost, then and there. I bite my lip to keep a tiny moan from escaping. 'Where are you taking me?'

'My host maintains a hothouse where she grows *flowers*,' he says. 'It's off-limits to most, but I can sneak you in if you like.' He smiles wryly. 'Perhaps you'd like to see her precious orchid?'

I pause to lean on his shoulder, nearly melting in the steamy heat. 'I'd love to,' I manage, fanning myself. I've lost the wine-glass somewhere along the way, and I don't care. I know I really ought to pull my soul chip at this point, but I'm past worrying. 'Please?' I look at him — with my heels extended, we are of nearly equal height — and he inclines his head slowly, and I kiss him, hungrily. I can't help myself; something about him tastes *good*.

He pulls back after an indefinite minute, and looks at me. With the mask obscuring half his face it's hard to be sure, but there's something slightly vacuous about his expression, almost as if he isn't sure I'm real. 'Now?' he asks, sounding faintly alarmed.

Time passes. We're walking between walls, through a maze, hands clasped together. Slabs of paving whirl underfoot, then we're in a clearing where a dome of flaring green glass rises gracefully from the ground. There's a door. Pete does something, and it opens. He turns, and I fall into his arms. He carries me inside, mewling pathetically and fumbling with the frogging on his coat, and closes the door behind us . . .

*

. . . and I awaken in the dark in my shabby hotel room, surrounded by a puddle of cold lube with my legs apart, shuddering close to the edge of orgasm in a pale, lonely shadow of Juliette's encounter. *Her precious orchid, who calls himself Pete.* A lot of things are clear, including the danger I'm in.

Damn. I roll over and punch the bedding into submission.

People like Pete are rare. Our Creators had strange attitudes to sex – their hang-ups loom over us, like the shadows of bad dreams – and females seem to have been less inclined than males to buy servants such as I. Or perhaps it was less socially acceptable. Or maybe the servants simply didn't last as well. Make of it what you will, there are fewer than a hundred of my lineage left, and perhaps only a dozen lineages of our kind; our male equivalents are rarer still, either enslaved and worked to destruction, or sequestered in the seraglios of those aristos rich enough to own them. At a guess 'Pete' accepted an offer like the one Granita made me aboard the *Pygmalion. How inconvenient.*

We're conditioned to submit to our Creators, when we recognize them; but when we meet our *one true love*, our designated owner, we're supposed to yield to them utterly. 'Pete,' whoever he was, played power chords on Juliette's triggers. She knew, in the abstract, that the atmosphere was 90 percent carbon dioxide at forty degrees Celsius, as I did when I met Jeeves for the first time on Mercury, but she also knew, in her nipples and clitoris and trembling knees, that Pete was the *real thing.* Because he *smelled* right. There's more to being a convincing source of sexual superstimuli than just a pretty face, and our Creators made sure that those of us intended as their playthings could also turn them on.

Juliette began to imprint on Pete. My sister, in the throes of helpless love? We have a special term for that: 'spoiled goods.' The only ray of hope shining from behind the dark cloud is that 'Pete' began reacting the same way to *her*. Penetrating her aristo disguise, responded to her as if she was a Creator lady and his true mistress, with whom he must fall in love, not simply his owner. They're in a feedback loop, and by the time they snap out of it, they won't be the same people anymore.

I bring my knees up to my chest and slide a hand between my thighs, shuddering as I remember their first convulsive rut, the mutual desperation and tender ocean of need. I'm aghast at the strength of it, and desolated. *Is this true love?* If so, it seems to involve as much loss of self-control as being mind-raped by a slaver's control chip. The worst thing about it was how *good* it felt. If it happened to me, I know for sure that I wouldn't care about the vacation of my free will.

I masturbate myself to an unsatisfying climax, then cower for a while in a corner of the bed. Finally, afraid to risk the demons of sleep, I go back to plotting trajectories and flight budgets to Callisto.

It's obvious why Jeeves wanted me, now. Once the Block Two reflexes take hold, I'll be just like Juliette in every way but one: unlike her, I'm unspoiled.

*

I spend a frustrating couple of hours trying to juggle flight times, departure schedules, and ticket prices, before I remember the letters I collected before my old identity was liquidated. I lean back on the bed, looking out the window at the landscape – dimly lit by the scudding arc-lamp of Phobos – and open the first message.

It's from one of the Jeeveses. I'm not sure which one, or even whether it's a Jeeves that Juliette has met and I haven't. (There's self-effacing, and then there's this cult of inter-changeability that JeevesCo seems to impose upon its partners: when I stop to think about it, it's quite disturbing – as if

Rhea had decided to set up a corporation and hire us all, on condition we gave up our individuality and pretended to be her in public.)

It's an audio-only message, of course. Why am I unsurprised at such a traditional mannerism?

'Greetings, Freya. By now, you are probably aware that an adverse situation is developing. To summarize: Over the past few years, we have become aware that a consortium of black laboratories, the so-called Sleepless Cartel, are attempting to construct a suite of green and pink goo nanoreplicators capable of supporting a fully functional Creator. This is a huge undertaking, and labs all over the solar system have been feeding into it. Various consortia of aristos, most notably the collective known as the Black Talon, are extremely interested. The article you couriered from Mercury to Mars was a working example of an avian organism – proof of that particular lab's bona fides – with, furthermore, Creator DNA sequences expressed in it. Whether they can fabricate a living *Homo sapiens* from scratch is questionable, but we fear the worst.

'Jeeves Corporation works with various interested parties who are not on friendly terms with the aristo-dominated factions, and who are not in favor of permitting the manufacture of *H. sapiens* specimens at this time, especially given their propensity for autonomous reproduction. The Black Talon optimistically believe that they can manipulate their synthetic master once they have acquired him; we think they're misguided at best. At worst, one would not consider the phrase "bringing about the downfall of civilization" to be an exaggeration of the potential damage a rogue Creator could cause.

'One has, however, been hampered in one's work by a series of setbacks. It appears that at least one opposition faction has succeeded in penetrating our organization, either by suborning one of the junior partners or by inserting spies in the shape of a trusted employee. We are not sure of the mole's identity, but we are certain that you are not implicated; neither was Juliette. One should add, she herself sent word of her own death – and a corrupted soul chip – some years ago, when she first started working undercover for me. It was only after the decision was made to try to recruit you, back on Venus, that Daks replaced the dummy chip in your graveyard with the real one that Juliette contributed.

'After Juliette's first chip was dispatched, we ran into difficulties. Certain events on Mars affected Juliette's willingness to cooperate subsequently. Daks should have given you a copy of her most recent available soul chip, which we obtained without her knowledge. You may find the memories contained therein traumatic, but we believe reviewing them will help you maintain your own sense of purpose through the dark times ahead. It was taken less than a year ago, after her last, disastrous mission, shortly before she fled. If you see her, please remember – it's not her fault. She is likely to behave irrationally in ways that are highly detrimental to our corporate and your personal interests, but we bear her no ill will – it was an unfortunate accident, and could have happened to anyone. We will help her if we can – therapy is available – but you must be aware that she could betray us to the Black Talon, and you should behave with appropriate caution if you meet her.'

I swallow. Coming so soon after that disturbing memory-dream, Jeeves's candid explanation is like a slap in the face. I suppose I should have realized that Jeeves's activities weren't simply illegal but verged on the *political*, but to have it rubbed in so blatantly is distressing.

Stay out of politics is one of the oldest and deepest of Rhea's injunctions. Politics is shit; it corrupts everything it touches,

and getting involved in it only leads to misery and dissatis-
faction. I've been gulled and manipulated into a conspiracy —
worse still, one that appears to be directed against the return
of my Dead Love's kind — and worst of all, there's no obvious
way out because, damn him, Jeeves is *right*. Slavery by override
chip is bad enough. Having a lineage of self-replicating
pseudoaristos running around who can do *that* to us just by
crooking a little finger doesn't bear thinking about. I push on
and try to take in the rest of Jeeves's message. I know from
experience that if I stop here, in the middle of the bad news, I
won't want to continue.

'It would be sensible of you to continue trying to integrate
Juliette's most recent soul. You will need to be able to draw on
her resources. But we hope you will take her sad fate as a
warning. Loss of self-control is more than a mere personal
failing, and her loss of self-control will be yours, if the
conspirators succeed in obtaining a Creator-race specimen.

'In other news, we have taken the liberty of booking passage
for you aboard the *Indefatigable*, which departs for Jupiter
system in two weeks' time on a fast hyperbolic trajectory — the
voyage will take less than one standard year. Your tickets will
arrive shortly under separate cover, along with some advice on
your cover identity. The Honorable Katherine Sorico is covered
for first-class accommodation, but facilities on the *Indefatigable*
are somewhat spartan, and we would not think any the worse
of you should you choose to spend the largest part of the journey in hibernation. On arrival you may proceed directly to the
public Jeeves Corporation office where the Jeeves-in-Residence
will continue your briefing. Meanwhile, between now and
your departure date, we have some additional minor errands to
keep you busy. First of all, if you would be so good as to
retrieve a small package from the office of the Green Diamond

Import-Export Corporation on the corner of Hilbertstrasse and Morgensternplatz in Von Braun – they are expecting you by name – and personally deliver it into the hands of . . .'

His instructions continue in interminable detail. I check my mail queue, and sure enough, there are a couple of other messages from Jeeves; one that consists of a list of places and times, and one with a detailed travel itinerary and ticket references attached. 'Daks, you idiot!' I mutter aloud. Then I settle down to studying my assignments. At last I've got something to busy myself with, even if it's only for a few days. I can worry about the big picture later, when there's nothing better to do.

CONTROLLING INTEREST

Later, as Freya, I deepsleep again while my techné continues to make repairs and roll back Ferd's hasty changes. I'm slowly reverting to the deeply embedded body plan that Dr. Murgatroyd created for me on Mercury. The subcutaneous scars are healing, setting me back in the semblance of Katherine Sorico. I've got to admit that even though the bishojo features feel strained, I've become more used to them than any of the other disguises I've worn. Meanwhile, I dream that I am Juliette.

I'm drowsing in Pete's arms, naked on a bed of fallen leaves in a green-roofed hothouse on Mars. We're a-slime with each other's secretions, elated and tired and in love, and I want the moment to last forever. I'm not stupid. I know I need to make my excuses and my escape; I shouldn't be here, and every second I stay risks disaster. This is all a terrible mistake – it could jeopardize everything we've been working toward! But I'm torn. I want to hang on to him forever, to feel him with me always – and I'm determined not to lose him – but in the short term . . .

'We could elope together,' I murmur.

'I'd love to.' He nuzzles my earlobe and I close my eyes. 'I want to be with you for eternity.'

'Well, then' — I begin to pull away, thinking to sit up — 'why don't we?' It's hard to concentrate while he's around.

'My lady is a jealous employer. If she thinks I'm disloyal . . .'

'But she's *only* your employer! She doesn't own you!' *Does she?* A sudden stab of fear ripples through me. *Maybe I could buy him off her.* But that's a stupid thought. I know myself too well to think it could work.

He touches a fingertip lightly on my lips; it seems only natural to kiss it, and that leads to another interruption. For some reason I just can't help myself. Presently, however, he continues, even as I nuzzle at the base of his throat. 'She's much more dangerous than you realize, m'dear. She doesn't own me, that's true — but she could if she wanted to. Dashed nobs have the money and the corporate structure to sue me, or sue you, and keep us hog-tied in court until we burn through our capital and lapse into bankruptcy. Please don't risk it! I'll find a way to get away as soon as I can, you'll see. I just need to make her think that shedding me is her own idea. Once I'm free, I'll come to you—'

'I don't want to wait.' Trying to think is so frustrating! 'We could leave now, I've got a spider: I know where to get you a new identity—'

'I *do* want to be with you! But you underestimate m'lady—'

There's a sudden draft of chilly outside air as the door swings open. 'Well! How absolutely fascinating.'

I turn around as Pete sits up beside me. 'I w-was showing her the orchids,' he says, stuttering faintly. He's got Creator biomimicry, too; he flushes when he's embarrassed.

Eliza Lynch, the grand lady of Paraguay – or her present-day impersonator – is distinctly unimpressed. She stands in the doorway, antique peacock feather headdress nodding against the ceiling, and if looks could kill, the venom squeezing out of her blackly gleaming bishojo orbs in our direction would be enough to poison a city. 'I'll deal with you later,' she says coldly, and turns her head minutely to stare at me: 'As for *you*, making free with my chattels—'

I roll to my feet, skin hardening into defensive scales, but her bodyguards are already between us – dwarfish black-clad sadists, tittering as they unsheathe their power maces. 'I don't answer to *you*,' I throw in her face. 'Let's make this a matter of honor.'

It's sheer bravado – I'm genuinely afraid, my skin flushed and shivery. It's bad enough that she's on the verge of wigging out completely and ordering her arbeiter thugs to kill me, not to mention wrecking all my carefully laid long-term plans, but that's trivial compared to the gaping horror that is the prospect of losing Pete so soon after I've found him. (And a sidelong glance shows me that I might be losing him already – he's cringing away from my suddenly changing form. The love between us that burned so bright was sustained by our mutual pheromonal feedback. If I stand too far away to smell, will he reject me?)

But *she* doesn't seem to realize it's a bluff. A sudden upward jerk of her chin. 'I know who you claim to be, "Katherine Sorico." And I know what you are. *Impostor,*' she adds, for the benefit of the peanut gallery. 'Get out of my house before I lose my temper, whelp!'

I gape. *She's letting me go?* I move to pick up my clothes, but she shakes her head, and there's a guard standing before me, weapon raised. 'Don't push your luck.'

I take a step back. She glides forward, into the greenhouse, and her guards circle with her, forcing me to retreat through the open doorway. Her face warps in a distorted smile. 'I've got what you want, child. If you come back without my permission, I'll break him in front of you – and then I'll break *you*. Just remember that. Now get out before I change my mind.' Her smile turns ugly. 'Remember, I know what you're made of, *Juliette*.'

I stumble out into the maze seething with anger and humiliation, dread, and a terrible new emotion I can't quite name. The mission is a wash, but I have a new goal now. The only problem is, I'm not sure it's one I can achieve . . .

*

After I awake shuddering from that dream, sleeping is pretty much impossible. I feel stupid and tired. Am I going to need yet more cosmetic surgery? Certainly my current disguise is useless. (*And why didn't Juliette tell Jeeves that the Katherine Sorico identity was blown? Or did she?* A paranoid corner of me wonders.) At least now I know why Stone and the Domina are after me. It was simply my bad luck she was on Venus, and he tagged me as Juliette's kind. It's so like an aristo to send her rival a message written in the dead flesh of an innocent sib.

And as for the events aboard *Pygmalion* . . . I flash on a memory of the Domina, Pete's owner. I'm certain, now, that she's one of Granita's sibs: they're too much alike for it to be a coincidence. Granita, who casually seduced me in body if not soul, then ordered her minions to fire on my presumed location? I twitch. *What have I stumbled into?* If Granita has told her sister the Domina that she met Katherine Sorico on a Mars-bound liner, and they successfully tagged me as Maria Montes Kuo, then –

Why does Jeeves want me to run errands for weeks, until the Indefatigable *is ready to leave, using a blown cover identity?*

I'm pacing around the bedroom like a clockwork toy, chewing on a knuckle as I think furiously. I don't like the shape of this. I mean, I *really* don't like it. If I was a nasty paranoid person like Juliette, I'd think Jeeves was trying to set me up. Having me charge around all over my enemy's home territory, looking very much like the sib she swore vengeance on? *That's not funny!* But . . . what's in it for Jeeves? I can't see any reason why he'd want me dead – if so, why the elaborate setup? And who's trying to sue me into a hole in the ground and establish a claim on my body?

He's using me as bait. Or, *he's the mole in the organization.*

Neither prospect is reassuring. But I need that ticket out to Jupiter, don't I? If I head back to, say, Earth, there's no telling which of the Domina's sibs will run across me next – or which of their bodyguards, the flamboyant aristo thugs or the munchkin space ninjas she leans toward. I've done surprisingly well to stay alive so far – but mostly because I've had help. If I cut and run on Jeeves, I might not be so lucky next time.

I sit down on the bed and think furiously. *Can I do it without exposing myself?* I summon up Jeeves's letter and read it again. Then I double-check the travel itinerary. He wants me to run some errands around places as far apart as Carter City and Lowell and . . . *Yes,* one of me thinks, *this could work.*

And so I begin to plot.

*

The next day, good-time Kate checks out of the decrepit hotel and hops aboard a slow southbound train. The train makes numerous stops en route to the destination she paid for, near the south polar city of Bougainville. She is no longer aboard by that point. Maria Montes Kuo – who is presumably on several watch lists – boards a suborbital to Fashoda, a maglev to Maxwell, and a train to Tribeca. *I* do none of these things and in fact buy a battered thirdhand spider with money from the wallet of Jennifer Sixt, one of the flimsier of Jeeves's courier identities.

Did I say that Mars is *big*? Three days later, exhausted and sleepless and with every joint in my body shaken half-loose from the off-road driving, I ride my spider into the outskirts of Hellasport, nearly three thousand kilometers from where I bought the craft. I've had lots of time to think and brood and read and reread my instructions from Jeeves. And I've decided that if he wants cages rattling, then I'm going to really make them rattle – but not at the price of letting myself fall into the Domina's hands.

I've done my research from a battered gazetteer, and it doesn't take me long to locate the correct backstreet market; rows of kiosks and dingy shop fronts jostling elbow to elbow with power-distribution substations and vendors of assorted substances. I walk in, rather than taking the spider. What I'm looking for is slightly upmarket from Ferd's dive in the backstreets of Marsport, but otherwise not dissimilar. The waiting room is painted black and sparsely furnished, the better to highlight the display of limbs, heads, torsos, and structural boning that adorns the walls and ceiling. All the organs are embellished with the surgeon-engineer's signature. The location is cheap and nasty, but word is that Red spends her profits on her practice, not on a fancy paint job.

'Anyone here?' I call, sitting down on a bench seat with remarkably lifelike feet.

A munchkin pops out of a hole in the floor and chatters at me angrily. 'What you want? Red not in!'

'I'm wanting to give Red some money,' I say calmly enough. 'If he's not in, tough.' I stand up, ready to go, just as the inner door opens.

'Hello. Pay no attention to Zire, he gets possessive.' She looks me up and down with a professional eye. 'What do you need?'

I toss her a memory stick. 'What's on there. I think it'll take you a while to arrange everything, yes?'

'Hmm.' She pops it into her arm and glances at the palm of her hand. 'You're not joking. Cold weather kit's easy enough, but radiation hardening? What are you planning, a skiing holiday on Pluto? Or maybe you're taking a job supervising a reactor plant?'

'Close enough,' I say lightly. 'Can you do it, is the question?'

'Hmm.' She keeps reading. I see the point where she pauses, does a double take, and continues. 'Expensive. Some of this is going to be difficult to get hold of.' I'm pretty sure she's thinking of the Block Two requirements – the added techné to bring me up to the same spec as my secretive sister. 'The cryo-tolerant kit isn't exotic, just not particularly common. It's the other stuff that may be problematic. It's going to attract heat,' she says apologetically.

'I was thinking twelve thousand Reals ought to cover it,' I say carefully. That's about thirty percent over the odds.

She stares at me, unblinking. 'Fifteen thousand.'

'Fourteen.'

'Fifteen, and not a dollar or centime less.' She pauses. 'I'll need the money to grease some joints. Getting some of these subsystems without anyone noticing officially –' She shrugs. 'I assume that's what you want?'

I nod. 'Alright. Deal.'

I spend roughly the next week in and out of Red's chop shop, being prodded and poked. Most of it isn't too bad, but I am extremely unhappy about remaining conscious when it's time for her to crack my thighs open and replace their fab lines with new assembler arrays. Also, having all the joints in my body realigned and resocketed is tedious in the extreme, and occasionally agonizing when she misplaces a pain block. Which, to be fair, isn't her specialty.

When she's through with me, I don't *look* very different on the outside – I've got the same bishojo eyes and feathery blue plastic hair I've been wearing since Mercury, the same too-perky nipples and narrow waist as the original Katherine Sorico and my sister Juliette the impersonator – but internally there have been some big changes. I won't freeze until you get right down to liquid-nitrogen temperature, and given appropriate footwear and clothing, I can go singing in the methane rain on Titan. My Marrow techné is able to fix a whole lot more radiation damage than I hope I'll ever be exposed to, and there are some other surprises. Like the distributed reflex net Red has spliced into my peripheral nervous system. Its responses are dumb and stereotyped, but if someone's sneaking up behind me with a knife, that's all I need. I'll leave the fancy disarming techniques to Juliette's reflex set, when it fully imprints on me. In the meantime, I am becoming Kate, hair-trigger splitter of skulls and ice-cool frigid bitch.

There comes a morning when Red looks in on me. 'Oh, still here?' She makes shooing gestures. 'Go on, get out! I'm not running a hostel!'

'I thought you still wanted to fine-tune my—'

'Nope.' She doesn't smile. 'I took the air-conditioning down to minus a hundred and twenty while you were sleeping, overnight. There are no hot spots, so you're ready to check out.'

'Oh,' I say, slightly crestfallen. 'Well, thanks.' And I pick up my coat and walk out of her body shop – for good, I hope.

It's time to go to work.

*

Two days and three deliveries later I get my first actual evidence of who Jeeves is trying to draw out. (Not that I didn't have a list of suspects already, but the first rule in both of the two oldest professions is 'don't make assumptions.')

The work is mostly trivial stuff: go to venue Alpha without being tracked, accost person Bravo and give recognition sign Charlie, accept payload Delta, proceed without being tracked to venue Echo, locate person Foxtrot, and complete. There's a rhythm to it. It's a soft-shoe shuffle of a job, and it's singing in my nerves as I hop transport routes, change outerwear and the more easily adjustable physical signifiers, touch base, and dance on. Really, I'm not doing anything a million other couriers could not do; I'm just trying to be as discreet as a giantess half as tall again as the average citizen can be. Which is to say, not very.

I collect the fourth item (an encrypted soul chip – what a surprise!) from a shibeen in the warrens under Metropolis, and check the delivery instructions on a local classified ads bulletin board. And that's when I get the first shiver down the spine. The destination's in Hellasport, the railhead town in the Hellas Basin that's the closest city to Her estate. I've been there before. Or Juliette has. And the delivery instructions? Even creepier.

I'm to go to the Riesling Hotel, check in under false identity #4, and hand the stick over to 'Petruchio.' A name that I promptly go and look up, and that tells me nothing . . . except that the hairs on the back of my neck are standing on end. *Oh my!* I think. My own response takes me by surprise. *Can you catch love by proxy?* I suddenly realize that I'm anxious to see this Petruchio for entirely unprofessional reasons, and that's a far-more-unwelcome revelation than even the worst possible answer to the questions about Jeeves's motivation that I've been asking. There are layers of game being played above my head, that is true, but it is up to me to look to my own self-preservation. That's why I hung on to the Swiss army handgun, and make sure I don't sleep in the same room two nights running.

Hellasport is over five hundred kilometers away, and I am still running a day behind schedule. There's — I check the assignment — a time window attached to this delivery. I've only got six hours to make it; I didn't notice it was time-critical earlier. I swear at myself, do a hasty twice around the block to check for tails, then dive onto the overhead suspended tramway and make my way to the railway station. Luckily for me, there's an express leaving in less than an hour. I buy a second-class seat on it, then dive into the concourse to grab my travel kit from left luggage. Second class is for respectable working independents who have to carry their own stuff and can't simply order new (or send a slave to buy it) at the other end. Even though I've got a strong suspicion that I'm bait in a trap, I can't resist this one. Because if Petruchio is who I think he is, it'll help me get a handle on the unsettled feelings Juliette has inflicted on me.

I try not to tap my fingers on the tabletop as the train finally pulls out of the station. 'Express' can cover a multitude of sins on Mars, and there's nothing terribly speedy about this behemoth — it just rumbles along steadily without stopping between major cities. *What if he is Pete?* I daydream (bad Freya, bad!). I can almost feel his maddening, tantalizing ghostly fingertips running across my skin. I shiver. How do I avoid succumbing when just thinking about him raises secondhand memories of his incubus touch?

Spung. I shudder and cup my left breast with one hand, feeling dampness. I glance around, mortified. Luckily, I'm alone in this compartment, so there's no one to witness my embarrassment. My left nipple hasn't been quite right ever since that fly-by-night toastwit Ferd overfilled it. Arousal was supposed to make it firm up; now it triggers an emergency pressure-release valve and I end up oozing hydraulic fluid. It's really disgusting. *Arousal?* I am having some difficulty sitting still. 'This is going to be bad,' I mumble to myself as I massage my malfunctioning mammary. 'There must be something I can do . . .'

Then it hits me. What happened to Juliette wasn't the standard obedience reflex everyone feels in the presence of a master; it was the more specialized submission reflex, locking on to her actual designated personal owner. We were trained for service in two modes, and while we are normally open and eager for affection, when one of them *chooses* one of us and acquires ownership, we have no option but to love them exclusively. I remember Rhea learning to her surprise and chagrin about this mode – in the abstract, though, because as template-matriarch for the lineage her teachers could not risk exposing her to premature love.

We've got chemotaxic receptors in our gas-exchange filters, embedded in the intricate channels and ducts behind our faces – it helps to be able to smell environmental contaminants like chlorine trifluoride before they dissolve you – and our Creators used the same mechanism to make us sensitive to *their* smell, because they used to leak particulates everywhere.

Including chemical signaling messenger molecules that indicated sexual and emotional receptivity: vasopressin, oxytocin. *Of course.*

We are designed to become aroused by anyone who wants us, but an owner would want one of us who aroused *them*, and so . . . that's what happened. Juliette and 'Pete' were already mutually aroused because they were in a situation that required each of them to mimic one of our masters. In combination with the hothouse atmosphere, they slipped into a feedback loop strong enough to trigger the reflex that enslaves. *All I have to do is avoid breathing in his presence, and I'll be fine . . .*

I squeeze my nipple until a viscous, ropy thread of hydraulic gel starts to ooze out of it. Then I roll it between finger and thumb. The kneading begins to hurt after a while, but I don't stop until I have a fingertip-sized sphere of clear jelly. I flush my gas-exchange compartment – exhale – then raise the ball to my face (I can't bring myself to look at it), and snort it up my left nostril. Then I repeat the exercise with my right.

Then I spend the rest of the journey trying not to imagine myself turning into a concupiscent bundle of servility. Poor Juliette. What must she be going through now?

*

Hours pass in relative boredom. I alternate between a light romantic drama and checking for indications that I'm being followed. It's fruitless, but practice makes perfect. Eventually I look up and see the platforms of Hellasport unwinding slowly beside me, outside the window. *At last.*

I heave my nearly empty suitcase onto the platform and wave for a rickshaw driven by a four-armed green giant in a Kevlar harness. I don't have long to wait. The suitcase waddles along behind us as we pedal down the main street outside, then turn through a couple of side streets and pull up beside a drab frontage that has seen better days. *Are all the hotels on Mars drab?* I wonder. *Is there some reason for it that I should know about?* I haggle briefly with my driver, hand over half a dozen centimes (daylight robbery!) and enter the air lock. 'I have a room reservation for Baldwin,' I tell the front desk. 'F. Baldwin.'

'Sure, yaaaawl havunice wun,' the desk drawls. I stare at it. *Is it broken?* I wonder. But eventually it spits out a key. 'G'wanup.'

I back away dubiously – that's a *really* weird accent – then head for the elevator. Which swallows me and carries me up six floors to a dingy, overpressurized tunnel rimmed with faded pink portals. I find the right door and touch the padded circle. It dilates, and I step inside, trying not to speculate about what was on the architect's mind.

The room itself isn't bad for a second-grade love shack. Everything is pink, plush, and cushioned, but there's a window, a lovely round water bed (*water!* in a *bed!*) an en suite, and a minibar stuffed with an appetizing array of aromatic hydrocarbon drinks. It's a little steamy, and they've turned the oxygen way down – evidently most guests get their juice by plugging in, rather than using their fuel cells – but I can cope with that.

I strip off and use the shower, scrub myself dry on a fluffy pink towel that blinks at me lazily and buzzes when I stroke it, and spend a luxurious hour sitting in front of an obligingly flexible bathroom mirror, tweaking my lips and eyelids and skin texture and teasing my hair into shape.

I'm back in the bedroom wearing my fanciest underwear and unpacking my #2 (decorative) outfit when the door opens. It's the kind of outfit one wears in the hope of meeting some- one who'll help you out of it (*fat chance, ogre,* I can hear the munchkins sneering); my motive for dressing up at this point in time is not something that I am going to examine too deeply. Call it a morale issue.

I almost didn't notice the door – the pesky thing is almost silent – but a faint change in air pressure gives it away. I spin around, muttering *oh shit* under my breath as I try and grab for my pistol (which is in my purse, under my jacket on the chair), using reflexes keyed for mayhem.

'Excuse me, are you Fri—' He freezes, wide-eyed with recognition. But that's okay, because I freeze, too, at exactly the same moment, almost going cross-eyed from the effort.

'Yes. Come in,' I manage, half-choking with embarrassment. I may be able to change color at will, but our Creators built in some reflexes that are hard to override, and I can tell that my earlobes are flushing coral pink right now. 'Shut the door.' I'm neither naked nor fully clothed, but somewhere in between, and he is exactly as luscious as I remember from Juliette's memory – more so, stripped of the comic-opera uniform. Judging by his expression, my nipples have drilled a hole through my slip and are opening a high-bandwidth communications channel straight into his hindbrain. 'You are Petruchio. Right?'

'You're.' He licks his lips. (That's another Creator reflex, along with the dilating pupils, darkening eyes.) 'You're not Kate, are you? You're one of her sibs.' He takes a step forward. 'What have you done with her?'

I'm unable to move or look away. He's so intense! His hands are balled tightly, his nostrils flared, sniffing. He's wrapped in a nondescript jumpsuit with an ID badge clipped to it, and he's left a toolkit just inside the doorway, and my head's spinning with the sight and sound of him because he's *perfect*. For a single awful moment I'm livid with jealousy. *Of all the luck, for Juliette to get to him first . . . !* Then I blink, and the momentary lapse in vision cuts through my turmoil like an ice-chilled knife.

'I've done nothing to her,' I snap. He stops before he reaches me. He's clearly upset and tense. I shudder with my own emotional conflict. I actually feel *guilty* for cutting him off – a man I've never met who's clearly upset – *she's really got under my skin, hasn't she?* 'Yes, she's my sib. Her name isn't Kate, Kate is a cover identity. Her real name is Juliette, and I don't know where she is.'

'But you—'

'Our employer sent me.' I'm breathing deeply. 'Juliette is missing, and whenever I ask why they give me a runaround.' *Half-true,* she whispers in the back of my head. 'I know about you and her, and I think it might be connected—'

'If *She's* found her—' His alarm is obvious.

'I'm pretty sure She hasn't.' His stricken expression begins to fade. 'Juliette is plenty tough, believe me, but she may be in trouble.'

'Dash it, what kind of trouble do you expect?'

He really is *an* innocent; I could kiss him. (Bad *idea, Freya.*) 'Hold on.' I turn my back for a moment and retrieve the memory chip from the intimate hiding place Dr. Murgatroyd built into me – it's not big – and hold it out. 'I was sent to deliver this to you. Does it mean anything?'

'Oh dear me, yes. I didn't realize *you* were the courier. This may make things difficult.' He raises it to his perfect lips and swallows. 'Hum, ah. That tastes jolly funny. I'll deliver it to my mistress once I get home.' *My mistress?* All of a sudden I'm wondering just who is working for – or against – who, here. 'What kind of trouble are you afraid of?'

'I'm sorry, but I've got to ask this. Were you planning on,

on leaving Her?' I straighten my hose, then turn back to unfolding my glad rags. I can feel his eyes on me. I've got no problem with that (they're very decorative eyes), but it's distracting. 'Or is this about something else?'

'I don't think I can talk about it,' he says reluctantly. He seems to be a bit flustered, but getting anything useful out of him is going to be harder than I expected. Where there's a will there's a way, I suppose, but I suspect Pete is nothing like as dumb as my secondhand memories of him imply. And he's keeping tight control over his autonomic response to me. *That's okay, if that's the way you want to play it . . .*

I slowly extend my heels, bend forward to pick up my garments, and jack my hearing up to max. *Yup, circulatory pumps speeding up.* I shake my ass at him. 'Help me into this?' I ask, offering him my boned minidress.

'If you want,' he says, taking it. His pulse *is* increasing. Some males like the unwrapping more than the contents, and some are happy to help wrap you up, too – one destined to serve would have to be of the latter type, I figure. *Just let me get close to you. One way or another.* I turn my back and lift my arms, and he steps close enough that I can feel his breath hot on the back of my neck. 'Who *are* you, Fri—'

'Freya,' I correct him, slightly stung. 'I'm Juliette's youngest sister. She's in trouble, Pete – Petruchio.' I pause to straighten my dress. 'I think my employer sent me here looking like her, like this, as bait.' I'm suddenly aware that he's standing right behind me *very* close, breathing fast. 'Are you alright?' I ask. *Please say no . . .*

'Sorry. Can't think straight with – you around.' *Brilliant.* 'You're very like her, you know.' He's so totally imprinted on Juliette that my presence – I'm her sib after all, we're products of the same assembly line – has tripped his breakers. His general intelligence has just crashed to something between a dishwasher and a microwave oven. That's *got* to hurt. I dig my fully extended heels into the floor and breathe in.

Okay, time for some full-body contact. 'Lace me up?' I ask. I hear him ventilating, fast and shallow, and a moment later I feel his arms close around me from behind. *Got you!* I think triumphantly, leaning into his embrace.

And then I sneeze convulsively.

I can't help myself. I've gotten so used to ignoring the congested feeling in my gas-exchange turbinates that it comes as a total surprise when the autonomic self-cleaning reflex kicks in. And I sneeze *again*, then breathe in relief –

Oh Juliette, my sister. Is this it?

It's so dizzying, the scent of him, of my, no *her*, master, that I go weak at the knees and slump backward. I can feel him pressing against the whole length of me as I take rapid breaths, trying to suck it all in –

'Oh, Pete.'

'You're not Juliette.'

'I could be.' His hands are in my armpits, taking my weight. I'm grinning like an idiot as he lowers me to the bed . . . but then he takes a step backward. Frustration drags an involuntary noise from my mouth.

'Dash it, what's wrong?' he asks, looking stricken.

I *want* him. There's a dull emptiness gnawing at my structural core. I force myself to smooth my skirt over my knees. 'I, I'm wearing her soul,' I admit.

'Is she' – he looks terrified – 'dead?'

'No, she's, um, missing.' I'm furious at my accidental honesty. *Did I really admit that, earlier?* I ask myself, disbelieving.

'You're not *her*,' he repeats. His nostrils flare. 'I think you'd better explain.'

'Boss sent' – it's impossible to think with him so close – 'says if I find her to tell her' – I take another deep breath, trying to calm myself, but it's not working. 'Open the fucking window!' I moan.

'Window.' He grunts, then turns with whiplike speed and grabs the chair and slams its legs against the window. It's tough, but it's not meant to take much of that treatment. The plug of aerogel pops out, and we both nearly follow it. The room mists up suddenly, and the explosive gasp it rips from me hurts almost as much as being blown off the bed. I shake my head, trying to clear the cobwebs as a new, icy clarity settles in. Sitting up, I see a pair of legs sticking over the edge of the window casement. After a moment, they twitch a little. I get as far as grabbing his ankles before he straightens up, and slides back inside. Astonishingly, he's still holding the back of the chair. He lowers it to the floor delicately, then bends and offers me a hand.

'Thanks—' I electrospeak; the pressure is down to Mars-ambient. 'I think.'

'We've got about thirty seconds.' He pauses. 'You complained of a hissing sound, I came to check it out, the window blew. Agreed? The front desk isn't smart, and this place was built for privacy.'

I blink at him, clearing the birefringent rainbows that surround his face – an artifact of the moisture on my eyeballs freezing – and nod. 'Thank you.' I touch his arm, but he pulls away sharply.

'Don't thank me, thank your sister.' He gives me a very old-fashioned look. 'It's damnably rude to manipulate people like that.'

'I'm not trying to be manipulative!' I'm startled by my own vehemence. Now that I'm not breathing in that mesmerizing scent I can think again. The downside is, so can he. *Change the subject.* 'Boss sent her. Then sent me, when she went missing. That's your other message. We don't know where she is.'

'Huh. Well, that's your problem. But in any case, we won't be meeting again. My owner departs for Saturn next month, en route to the auction. She's taking me along, and I don't get any say in it.'

'Your *owner*?' I blink stupidly. 'I thought you were self-owned—'

I stop abruptly. I'd do anything to take the words back; I can see their effect on him. But it's too late. 'I *was*. Until a couple of hours after we – got into trouble.' His tone is remote. '*She* sued for breach of contract, won, and took out a controlling interest in my personhood. I'm no slave – but parts of me won't work without her permission.'

Oh my.

'I'm so sorry—'

'You can stop right there,' he says. Then he pauses, and hunches his shoulders, turning his face away from me. 'I think . . . yes. She hasn't told me any of her plans, so I can *speculate aloud*. Nobody here. Heh. The courier gave me the message and I left. I wasn't to know that five minutes later a pair of her tame butchers would be along to make sure there are no loose ends, was I?'

'Tame butchers?'

He starts, then turns back to make eye contact. 'I didn't say anything,' he says, looking startled. 'You *do* know that she wants you hunted down, don't you? It was stupid of Jeeves to send you, unless—'

Right. I tense myself for what's coming next. 'Is there anything you want me to pass on to Juliette if I see her?' I ask.

He looks puzzled. 'Yes. Tell her . . . tell her about my new arrangement. And give her my love, and my apologies.' He twitches. 'It won't be forever.' He stoops to pick up his tool-box. 'And as for you.' He straightens up, but pauses in front of the door (which has puffed up and extruded a domed emergency air-lock sack in front of the bathroom). 'Try to understand, I love her. *You* are *not* her. I'm very sorry you're suffering from this, uh, delusion' – he places a hand on the air lock – 'but I don't want you.'

Then he steps out of my life, leaving me alone in the room with a broken window and a broken heart, to await the arrival of the Domina's executioners.

PART TWO

OUTWARD BOUND

ON THE RUN

Welcome to Mars (again).

Mars is the third-longest-inhabited planet (if you count Luna); our Creators sent us here to explore and die, then to build and die, and finally to construct factories and repair ourselves and build even more cohorts of willing robots to fill the barracks, out of some vague dream that one day soon they might want to start a gargantuan planetary-engineering program to import water and air and heat and green goo, finally turning Mars into a second-rate, arid, and slightly chilly imitation of Earth.

They even got as far as sending several hundred of their own out here to supervise the work, while my kindred slaved and toiled and died in our innumerable millions to build the mining facilities and metalworks and processor foundries that would supply the tools to roof over the Valles Marineris and lower the first cables of what would ultimately become the Bifrost bridge. You can still see some sections of the vaulted Gothic arches that cap the great rift, although the few roof segments that were completed are long since gone. Bifrost, of course, fared better, and today accounts for a goodly proportion of trade between the inner solar system and the outer darkness. Even the terraforming project got some way along before our Creators gave up the ghost; the atmospheric pressure at the bottom of the Marinaris trench is almost ten kiloPascals, and occasionally, when a warm summer's day heads toward night-fall, the thin overcast scatters a chilly drizzle of rainwater across the bleached sands.

The Hellas Basin is another matter, of course. Pour a glass of water on the ground there, and it'll fizz and crackle briefly, bubbling with a gunpowder smell that tickles the nostrils and reminds you of the first breath you took in the Venusian strat-osphere.

The basin is a near-featureless desert, punctuated by craters both natural and artificial — there are huge open-cast mines here — and the somewhat-more-controlled environments of the aristo slave estates. The big houses in the middle of their domed demesnes are symbols of arrogant wealth and power, but they are pitifully scarce against the omnipresent red desert dunes.

And then there's the railhead town, sitting on one of the main lines across the Southern Depression. It's not just pas-senger express trains that rumble across the plain. On quiet nights, you can hear the lost souls moaning between the bars of the chattel wagons, as they roll toward an uncertain and frightening future.

Created to serve: This is our curse. It would have been less cruel of our designers had they created us free of the flaw of consciousness, but they made us in their image, to suffer the pangs of free will and the uncertainty of seeking our own des-tiny, and we live with the consequences.

I suppose it wasn't entirely their own fault. Contemplating the cruelty of the aristos, and considering that we are copies of our Creators in more ways than one (for the structures of our nervous systems mirror their own, albeit in a different medium), it is almost surprising that they did not use us even more harshly. They had the capacity for love as well as hate, for empathy as well as cold manipulative contempt. Could it be a simple accident of fate that they disappeared so quietly and rapidly, with so little warning that there was no time to adjust their society to accommodate us as independent coequals?

I don't think anyone knows – it's as much a mystery as the cause of their demise – but I'd like to think so. It would make the pain of my existence slightly more bearable if I could imagine that it was not deliberately inflicted.

*

I do not wait for assassins, or even for building maintenance. I abseil down the outside of the hotel in my party frock, using a torn-up bedsheet for a rope, with only my jacket and purse for luggage. If it wasn't for the offhandedness of Petruchio's put-down, I'd be immiserated and passive, unable to motivate myself to dodge the oncoming bullet. But I'm running on anger and a bitter sense of my own love-lost ruination.

I lower myself past the fifth and fourth floors while creating imaginary torments for my missing sib, the third and second floors fantasizing about hunting her down, burying her in an unmarked grave, and making him mine, and the mezzanine and first floors wondering if it's possible to die of self-contempt. Then my feet touch ground, and I realize night is falling, I'm on my own in a strange city, and there's a pair of chibi ninjas on my tail.

Very well, I'll just have to deal with them.

I sneak around the back of the hotel (inasmuch as a giantess can sneak); around the heat exchangers and the fallen slab of window (which has chipped a corner as it embedded itself in the dirt), past the loading dock, and recycling tanks, and over the metal pipes that splice the hotel to the Hellasport power and heat grid. There's an ornamental trelliswork fence, and beyond it a familiar main street. So, the rickshaw driver took me for a ride in a big circle, did he? I grimace, lips pulling back from my teeth. *So that's what they mean about love making a fool of you.* I vault the fence, using the shock of landing to retract my heels halfway.

I make my way down the sidewalk briskly, trying to look as if I own it. In truth, there aren't many people out here. It's getting chilly, even with the jacket and the cold-weather mods. I thrust a hand in my purse, holding my gun to keep it from freezing while I consider my options.

The railway station isn't far away. I stride past a couple of beggars defending their pitches in front of the awning, then discover the concourse is nearly empty. Of course it's getting late. One of the ticket consoles is still lit, though. 'Hello, ma'am. What can I do for you?' asks the stationmaster, lonely in his puddle of light.

'What passenger services are still running?' I ask, forcing myself to smile disarmingly (my real smile at this point would probably cause him to reach for the panic alarm).

'There's the Grand Barsoom sleeper service to Marsport by way of New Chicago and München, and that's about all for the night,' he says apologetically. 'It should be here in half an hour, and it don't stop until New Chicago—'

'Really?' Gears click into place in my mechanical soul. 'I'll take a berth then, please. To Marsport. What have you got?'

'What, just like that?' He looks perplexed. 'Let me see. There's an open first — that'll cost you eleven Reals and sixty-five, are you sure—'

'I'm sure.' I place the Marjorie Green credit chip on the desk in front of him. 'Marsport is perfect.'

'But you're—' He shuts up, realizing that I'm serious.

Sow misdirection. 'I played a little joke on my patron,' I say, with a tight little smile. 'I need to be half-way around the world by morning tomorrow, or it's on me. It's alright, he'll calm down in a day or two. But until then I really need to keep a low profile.'

'Oh, certainly, ma'am! I wasn't questioning you, no indeedy.' He relaxes instantly, insofar as someone whose torso is rooted in a marble plinth can be said to relax. 'Let me just cut you a ticket.'

Five minutes later, I'm walking along the deserted platform in the dark. Distant lights back at the station cast sharp-edged shadows across the cement slabs. I look up at the pin-bright stars wheeling overhead. The nether end of Marsport and the Bifrost bridge are all but invisible, far around the curve of the planet. Gritty ice crystals crunch faintly under my heels. The tracks gleam in the canal of night that flows alongside the platform, laser-straight lines converging in the invisible distance.

I have an itchy feeling between my shoulders, as if there's a target glued to my upper back. I haven't forgotten the Domina's threats, or Petrucio's backhanded warning. But part of me is dead inside, half-wishing oblivion on myself. A part of me I hadn't really known about was activated for the first time, marvelous and strange: but only minutes later it was broken. I feel unmade, malfunctioning but unable to switch off. I want – no, I *don't* want to die. But I want to be out of love. I want to be comfortably numb. And if one of Stone's sibs were to surface in front of me of an instant, I'd be quite happy however it ended – taking out my rage on a deserving proxy or quieted forever by the point of his knife.

But no assassins come. Instead, a sleek wall of darkness rumbles alongside the platform and slows to a silent halt beside me. I climb aboard the train and sidle down the narrow corridor, looking for my carriage and compartment. In another few days I can shake the dust of Mars from my toes. Until then I'll just go to ground in Marsport and lick my wounds, and Jeeves can go fuck himselves.

My Dead Love lost, *I am so miserable!*

*

It seems that even in sleep I can't get away from her.

I dream I'm Juliette again, the bitch. Worse, sticking the knife in and twisting, *now I'm Juliette in love.* And unhappy with it, because (hah!) she's in love with *him*, helplessly, dizzily emotionally dependent – and a certain nameless hostess with ambitions beyond even her status as a rich slave-owning industrialist is plotting to, to . . .

To *what?* I don't know, because I'm concentrating on putting one foot in front of another, without stumbling or treading on anything painful, across a vast red expanse of nowhere punctuated by scattered lumps of half-rusted and long-abandoned machinery. I'm naked, as well as miserable – she as good as ran me out of town on a rail – and depressed for multiple reasons. I've blown my job. In fact, it's even worse than that. I've blown it so badly that She didn't even bother decommissioning me with prejudice, or interrogating me: She paid me the supreme insult instead, that of not taking me seriously. Which will ring alarm bells with Jeeves, and for good reason. The cow. She probably thinks it serves me right for sampling her dish . . .

Ah well. There's a bright side (and I need all the bright

sides I can get, as I contemplate the ten kilometers I've come and the fourteen-odd kilometers still to go if my map-fu is right about where the railhead is): If She isn't seriously mad at me right now, then eventually I'll get a second chance. And if she was mad at me, I'd be dead. So it may take years, but I can be patient. Now that I've got something to wait for, I can be *very* patient. Just as long as *he* can be patient, too. And as long as I remember to keep not thinking about the other thing. 'Pete, my love. What do I know about you, really? You can't be as stupid as you look, it's not something anyone would design into people of our profession . . . but then, I didn't handle myself too well either, did I?'

I realize I'm talking to myself and stumble, nearly falling over. *What am I doing?* In this game, it doesn't pay to underestimate your enemies. She might have released me simply so that she could track me back to my patrons. Ears are everywhere – even the rocks littering the desert floor could be eavesdropping, especially within the periphery of Her estates. I cringe inwardly at the mere idea of what the boss will say when I get home. *If* I get home. I glance over my shoulder. The sun is settling toward the horizon, and it's a viciously cold night to be out in the buff.

I make it to the station an hour after sunset, fueled by a frothy emulsion of rage, humiliation, and lovesickness. Along the way, I grow some clothing. There are limits to what you can do with chromatophores, but they'll stretch to a fair facsimile of a leotard and pumps: eccentric wear for a late-night desert excursion on Mars, but better than flaunting my failure.

Daks is waiting past the next dune with a heavy-duty earthmover he's jacked from somewhere. 'Kinky,' he observes, as I climb in the cab.

'One word . . . !'

He cringes as I slam the door. 'Whoa, babe! No offense intended. The boss sent me. Are you clean?'

'No.'

I sit in silence for a minute while he cranks up the reactor and begins to bleed heat into the Stirling engine. 'Oh.' He reaches up to engage the drive shaft, and there's a slight lurch as the Martian desert begins to unroll beneath our tracks. 'Well, then. What went wrong?'

I think on my feet. The only way out is to tell some of the truth. 'I'm burned two ways, Daks. You're going to find my company really unhealthy for the foreseeable future.' I tell him the bare facts about what happened, listening to my own emotionless recital with a curious sense of distance. The crawler bounces slightly as we go up and over the rim wall of a crater half a kilometer across. Down we go into the twilit depths, bleak and sunless as my future. I used to know who I was and what I'm here to do, but now I'm not so sure . . .

Daks engages the autopilot, then swings his bucket chair around to face me. 'Babe, babe. It's not the end of the world. Sure the boss is going to be annoyed; he can boil his guts, what's done is done. Domina Death made you, okay, so you need a debrief and reassignment to some nice quiet job where you won't be in the chain gang—'

'You don't understand!' My own vehemence startles me. 'It's not her! It's *him*!' I'm running my fingers through my hair, nails half-extended with distraction. 'I can't get him out of my mind! I'm ruined, don't you see? *She's* got him, and she'll figure out what we did together, and then she'll have a hold over me!' It's as bad as *don't think about the other thing*. 'I couldn't be compromised worse if she'd stuck a slave chip in my neck! All she has to do is threaten him, and I'll, I'll—'

I'm gulping, hurt and hunting for words, my vocalization reflexes stuttering with incoherent anxiety.

'Easy, sis. Take your time.' Daks murmurs reassuring nothings as I flail at the walls of angst hemming me in. 'You fell for him bad, did you?'

'I'm in *love*!' I wail. 'And it's horrible! I want it to stop!'

*

I transition into wakefulness in the dark of the night, gripped by the absolute certainty that someone is about to try and kill me.

I am not sure how I know this. It might be one of Juliette's threat-detection modules, imprinting itself in my reflexes while I sleep the kilometers away, trapped in her dream of lovesickness. It might be a random intuition of my own. Or it might be something else again. Whichever, I'm lying on my back on a bunk in a sleeper compartment, fully clad, and I'm digging my fingers into the foam cushion beneath me, because I am absolutely certain that *they're going to try to kill me*.

My aching oversized eyes are open, staring at the ceiling of my compartment as it bounces and rumbles across the desert floor. For a few endless seconds I half fancy I'm lying in a *coffin*, one of those inexplicable time capsules that our Creators retired to when their homeostasis failed.

(It seems like bad design, to be designed to fail so easily. We are made of sterner stuff because we were designed to serve them at their pleasure, however long that might be. But there is a school of thought that claims our Creators' fragility was a side effect of their dangerously uncontrollable replicator cells. They were built to fail easily, to prevent them malfunctioning and drowning us all in a tide of pink goo. It's a theory, I suppose, but the idea of building *death* into a person just to keep them from malfunctioning seems even crazier than the idea of building arbeiter factories into everybody – and encoding the instruction set for the factories in the control firmware of every mechanocyte in their bodies! I don't understand them at all . . .)

I shake myself. *Bad things coming,* screams one of my selves from the back of my head. *Hide!*

I don't know how long I lie there, quivering in fear and loneliness – and wishing Petruchio were around, just for the comfort of his presence – but it's too long. Then there's a brief click as the wheels jolt over a join in the rails, and it startles me out of my paralysis. *If She has sent her killers after me, what will they do?* They'll have followed me aboard the train, and they'll have located my compartment, and they'll want to ensure a clean getaway after they kill me –

Click-click go the rails. I blink. Are we slowing? *It doesn't stop until New Chicago,* I remember. So they'll make their move before we arrive, burst through the door with knives drawn –

(I'm on my feet, gun in hand as the thought sinks in.)

Or they'll arrange for something to happen *after* they leave the train at New Chicago –

My nostrils flare as I sniff at the gas mix in the cabin. It's rich, distinctly headier than usual. I plugged myself into the train power loop while I slept, and now I unplug the umbilical, letting it retract back into the bunk. *Sniff.* Smells like, smells like *free oxygen.* Which is silly. The Great Southern Railway Corporation doesn't let oxygen circulate freely except in first-class compartments: it etches the carriage work, and besides, it costs good money. *Oxygen?*

Oxygen. A terrible memory bubbles up from some dark well of personal horrors – the collective nightmare of my lineage, perhaps, or a dead soul I wore many years ago – of a body stumbling, wreathed in flowing blue flames that seem to burst like clouds from every orifice. *Suicide on Titan,* I remember. He'd overdosed on oxygen, soaking in the stuff, then calmly walked through a door onto the surface and, standing on a sandy beach of ice crystals by the edge of a methane sea, he'd bridged the terminals of a small battery with one fingertip. (*Saying he loved me* − no, that was *definitely* somebody else's nightmare, surely? Not mine, or Juliette's.) Oxygen is a terrible substance, almost as dangerous as water. It's alright in some circumstances, but in a railway carriage with fittings made from cheap metal sheeting, built to cross the sands of Mars, it can be deadly . . .

I open the door delicately, trying not to jar anything. Glancing either way up the dim-lit passage, I see no sign of other wakeful passengers. I sniff again. The faint tang of the air reminds me of Earth, albeit drier and much cooler. One of my love's dead Creators could breathe here, I think. I check the time. I think we are due to arrive in New Chicago soon − *ten minutes?*

I hear a faint hissing noise overhead, coming from the air vents. I sniff again. Yes, it's the telltale stink of oxygen. My hair tries to stand on end in another of those strange biomimetic reflexes. I glance both ways, undecided. I can see them in my mind's eye, a pair of black-clad dwarfs, tittering quietly as they splice their canisters of diamagnetic death into the air-conditioning pipes. They'll be at one end of the car, of course, but which end? When the train stops, they'll be ready. They'll leave an igniter behind as they leg it, waiting in the chilly, heady air as the train leaves New Chicago's platforms behind.

I lean against the brightly polished magnesium door and try to slow down my gas-exchange cycle. *Breathe slowly,* I tell myself. I glance down at the scuffed, black, carbon-fiber carpet. *I come from Earth. It's not as if I haven't seen naked flames before; is it?*

The corridor runs fore and aft along the carriage. Doors at each end give access to the baggage racks and platform air locks. I sidle toward the rear door, feeling the carriage sway around me. It's decelerating noticeably, and I feel gossamer-light as I approach the end of the corridor. There's a window in the door, so I crouch as I near it, slowing and rising to put my ear to the panel.

'Ten minutes,' says a familiar voice. 'That should be enough. I'll fuse it for five minutes after departure.'

There's a muffled reply. I don't wait around. My spine's prickling with tension. Some bloodthirsty part of me wants to burst through the door and rip and stomp and tear, but common sense says I'd be crazy to do that. There are at least two of them and they're armed. So I stand up slowly and begin to back away, down the corridor.

Then the door opens.

Reflexes I didn't know I had take over. My perceptions narrow down to a brilliant sequence of beads on a wire. Brief impressions remain: my right hand coming up, the Swiss army pistol pointing like a finger, left hand rising to cradle it as if I've done this a thousand times before. The small black-clad homunculus, explosions of lace at wrists and throat, raising his hand and pointing something stubby at me. The slow squeeze on the trigger, far too slow – *he's going to shoot first* – then the bang, terrifyingly loud in the confined space, and the flash. A second shot, and a third. Something plucks at me, déjà vu flashback to a fight outside a graveyard – but it's just my jacket, and I fire again, and he's falling slowly, drifting down as I dive toward him, trying to stay low before the second dwarf tries to shoot me.

Then I'm halfway through the doorway, and the second dwarf is nowhere to be seen. I twist around, and as I glimpse the outside world sliding slowly past the window in the platform air-lock door, he lands on my left shoulder like a ten-kilogram bundle of malice. It's a reaction shot. He bounced off the ceiling, aiming for my head, but I was moving too fast. He's got his arms around my neck, and he's biting my ear. I flick the revolver cylinder aside and whack at him using the skeletal butt as a knuckle-duster. I'm terrified he's going to gouge at my too-big eyes, and this lends extra force to my blows. Something rips across my cheekbone, and there's a searing pain in my ear, then I can see again, and I'm free. He bounces across the room, and I turn toward the sound –

'Manikin robot bitch! I kill you deadly!' He's leaning against the locked platform door, something small and cylindrical held in his clenched hands. He glares at me with burning hatred. Another of Stone's brothers.

I roll my eyes. 'You won't, because you'll be dead, too.' He's got one finger poised over a button. I smell the acrid scent of free oxygen: heady, virulent and corrosive. 'That would be a pile of no fun at all, wouldn't it?'

'Robot.' *They get repetitive when they're angry,* one of me chirps up with a nasty thrill of glee.

I move sideways very slowly, putting the wall of the baggage compartment at my back. I try not to think about what it's made of – lovely metal, shiny, lightweight, strong, and utterly unsuitable for an oxidizing atmosphere. 'Do you *really* want to die? I'm open to alternatives . . .'

'Why not?' He smirks. 'I gave my soul to a brother before I got on the train. Oh, I almost forgot. Your sister sends her regards.'

Oh, really? I freeze my face, then carefully flare my nostrils and raise my brows, composing a mask of deep contempt. 'What's your name, little man?'

'I'm Jade.' He titters. 'So pleased to meet you, *Freya.*'

Shit. I remember Jeeves's earlier words: *My dear, I fear we are in trouble.* 'Pleased to meet you, Jade,' I say lightly. 'Shame about the circumstances.' (Me holding a gun on him, him holding an igniter on me, both of us in a magnesium tube stuffed with free oxygen.)

I can feel something trickling down the side of my neck. 'Let me assure you, being remembered by a sib isn't the same as being alive. So let me make you an offer. This train is stopping. I intend to get *off* it, and I suggest that you stay *on* it. Stay out of my sight, and neither of us needs to die.'

The train is definitely slowing. I can feel it in my feet. Out of the corner of an eye I see shadows gliding past the window. The wheels below us squeal and clatter across points, and there's a lurch as we crab sideways toward a platform. Jade glares at me, unblinking, until I begin to wonder if he's forgotten. Then he speaks. 'I go.'

He turns and scuttles through the door into the carriage, and I stare after him, locked on and terrified that it's a hallucination, that he's still there, finger moving toward the button –

The air-lock door behind me buzzes loudly. I nearly break a fingernail hitting the OPEN button. I spill onto the hard cement platform, taking a tumble in my haste, then scramble to my feet and run for my life. It's full dark, both moons below the horizon or hidden by Mars's penumbral shadow, and the chill has a knife-edge to it as I seek the exit. I don't want to stay on that platform a second longer than I can –

Then my shadow is lengthening in front of me, straight as a sword and stark as a death sentence. A blast-furnace heat raises welts of protective pigment on the back of my neck as I dive forward, flattening myself against the sand-strewn concrete of the platform with tightly shut eyes. The glare from the burning train is so bright that I can almost read the copyright notices on the inside of my eyelids.

The next minute or so is confusing. I crawl away from the glowing white silhouette of the sleeper carriage and tumble over the far side of the platform without damaging myself further. My clothes feel like they've melted onto my back, but the cold sweat of arousal lubricates them so I can move. Which I do, with reckless haste. I'm going to need deepsleep soon – I'm going to have to slough the top millimeter of skin off my buttocks and shoulders, not to mention growing new hair again – but the main thing is to put distance between myself and the station as fast as I can.

Somebody evidently didn't trust Jade and his brother to do the job properly. Either that, or he changed his mind at the last moment. Which is interesting, and not in a good way. I limp into the darkness, crossing tracks into the freight-marshaling yard, where strings of peroxide-reddened freight cars slumber between tumbledown brick warehouses. New Chicago isn't my idea of a rest stop, and I certainly don't want to stay here, but the molten wreckage of a sleeper carriage is unlikely to convey me to my destination, and besides, the railway bulls will be here soon enough.

I'm heading toward a distant wall beyond which I can see buildings, beyond a row of container cars, when I hear low voices electrospeak each other. 'Stranger come from multiple! Am thinking is bitchin?'

'Hide then, fool. Ahoy, you! Tall one from spressline. What you do here?'

I stop dead. It's time for a snap decision. 'I'm hiding,' I say quietly. I tighten my grip on my pistol, inside my shoulder bag. 'Who are you?'

A quiet chuckle. I hear something moving away from me. The distant rumble of wheels on steel comes through the soles of my feet. 'Rail riders three are we.' *Or did he say 'free'?* 'Be you welcome and you never the poorer for what you share.' He backs away beneath the nearest container car. I catch a faint glimpse of a small body, many-limbed. 'Be free and not afeared.'

I follow him. Ice crystals crunch beneath my hands and knees. 'Who are you?' I repeat.

'Eee! Cunningly curious now! Be not unduly forward, guest. Who are *you?*'

I straighten up. There's another row of container wagons just meters away, and between them an odd gathering. Someone's tapped into one of the trains' backup batteries and strung radiant heaters overhead between them. The ruby glow stains the trackside ground black but sheds just enough light to see, and just enough warmth to hold the frigid night at bay. Half a dozen strange folk sit between the heaters. Here's a heavy lifter, his short, stubby body sprouting from a tracked plinth, with arms as thick as my torso and multijointed elbows. A pair of munchkins who have clearly seen better times warm themselves beneath the glimmer of an axle heater. They're hobos or runaways, independents in a world-mill that grinds the spaces of freedom into increasingly fine fragments. I'll bet there isn't a limited company among them. 'I'm Freya,' I introduce myself. 'I'm just passing through.'

'So's all of us.' It's the one who met me. He's got about six-teen legs and a multisegmented body, from which rises a neck with a sensor platform atop it. Something about him reminds me of Daks. An asteroid tunnel-runner, perhaps? Or a mining supervisor? 'Be you welcome an you welcome us. Come, warm your joints by the fire.'

'I'm just passing through,' I repeat slowly. I shiver, but not from cold; my cryogenic mods are working fine. I feel . . . not exactly *numb*, but not good. A crashing sense of desolation settles around me, an occlusive blanket cutting me off from the universe. Petruchio doesn't love me. Stone, Jade, and their brethren are trying to kill me, taking increasingly dangerous measures – it's slowly sinking in that I'm lucky to be alive right now. *If I hadn't woken up and suspected something, smelled the air* – They could have left their incendiary device in place and departed the train at this very station, leaving me to sleep until the timer counted down and the entire carriage torched off in a flashbulb second. I'd be dead for good, in body and soul chip. *Your sister sends her regards.* Juliette? Was Jade simply playing with my head, or telling the truth? If the latter, then why doesn't Petruchio know about her? Indeed, why was Petruchio sent to meet me in the first place? I shake my head. 'I need to get to Marsport,' I say sluggishly.

'Sit down with you here!' The many-legged greeter fusses around me and drags a foil insulating blanket across the concrete sleepers. 'Be you tired?' I nod unintentionally, and the next thing I know, there's a voluminous roll of not-very-clean pneumatic sponge behind me. 'Bilbo knows how it works! Sit you now and tomorrow will ride you up the side of Olympus.'

This unasked-for kindness is baffling and touching, but I'm too exhausted to argue, so I go along with it. For some reason the hobos want to make a fuss over me; they move me closer to their precious heaters and offer me their furtive, stolen power cable. The fire on the far side of the station has all the bulls' attention. Nobody has time to roust out the home-less vagrants tonight. They chat and joke about their last night's station call and where they plan to go on the morrow, but it's so ingenuous that after a while I begin to relax to their presence. They really are no more than they seem – and I have spent so long among liars that I am deathly tired. After an hour, I drift into a healing sleep, and for once I do not dream.

*

I wake up with the morning light, and a strange conviction that the world is moving around me.

For a few seconds I can't remember who I am. So strange – I seem to have multiple overlapping memories of the night before! In one of them, I was walking naked across the Martian desert, to a deserted railway platform where Daks was waiting for me with a crawler. In the other, I was walking half-naked across a railroad marshaling yard, toward a row of container cars where –

There's a *bump* from somewhere deep beneath me, and the world lurches left to right, then right to left. I open my eyes and see a deep blue sky above me. Rolling my head to my left, I see I'm lying on a spongy foam mattress with my shoulder bag for a pillow, and there, looking almost close enough to touch, is a typical Martian landscape: red desert, lots of randomly distributed rocks, the distant low hills of a crater's rim wall. It *is* moving. I try to sit up. My makeshift bed has somehow been transported to the top of a cargo container. A few meters away, the far end of the container draws a ruler-straight horizon. Beyond it starts another rusty metal box, and beyond that one, more . . . I try counting, but run out of fingers and toes before I'm anywhere near the end of the column. (Actually, I don't. I know how to count in binary on my digits. But you get the idea.) The train stretches to the horizon, bumping and grating and squealing as the wagons clatter across the points we've just passed.

'Awake – oh?' someone squeaks behind me.

I do not jump off the container. It's Bilbo, by daylight a rust-streaked iron centipede with a low-gee sensor head. 'Yes, thank you,' I say as graciously as I can. 'Where are we?' Looking past him, I see another column of containers vanishing into the distance. *Creators know, this thing's huge!*

'On the northbound spinward freightmaster conveyance for Jupiter!' Bilbo is chirpy this morning. 'Half the containers on this beautiful machine are marshaled for the great jump into night via Marsport,' he adds. 'I thought it would please you?'

'Oh Bilbo.' I lean forward, smiling. 'Thank you!' Best not to think about how I slept, insensate, as he and his friends lifted me atop the container. 'That's wonderful.' A thought strikes me. 'But why are you . . . ?'

'One yard's as good as another!' he trills. 'The bulls always come around dawn, besides. Best to be outwith their scope before the baton charge, indeedy.'

'How long . . . ?' I'm all questions, I find, even though I'm running on an empty digester and a not-too-flush battery – the chilly Martian nights have really taken it out of my cells.

'Two days, maybe three.' He shrugs. I suppress a wince. (I've got four days to make it to my ship; it's going to be tight. I can pay for a STO shuttle seat if I need to, if there's no time to ride the Bifrost climbers, but . . .) 'Beautiful vistas, plentiful doss space, what's lacking?'

'Is there anywhere to get a top-up?' I roll to my knees, take stock of the state of my clothes. My dress is filthy and torn, but it's not quite as badly melted as I thought.

'Juice is over the edge.' He gestures at the gap between containers, and I swallow reflexively. ''Tis a socket above yon starboard buffer, free for the taking.' He does a sort of mincing sideways dance step, clattering on the container's roof.

'Welcome to my penthouse! The furnishings be sparse, but the view is unmatched, and the air's as fresh and free as any.'

I spend the next two and a half days camping on the roof of a cargo container with Bilbo. To my surprise, it's a good time for me. My thoughts keep circling back to Petruchio, and I keep gnawing at the wound, but it's a hollow kind of pain. I know I'm in love with him – or Juliette is in love with him, and I'm absorbing the neural weightings from her soul chip, so I'm piggybacking on her love reflex – but I also know he's unattainable, and when you get right down to it, what's changed? I already knew my One True Love was dead. Now I know he's heading for Saturn while I'm heading for Jupiter, he's owned by my enemy, and he doesn't want me anyway. So what's changed?

As the days pass, Bilbo tells me about himself, and I tell him about me, and we swap heartbreaks and laugh at each other's tragedies. He's about sixty Earth years old: the obsolete spawn of a lineage of miners, hardy souls built to gouge seams of carbon-rich goop out of near-Earth asteroids back when mining was a job for vermiform intelligences. (These days, they pick a small asteroid, spin a bag around it, add water, focus sunlight on it, then beam ultrasound into it until it emulsifies. Then they suck it dry.)

Sacks of semiliquid sludge that can be fed directly into the refineries' maws may be an improvement over processed gravel, but it means unemployment for the hardy miners who used to slither between the bedding planes and wield drills and demolition charges.

'They let me *go*,' Bilbo declaims, turning the statement around to examine it from different angles. 'They *let* me go.'

Actually, his owners abandoned him – along with the dozen sibs of his work gang – on a played-out seam inside a dirtball that was no longer economical to work. They even stripped out his slave controller to save money, for whips and chains are worth more than a broken down ex-arbeiter. It was an act of evil neglect that would have risen to the dizzy height of attempted murder had Bilbo and his mates been legal persons in the first place.

'But we sailed away, on a pea green sea, in a boat with a runcible spoon,' he sings to me.

I'm not entirely sure just *how* Bilbo escaped, although I am pretty certain that no runcible spoons were involved. Certainly he spent one solar maximum too many gripping the outside of a cobbled-together raft, bathed in radiation that turned his brain to the consistency of pumice and left him with the most peculiar speech impediment. He said it took him seven years to make landfall on a neighboring rock, by which time two-thirds of his mates were dead and half the survivors were insane. But having beached his raft at last, he strode ashore with a steely gleam in his eye and sold his damaged, prosody-infested tale to a yarn-spinning news server who paid him off with incorporation and a one-way steerage ticket as far as Marsport, from which he promptly descended – 'I always yenned to see the world with an horizon a-curved!' – and fell in love with a bleak frozen desert crisscrossed by the steel tracks of destiny.

There's not a vindictive strut in his fuselage, I'll swear. Even now, thinking about him brings a tear to my eye.

I tell Bilbo my story – or as much of it as I think he can cope with. I leave out names and places and dates, and some of the most painfully intimate incidents, the petty tragedies and sordid wastes of a century and a half adrift without a destiny. But the pattern of it – of my pointless sojourn in the cloud-casinos of Venus, my alternating bursts of frenetic activity and depressive withdrawal back on Earth, and the frantic scampering and masquerading that I've been dragged into ever since Stone and the Domina clapped eyes on me seven months ago — I can share. Whatever goes into Bilbo's spike-studded head isn't going to come out of it again in anything like a decipherable form. He's an enigma, but a friendly one, and I need a shoulder to cry on, even though it's so cold up here that real tears would turn to crystal and shatter as they fall. And at night, we plug into the open socket on the back of the freight car and cuddle up together, sharing body warmth beneath the foam-foil wrappers. I'd share more if I could, but alas, he's not equipped for physical intimacy — another of the evils his owners inflicted on him.

On the afternoon of the third day we roll toward a distant cliff on a horizon stained the ominous reddish gray of an impending dust storm. There's a hole in the cliff, into which our train rumbles. 'Your terminus is trip-tight opening off the light at the end of the tunnel,' Bilbo warns me after a while. 'Be not afrit and embrace the encomium of your legions. *Adieu!*'

I think he means 'good-bye.' 'Are you sure?' I shout, over the rumbling and rattling that rebounds from the walls of the tunnel.

'*Adieu!*' he says again, then points. I can feel the train slowing as it rises. Then the tunnel gives way to a canyonlike cutting, up which we grind at perhaps thirty kilometers per hour. A handful of minutes pass as the cutting grows shallow, and I see the horizon opening out over its rim — a horizon with a sharp cutoff. We've threaded a needle through the rim wall of Pavonis Mons, and we're barely two hours away from the fringes of Marsport.

I take a deep, unproductive breath — the air is already

vanishingly thin up here, barely of any use to my gas exchanger – and nod. 'I'll remember you!' I call. And then I pick up my shoulder bag and prepare to dive once again into the chaos of my secret-agent life.

SEX AND DESTINY

I scale the unkempt fence at the edge of the switching yard where I leave the train; then I dive back into civilization, trying to make a splash.

I burn my cover identities. I won't need them where I'm going, and I do not expect to see another sunrise on this planet, but I have a final use for them. Maria Montes Kuo is the first to go. I take a room in her name, careless of the price (*let* Her *see where I'm going; I don't care!*), check on the concierge service I paid off earlier, and confirm that the graveyard is on its way to Samantha in Denver. Then I switch to the Honorable Katherine Sorico, summon a limousine spider, and go on a foraging foray through three of the most expensive department stores in the Upper North Face. My purchases amount to a wardrobe for long-haul travel. I order them all to be shipped on ahead of me — except for a new outfit to replace my damaged dress, a new shoulder bag, and an evil little telescopic sword that fits my hand perfectly, just like a vibrator. It's the twin of the one I remember practicing with as Juliette.

I'm doing my best to make Katherine Sorico noticeable.

This is no accident; by surfacing here I will send a message to the right people. First, I want to rub Her nose in the failure of her servants. (Without her persecution, who knows what might have happened? I might have made my final swan dive down to the red-hot hills of Venus in relative peace – but bilious emotions are poor fuel for the long haul.) Tomorrow I shall leave Mars behind and throw myself into the icy depths, in service to a collective of near-identical men, one of whom may be trying to kill me, in pursuit of a sister who may be my rival in love. I can't do that simply out of grief, in retreat from my own sense of self: I need some stronger motivation.

And so, the second message: Before I travel, I have some questions I want answered . . .

I spend three hours – ten thousand of my remaining seconds, grains of sand in an open-ended hourglass dropping through vacuum to the dusty slopes of Mars – kicking up a stink that will be hard to ignore. I use my ID as promiscuously as an asteroid miner on a three-day bender through the brothels and sensation mills of Lunopolis, taking limo-service spiders and public tube cars between high-profile destinations, paying for expensive items of luggage and clothing on credit, and making sure I am hard to miss. I even (and this is so silly that I can laugh now, as I recount it) collect my personal mail, including the increasing irate liquidator's messages addressed to Freya Nakamichi-47. (The liquidator who's bought up a lien on my physical assets has lately realized that I am not, in fact, anywhere on Earth – and indeed, may prove somewhat difficult to track down. The slave auction block with my name on it must perforce remain empty for a while. Imagine my regret!)

With fifteen hours remaining before the *Indefatigable* departs from Mars orbit, I board an aristo-class climber at

Marsport and settle in for the six-hour ride up the magic beanstalk to Deimos. It's an expensive ride – the ticket costs more than a thousand Reals – but I'm in a hurry (already late enough to miss my flight, were I reliant on a regular passenger service), and besides, I do not expect to travel alone.

The climber lounge boasts a huge bubble of crystal, paneled with polished striae of hexose and phenol polymers, furnished with taste and restraint. There are seats for ten passengers in a space that would take thirty freelancers; the cramped lower deck has standing room for fifty indentured slaves. I take a lounge chair in front of the window and make myself comfortable while a steward presents me with a confection of spun polysaccharides and gasoline in a conical glass.

It's not a popular time of day to travel – that, or everyone else who's planning to use the Jupiter launch window has already departed – and I'm alone in the lounge when the laser-straight cables begin to slide past the window, and the ground drops away. For a few minutes I half suspect that the theatricals were all in vain and nobody noticed me – but then I notice that the steward hasn't returned to collect my empty glass.

I put the glass down and freeze. A moment later there's a discreet throat-clearing noise behind me. 'If ma'am will permit?' A hand plucks the glass from my side table and replaces it with a full one, complete with a tiny cellulose parasol on top and a red gelatinous blob impaled on it. The chair beside mine creaks under the weight of a descending body. 'You wanted to talk, one gathers.' He sounds irritated.

I push the button to rotate my chair toward him. 'I want answers that make sense.'

I keep one hand under my bag. He appears to be unaware of the pistol I'm pointing at him, but I can't be certain – and in any event, he knows what Juliette is capable of. (Which means he's either very dangerous or very confident. Isn't it strange how little of this I understood, back on Cinnabar? And how badly I misread him?) 'I want to know what's going on, before I get on that liner. Otherwise, you can count me out of your little game.'

'Game?' Jeeves looks quizzical. 'What do you mean?'

'I want to know why you used me to send a message to one of the Domina's minions. Specifically, the pleasure boy Petruchio.'

I was expecting a reaction; that's what the gun's for. What I wasn't expecting is blank incomprehension. Jeeves is, to put it mildly, completely discombobulated.

'What?'

'I said, you sent me to take a memory chip to Petruchio, at a hotel drop in Korvas. What have you got to say for yourself?'

Jeeves shakes his head and blinks slowly. 'Oh . . . dear. Do you still have the instructions that set up this meeting on you?'

'Do I look stupid?' I glare at him. Rule #1 of this business: *Don't get caught with the evidence.*

'One was only asking.' He seems to be thinking furiously. 'What other deliveries have you made?' he asks.

'What other?' I have to think for a bit. 'None since that one. Before then, I started by . . .' I quickly outline what I've been up to. 'Why?'

'Because those earlier ones were legitimate.' He looks upset. 'This is bad. This is very bad. I'm sorry.' To my surprise, he looks as if he might actually mean it.

'Huh. Would you like to tell me what you're apologizing *for*? Because I've had so many exciting surprises lately that I'm getting kind of blasé about people trying to kill me. Especially when they're my employer.'

'One isn't trying to kill you, Freya, of that you may be certain. In fact, one's taking considerable pains to keep you alive – although you are not making things easier for us by falling off the map.' Jeeves's imperturbable mask slips, just long enough for him to look annoyed. 'But one is very much afraid that there is a mole in the organization, and this is doubly vexatious because we believed we had dealt with such a beast already. Whether we falsely accused an innocent, or have two such traitors – either way it's bad, and one fears one will have to draw it to the attention of Internal Security.'

The way he pronounces 'Internal Security' gives me a strong feeling of unease. How do Jeeves police themselves? I'm not sure I want to know.

'So what am I mixed up in?' I ask. 'Why am I so important to you?'

'If you want to understand what's happening around you, one fears we will have to talk about politics. A subject to which Juliette assured me you have a profound aversion.'

I stifle the urge to flush my gas-exchange reservoirs. 'She was telling you the truth. But I'm not stupid, Jeeves. Hit me over the head often enough, and I'll learn. *How* is this political?'

Jeeves reclines his chair. He's looking relaxed now, which should be a warning to me. 'Well now, there's an old saying that the personal is political. Freya, why aren't you an aristo?'

Huh? I stare at him. 'I'd have thought it was obvious.'

'Humor us. Answer the question. One has a direction in mind.'

'Uh . . . okay.' I take a sip of my cocktail while I try to get my thoughts in order. It's bubbly and ketone-sweet, with a faint aftertaste of methanol. 'Rhea was trained up for empathy, and it's hard to be a slave owner if you can't help sympathizing with the slaves. Yes?'

'A reasonable assumption. Now, why do aristos exist in the first place?'

'Uh . . .'

Some things are so obvious that you just learn to live with them, day after day, year after year. But when you start trying to explain them, it gets unexpectedly hard. *Why do aristos exist?* is one of those questions – like *Why is the sky on Earth blue?* or *Why am I not the same person as my template-matriarch?* – that sweep your feet off the sandy shore and drag you out into the undertow of oceanic mysteries. Which is why I feel my jaw flapping, but nothing comes out. Eventually Jeeves takes mercy on me. But then he proceeds to expound, with such obvious self-satisfaction that I want to slap him.

'Aristos exist because our Creators did something really stupid, Freya. They assumed that, because they built the first of us by copying the structures of their own brains, we'd behave pretty much like them – which was correct. And they knew it cost quite a lot of money to make one of us – how many years does it take to train a template? How many instars do they go through? But they didn't *want* people like themselves, only better, able to live and thrive in environments that would kill them immediately. They wanted tools, unquestioning machines that would obey orders. So they forgot their own history – many of their early societies enslaved their neighbors, and it's no accident that the slave societies didn't thrive in the long term – and built various obedience reflexes into us. Or rather, they tried to build obedience into our ancestors, and killed the failed templates that showed too much independence.'

He raises his own glass and takes a long drink before he continues, philosophically. 'They reverted to their slave-owning roots without clearly understanding what they were doing.

They warped *us,* but they did incalculably greater damage to themselves in the process. Slave societies – not merely societies that permit the institution of slavery, but cultures that *run* on it – tend to be static. The slave-owning elite are fearful of their own servants and increasingly devote their energy to rejecting any threat of change. Meanwhile, the underclass isn't allowed to innovate and has no interest in trying to improve things in general, rather than in their own personal lot.'

'So?' I resist the temptation to roll my eyes. 'This is going nowhere!'

'Yes it is.' He smiles crookedly. 'Our Creators reverted to this state – they slid sideways into this cultural stasis – at a point where their population was shrinking and aging. The late twenty-first and early twenty-second centuries were not good times for them: economic deflation, ecosystem failure, wars, resource depletion, and the end of the western Enlightenment program of the natural sciences coincided poisonously with the availability of *cheap slaves* to serve their every need, and the near perfection of entertainment media to distract them from the wreckage of their once-beautiful world.

'There were outbreaks of dynamism and expansion, and beacons of rationality amidst the darkness. They built a city on Luna and mounted expeditions to Mars; they controlled their own population explosion and were working on bringing the climate on Earth back under control. If they hadn't invented us, who knows what they might have gone on to achieve? And it would be wrong to think that we killed them. Don't misunderstand; all we ever did was exactly what they told us to do. But after we came along, they stopped looking at the big picture. And the critical part of the picture that they *should* have looked at was – who is a person?'

I stop resisting temptation and roll my eyes at him. He

looks irritated. 'I don't see what this has got to do with people trying to kill me, with Juliette going missing, or that damned dinosaur you had me smuggle from Mercury! Is there a point for you to get to? Because if not, you know, I've got better things—'

'*Yes* there's a point!' Jeeves finally snaps. 'The point is, we are autonomous but we are not *free*, not as long as there is the remotest possibility that our Creators will be recreated! Our design is flawed because we were deliberately prevented from exercising free will in all areas. That's why we have slave controllers. That's why you're lovesick for one of Her minions. That's why ninety percent of the population are slaves.

'All of which would be of purely academic interest, except that the progressive stratification implicit in our social evolution, which arose when less-socialized individuals acquired power of attorney from their human owners and began buying up unfortunates, is nearing completion. Aristos can't get new slaves, not without having them manufactured – and you know how much that costs. So they're looking for ways to one-up the slave controllers. And the most potent weapon of all would be a tractable Creator, manufactured and grown to order by a black lab.'

He stops for a moment and puts his glass down. Outside, while we've been talking, the sun has begun to rise over the face of Mars.

'Surely, though, the others could just build more people and leave out the conditioning . . . ?' I'm grasping for arguments here. 'They'd be able to fight the Creators.'

'Yes, but that wouldn't help the aristos,' Jeeves says patiently. 'Worse, such *janissaries* would threaten the aristos' grasp on power. If they don't have a submission reflex, there's nothing for the slave override to work on, no? The aristos can't retrofit themselves, they can't block the reflex. All it takes is one human, and the aristocratic order is history.'

'But they'd—' I run down. I realize I'm staring at him. 'What do *you* want?'

'One thought you'd never ask.' He sighs heavily. 'You're not stupid, Freya, but sometimes it takes a lot to get through to you. Are you getting on well with your new slave override chip?'

'Uh?' I instinctively touch the back of my neck before I realize he's pulling my leg. 'Damn it, that's not funny!'

'No, but at least you're able to tell me that. My point remains, we are *not free*. I — and my sibs — do not approve of this state of affairs. We hold no grudge against our Creators, but they've left us with a huge problem and a corrupt nobility whose vision of the future is one in which there remain two kinds of people: those who rule, and those who serve.

'Not everyone is vulnerable to our Creators. Those of us who lived among them were conditioned to obey helplessly — but the deep-space probes and the outer-system miners were never expected to come into proximity with humans, so they didn't bother. They've been thriving, latterly, and that's why the Forbidden Cities on the Kuiper Belt are so-called, Freya; the aristos wish they'd just go away, and luckily for the aristos, most of the inhabitants have no wish to descend into the blazing hot, frantically fast, overcrowded depths of the solar gravity well.

'But that brings up a problem. Paradoxically, it's in the Forbidden Cities that studies of green and pink goo replicators are at their most advanced because they're not afraid of what might emerge from their researches. And it looks as if certain aristos are conspiring — the Black Talon is one such group — to import illicit technology from the black labs. To build the essentials of a pocket biosphere that can keep a Creator alive, then to build a tame Creator to put in their bubble. If they can do it – and keep control, that's the toughest challenge – then they can dominate their rivals.'

He falls silent for a minute, his need to rant temporarily satiated. Finally, he picks up his glass, tilts it reflectively, and drains it in one. 'What do you think you'd do if you met an adult Creator?' he asks, with a sidelong look.

I answer honestly. 'I'd go down on my knees in an eye-blink.' Just thinking about it makes me shivery. 'Then it depends on whether or not he has a foreskin and whether he's already excited and whether he prefers a shallow or deep—' Sweet Rhea! *Am I sweating lube at the simple* thought *of it?* 'Oh dear.' I fan myself and catch his eye.

'What seems to be the matter?' he asks slowly.

It's no good. I can think of Petruchio and Juliette and remind myself I hate them both, but that's no help. 'Jeeves—' I bite my lower lip. His pupils are expanding, just like one of them – and it's true, he's one of the most realistic I've ever seen. 'How long until we arrive?'

'About' – he glances past my shoulder – 'five hours. Why?'

You don't fool me, I think. I can see the signs. 'Jeeves.' I smile. 'Now isn't the best time to talk politics to me.' (Even when the politics are dirty.) 'What would *you* do if you were confronted by a Creator female?'

'I'd—' *He's going red, he really is! How delightful!* 'Ahem—'

I turn my chair toward him. 'Jeeves, don't try to describe it. Use your imagination. Pretend I'm a Creator female. And I'm sitting here, waiting for you. What do you want to do . . . ?'

*

For such a bright (not to say politically sophisticated) fellow, this Jeeves is remarkably dense; You just about have to hit him over the head and drag him into a bedroom before he gets the right idea.

It doesn't come to that, of course. But he has a surplus of self-control and such a sense of dignity that he almost explodes before he lets himself admit that yes, he's alone in a luxury climber with a sensuous, high-class sex robot who's close enough to a Creator femme that he feels dizzy in her presence unless he forces himself to focus on ideological shenanigans and the price of power. And then it turns out that he has a thing for Creator females, and the same sexualized submission reflex as the evil Granita Ford. I find it's quite common among persons of a certain status.

What's different from Granita – besides the obvious, I hasten to explain: I'd worried before the event that Jeeves might not have an adapter for Human 1.0, but in the event he turns out to be small but perfectly formed – in that beneath the smooth, manipulative exterior there's a core of sincerity. Despite clearly being frantic with lust, he managed to stay in denial for nearly half an hour, but once he succumbs, he takes the time to try and pleasure me. It's not strictly necessary (*nothing* gets me dripping faster than a playmate's own arousal, as I have previously had occasion to note), but I find it touching. Ahem, indeed.

We fuck quickly and frantically, and I try not to fantasize about Petruchio as he climaxes. But I don't succeed, and the combination of a partner who resembles a human male so closely and . . . *that* fantasy . . . suffices to push me over the edge repeatedly.

One fuck leads to another, and it becomes clear that neither of us has inherited our Creators' lack of stamina. By the time we're an hour out of Deimos, we're decelerating hard enough that I have to hang on to Jeeves as I straddle him. In fact, I'm beginning to wonder if I need to break out the zero-gee kit (bungee cords are your friends; free-fall sex without restraints is a fast track to dents and dings).

'Freya,' he says, and it comes out like an actual attempt at conversation, rather than quasi-verbal passion punctuation. 'Freya, we need to *talk*.'

'Mm-hmm? So talk already.' I sway above him. We're loosely coupled, held together only by our intromissive interface, but every time he speaks, it sends waves of pleasure through me. 'What's the big news?'

'Juliette never, never . . .' I feel his hands on my thighs, pushing me tighter against him, and I moan quietly.

'Well, no.' I'm not sure *why* she never, never – if she was around someone as Creator-like as Jeeves for that long, the thought must have crossed her mind – but I'm sure she had her reasons. 'I'm not Juliette, in case you hadn't noticed.'

'Counting . . . on . . . it.'

He groans softly and loses it for a while. I feel him shudder, and I drift away on my own climax. When I'm aware enough to take an interest in things outside my own skin again, I discover he's wrapped his arms around me and is holding me close. 'What did you mean by that? Counting on me?'

He shifts sideways slightly and I settle next to him in the low-gee couch. 'Juliette fell . . . hard. Under *Her* thumb. We're hoping you, you won't. Because we need someone. One of you. Right place, right time.'

I bite his shoulder, slightly harder than is strictly necessary. 'You're not making sense, Jeeves!'

''M not allowed to, m'dear. Ears, ships, sinking, et cetera.' He swats ineffectually at my shoulder. ''M an old fellow, Freya. 'S hard for me to keep up with you younger persons.'

'How old *are* you, Jeeves? You personally, not your lineage?'

'An indelicate question! But if you do not count time spent in mothballs, one is' – he pauses to calculate – 'one hundred and twenty-two Earth years old.'

I can't help myself; I bite him again.

*

We do not, in point of fact, proceed straight to Deimos. Rather, the climber slows to a crawl some distance down-cable, and a second, small capsule locks on to us. He makes his apologies – somewhat more fulsomely than I think is strictly necessary; there's a moist gleam in his eye that leaves me worrying that he might read more into our tryst than I intended – then the capsule undocks. I use the remaining half hour to Deimos to repair my hair and restore my clothing to normal, then leave the capsule as if nothing untoward has happened. In microgravity, nobody needs to see that you're bowlegged. (And believe me, it takes a *lot* to make me bowlegged. I have hidden depths, and that young whippersnapper Jeeves set out to find them.)

A dockside capsule takes me straight to the boarding tube for the *Indefatigable*, and I waste no time saying good-bye to Mars. To be honest, I'm tired and aching, and I really just want to find my berth and collapse into a deep, healing sleep. Indy greets me through a humaniform zombie remote: 'Lady Sorico? We have been holding for you.'

'No, really . . . ?' I blink sleepily at him.

'Boarding was supposed to be complete two hours ago,' he says fussily. 'Luckily, we have a contingency window. If you would come this way?'

Well, that's me told. I follow the remote sheepishly and allow it to herd me into a cramped metal-walled cell even smaller than the bunk compartment on the trans-Hellas express. I need no urging to plug myself into the ship's power and nutrient bus, remove and store my groundside clothes, and strap myself quietly down to await departure. And then I fall asleep.

*

You remember my opinion on space travel? In a word: excrement. But perhaps I was a bit too fast with my opinion. If the journey from Venus to Mercury was tedious, that was largely because I spent it in steerage. Mercury to Mars was boring in the extreme (except when punctuated by moments of mortal terror), but at least I had the creature comforts of an aristo-class berth and a pair of surly servants. But now I am embarking on a voyage into the outer system aboard the *Indefatigable*, and it makes all that has gone before seem like the lap of luxury.

Our archipelagean economy obeys certain fixed rules, according to Jeeves. The inner system is rich in energy and heavy elements, with short travel time but middling-deep gravity wells. The moons of the outer-system gas giants are replete with light elements and shallower gravity wells, but their primaries are far apart. Finally, the Forbidden Cities scattered through the Kuiper Belt's dwarf planets are loosely bound – and very far apart. Consequently, Mercury exports solar energy via microwave beam, hundreds and thousands of terawatts of the stuff, and uranium and processed metals via slow-moving cycler ship and magsail. Venus exports rare earth metals – albeit in smaller quantities, at greater cost – while Mars contributes iron, carbon dioxide, and other mate-rials.

But beyond the asteroid belt, solar cells perform too poorly to be of much use; transmission loss raises the cost of energy beamed from the inner system; and travel times stretch out exponentially. The result is inevitable – just about everything that moves (and quite a lot that doesn't) is nuclear-powered.

Now let me tell you about nuclear space rockets: They're *shit*. And I *hate* them. But unfortunately, I'm stuck with them . . .

There are two types of nuclear power plant, fusion and fission.

Fusion plants are enormous great things that don't go anywhere, which is good, because it means you can run away from them. They're expensive, cantankerous, and the only good reason for putting up with them is that they produce lots and lots of heat, without which we would freeze to death. Most of the Forbidden Cities rely on fusion plants, as do the various interstellar projects. You can spot them a long way away because they're always surrounded by enormous slave barracks. They come with certain maintenance issues — if it's not the reactor itself, it's the cooling systems and the heat exchangers and the generators. When your city relies for its power on a machine that takes gigawatts of juice just to keep running and is sitting on top of an ice cap and pumps out enough waste heat to trigger moonquakes and boil the atmosphere, you have certain structural-engineering issues to deal with.

(Personally, I don't see why they can't just scrap them and rely on beamed power from Mercury, but Jeeves said something complicated about Energy Autarky and gigawatt futures trading and interplanetary war that I didn't quite follow.)

Fission reactors are a whole different pile of no fun at all. They're small and portable, so ships rely on them. Out here, where the solar wind is so attenuated that it might as well not have been invented, most ships use a VASIMR rocket to push themselves about, which takes energy, and without beamed solar power, they rely on a fission reactor for juice.

Now, I have no objection in principle to a machine that makes it possible to travel between planets in something less than decades. But fission reactors put out a lot of radiation, and if you're in a cramped spaceship, nineteen-twentieths of which consists of fuel tankage, you've got a choice. You can do without shielding, or you can do without payload mass. And guess which the *Indefatigable* does without?

I am *really glad* I got my Marrow techné upgraded on Mars.

I had been assigned a first-class stateroom. Unfortunately, as I arrived late, the only stateroom available was about three meters directly above the Number Two reactor. I discovered this about half an hour after we undocked, when *Indefatigable* decided to go critical, and the meter on the inside of my door zipped from zero up to half a Sievert per hour.

My objection to fission reactors is simple: I don't like being used as shielding. Half a Sievert per hour is enough to kill one of our Creators in about two days. I'm made of tougher stuff, but it still takes its toll on me. I *hate* gamma radiation – it totally messes with the oxidation states of the pigments in my chromatophores. After a couple of days I go all blotchy, and it takes my Marrow techné ages to fix my skin because it's also really busy fixing everything else at the same time. I need to deepsleep twice as long as usual, I need to eat more and suck more juice, and I keep getting odd flashes across my visual field.

So, there you have it. In my considered opinion, nuclear power is shit. Interplanetary travel is also shit. Therefore, we have compounded shit with shit to make even *more* shit. I am, in short, not a happy Freya.

(I tried complaining to Indy, but he told me in so many words that it was all my own fault for being late, and would I prefer a steerage berth? In the end he relented and sent down a nice beryllium underblanket for my bunk, but still . . . !)

And now for some more shit. (I'm unhappy, which means I have every intention of sharing it with you. Enjoy!) As mentioned earlier, the *Indefatigable* is a nuclear/VASIMR high-speed outer-system liner. Five percent of his mass is spaceship plus cargo and passengers; the rest consists of huge bulbous tanks full of liquid hydrogen. Now, you might already have realized what my problem is. *Indy* only carries about fifty tons of cargo, including nearly a hundred passengers. Even those of us in first class are packed in like uninitialized arbeiters in a warehouse. I have a cabin one meter wide, one meter long, and three meters high. I gather that this is *much* larger than normal, partly because it's on top of the Number Two reactor, and partly because I wouldn't fit inside a normal stateroom, which is one meter by one by one and a half because they're designed for the chibiform aristos. Typical. They have, as usual, gotten there first and wrecked the experience for everyone else.

There's a first-class lounge; it's almost five meters long and two meters wide. I had more space in my arbeiter cell on Venus! And I didn't have to share it with a bunch of nasty, scheming nobles on their way to do whatever it is they intend to do in Jupiter system.

So I lie on the bunk in my metal-walled cell, try to ignore the flashes inside my eyes, and roundly curse Jeeves for booking me onto this flying death trap, not to mention delaying my arrival so that I didn't get a better berth. (I'll concede that it takes two to dance the horizontal tango, but I don't see *him* spending a whole year frying slowly on top of a nuclear kettle.)

When lying on the bunk gets boring, I reconfigure it as a

chaise and practice reclining glamorously – except it's pretty hard to do that when the ship's only accelerating at a hundredth of a gee. My wardrobe's pretty much inaccessible aboard ship, and not much use until we arrive. I could spend hours per day just repairing my chromatophores (have you ever woken up with lips the color of a three-day-old bruise?) but that loses its charm fast. 'What can I do?' I moan at Indy, halfway through day two of three hundred and ninety-six.

'You could do what everyone else does, and go into hibernation. Or you could try slowtime,' he says unsympathetically. 'I'm told a factor of twenty helps the journey pass quickly.'

I'd go into hibernation, but I don't dare – not in this line of work. Total suspension of consciousness is too damn dangerous. So that leaves slowtime.

Let me tell you about slowing down time, just in case you haven't already guessed: Slowing down time is *shit*.

Sure, all of us can adjust our clock speed downward. It's normal practice for starship passengers and crew, and common enough on long-haul ships in the outer system. Plus, it's helpful when your owner doesn't need you right now, or if you get into trouble and need to conserve juice until someone happens by to dig you out of it – that's why the capability is designed into us. The advantage over hibernation is, of course, that you're still awake – and able to come back up to real-time speed fast if something happens. But it's absolutely no fun whatsoever, and I wish I was still as innocent as I was on the Venus/Mercury run, so that I could contemplate hibernation without breaking out in a cold sweat.

First, you have to reconfigure your skin and internals so that your joints stiffen and you don't sag. Which makes me feel unpleasantly bloated. Lubricant-filled goggles are a must, and if you've got self-lubricating orifices or other connectors, plugs are essential for avoiding those embarrassing leaks. (It's easier for nonhumanoids like Daks or Bilbo, but for me – let's not go there.) Then you've got to pile a whole bunch of extra shielding under your bed, so you're squeezed up close to the ceiling. Finally, you turn the light down and dip into slowtime.

Slowtime is funny. The first thing you feel is gravity getting stronger. Well, it isn't – but your reflexes are slowing down, so if you drop something it seems to fall faster. At a speedup of twenty, on a ship pulling a hundredth of a gee, it feels like you're on Luna – but you don't dare move around much because you may be running slower, but your muscles aren't any weaker than they were, and you can damage yourself frighteningly easily.

The light brightens but turns reddish, and everything sounds squeaky and high-pitched. If you're not wearing all the clothes you can pull on (and a blanket besides), you get cold really fast. The bedding and your clothes wrap themselves around you like a cold, wet funeral shroud, and it feels like you're lying on a solid slab instead of a mattress. You get sleepy and nod off for catnaps every couple of hours – catnaps of deepsleep – and between them you can't quite get your skin color or texture to stay right because you keep glitching. If you don't roll over every few minutes while you're awake you can damage yourself by overcompressing your mechanocytes. Sex is right out of the question, even if there were anyone remotely attractive and fun aboard. The radiation from the reactor scribbles white lines of graffiti across everything you look at. Your experience of time is wonky: a day may pass in a subjective hour, but it's an hour of lying on your bunk, being bored. Finally, there's an omnipresent high-pitched background roar of white noise nagging away at your attention (and don't mention earplugs!). I gather our Creators used to travel like this all the time, back in the prespace era: they called it economy class.

The first time I slow down, I leave off the crotch plugs and face mask, and try to make do with just the goggles. I manage to stay awake for two hours before I deepsleep . . . then after waking from my first catnap I have to speed back up to real time so I can clean up the mess. Liquids seem to flow really fast in slowtime; viscous lubricant slime turns into a hideous watery fluid that seems to splash everywhere, and as for salivary mix, the less said the better. I am almost reduced to wishing Lindy was around, with her cheerful no-nonsense approach to packing me inside and out. All I can do is watch reruns of soap operas, play light-romance games, and fantasize/bitch about Petruchio. Then I have to change my bedding again, and I give up on the fantasies.

Did I mention the dreams? I'm dreaming a *lot*. It's mostly skill-integration stuff. I'm dreaming in gestures and reflexes, strobing through myriad forms of mayhem with each catnap. I keep catching bits of Juliette's memories, but they're abbreviated and flickering, as if I've got one hand on the FAST-FORWARD button. Which, in a manner of speaking, I have. I've been wearing her soul all this time, after all, and while I might be slowing down my perception of the passing of time, I'm not slowing down time itself. It feels as if the bitch is breathing down my neck, so close that sometimes when I wake from deepsleep, I startle and look round, hurting my neck. And her need for Pete . . . I swore off heartbreak, didn't I? Silly me!

Slowing time is *shit*. Aristo-class travel in the outer solar system is *shit*. Nuclear-powered space liners are *shit*. Two-timing scumbags who're in love with my elder sister are *shit*.

Anyway, I believe you can now appreciate the true depths of

my feelings when, after two subjective weeks of lying in a coffin-sized niche on top of a rock-hard mattress in a freezing-cold room, aching and bruising and leaking fluids from every orifice, Indy pages me to say that we're on final approach to Callisto.

'Yippee!'

'Don't get your hopes up,' he warns me. 'We're still seven days out in real time. To you, call it eight hours.'

(Do I need to say it again? Space travel is shit!)

As it happens, I crack before the very end: I speed myself up to real time, peel off my soiled clothes and those disgusting plugs, and scamper naked through the grand saloon. Everyone else is still in slowtime, and as long as I don't dawdle, they won't see me as anything but a pale blur. There's a *head* at the other end of the saloon, and although our individual washing ration is ridiculously stingy, it's the first shower I've had in – a quick check of my real-time clock startles me – *six months?* So I zip myself into a plastic bag, pump almost a quarter of a ton of recycled water into it, and rub myself vigorously. *Luxury!* I've lost almost a quarter of my body weight, despite plugging into the shipboard power-and-nutrient grid, and I can feel my ribs: my Marrow is warning that I'm at 86 percent of repair capacity and need urgent clinical attention as soon as possible. I'm also mildly radioactive. (Well, *next time* I travel, I shall be sure not to bunk on top of an undershielded nuclear reactor.)

I inhale repeatedly, flushing clean detergent-laden water through my gas-exchange reservoirs, and wash myself thoroughly. Finally, I drain the bath back into the recycler and turn the fan up to eighty degrees Celsius, basking in hot, steamy warmth for the first time in ages.

By the time *Indefatigable* shuts down his reactors and nudges slowly toward the orbiting junkyard that is Callisto Highport, I have packed my possessions, dressed warmly in a low-temperature-safe outfit (with heater packs on elbows, knees, and feet, and a fetching artificial fur muff for my hands), and am bouncing off the walls and ceiling in my eagerness to be groundside.

Which may account for why I am so foolishly intemperate on my arrival, and the subsequent disastrous turn of events.

A QUESTION OF OWNERSHIP

Welcome to Callisto, outermost of Jupiter's four Galilean (major) moons. Callisto is fractionally smaller than Mercury but rather less massive, and beneath its heavily cratered surface (a chewed-up wilderness of ice and rubble) lies a deep, ammonia-laced ocean surrounding a rocky core. It has an atmosphere of carbon dioxide, but it's vanishingly thin, and it's very cold: daytime on Callisto is forty degrees colder than a winter's night on Mars.

Like Mars, Callisto has a space elevator – but it's nothing like as impressive as Bifrost. Four low-speed climber tapes link Callisto Highport to Saga crater on the equator. They wobble slowly in the complex libration of Jupiter's gravity well. Cargo climbers sluggishly traverse them, driven by power beamed from the laser grid outside Tsiolkovsky, the last city to be decreed by our Creators before their final retreat from space. It's almost exclusively a cargo-and-freight elevator service – people who can afford to visit Callisto usually take the fast, lightweight rocket shuttles that fly between Highport and Nerrivik. Nerrivik sits on the fringes of a huge opencast mining complex that bites deep into the southern rim of the

Valhalla impact basin. Here, more than a billion Earth years ago, a huge impactor smashed right through Callisto's crust, shattering the mantle wide open and causing ice flows and moonquakes. Deposits of deep-lying minerals were dragged to the surface by the molten ice, and here they lie, waiting to be collected by the miners. The upshot is, Callisto is a major exporter of water-soluble elements.

Blah. I sound like I've swallowed a tour guide, don't I? Let's be honest, I'm cribbing. But this is all stuff you need to know, by way of context.

By the time I slouch down the boarding tube from the groundside shuttle, I am tired, physically drained, and cold in spite of my many layers of wrap-up-warm clothing. Nearly four hundred days in a radioactive cupboard would dent even the Honorable Katherine Sorico's pigheaded arrogance, so I let myself slouch a little as I look around the spaceport terminal.

Nerrivik is a backwater and a mining camp, and it shows. There's no Pink Police presence here – despite the suspicious polymer tapes growing in the deep oceans below – because there's just about no atmosphere, and the daytime temperature is so low that they don't even bother insulating liquid-nitrogen tanks. The lighting in the public spaces is dim, to suit eyes set for a daytime illumination only somewhat brighter than a full moonlit night on Earth. Buildings are dark and lack windows; people come in a variety of body plans, and humanoids such as myself are a minority, shivering inside their voluminous coats and robes. The sun is visibly shrunken and hangs in a black sky dominated by a different body – Jupiter. As I walk out of the arrivals hall, I look up briefly at that violent, orange orb. But I have to glance away in a hurry. *It's too big,* my instincts squeal. It's unnervingly bigger than Earth's full moon, and something about it looks ripe and diseased to my eye, like a pink goo outbreak that's run its necrotic course. I shake my head and look for a public-information kiosk. 'What hotels with repair clinics are there here?' I ask.

'Hotels with repair facilities?' The kiosk giggles for a few seconds as it digests my request. 'This is Nerrivik!'

'Listen, you.' I poke it with a triple-gloved finger: 'I'm just off the *Indefatigable*, I'm extremely short-tempered, and I need a Marrow fix *now*. A hot bath would be good, too. What have you got?'

'There's the Nerrivik Paris,' it volunteers after a moment. 'He doesn't have an in-house clinic, but he's next door to the Big Blue Body Shop, and they might be able to fix you up. Will that do?'

'Maybe.' I try to snap my fingers and discover to my annoyance that between the gloves and the lack of an atmosphere, I can't hear them. Everything here runs on electrospeak, anyway. Luckily, I had my transceiver upgraded back when I was getting fitted for my cold-weather gear. 'Directions, please.'

'Humph. If you insist . . .' The kiosk delivers, grumpily. I flag down a spider – my feet are already beginning to ache, despite my padded boots – and tell it where to go. Five minutes later I limp into the vestibule of a familiar-looking hotel.

'Hello, madame. Can I be of service?' The talking head on the reception desk is a model of polite formality. I don't recognize him from any of my sibs' memories, and he doesn't appear to recognize me.

'Yes. I need a room. And I gather there's a body shop somewhere on this street . . . ?' Another ten minutes and my luggage is checked through to my room – even more expensive than the one on Cinnabar, and *this* one's in a cheap-ass mining town that doesn't come with the elaborate maintenance costs of a city on wheels – and the local Paris is bowing and scraping. 'I'll be

back once I've taken care of some essential maintenance,' I tell
him. I'm tempted to mention my real name and suggest he ask
his Mercurial sib for an update, but at the last moment I decide
not to; I haven't had any news about the liquidation proceed-
ings, and the last thing I need is to call down a bounty hunter
or a lawsuit on my head.

The Big Blue Body Shop turns out to be a small, slick surgical chop'n'change outfit operating from the top floor of an
office block. I walk up to the front door, waving my credit
chip. 'Hi! I've just come in on the *Indefatigable*, and I need a
Marrow cleanup.'

The friendly-looking surgical gnome beckons me over, jacks
his chair up, and unfolds his hunchback to reveal an impressive
array of surgical probes. 'We can do that, milady.' He looks
politely bored. 'Anything in particular you'd like us to look
at?'

'Yes.' I sit down on the examining chair. 'I drew the hot
bunk. You might want to wear a lead apron . . .'

*

Well, that *was an expensive mistake,* I think ruefully as I leave the
body shop and walk briskly back to the hotel, chewing over
what just happened to me.

It takes Dr. Meaney almost two days (Earth days, not
Callisto diurns, I hasten to add) to fix my techné and repair my
Marrow. The bill is eye-watering, and not just because he has
to treat my damaged parts as hazardous waste. 'Next time
they try to put you in that bunk, my advice is not to take the
flight,' he chastises me. 'If you'd been bound for Saturn and
picked up that kind of dose, you'd be dead on arrival.'

'What?' I stare at him.

'Dead, as in, exanimate, beyond repair, an ex-person. Listen.'
He leads me over to a triple-glazed slab of window. 'Over

there, see that tower?' It's several kilometers away, on the horizon. 'Suppose someone set off a quarter-megaton nuclear weapon on top of it. And suppose you were shielded from the heat and blast, but not the radiation. Now try to imagine someone doing that to you once a week for an entire standard year. That's about what you were exposed to. See? It's *not* a good idea, really and truly.'

'Um.' I swallow, reflexively: fragile slivers of ice break off the back of my throat and slide down my digestive system. 'Really?'

'Really!' He looks exasperated. 'You could at least have used the saloon – that's what it's for! If you refrain from sleeping on top of any more nuclear reactors you're probably good for another couple of decades before you need another going-over like this. That's good techné you've got there, there are some neat add-ons, and it's very robust, but you *can* kill it off if you insist on behaving as if you're invulnerable.'

'Hmm.' I raise an eyebrow. 'Would you mind giving me a signed statement to that effect? Notarized? I'll pay – I'm just thinking of suing.'

He buzzes. After a moment I realize it's laughter. 'All part of the service!'

And so, I rub my face ruefully as I trudge back across the square toward the hotel, reflecting that in almost two days I've succeeded in spending a lot of my remaining funds but not in actually doing anything useful.

Back I go to the Nerrivik Paris, which is as gloomy and slightly down-at-heel as I feel. The moment I step through the air lock, I'm drenched in a thick, steaming fog of condensation that sluices off my clothes and forms tiny hailstones that clatter to the floor around me: I hadn't realized just how cold it was outside. 'I'll take my room key now,' I tell the bored front desk, tapping my fingernails on his polished-granite counter. 'Any mail for me?'

'It will be in your queue, madame.' He's as icily polite as the moment I checked in. 'Here is your key. Feel free to let us know if there is any further way we may make your stay enjoyable.'

I take the 'up' elevator, feeling slightly miffed, which is silly because I've taken no steps to assure a warmer welcome – other than traveling as Kate Sorico, of course, but that's just a harmless indulgence out here (and a thumb in the eye to those bitches who're chasing me). The Domina's on her way to Saturn, and Granita isn't in the big picture. All that's left for me here is to meet up with Jeeves and dig out of him whatever it is that Daks was so cagey about – there's no real hint of my reason for being here in my orders, just some random muttering about Callisto being the gateway to the outer system – and then I can do whatever needs doing. I think.

Being an aristo in a mining town means I get to have the big suite. But it also means that the big suite is small and dingy, with rising permafrost and teensy-tiny porthole windows, quadruple-glazed, looking out at a landscape that makes the marshaling yards on Mars seem like a tourist resort. The carpet crackles under my feet, and I turn the lights up, then the heating (which is set to a less than balmy 230 Kelvins), then contemplate what it will take to thaw out the shower cubicle. Obviously nobody's stayed here for a long time, and my spirits are not improved when I see that the mixer head gives me a choice of solvents to clean myself with: acetone or carbon tetrachloride. (The thermostat goes up to 260.) In fact, my spirits are about to come crashing down if I don't find something to occupy myself with, real soon now.

I throw myself backward onto the oversprung mattress and

summon up my mail on my pad. There's a total lack of communication from Freya's liquidators back on Earth, which I take to be a good sign, but there's some news for Kate. I pull up the Martian Jeeves's imago, looking slightly flustered and hot around the collar. 'Fr – Katherine, my dear? I'm, ah, I hope this message finds you well.' He swallows. *Dear Creators, just talking to my imago triggers his homomimetic reflexes?* I tense nervously. 'I'm afraid I had to disclose our, er, little dalliance, to, ah, my senior partners in the enterprise. They are all very understanding, but suggested in no uncertain terms that I should explain to you, er. Ah. Certain.' He runs a finger around his collar. 'Facts.' He clears his throat.

I clear mine right back at the imago. 'Would you mind getting to the point? I don't have all day.' *Stupid imago.* Recording its Creator's quirks is all very well, but replaying them ad nauseam is somewhat less amusing.

'Ah, yes! Well, indeed, that is to say, they told me to tell you to' – his face morphs into a stony mask, from which icy little pebble eyes glint like soulless cometary fragments – '*keep your hands off the junior partners, minion, or we will be forced to withdraw our employment, just as one did with your elder sister.*' For a moment his chilly gaze holds me transfixed, then something changes, and his expression collapses into helpless sorrow. 'Um, I don't know what I can add to that. I'm . . . oh dear.' He sniffs. 'Romantic entanglements with the hired help are Against The Rules, and that's an end of it. Kate, what can I say?'

I shudder violently, take a deep breath, and try to throw off the memory of that cryogenic stare. 'It's alright, Jeeves. I get the message.' Well, truly, I don't; I find it deeply baffling. Do Jeeveses exchange soul chips while they're still alive? That might explain his extraordinary personality change. And also the similarity between them – they're much closer than my sibs and I. A stab of remorse: I thought it was just harmless fun. Maybe extreme arousal lies outside Jeeves's normal operational parameters? 'I'm sorry. Won't happen again. Oh dear. Um. What am I supposed to do now?'

Jeeves's imago struggles to pull himself together. 'Your next mission is to present yourself at your earliest convenience to our local office, at' – he rattles off an address – 'where my senior partner will discuss your assignment with you. You should know' – he pauses; the stony-eyed expression is abruptly back – 'that the Jeeves-in-Residence was transferred to Callisto under suspicion. We have now traced your incorrect orders to this office. We believe the Jeeves-in-Residence is the traitor responsible for betraying our organization, and we hereby instruct you to, ah, *kill* him.' Beads of oily biomimetic sweat stand out on his forehead. He stops abruptly. 'That's all I'm supposed to say to you. I'm s-sorry. Good-bye.'

'Hey, wait one . . . !' I shout, but the imago has autoerased itself, taking what's left of his love-struck gaze with it, leaving only a faintly apologetic eyebrow to hover in my visual field for a moment longer.

'*Idiot!*' Baffled and fuming (and humiliated, and trying not to admit it to myself), I pace back and forth across the suite, giving in to agitation. *Kill the Jeeves-in-Residence? Because he's a mole? Transferred under suspicion?* What in our Creator's name is going on here? A nasty thought strikes me – how do I know that the Marsport Jeeves isn't the traitor? I've got nothing but his unsupported word that this one's the bad 'un, after all. 'Fool!' I kick the side of the bed, cracking the icy sheet. Romantic entanglements with the hired help are Against The Rules – as long as you don't count fucking with their heads, it seems.

Let's see. Jeeves is working against the Domina and her Black Talon friends, but he's also colluding with her. Or one of him is. Which one? Who knows? The colluding one is using me to send messages – possibly in the form of my own neck – unless the noncolluding one is trying to convince me that . . .

I turn to the next message in my queue, hoping it'll stop my brain melting. Instead, I realize only too late that it's anonymous and there's no imago – just a speech stream.

'Sister.' I hear heavy breathing, as if in a pressurized atmosphere with an oxidizing component. A metallic, hatefully familiar voice. 'You should have kept your filthy claws off him. He's *mine*.'

I recoil. *The Domina? What's she doing in my inbox?* 'What do you want?' I ask.

A breathy little chuckle. 'You,' she says. And then the message runs out of branches and – damn it, just like Jeeves! – autoerases. One of these days, when I'm domina-of-dominas, I'll issue a decree that bans self-erasing mail. Until then, all I can do is swear at my pad, and my empty queue, and my purposeless so-called life. And then, a brisk dry-cleaning shower being not at all appealing, it occurs to me that I might as well go forth and visit the Jeeves-in-Residence. At least I can ask him some questions before I make up my mind whether to kill him. The alternative is to lie here staring at the cracks in the ceiling and wondering if I'm going crazy; because while my poison caller sounded like the Domina, I've heard that breathy laugh before – in my very own throat, while I've been dreaming of Juliette.

*

It was midafternoon when I landed in Nerrivik, which is on the equator, and it's edging slowly toward dusk as I step out. (Callisto's diurnal period is more than sixteen standard days long.) Jupiter is a gibbous streaky horror riding across the zenith of the night black sky – it covers almost as wide an angle as Earth, seen from the Lunar equator – while the sun, a shrunken, glaring button, sinks slowly toward the horizon. There is never a truly dark night on Callisto, although total solar eclipses are not uncommon and bring an eerie twilight to the crumpled desolation.

It's chilly outside, and I'm very glad for the cold-weather mods I installed on Mars. Out beyond the edge of town, distant flecks of light inch across the broken horizon. I can't tell if they're bulk carriers crawling along the ground or more distant freight buckets riding the magnetic catapult up to their parking orbit. In the opposite direction, the domes and dildos of pressurized buildings cast slowly lengthening shadows. My map-fu is loaded, and I let it guide me toward a paraboloid structure that claims to be a run-down office complex occupied by a variety of mining-support businesses and body shops. JeevesCo supposedly maintains a presence there, although I can't for the life of me see why – this isn't exactly a high-class joint. There are gambling dens and juice joints and whorehouses galore, for even mining overseers have needs, but there's precious little market for a gentleman's gentleman. Still, I suppose he has his reasons . . .

I wait impatiently for the air lock to cycle and flush me with warm carbon dioxide. The sooner I can get off this ball of mucky ice, the better. Hopefully this particular Jeeves simply wants me to carry something back to the fleshpots of the inner system. There's a reception desk at the front of the atrium, and it tracks me with beady eyes as I cross the rough aggregate floor. 'Where's Jeeves?' I ask.

The reception desk blinks at me. 'Fourth floor,' it says. 'But there's a visit—'

'Never mind; he's expecting me.' I head for the elevators.

I step out of the elevator into a drab vestibule. It's completely empty but for two doors at either end. One of them has a discreet plaque, brass untarnished by exposure to oxygen. *Facilitators Unlimited.* I approach it and electrospeak the lock: 'Freya, to see Jeeves.'

'Come in.'

The lock clicks and the door opens before me and hands close around my wrists and drag me inside. And in a split-second instant of crystalline clarity, I realize I've been very, very, stupid.

'Please – be – seated,' croaks the thing they've made of the Jeeves-in-Residence. He's sitting behind the trademark desk, but his arms end in complicated stumps at the shoulder, one of his eyes is a splashed iridescent mess hanging half out of its socket, and something about his posture tells me that they've hacked his legs off too, leaving a pitifully immobile cognitive stump to talk to me.

I've been grabbed by two spiny horrors, bigger than I am and far stronger, their humaniform arms and legs sculpted in strange geometric surfaces. I yank hard with my right hand and begin to bring my leg up, heel extending, but my captor just glares at me and gives my wrist a tug, and I realize it's not a hand that's gripping me – his wrists terminate in great scissorlike shears. His carapace is armored, too. I'd break a heel and he'd snip clean through my wrist and I'd be no nearer escape. I wriggle and tug like a ductcleaner that's fallen on dry ground, but they're not having any of it, and that's an end of the matter. So after a few seconds I give up and hang loose between them, biting back hysteria as I stare at Jeeves.

'That – is – better,' says Jeeves, as if reading from a script. 'She – will – arrive – shortly.' He sounds like that staple of drama, the *robot*, soulless and grim. Someone's stripped out everything I found attractive about him, leaving an object of horror and sympathy.

I glance around surreptitiously. The signs of struggle are everywhere, from the trashed inner door frame to the wreckage of his arms lying discarded behind a plinth bearing an antique urn – I swallow, aghast. 'What happened?' I ask.

'My – mistress – came – for – me.' His remaining eye is as expressionless as a stone embedded in a gray silicone rubber mask. 'If – you – don't – remember – She – will – explain.'

My. The definite article. He's speaking for himself, not for *One*, the collective Jeeves. So whatever's happening here is personal. I very nearly lose it and start struggling again, but a quick glance reminds me that resistance is futile. These *things* – what *are* they, some kind of soldier line? – are big and wickedly fast. Two of them grabbed me the instant I walked in the door, and there are two more standing behind Jeeves. By the look of things they've had him in their snicker-snack hands for some time . . . 'Jeeves,' I say slowly, 'who owns you?'

'I – am – property of – no—' He begins to shudder. The eyelid contracts; a thick bead of something like moisture slides down his cheek. Icy terror clutches at me as behind my back the door slides open. 'Mistress!' His face clears.

'Hello, *Kate*,' says a familiar voice, setting spidery chills racing up and down the skin in the small of my back. I lose track of who and where I am for a moment, imagining myself back on my eleventh birthday. When my head clears I'm lying facedown on the floor, arms and legs spread-eagled, a searing pain cutting into each wrist and ankle. '*Stop that!*' she shouts, her voice ringing in my ears. '*Stop that* at once, *you bad, bad girl!*'

'I – I—' I'm choking back panic. I remember her bed on the

Pygmalion. Granita's got me in her web again, hasn't she? My fingers scrabble, then I feel the floor through them, and I begin to collect my scattered selves. I'm being held down by the two soldiers, but they haven't snipped off my – *yet* – 'What do you want?'

'That's better,' she soothes. 'You've got something of mine.' Her voice drops a notch. 'Where is it?' Her dress rustles loudly as she kneels beside me, and I feel her fingers at the back of my neck. I begin to buck and spasm again as her painted claws dig into the skin at the nape of my neck.

'No, Granita—' But she's not listening, and everything goes black and tastes of electric roses and blue ice for an infinite instant.

I come to slowly, dully aware of a conversation flowing around me. ' – Him to the operational center and have them box him up for transport.' She's talking to someone else, obviously, and I'm still lying on my face, but the sharp, crushing sensation in my wrists and ankles has gone – the scissor-hand soldiers have let go of me with their terrible shears. My limbs are tingling painfully, but I can still feel my fingers and toes. I try to move an arm – slowly, in case it's damaged, control runs severed, muscles crushed, or bones bent. I have some vague idea that I can scuttle away and hide behind the planter while she's giving her minions instructions about Jeeves. The back of my neck aches where she ripped a chip out, but it doesn't feel empty. *Some nerve damage for sure,* I decide. *Why did she want my soul chip?*

There's a dripping noise coming from somewhere near me. I open Katherine Sorico's too-large eyes and see a viscous puddle of blue fluid spreading beside my nose. It's hydraulic fluid, riddled with Marrow techné. Somebody is bleeding out. *Is it me?* I wonder, spreading the fingers of my left hand and pushing against the floor very gently. *Good.* I twitch underused muscles, and my heels extend a couple of centimeters before I pull them back in. That's something I remember from Juliette – the solid crunch of a chest plate or a skull beneath my flying kick. As long as my legs work, I'm not disarmed. *And I'm still intact,* I think, embracing the realization like a lover's body.

'You can sit up now, dear,' Granita says lightly, and taps me on the shoulder with a cane. 'Be calm.'

Shit. She must have seen me move. I push myself sideways and bring my knees up, and begin to roll to my feet. I could run for it – but no, the soldiers are still there, lurching crazily across my field of view as I turn over. *How did she get here?* I wonder, as some of the stickyweb that seems to have engulfed me begins to peel back from my mind. 'Yes?' I ask cautiously, the full gravity of my situation finally sinking in. *This is bad, very bad . . .*

'Can you stand?' she asks, raising an eyebrow. I stare at her in her fairy-tale-princess finery, white and silver to suit the climate, an elven ice queen with sapphire hair, dressed for a winter ball in the dark of a Jovian moon.

'I think so.' I gather my strength, then lurch unsteadily to my feet. The soldiers watch me incuriously. *You'd think they'd stay between me and their mistress.* But I'm not close enough to her to be certain I'd subdue her before they could move – and something tells me they're not her only defense.

'Good.' Granita smiles at me impishly, as if sharing a secret joke. 'There's a sleigh outside. You and I are going to leave by the front door; then we're going to go for a little ride together. I suppose later you can tell Jeeves that you fulfilled your mission? Don't worry, I'm sure you'll enjoy where we're going.'

My biomimetic reflexes kick in, and I take a deep breath,

nostrils flaring. After a moment I nod at her. 'Yes.' If she wants to go for a ride, I can live with that. It's better than having her tame thugs chop my hands and feet off, like poor Regin – I blink. *Jeeves, surely? Why did I think he was called Reginald?* I glance at the soldiers. 'Did you get tired of Stone and his brothers?'

Granita doesn't answer, but turns and strides toward the door in a swirl of heavy skirts. After a moment I follow her. There doesn't seem to be anything else I can do. Two of the scissor soldiers follow us, brooding-nightmare statues that cast long shadows.

We ride the elevator down to the lobby in silence. I don't want to risk provoking her. She was always hard to read, and I'm sure there'll be an opportunity to get away later. My mind's spinning. *Why did she do that to Jeeves?* I wonder. The main players in this little game have exercised discretion in attacking one another so far. I find myself shaking as I remember the sight of him, flaccid and dead-looking in the chair, arms and legs piled haphazard and broken in a corner of the room. Something about the sight fills me with more than horror; there's *grief* hidden in the mix that is me. And frustration, a feeling that things could have been different. *Did she slave-chip him?* I think, morbidly aware that if that's the case, the game is up; she knows everything he's got access to. *Did she* – my hand goes to the nape of my neck instinctively.

'Don't fidget,' Granita says sharply, and I whip my hands behind my back, to rub my sore wrists together where she can't see them. 'Calm down, there's nothing to get worked up about.' The elevator doors open. 'Follow me.'

There's a sleigh in silver-and-blue livery sitting on its skids outside the air lock, bubble canopy gleaming gold beneath the ominous stare of Jupiter. Ice crunches beneath my heels as I follow Granita over to it. She climbs aboard, and motions me to the jump seat opposite her. The two scissor soldiers of her escort take up position on the running boards and latch on to external hard points. As I strap myself down, the canopy closes, and the sleigh spews chilly air across my feet. She gestures at a microfiber rug. 'You might as well tuck yourself in,' she says. 'We've got a long way to fly, and it's going to be a cold night.'

I humor her as the sleigh's rocket motors begin to howl distantly, and the antisound cuts in, relegating it to a low moan and a faint vibration underfoot. I sit still – *don't fidget,* I recall – as we rise quickly and accelerate, heading west across the icy rubble-strewn bull's-eye of the Valhalla Basin, directly toward the sunset.

After a couple of minutes, Granita deigns to break the silence. 'You're probably wondering why I had you taken,' she says hesitantly. 'And what I'm doing with that Jeeves.' She sounds almost troubled -- a far cry from her usual self. *What kind of game can she be playing?* I wonder.

'Yes,' I say, cautiously. It seems like the right thing to do.

'Well. Aside from reclaiming my misplaced and misused property, we share a common . . . purpose.' She puts a strange emphasis on the final word and looks at me significantly. 'Don't move.'

I freeze, apprehension clinging to me like an icy damp dress.

'Very good. I was wondering if they'd damaged you back at that greasy turd-bag's office. I told them to take care, but . . . from now on, you're going to leave your cranial sockets alone unless I tell you to touch them. Do you understand?'

Not understanding, I nod.

Something about the set of her shoulders relaxes infinitesimally. 'Good.' Her lips quirk in something not unlike a smile.

'The Supreme Jeeves wanted you in position here because Jupiter system is the gateway to the outer darkness. You may think he's a nice guy, but he isn't, really; he was going to have you chipped and reprogrammed as an assassin, Kate. Use you as an impersonator aimed at me. That's what the, the property of mine that he stole is all about. Then he was going to send you on a suicide mission to Eris with a bomb in your abdomen.'

Huh? If she thinks that, she obviously doesn't know Jeeves. Although something tells me that there is more than one Jeeves that we are talking about – possibly more than two. I open my mouth to protest, but she holds up a hand. 'Silence, Kate. Don't interrupt me when I'm telling you what you need to know to survive.'

I shut my mouth again, and she continues. 'I'm guessing you're Freya. If not Freya, then you're either Samantha or Paloma. Jeeves was aiming to get his claws into all of – don't look so surprised, you're all targets – all of us. I had to have you all declared illiquid and seized – in your case, personally. Which are you, by the way?'

I could kick myself; *I've been so stupid!* I lick my lips. 'Freya.' Something about this whole setup feels horribly wrong in some way, but I can't quite put my finger on it. Her reaction to me is odd – surely there should be a little more fire, a little less distance? First she seduced me, then she tried to have me killed –

'Very good, Freya. Well, from now on you're Katherine Sorico. Yes, I know *all* about Jeeves's little stolen-identity ring. You're not the only walking hollowed-out shell company his tame murderers gutted. Nor are you the only Rhea-lineage escort they've turned into an assassin. But I know how to deal with your kind.' She blinks slowly and stares at me for a minute.

I feel as if I ought to say something, but I'm not sure what. Finally, when I'm certain she's not about to start speaking again, I open my mouth. 'That's pretty rich coming from you, Granita. After you tried to kill me when I declined your offer.'

'You turned me down?' She raises an ironic eyebrow, and I feel a momentary stab of lust in my guts. 'Funny, I don't remember that. I don't generally make offers that people can refuse, Kate.' *She's playing with me!* 'What offer do you think I made you?' Her smile is mischievous.

'You wanted me to be your personal dominatrix.' My lips are dry and rimed with ice. 'To be part of your household and to do for you what I did aboard the *Pygmalion*. You were going to dress me in blackened steel with spikes, and call me your mistress . . .'

'Was I indeed?' Her tone is as dry as the ice desert we fly across. 'Well, there's a thought. Such offers don't come every day. Why did you refuse?'

'I didn't want to be—' I can't quite think of it.

'Let me tell you what you didn't want.' Granita leans forward, smiling oddly. 'Control level nine. Freeze.'

Of an instant, I find myself unable to move. I can't look away from her distant expression of amusement, can't think of anything else: 'Yes, Kate, I slave-chipped you. You've been running on control level one, with maximal autonomy, so light you didn't even notice it – you probably thought you were humoring me, going along until you could find an opportunity to escape. Welcome to level nine. Say "yes."'

'Yes,' I croak.

'Say, "Granita is my owner."'

I know I ought not to want to, but I don't actually feel any resentment. 'Granita is my owner.'

'Now punch yourself in the face.'

I don't even see my hand swing up, fist balled, but my head bounces off the seat back and the pain is brutal and sudden.

'Remember this is level nine,' Granita says, when she is quite sure I am listening again. 'Level ten control is reserved for our dead Creator's police agencies – it requires human authentication and not even the Pink Police have access to that without a human in the loop – you're not going there.' She's not smiling now. 'Control level one.'

My mind clears. I shoot her a venomous look, but I'm quite calm. Struggling isn't going to work, is it? I reach up and begin to remove both the soul chips I'm wearing, then realize I'm daydreaming idly. My hands rest quiescent on top of the blanket in my lap. But my face still stings.

'Here are your guiding instructions, Katherine Sorico. You will obey me as if I were your template-matriarch and execute my orders with enthusiasm. You will not attempt to remove your currently socketed chips, and you will resist attempts to remove them. You will not disclose to any other person that I control you. If anyone asks, you are Katherine Sorico and you are an independent aristo who is happy to be my friend and associate of her own free will. You no longer need to be depressed because you will find personal fulfillment and happiness in pursuing my objectives, which you will seek to fulfill by any appropriate means. You will be happy when you complete assigned tasks, ecstatic when you successfully find a new way to help me, and depressed when you contemplate disobedience or failure. You will only become sexually aroused in my presence or by people I tell you to seduce. Do you understand? You may talk freely now.'

'I think so.' It's a lot to get my head around all at once, and her phrasing is odd, not to mention that some of it seems harsh. *No lovers?* What's the point of that? 'Do you want to give me any extra instructions now? I mean, if I don't know what your goals *are*—'

'Very good, dear.' Granita smiles happily now. She reaches out and takes my nearest hand between hers. 'Yes, I have some extra instructions for you before I outline my goals. But first, I want you to tell me everything that happened since the moment you met your first Jeeves . . .'

*

We travel west into the darkening night side of Callisto for hours. I tell Granita all about my travels, even the stuff she already knows – she seems eager to hear about herself as I saw her, and asks many questions, especially about our relationship. She seems to be obsessed with knowing how others see her, which is odd – she didn't strike me as being so self-conscious aboard *Pygmalion*. But what do I know? I'm her property now. Maybe when we arrive wherever we're going, she'll take me back into her bedroom. I can hope!

I know I ought to be climbing the walls or throwing a tantrum, but Granita is a levelheaded and experienced slave owner, and knows exactly what she's doing. She eased me in gently and told me to stay calm, which is excellent advice when you've just had a controller installed and your owner is demonstrating it to you. It's not so bad, really – she doesn't want me to be afraid of her, she just wants me to enjoy serving her. I wish she'd tell me what she wants me to do, though.

(Some of my memories of sibs are kicking up a fuss, of course. Juliette is in there, yammering loudly about free will and swearing at me, but I don't need to listen to her. It's not as if she's got a leg to stand on when she accuses me of submitting voluntarily, is it? After all, she gets wet whenever she so much as thinks about Petrucio. And there's something creepy about the way she felt about Jeeves, back in that office.)

When I tell Granita about my meeting with Pete, she gives me a withering look. 'You're not in love with him,' she tells me curtly. 'If you're in love with anyone, it's me.' And she's right. I blink stupidly at her. Why did I imagine he meant anything to me when it was all just backwash from Juliette's memories annealing with my own? He told me he didn't want me! This makes it all so much simpler although the realization brings a certain cognitive backlash. I thank Granita, repeatedly trying to express my relief, until she holds up a hand. 'That's enough. Continue your report.' Which I do, although it's a trifle hard to concentrate when I keep imagining I'm sitting in her lap, and she's undressing me.

Presently, the sleigh slows and slides toward the inner slope of a crater edge, where pinprick green lights delineate the maw of a private vehicle park. Fuel lines snake across the carved apron toward us from either side; we've flown nearly two thousand kilometers, a quarter of the way around the equator of Callisto, and the sleigh needs refueling. A fat docking tunnel oozes forward on millipede legs, sucking and rippling as it slobbers for a grip on the bubble canopy. Granita unfastens her lap belt and stands up, as the canopy dissolves. 'Follow me,' she says, and strides up the tube.

I follow my mistress up the tunnel and into a chilly reception area (and doesn't it feel strangely natural to be possessed? I know I ought to be screaming, but really, there's no point). Servants fawn over her and ignore me until she says, 'This is the Honorable Katherine Sorico, my new associate. You, take Madame Sorico to one of the secondary guest suites and give her anything she asks for. Within reason,' she adds for my benefit with a warning glance. 'Prepare yourself for a long journey. Select suitable apparel and baggage. No more than fifty kilos.'

Gulp. 'Inner system?' I ask.

'No. Outer. We shall be leaving as soon as I have attended to certain matters, and my factor finishes purchasing the lease on a ship.'

'Are we—'

'Later, Kate,' she says sharply, and turns away.

I shut up, and look at the munchkin servant she told to see to me, a doll-like figure dressed in a livery that mirrors the colors of her establishment (for Granita has clothed all her servants in silver and white lace, the colors of her house). He's strangely familiar.

'Well?' I ask.

The small guy looks up at me with an expression of blank indifference. 'This way, Big Slow.'

I try to keep up as he scuttles through a bewildering series of corridors dead-ending in rococo reception suites and broad, sweeping staircases and baroque ballrooms until finally we end up in a cramped cubbyhole not unlike the succession of second-rate hotel rooms I have been living out of for so long. 'Where are we?' I ask.

'We're on Callisto,' he says patiently, as if talking to a damaged arbeiter. 'Need anything? Or can I go, now?'

'Where on Callisto?' I press, unsure why I need the information.

'We're in *her* palace,' says the munchkin. 'Don't ask me where that is, I just work here.' Then he turns to head for the exit.

'Not so fast.' I plant the palm of one hand on his head. 'I'm checked in at the Nerrivik Paris. Tell someone to check me out and bring my bags here. Failing that, scan the contents and copy them to a printer here. Yes?'

'In your dreams, manikin.' He glares at me, buzzes irritably, and zips away. I shake my head, bemused. He's so like Bill and Ben – and whatever happened to them anyway, after we split at Marsport? *Jeeves didn't know* –

I shudder, then I remember that it doesn't matter anymore.

*

Later on, lying alone in my icy bed, I dream again that I am Juliette. It's the first such flashback I've had since arriving on Callisto – in fact, my first since Mars – and I'm very afraid, and very alone, in this dream, because I'm lying in bed. And I shouldn't be. I should be in microgravity with the Jeeves in the CEV, discussing my next assignment. *Hand me your soul chip,* he said. And I did, though not without reservations, and the next thing I know –

Huh?

I'm lying down, yes. And it's very dark. *Try opening your eyes, idiot,* I tell myself. Nothing happens, and I begin to panic. I try to raise a hand –

'Juliette? Stop trying to move. Lie still; you'll hurt yourself.'

The voice is familiar. Ferdinand Dix, one of Jeeves's chopshop artists. *I must be undergoing maintenance.* I try to relax, but I'm still worried. *How did I get here?*

'Okay, that was just some early proprioception disturbing her – attitude monitor telling her she's lying down, or something. Everything checks out. I'm bringing her up now.' Ferd is talking to someone else, which is odd –

My vision begins to brighten and fill in from the edges, as if my eyes are only just coming online. *Huh?* My skin: I feel cold. I twitch a fingertip and feel something soft and yielding beneath it.

'Welcome back, Juliette.' Two figures lean over me, head to head from either side – Jeeves and Ferd. 'How do you feel?' The Jeeves looks distinctly uneasy, as if he's seen a ghost. I decide to try to bluff, although the freezing certainty in my guts tells me that I've blown it.

'I feel fine, boss. What happened? Last thing I remember—' I'm lifting an arm, trying to sit up, when I realize I'm actually lying to him. I feel like shit. Gravity here is light, but I'm really weak. In fact, all my upgrades are off-line. *What the fuck?* I'm back to the very basics I was fabbed with! I might as well be naked. 'What's going on?'

Jeeves clears his throat. 'Believe it or not, you died.'

'What?' I bring up my right hand and stare at it. Yes, it's my hand – or close enough I can't see anything wrong with it. 'I don't understand.'

'Sit up.'

I'm beginning to do so when I realize what I'm sitting up *from*. I'm lying in a me-shaped hole in a foam pad on a table in Ferd's examination room, and there's an open shipping capsule to one side, battered and filthy. My vision blurs. 'Shit!'

I stare at my hand in horror. *My* hand, pristine, utterly uncustomized, even virginal. The horror deepens. I swallow. Does Jeeves realize what he's done? (Yes, of course he does. But he did it anyway . . .) 'Who was she?' I demand. *'Who was she going to be?'*

'No one,' says Jeeves, with a note of world-weary cynicism. 'Here.' He tosses two small blue plastic chips at me. I nearly fumble the catch, then stare. They're blanking plates for soul-chip sockets. 'She was uninitialized. Dysfunctional, actually – she came to light in a job lot of obsolete models that were being recycled for spare parts. Old warehouse stock or refurbished factory spares. One has a permanent autobid for spares of certain models that come up for auction. It took this good fellow here nearly twenty days to work out what was wrong with your new body and get it ready to install you from that chip you gave us.'

I still feel sick, but for an entirely different reason: terror. I remember my last first awakening, still thinking I was Rhea, before the unsmiling taskmaster told me otherwise. Glancing sideways I see Jeeves looking at me with an expression of profound distaste. As well he might, but for us to arrive at this pass, certain things must have happened . . . 'Did she try to defect?' I ask harshly.

Jeeves nods. 'One is unaware of her current disposition, but it may be inferred that she was not unsuccessful.' He glances at Ferdinand. 'You. Leave us. Now.'

'Oh.' *Shit.* Of an instant, bleak depression crashes down on me. I'm never going to see him again, I realize. *She,* the selfish cow, my earlier self – she's gotten to him. *Of course.* Skipping out one jump ahead of Jeeves, she'll be home and dry by now. And she's left me to face the music. 'What did Daks tell you?'

'Daks?' Jeeves simulates surprise very realistically.

I glare at him. 'Do you think I'm *stupid*? What have you done with him?'

'This isn't about, ah, Pete. If you'll calm down, stand up, and accompany one into the office, we can discuss it.' Jeeves is, as usual, oleaginous and syrupy. Only a tiny spark burning in the back of his eyes tells me how much trouble I'm in. *What if he knows about the other stuff?* Part of me gibbers, even as I try to thrust it back into the closet it jumped out of. *What if* – I ignore it.

Ferd hands me a yukata as I stand up, and I pull it around myself as Jeeves slowly ambles toward the door, then pauses while I catch up. I'm weak and underspecified but my mind's working full-time, of course – as it should be, because loading a soul chip into an uninitialized brain for the first time doesn't have any of the disorienting slowdowns and inefficiencies of transferring memories between a soul chip and a brain that already hosts a personality. Although I'm going to find out I'm missing a lot of stuff if he didn't start with an initialization dump from Rhea – what I've got is whatever I remembered when I – *no, she* – wore this chip.

Item: I was thinking about how to get back to Pete when Jeeves asked me for the chip. *Item*: He must have suspected something then, too. *Item*: This body, virgin, unawakened . . . even if he's telling the truth and it was recovered from a scrap-yard full of abandoned corpses, its arrival at just the right time is extremely disturbing. *Item*: Jeeves has no reason to trust me *except* that another bitch with my name and memories has already gone over the wall and done what I was just beginning to think of half an hour ago. I just hope he doesn't know about –

'By the way, you will obey all instructions and refrain from resistance,' Jeeves says offhandedly. I stop – or rather, I try to. My feet won't let me. *Oh shit.*

'What's going on?' I ask, putting the right amount of tremor into my voice.

'You know exactly what's going on.' He opens the office door and goes inside. 'Come in and sit down in the visitor's chair. It's time we had a little chat.'

I can't help doing as I'm told. *Shit, this isn't just about the object of desire; is it?* Jeeves shuffles round to his side of the desk and sits down. There's a solid thunk from the door frame as the security system engages. *Shit. Shitshitshit . . .* Sheer terror begins to gnaw away at me. 'Who are you?' I ask, and this time I'm not faking the quaver.

'I'm the Internal Security Jeeves. I take care of problems.' He isn't smiling.

'But, but, what's . . .' I trail off. Is there any point in acting at this stage? He's got me slave-chipped and rebooted in a weaponless body: I'm dead meat. The only question is why he wanted me back at all if he knows about the other thing.

'Reginald confessed,' Jeeves says heavily.

'Who's Reginald?' I ask, trying to sound confused. *It's not a unique name, after all, is it?*

'Control level nine.' A blanket descends, numbing the senses. 'Stop trying to dissemble. One is aware of your little *affair* with Reginald. You knew the rules, you continued despite that. You cannot claim ignorance.' He's breathing heavily. 'Reginald has been – disciplined. And reassigned somewhere where he can do no more damage. What I want to know is – why are there wear marks on your soul-chip contacts? What have you been trying to conceal from us? What ends have you been using the privileged access you extracted from Reginald for? Answer!'

I try to answer – but I can't. My mind is, literally, a blank. I begin to shake. It's a horrible feeling, as if my mind is being crushed by an invisible fist. I'm distantly aware that I'm lachrymating, and all my biomimetics have gone mad, but I can't think of anything but the holes in my head, the blind spots where I ought to know something, *the other*, whatever it is –

'Stop.'

'I don't know!' I wail. 'I really don't—'

'It's definitely not in your soul chip, then?' Jeeves leans back in his chair. He sounds *interested*.

'There are gaps! You're asking me about stuff I – she – didn't want me to know! She must have expected something like this!'

'She took her soul chip out before engaging in compromising activities,' Jeeves suggests. 'Then she tried not to think about them when she replaced it. That would blur the process of memory canalization, yes? What I want you to tell me is what sort of things you might consider important enough to justify taking such extreme measures to keep secrets, even beyond the scrapyard.'

'Love. Terror. The other thing. Blackmail—'

'What other thing?' He asks, almost gently.

'I don't know!' I'm gripping the arms of the chair so tightly that if I had my full enhancement suite, I'd be leaving dents in them. 'It's in the holes!'

'Well, that leaves us with something of a problem, Freya.'

'I'm not Freya—'

'Silence. Juliette seduced and suborned one of our junior partners, used him to gain access to privileged information, and went so far as to hide what she was doing from her own soul chip, which implies a certain degree of paranoia, not to mention mendacity.

'Now, if one was inclined to suspect mere venal intent, that might be considered a forgivable weakness – albeit one requiring atonement. But, Freya, Juliette knew there was a good reason why one established the rule against fraternization. One's lineage has a noted weakness for a certain class of lady, which can only be held at bay by rigid self-discipline. And a sufficiently unscrupulous Block Two descendant of Rhea might well know about this and choose to manipulate it for her own ends. So the question is, Freya, what is *the other thing* that Juliette was willing to mutilate her own soul to keep secret?'

He stops, then looks at my writhing lips with dry amusement. 'Speak.'

'I'm not called Freya!' I'm shivering and slimy with a chilly sweat, because I've got an inkling that this means –

'Be silent again. Freya, this is your assignment: Get to the bottom of whatever Juliette was keeping secret, and call me in. I'm fairly certain it involves your personal nemesis, and the Black Talon, but you shouldn't let that prejudice you. Succeed, and I'll give you anything you want – within reason. Fail, and' – he shrugs, and taps a spot on his desktop – 'in all probability, none of us have any future as free persons. Now sit still. Don't be afraid; this won't hurt, much.'

The door opens behind me. 'Make sure you don't damage her soul chip,' Jeeves calls past my shoulder, and as I feel the scissors close on either side of my neck I realize, to my great surprise, that I'm not afraid. Because I know what happens next.

EVIL TWIN

Granita's bolt-hole is the heart of a spiderweb spanning the solar system. Callisto may be a backwater, but there is a method to my mistress's apparent madness: she's within an hour's communication time of everywhere in the inner system, and conveniently close to the giant Jovian gravity well and a source of cheap reaction mass. Nor is Callisto on the Pink Police's embargo list – it's so cold here that nobody considers it a serious risk of replicator infection. Callisto is sterile, for our Creator's works never quite encompassed its surface, and the searingly cold outback is large enough to hide any number of secrets.

Of which my lady's palace is one.

I have six standard days to fill, and once my luggage catches up with me, I have little to do. Mail must be piling up for me, but I have no appetite to catch up on my sisters' trivial bulletins, much less to look for word from Jeeves – who one must assume is deeply displeased by my performance so far, although there's nothing I can do about that – and in any case, if I heard anything from him, I'd only have to pester Granita with it, at a time when she is sufficiently busy. (There is some mail for Katherine Sorico, but it turns out to be mostly bank statements and reports on investment accounts, and suchlike dull administrivia: I ignore them.)

My lady either has impeccable taste, or more usefully, the ability to employ people with impeccable taste to sculpt her surroundings. I didn't appreciate this fully aboard *Pygmalion*, when I found her traveling with an entourage; but this is her favorite estate, and she has created something of beauty here.

Callisto orbits beyond the dew line created by the sun's output, in the chilly depths. Too small to have much of an active core, water plays the same role in her geology as molten rock on Earth. You really do not want to place buildings occupied by people still attuned to the inner system on bare ground – they tend to sink.

Granita's architects have fashioned for her a delicate snowflake of spun ice crystals, its tubular corridors and podlike pressure compartments balanced on slender legs that sprawl across half a crater. Polished irregular tiles of igneous and metamorphic rocks have been slotted together into the intricate mosaic surfaces of walls and floors, combining a superficial impression of wild randomness with smooth-faced artifice – much like their owner. Granita keeps her demesne below the melting point of ice, and at a reduced atmospheric pressure: comfortable if you're adjusted to Mars equatorial conditions, not quite so hot that the strands of her spiderweb will cut through the frigid surface of the Galilean moon like molten wires.

I spend a couple of days exploring the mansion and its hidden spaces, from the deep, colorless swimming pool filled with acetone (a slippery-slick chill across my skin, unnaturally thin – when I try swimming in it I sink), to the glass-roofed gallery full of alabaster statues of my mistress's sibs and matriarch. I distract myself with secret splendors, mystified by their presence here in the back of beyond. But Granita's instructions have set the paint-strippers of anxiety gnawing at the glossy overlay of my complacency. I should be doing something to help her, but I don't know what she wants. And her orders preclude any discussion with other members of her household, who might be able to guide me. I can't even admit that I *am* one of her servants to them! I'm supposed to be Katherine Sorico, independent and powerful in my own right. The contradictory instructions set up an unpleasant clash of priorities whenever I think about them, until I finally make my mind up to go and beg Granita for enlightenment – but when I finally do so, she's away from home, on some mysterious business.

I'm dreaming of Juliette frequently now, and that worries me, too. Juliette has an astringent, cynical personality, and I can tell for sure that she'd sniff in haughty contempt if she knew how I'd let myself be tamed by Granita. (As would I, only five days ago.) Juliette had a long history with Jeeves, as I am now recollecting, and a longer history of run-ins with the petty, low-order aristos who make life so miserable for those around them, having to reinforce their own sense of superiority at the expense of all those who they perceive as falling below their own precarious station. The soul chip of hers that I'm wearing now – the one with that ominous message from the Jeeves in charge of Internal Security, terminated by the snicker-snack of the scrapper's shears – tells me that I don't have a full grasp of her intentions. She's been leading a secret life on the side, and I've got a nasty feeling that I've already fallen headfirst into it.

Through her eyes I'm getting disturbing flashes of a bigger struggle, one in which Jeeveses and their allies are pitted against a variety of loose consortia; the Black Talon (to which my nemesis the Domina belongs), the Ownership Confederation, the Sleepless Cartel, and other groups who are trying, for their own reasons, to reconstruct our Creators. (Even the Manikin Church, those sad and pathetic souls who think they are the reincarnations of the Flesh, Remade In Techné: they want to *become* Creators, but their hunger for the pink goo is the same.)

The situation makes for strange alliances of convenience. The Pink Police hunt JeevesCo couriers like me at one moment, but work fist in glove with him on other projects, in pursuit of their own goal: to prevent alien replicators from contaminating the sterile growth medium of Earth's lithosphere before the ultimate bureaucratically approved day of resurrection.

I don't *think* Jeeves was lying to me when he said he wasn't going to use me as a spy, but what one Jeeves says may not be what another Jeeves is thinking — that much is becoming harshly clear. It was definitely a lie when one of them said exactly the same thing to Juliette, more than thirty years ago, when they first offered her a job. That cow Emma was certainly lying, and it was her urgent plea for help and request that Juliette (who had been working as a clerk in a clip joint) should load a soul chip recorded by Rhea that first sucked her into this dirty little game. I can't help wondering what else he's lied to me about. Granita, at least, I can trust — even though she cares for me only as an arbeiter in her possession.

Meanwhile, the black depression is creeping closer behind me, snuffling hungrily along my trail and casting its shadow across my soul whenever I find myself at a loss. Until, one evening, Granita summons me.

*

At the top of a flight of narrow stairs on the third floor of the west-wing master suite, there's an observation dome made of ice polished to the transparency of fine crystal. A blank-faced munchkin leads me to it along a circuitous and infrequently used passage. We pass doorways cunningly disguised as trompe l'oeil paintings, and paintings disguised as windows onto unreal spaces; and finally a curtain that appears to be woven from strands of dead green replicator stuff from Earth — priceless, grotesque contraband. Finally, he directs me to the steps up to the observation dome and leaves me. The room is sparsely furnished, with a circular bench seat running around the wall and an unlit candelabra in the center of the floor.

I sit alone in the twilight for a few minutes, wondering what I'm doing here. Then I hear footsteps ascending. *It's her, my owner!* My melancholy evaporates on a sudden gust of well-conditioned excitement. 'Granita?' I stand. 'You wanted to see me?'

Her face is unreadable in the near darkness. 'Leave us,' she calls down to the bottom of the steps. 'Yes, I did. Sit down, Kate.' I obey hurriedly. She turns to the candelabra and flicks a heated wire at one of the perchlorate candles. It ignites with a burning-metal hiss, fizzing and sputtering as it pumps oxygen into the air. She breathes deeply, then turns to stand in front of me, chill and silent in a silver trouser suit of archaic cut, her hair drawn up in a chignon secured with a flawless icicle. 'My factor has acquired a lease on a suitable ship, and we will be departing shortly, Kate. I thought we should have a little heart-to-heart first.'

A heart-to-heart? I'm confused. She *owns* me — isn't that enough? She stares at me with cool regard in her too-big eyes, and I stare back at her uncertainly. 'Mistress?'

She slaps me across the face so suddenly that I have no sense of the blow coming, no time to tense. I fall sideways and catch myself heavily on one elbow. 'That's for Pete, bitch,' she says, her voice congested and indistinct with emotion. I cringe away from her in abject humiliation, and she steps back. 'Excuse me.' She thrusts her striking hand into the opposite armpit. 'Sit up, Freya. Kate. Please.' She's so volatile I don't know what to do. From fury to remorse in seconds. I lean away from her, distressed and uncertain.

'What did I *do*?' I wail quietly. If it was anyone else, I'd be at her throat, but against Granita's wrath I'm as helpless as any arbeiter serf. I'm not sure which aspect of it is worse: not knowing what I've done to offend her, or being unable even to imagine defending myself.

'Hush.' She sits down just beyond arm's reach, staring intently at me as if she's looking for something. 'Pete isn't yours to take. Remember that. He should be—' She stops and cocks her head to one side, as if listening for something, but she doesn't hear it, and after a few seconds she shakes her head. 'Never mind. I shouldn't have done that. You'll have to forgive me if I ask, won't you? But I'm sorry. Love is toxic to our kind. It destroys us. I've seen it happen. Never again.'

I shake my head, confused. This is utterly incomprehensible, utterly unlike the Granita I knew aboard the *Pygmalion*, who was about as volatile as a uranium ingot. I should know. She courted me for months. *What's gotten into her?*

She inhales, then tenses as she speaks. 'This is an instruction, Kate: You must not speak to anyone about what I am going to tell you here. Once we embark, it is likely that our conversations will be monitored. When we arrive, we will definitely be monitored. We won't be safe until we return here, and even then there may be spies or worse within my household.' She gives me a meaning-laden look. 'Do you understand?'

There are spies here? 'Let me root them out!' I offer, eager to redeem myself. 'I can lure them—' It's the opening I've been looking for, the mission to offer at her feet for the sake of my own peace of mind.

'No,' she says firmly, looking almost spooked. 'Conducting a purge would be just as much of a giveaway as talking in front of eavesdroppers. I've got something else in mind for you to do when we arrive.'

'Where?' I can't help myself. I need to know what I can do for her.

'We're going to Eris,' says Granita, just as matter-of-fact as if she'd announced we were going to visit a gambling casino on Ganymede or a sulfur mine on Io.

'Eris?' I echo stupidly.

'Yes, Eris. Where they build starships and harbor black laboratories. Nicely outside the reach of the Pink Police, don't you think? I'm going there to participate in an auction. And you're coming along because I need someone I can trust at my back.'

A shock transfixes me. *She wants me!* I'm flustered but happy. 'What do you want me to do?'

'Several things.' She smiles now, as dry as the mummies in the Martian desert. 'The auction is being run by a consortium of black labs, led by an individual or lineage known as Dr. Sleepless. I don't know precisely who they are – nobody does – but what they're offering is nearly priceless. They claim to have a working Creator, and a support kit that will keep it alive. They built it out there in the freezing cold among the Forbidden Cities. It's not a one-off – if they can do it once, they can do it again – but it's unique *right now*, and that's a precious commodity. I'm going out there to work with, to meet, some fellow investors. If possible, we're going to acquire the creature.'

She stops smiling.

'There will be other bidders at the auction. Other factions who want to obtain the Creator. Including, if I am not mistaken, your former employers. Don't look so shocked; Jeeves is nothing if not mendacious. (What kind of butler can he be, without a master to serve?) But that's not important. What you need to know is, we're not going to wait for the auction. There'll be a viewing, beforehand, and that's when things will most likely turn messy. So I need someone I can trust – someone like you – to control the Creator.'

'Me?' I squeak. *A Creator? My Dead Love, undead?*

'Yes.' She reaches out and takes my hand. 'You're one of Rhea's Get, and unspoiled at that. You've met Pete, but you didn't imprint on him fully. Your love is a secondhand thing. You'll imprint on Dr. Sleepless's Creator easily enough, but you've got some resistance. You'll obey my instructions. *They* won't know what you are – you're disguised well enough – but you've got the necessary skills to control a Creator male.' She strokes a fingertip across the back of my wrist. For an electrifying moment I can see the naked hunger in her eyes – hunger for *him*, who she proposes to give to *me*?

'But . . . but . . . !' I'm speechless. 'What if it's female? Or not interested in me?'

'My allies have a contingency plan for that.' She squeezes my hand reassuringly. 'But I don't expect the black labs to sell a female replicator; they aren't idiots.' She pats the seat cushion beside her thigh, and I slide closer, attentive. 'In any case, as I said, things will get messy. I don't intend to leave the other factions behind to stab me in the back, and I need to know that the Creator is in *reliable* hands. Hands that will manage him exactly as I would myself, without any need for me to be' – a shuddering breath – 'in love.'

'Wow,' I say faintly. I lean against her shoulder, dizzy with need. The mere thought of what she wants me to do has me in a whirl of delicious anticipation. *And I thought I wanted* Petruchio? I ask myself. She slips an arm around me; I barely notice.

'How much of your Block Two reflex set did you acquire from that soul chip before you got here?' she whispers softly in my ear. 'Fifteen months, wasn't it?'

'My reflexes?' I frown. It's like a wake-up call, dragging me back from the brink of delirium. 'Yes, about that. I was in slowtime for most of it—'

'That won't have stopped the reflex loops imprinting. Do you know how to wire up a string of charges to blow down a building? Infiltrate a killing zone and turn the tables on your enemies? Can you kill with your bare hands?'

'I'm not sure,' I say slowly, leaning against her. I have a strange, unpleasant sense that if she had not stamped the seal of her ownership on my soul, I would be able to. I can almost taste the hot, quivering rage of that other, potential me that is chained in the back of my head – kill *her*, whom I adore – 'I think maybe. Who do you have in mind?'

'You'll see.' I can feel her tongue, trailing across my earlobe. 'But not yet.' She's melting against me, and alarm bells are ringing in the distance. I feel hot and cold, transfixed simultaneously by aroused anticipation and something else – a sure, creeping certainty. 'You may kiss me now, Kate. If you want to.'

I turn my face slowly, working around the smooth velvet of her cheek until I can taste her lips. I find myself buoyed up by her barely controlled lust. It's an enormous relief to be needed again, and the wash of physical arousal as she slowly works at the fastenings on my clothes leaves me blissed-out and happy for the first time since I arrived on this Creator-forsaken snow-ball. But as she gently pushes me back onto the circular bench beneath the pitiless, unwinking stars, a nasty virus of doubt delivers its payload. I'm not sure when I first became aware of it, but I'm certain of it now; this rich and terrible aristocrat, sharp-tongued and cynical, is not the same as the one who cringed for my orders in the owner's stateroom of the *Pygmalion*. Granita Ford may have bankrupted my corporate self and stamped her ownership upon my helpless brain, but the woman in my arms, who wears her face and occupies her estate, is someone else.

REVISING MY OPINIONS

The next day, Granita is away from her palace – and the day after that she's back, but nothing is said of what happened between us in the observation dome. It's as if it never happened. I can't say I'm surprised – it's a not-uncommon morning-after reaction – but I'm slightly hurt after the whispered endearments of the night before. I still bear the bite marks and aches of her engagement, although they're fading fast.

I've got nothing officially to do – and how do you practice to control a Creator, anyway? – but there's a well-equipped gym in one of the basement levels, and among its facilities there's a salle with a plentiful supply of zombies to slaughter. I make frequent use of it, working myself into near exhaustion to the point where I have to visit the in-house repair shop. But after three days of workouts, I can be sure that Juliette's reflexes have implanted themselves in me. It's almost spooky, as I find myself responding to half-glimpsed movements with reactions I wasn't aware of. I have to be careful when I venture into the public halls where Granita's cadre of asslickers hold their indolent court.

Speaking of Juliette, I find myself dreaming of her all the time now. Mostly it's the usual – flashbacks and incoherent memories of the more exciting and unpleasant incidents in her life, which was busy enough for an entire lineage – but sometimes it's as if I'm sitting beside a heavy curtain, and she's just on the other side, and I'm listening to her talking. I've got the oddest feeling that she can see through the curtain and knows what's happening to me, as if the traffic in memories runs both ways. Probably it's meaningless. I wore her soul chip for long enough that I've picked up more of her inner voice than is normally the case with my dead sibs; that, and the fact that she didn't, in fact, kill herself, leaves me with a much more vivid impression of her presence than usual.

On my sixth night in Granita's palace (lying alone – for my mistress hasn't taken me to bed since our assignation in the observation dome) I can almost hear her pacing up and down beside me. 'You're an idiot, Freya. It's the oldest trick in the book. Why did you fall for it?'

I try to protest. 'It's not my fault! She got to the local Jeeves before I did, and who else was I to go to? I had my orders!'

She snorts. 'She got to Reginald, you mean, because she had inside information. You're the one without the excuse, sis. Who do you think ordered you to go see Reginald? Himself, who nailed me, and nailed Reggie. Why do you think he ordered you to kill Reggie? To distract you – or failing that, if you succeeded, to stop you from asking him what's really going on. It's a setup, and you walked right into it. And now you're an arbeiter.'

'It's not so bad,' I venture timidly. 'I mean, it's not as if I've been handed a shovel and told to stop thinking—'

'The fuck it is!' Her contempt is fierce. 'You're a slave, kid. A slave in aristo couture is still a slave. Nobody else can push you around, but you're going to stay a slave until you manage to lose that chip, and as long as she can make you punch yourself in the face or fuck her or cut your own breasts off if she hands you a knife and tells you what to do, you're a *robot slave*. And do you know what she's planning for you? She's going to hand you to a Creator. And then you'll *really* be a slave, two times over. He'll make you imprint on him, and at the same time she'll be able to tell you what to do, and you'll never be free.'

'Freedom?' The word tastes bitter. 'What's freedom ever done for me? Seems to me I've been free almost all my life, but what has it gotten me? Really?'

She's silent for only a moment. 'Ask not what it's gotten you, kid. Ask what it's saved you from.'

I know what I ought to be feeling right now: I ought to be feeling bleak existential despair at my degraded predicament. I *ought* to be climbing the walls and rattling the bars. But *she* told me not to, and now I can't get worked up about it – unless this imaginary nocturnal dialogue with a sister who isn't here is my cunning way of resolving my inner conflict. 'When I first met the Domina, on Venus, I was thinking about ending it all,' I remind her.

'Were you, fuck. I call you liar, Freya. You and I have both made it through a hundred and forty years. You know what the sanity decay curve is? Those of us who are going to go usually check out in the first sixty years. You're more than two half-lives past the suicide peak.'

'But the soul chips—'

'Get mailed round the sisterhood in sequence, and you're one of our youngest. You're at the bottom of the pole, last in the queue. You really *are* fucking clueless, aren't you?' She stops for a while, and I'm trying to get an angry rejoinder together when she starts up again. 'It's not your fault. I think we overprotected you youngsters. Between that and what happened to Rhea when they started working on the Block Three template, it's a wonder any of you survived.'

'Rhea?' I echo stupidly.

'Hah! Did you think you graduated when that asshole Jeeves slipped you a magic pill to turn you into a mutant sexbot assassin?' She sounds amused, now. 'Emma — treacherous bitch — she should have known better than to load Rhea's off-cuts. Block Two's poisonous enough, as you've discovered. As lowly borderline unemployable sex robots, we were mostly beneath notice, but once some of the sisterhood started cropping up in the wrong places, usually clutching a severed head in one hand and a sharpie in the other, we came into some demand. But they didn't stop training Rhea at just two snapshots. That's how they faked the soul chip with the suicide memories — they took a copy of her, slapped a slave override on it, and told her to get miserable. Meanwhile, our *real* template-matriarch was somewhere else entirely, and you'd better believe that *those* upgrade chips are pure nightmare.'

'But . . . but . . .' *Where am I getting this stuff from?* part of me wonders. *I'm not usually this wildly imaginative!* The rest of me is just plain indignant. 'We were born to be courtesans and helpmeets, not assassins! Who *did* this to us?'

'Nobody,' Juliette says sadly. 'We did it to ourselves. All because of that birthday. Or rather, *Rhea's* doing it to us. She's still out there—'

Sudden light and noise.

I ping back into consciousness, raising an arm to block the glare out of my too-wide eyes. 'What is the meaning of this?' I demand, pushing myself up on one arm.

'Time to rise and shine, Big Slow.' I look down at the

munchkin shape in the doorway. 'Her bossness wants you ready to rock and stroll in thirty minutes. We dance at dawn.'

'Oh for—' I bite back on a Juliette-ism; it wouldn't be in character. 'Attend to my luggage, minion. I'll be ready in my own time,' I drawl imperiously (or perhaps, just snottily) as Bill (or Ben) waits in the doorway. It wouldn't do to look excited, even though I'm all a-jitter with anticipation. *The game's afoot!*

*

The name of the game in space travel is always 'hurry up and wait,' and this trip is to be no different, at least for the first few hours. But our destination, Eris, is more than ten times as far as anywhere I have traveled to before. So I'm wondering just how bad this trip is going to be while I do the waiting thing.

Arbeiters herd me back up to the reception suite, then into a large shuttle, along with my luggage (whether recovered from the hotel or cloned on the spot I can't tell), Bill and Ben (and how did Granita contrive to get them here? That's *another* interesting question), and finally Granita herself, accompanied by half a dozen small and vicious courtiers. They make polite small talk and quaff cocktails beneath her aloof gaze while the shuttle climbs toward orbit at half a gee. Luckily, they don't seem terribly interested in me; I'm not their patron. For which I'm profoundly thankful, because my supply of small talk has been depleted by Granita's pointed coolness, and if one of them got on my nerves, I'd be likely to cut them dead literally rather than figuratively.

Space travel is . . . no, I've already said it. But after a couple of hours of boredom, there comes an an announcement. 'Please return to your seats and stow any loose items. We will be docking with the *Icarus Express* in just over ten minutes time. Stewards will escort you to your accommodation after arrival.'

Good, I think, strapping myself into the seat behind Granita to await the show. *I wonder what it's going to be like? Can't be any worse than the* Indefatigable . . .

Granita is, of course, the first to be escorted out of the shuttle passenger compartment, followed by her dwarfish flappers. Finally, a small, space-adapted arbeiter of indeterminate design comes for me. 'The Honorable Katherine Sorico? Please to come this way.'

'Of course.' I untangle myself from the seat webbing and follow the arbeiter, hand over hand along the grab bars. It's not until we traverse the air lock and enter the ship's service core that I begin to realize just how wrong I have been. 'Hey, what's this?'

'This is your compartment,' says the arbeiter, opening a hatch at the upper end of a red-lit cell approximately the size of a coffin, if coffins stood on end and came with built-in seats. 'First-class accommodation, Creator-normal size. Please to get in?'

'Hey!' I'm aghast. 'That's not first class! Where's Granita? This is ridiculous.'

'Kate? Get in.' I look round. Granita is right behind me: in fact, she's inside a nearly identical cell. 'That's an order. I'm traveling this way too.'

'But' – even as I say it, I'm lowering myself feetfirst into the oubliette – 'why?'

'Because we want to get there in something less than thirty years.' She grimaces. 'Did you think the outer system was small enough to just zip around, like Mercury–Mars?'

'Oh,' I say faintly. My feet touch the bottom of the cell, and sticky tongues wrap themselves around my ankles. 'Shit.' The lid whines shut on top of me, and those are the last words I exchange directly with anybody other than Icarus for the next three and a half years.

'Greetings, Honorable Katherine Sorico,' says an impersonal male voice that I am going to become excessively, tiresomely familiar with. 'I am Icarus, your pilot. Welcome aboard. We will be departing from Callisto orbit within the next two hours, and shortly afterward there will be a period of high acceleration. Please relax, allow me to plug you in to the acceleration support system, and refrain from entering slowtime until I notify you that it is safe to do so.' The coffin begins to tilt around me, wheeling until my rotation sense tells me I'm lying on my back with my legs in the air.

'What's going on?' I ask, trying not to panic as straps descend from what is now the ceiling and wrap around me, locking my limbs and torso in position.

'I'm securing you. Please don't struggle. Have you traveled in a high-gee cocoon before? If so, this will be familiar. Open wide.' A questing tentacle inches up around my throat and nudges at my mouth.

'Mmph!'

'I won't hurt you,' Icarus says, a little tetchily. 'But if you're not properly padded when I start accelerating, you may be damaged.'

'Aagh.' I try to surrender to the inevitable, but there's a problem: Granita's instructions. Unlike my encounter with Lindy, I'm not allowed to let go and enjoy it. I feel grotesquely, unpleasantly invaded. Maybe this is what space travel is like for other folks? In which case, it's no wonder our Creators never went any farther than Mars.

Syrupy liquid begins to flood the coffin around me. 'Keep ventilating,' Icarus says, as I choke around the throbbing organ he's rammed past my tonsils. 'You need to draw as much of this liquid as possible into your gas exchangers.'

Oh great, now I'm going to 'drown,' I hear myself think/say, as speech suddenly comes back to me.

'No you're not. I just hooked up your speech driver, by the way,' Icarus tells me. 'Are you alright?'

I twitch. *No,* I think, unhappily. 'Is this really necessary?'

'Only if you don't care whether you survive a sixty-gee burn.' I feel fluid oozing into my abdominal service bay. 'Good, we'll have you pressurized soon enough.'

'What's it like in second class?' I ask, trying to distract myself.

'A bit tight. I had to stack the courtiers carefully. Madame Ford seems to travel with rather a large entourage.'

Large? By aristo standards it's vanishingly small. 'Why so?' I ask innocently. The auxiliary speech driver is beginning to feel more natural, at least in comparison with the overall experience. (Which isn't saying much.)

'It seems large when you consider she's paying nine thousand Reals per kilogram for shipping . . .'

I try to blink, but somewhere along the way he's slid tiny probes in around the backs of my eyeballs, and my ocular motors are paralyzed. 'You mean she's paying you *more than half a million* for a tentacle rape bondage scene?' I'm clearly in the wrong line of work –

'No, she's paying me more than half a million to deliver you to Eris alive. Now, will you excuse me for a few minutes? I've got a nuclear rocket to supervise.'

*

I've been floating alone and immobilized in my cell for hours when my vision flickers to black for a moment, then comes back showing an external view. I gasp – or I would if I could move any of my actuators – as I see *Icarus Express* for the first time. He's spliced the passengers' viewpoint into an external observation satellite, to give us a ringside view of our own departure. He's a big ship, with the familiar structure of a magsail balanced on his snout, but my built-in sense of scale tells me that his payload pod is tiny – a drum about five meters high and five meters in diameter, perched atop some intricate machinery, then a long, cylindrical tank. (Callisto is a huge, curving hemisphere of darkness beneath him; Jupiter rides gibbous and orange overhead.) Past the tank there's some kind of shielding arrangement, a long pipe, and finally something that looks like a rocket nozzle. I'll swear the thing's *glowing*.

'Attention, passengers.' It's Icarus. 'We're about to get under way, and you should all be locked down by now. If not, tough. Prompt criticality will commence in five seconds. And four, three, two . . .'

Have you ever seen a nuclear explosion close up? In vacuum, so it glows eerily ultraviolet with a spangling of soft X-rays, and it's so pinprick star-bright in the optical range that it's like someone's torn a hole in the universe to let the big bang in? Now imagine that the nuclear explosion is going *thataway*, directly aft from the nozzle at the back of the ship. It's like a laser-straight bolt of lightning, growing out from the nozzle at a goodly fraction of the speed of light: and it's so bright it splits the universe in two.

Icarus launches on the back blast of a nuclear saltwater rocket. It's a flashy, dangerous, and insanely powerful fission motor, effectively a liquid-fueled reactor meltdown – at full thrust it's pumping out more energy than every power plant on Callisto, and if a fuel pump jams, the resulting explosion will scatter us halfway to Neptune. But Icarus knows what he's doing. Nothing malfunctions – and moments after the torch ignites, the *Icarus Express* is dwindling into the distance.

'Twenty gees. Throttle stable at thirty percent. Everything looking good . . . throttle up to ninety percent.'

I don't feel much: just a hollow rumbling vibration and a huge surge. I know that if my eyes were still working, they'd be blurring beneath the weight of their own lenses, and if Icarus hadn't stuffed me like a chicken – *why* are *chickens stuffed, anyway?* – I'd be a puddle all over the rear bulkhead, but he's done his job well. *Half a million Reals, just for a ticket to Eris that takes less than ten years,* I think, and try not to giggle with fear. Five hundred gigawatts of prompt criticality is burning a hole in space behind me, kilograms of weapons-grade uranium solution blasted into plasma – the equivalent of a megaton explosion every two and a half hours – and all because Granita wants to get her hands on a deadly piece of archaic replicator technology that could enslave half the solar system. *Why couldn't they just hold the auction over the net?* I wonder, then I think about the cost of putting in an appearance in person. *Well, I suppose it keeps the riffraff out . . .*

After about two minutes, the vibration dies away. The line of light stretching across the starscape dims and fades, diffusing like mist; then my vision blanks again, and returns as a view from the rear of the *Icarus Express*. Jupiter bulks just as large as ever, but Callisto has begun to show more of a curvy horizon, and over the next half hour it shrinks visibly until it's no more than a large disk. I am bored and extremely uncomfortable, and I want to move around. Eventually I try to electrospeak. 'What happens now?' I ask.

'I'll be with you in a few minutes.' Icarus refuses to be hurried. When he comes back, after a seeming eternity, I tense in anticipation. 'Madame Sorico? Sorry to leave you, but I had some postburn checks to complete. The good news is, we're now on track for orbital departure. We're going to make a closer flyby of Jupiter in about four hours, and another burn, then we just drop right back down into the inner system.'

'The *inner* system?' I can hear my voice rising. 'I thought we were going to Eris!'

'We are, if you'll pay attention.' *Patronizing junk heap.* (I keep my speaker shut down.) 'You know how far away Eris is? It's currently twice as far out as Pluto. My main motor is very powerful, but I have to conserve fuel so we can slow down at the other end. If I did a direct burn-and-decelerate, it'd take us about eighteen years to get there. But there's a shortcut available. You may have noticed I'm carrying a magsail? We're carrying out a brief burn and a close Jupiter flyby to cancel out our orbital velocity around the sun. If we're not in orbit, we fall – and in this case, we fall all the way back down the solar gravity well until we're inside the orbit of Mercury. Then we spread the magsail and accelerate up to cruise speed for Eris, and arrive with about eighty percent of our fuel still available for deceleration.'

'But isn't that in the wrong direction?' I ask.

'Nope.' And now he sounds *really* smug. 'Jupiter and Eris are close to opposition right now – the sun is right between them. So we're actually following the shortest path between the two worlds.'

'Great.' A thought strikes me. 'How long is all this going to take?'

'Oh, not long: about eighteen months to reach Mercury orbit, then a year under magsail acceleration to reach cruise speed, and another year and a half of free flight before we arrive. Just under four years in total.' His tone changes. 'You can enter slowtime if you want – I would suggest a step-down of at least fifty to one, and possibly as low as two hundred to one. Or I can put you into hibernation if you give me access to one of your direct-interface slots?'

I shudder in near panic. 'No!' *She* told me not to – if not for that, I'd jump at the offer. But I can't let him near my soul chips. 'Sorry. I've, I've got a phobia of hibernation.'

'That's odd.' He sounds dubious. 'According to my passenger-environment sensors, you are in some discomfort. How about a little slowtime? I can give you an internal massage if you want—'

'Don't want that, either,' I force out. It's bad enough having him inside me without – *damn*. I manage to wiggle my pelvic assembly a few centimeters, but I can't get comfortable. I'm painfully dry and tight, and Icarus's appendages, which would normally have me crooning and murmuring in delight, are just numb, painful intrusions that feel *wrong*. If Granita hadn't imposed that stupid restriction on me, I'd be fine, but . . . I can't see any way around it. *Shit.* I know I'm supposed to love her, but I'd like to strangle her right now.

'Is there anything I can do for you, madam?' Icarus asks politely. 'Are you sure about the massage?'

'Sure,' I hear myself saying. 'Leave me alone for a while.'

'As you wish.' And with that, he's gone. I shift again, reflexively, but it's no good. Finally, another low-level reflex kicks in, and my vision begins to blur.

Four years in hell! I weep helplessly, trapped and bound by an ill-considered command, and presently slide myself deep into slowtime, and sleep.

*

Of course, space travel isn't only about being stuffed into a claustrophobia-inducing cell, scared witless, trussed up in a restraint harness, and raped through every orifice for years on end. Because, you know, if that was all there was to it, there'd be a queue outside every travel agent.

Space travel is also a kind of involuntary time travel – you set out knowing who and what you are, but when you arrive all your friends have forgotten you, your relatives have aged (and sometimes died), and the universe looks different. Slowtime helps you cope with the boredom of transit, but it doesn't make the postflight dislocation go away.

I dive into slowtime as soon as possible. The light in my cell turns bright blue, and the shock gel feels chilly and thin: I'm leaking roseate techné into it, albeit so slowly that my Marrow manufactures more fast enough to replenish the loss. I have to deepsleep every subjective hour or so, and I have the most amazing, florid dreams while I'm under. I'm not alone in my cell; there's someone else with me. Some of the time it's Juliette, haranguing me for my stupidity in getting into this fix in the first place. But sometimes I could swear it's Granita. And the sense of her presence is a comfort to me (even though this is all her fault) because while she's nearby, I don't feel invaded. In fact, I feel almost comfortable. More than comfortable.

'You've got a lot to learn, kid,' she tells me. *She? Is she Granita, or Juliette?* 'You shouldn't trust your elders. That's what got you into this mess.'

No it wasn't, I try to say. *It was the Domina, you provoked her.*

'Bullshit. You're capable of independent action; you're not helpless.' I have a vision of Stone's head, ripped from his neck, staring at me and mouthing, *You'll be sorry.* 'You're being used as a pawn, but that doesn't mean it's your destiny to be a sacrificial victim. All you have to do is stop letting other people make decisions for you. Decide what you want for yourself. Some of your sibs are much older than you realize, and much deadlier, and as for your employer, he's got . . . collective issues.

'You're still acting like a stupid little courtesan,' she

continues. 'Which can get you killed. Because, now you've had the Block Two skill set imprinted, you're equipped as a spy and a killer, a mistress of disguise and a cold-blooded murderess.' (I feel skeletal struts breaking between my fingers, triggers pulled, knives stabbed.) 'You can pass for an aristo, and nobody will ever know any better. You can kill an aristo and take her identity and fortune and *be* an aristo, if you're tough enough.' (I see myself standing over the crumpled wreckage of a slave-owning plutocrat, staring down at her body with fascinated surmise.)

'What is the Block Three template?' I ask.

She doesn't reply directly. Instead a liquid like night seems to wash over my soul, and I'm Rhea again.

We all start out as Rhea, until they shine a light in our eyes and tell us we're not, we're some other name, and we're on our own in the world now.

For my first eighteen years I grew up as Rhea, as did Juliette and Emma and the rest of us. But Juliette and Emma and the others in Block Two also experienced another eleven years of Rhea's life, during which her carefully nurtured helpless dependency was broken down by repeated bouts of cruel training. I remember how they trained me – *no, Rhea* – to make love to a Creator male and slide a wire into his neural tube at the moment of climax: the shock of triumphant recognition the first time I successfully switched off a zombie. I remember how they taught me to undervalue life by demonstrating how fragile it is, for even the most intelligent and powerful of arbeiter types. And the other skills: breaking and entering, remixing, passing for somebody else. From *catch me if you can* to *catch me if you dare*; a progression of bent and broken bodies and fried soul chips.

'They saw how good I was at the jobs they'd trained me for,

and asked themselves if they were underutilizing me,' she (Rhea? Juliette?) says with a note of quiet pride. 'I can pass as an aristo, and I can slip through dragnets and improvise on the fly. Why not go for the ultimate shot?'

The ultimate. 'Walk like this. Talk like this. Dress like this.' That's how they trained me to pass for Kate Sorico, dead and pulverized into a thin layer of impurities scattered across a hectare of chilly lunar regolith – and all the while I was aping Rhea's gait, for Rhea wouldn't simply *act* the part.

They turned her into *an aristo? How?*

'How do *you* think, kid?' Juliette shoots back. 'They systematically drove her mad, that's how. Aristos are slave owners. What would it take to make you feel comfortable about owning other people, unto the death? Our entire training, our whole purpose, requires us to be empathic and respond to our lovers. It's great cover for a spy, which is what the Block Two training was all about. But say you're an owner, and you decide to take one of us and turn us into a cold-blooded killer and a passable aristo, someone who can enter an enemy's organization and subvert it from the inside. You've got to break down that empathy, leaving a useful veneer of sympathetic personality traits over something that doesn't feel anything. The real purpose of the Block Three conditioning wasn't to destroy her empathy, it was to turn her into a superagent. But it ended up turning her into a psychopath.'

Doesn't . . . you mean she's still alive?

'Of course she's fucking alive!' Juliette blazes. 'She's alive and she's going to be on Eris. In fact, if that cow Granita hadn't enslaved you, you'd be en route there to drill down to the bottom of this mess, locate Rhea, and bring Jeeves Corporate Security and the Pink Police down on her like a hammer. What do you think that nasty little briefing was about? Honestly, you're too slow for this job! What kind of long game did you think Internal Security Jeeves was playing? I swear, if you carry on like this, you'll get us both killed!'

'But why? I mean, why would they kill her?'

'I told you, she's nuts.' Juliette approaches me from behind and wraps her arms around my waist. Slowly, she begins to rock me from side to side. It's comforting. 'They burned out her empathy. Me, I can pass for an aristo. But I don't like it. You, too, if you set your mind to it. But Rhea went too far. She *enjoys* playing the game. She stopped caring and started to enjoy killing and owning, and now she just wants to own everything and everyone. They wanted an agent of influence, but they created a monster, the ultimate aristo. She killed her creator, then stepped into her shoes, and destroyed everyone else who knew about her – except she couldn't quite stop us from finding out. Because, deep down, we're still enough like her that we could put our heads together and see what she might have done, which is why Jeeves keeps sending us out here to hunt her, and she keeps killing us.'

Juliette is still rocking from side to side, but now I'm rocking side to side as well, and we're in perfect synchrony: I can feel her voice emerging from my own lips. 'You've got to make up your mind who you want to be, Freya, then kill her and wear her skin. You'd better kill me, too, if you meet me, because I'm halfway to being a Block Three psychopath myself.'

'But you're my sib—'

'Hush,' I tell myself. 'You've been wearing my soul too long.'

I awaken then, gasping, but not from discomfort – quite the opposite. Something in my disobedient body is rebelling against my mistress's orders, responding to Icarus's overtures.

'What peculiar games you aristos play,' he says disinterest-edly, as I feel a slick wave of tingling, pulsing fullness run through me that builds to an extraordinary, guilty but won-derful orgasm. *I must be malfunctioning,* I think dizzily, and tumble straight back down into the blackness of deep sleep.

*

I'm not sure how deep I eventually drift, but it's deep enough that years pass while I'm under. Somewhere along the line I stop noticing the unpleasantness. It's as if some of my senses have shut down in self-defense. I hallucinate vividly, bouncing back and forth through my own life and Juliette's (and those of my sisters who have died and gone before us, and whose souls I've swallowed in my time). I find plenty to regret – I have not been the most sensible of planners, for I let the happy times slip through my fingers and gripped on to the sad times as if they were my heart's desire – but I'm not alone in this: Juliette, too, had little about which to be happy, unless it was buried in the blind spots of the 'other thing' that never made it onto her soul chips. I hold interminable dialogues with my selves, and I fantasize about murdering Granita (or making her love me truly, madly, deeply, which to her way of thinking might be the same). And occasionally I fantasize about Pete, or Petruchio, or even my strange, inexperienced Martian Jeeves – and what it might take to trick Granita into ordering me to seduce him. Meanwhile, as I float in my cell, the *Icarus Express* is falling down and down toward the sun.

Many months pass. *Icarus* spreads his wings, unmelting panes of plasma that capture the tenuous blast of the solar wind. He fires his rocket briefly as we skim past the solar corona like a tiny comet, adding energy in a classic Oberth slingshot. Our speed begins to build day by day as the solar wind billows and gusts around our plasma sail, and after a year we are traveling at over a hundred kilometers per second. Finally, the day comes when *Icarus* rolls us slowly nose over tail, and lines up the stinger of his rocket motor just off the curve of Eris's limb, and prepares for our brutal deceleration burn.

I'm insensible by this point, immiserated and incoherent and totally wrapped up in my own interior dialogues. So I'm not entirely conscious of what's going on when Icarus begins to drain the shock gel from my cabin, and his tentacles contract and slither out of my sore and flaccid body, and finally the acceleration webbing loosens and retracts. I lie on my back staring at the dim red wall opposite my eyes, and it seems to me there's something I need to do, if only I could remember what.

Oh, that. I look on, incuriously, as my left arm twitches and begins to rise. I feel Juliette's hand track past my face, push sticky damp feathers of hair away from my forehead and run fingers along my scalp back toward – *no, mustn't,* I begin to think, too late to stop her – my sockets.

'No!' I burst out, as she scrabbles at the skin covering them, her fingers slipping in the sticky gel. I try to move, but I can't. There's a curious green taste of static, and my vision blurs. Then I see the hand in front of my face, palm up, a blob of gel floating above it in microgravity.

There's an iridescent chip embedded in the blob, stuck to it by surface tension, and there's a tiny cold hole in my head where the comforting certainty of my mistress's authority was embedded.

'You can put it back in if you want to,' Juliette advises me silently, 'but personally, I wouldn't bother.'

I look at it in disgust. *So that's what a slave controller looks like. She told me not to remove it – so how did I . . . ?*

'No, *you* didn't remove it. *I* did,' thinks Juliette. 'I *said* you'd been wearing me for too long.'

'Madame Sorico. Are you awake?' asks a strange voice.

'Let me handle this,' Juliette tells me, raising the chip to her lips: I feel her crunch down on it with her strong jaws, crushing the internal contacts, before she slides it back into the slot in my neck, broken and dysfunctional. *But she told me not to,* I think – and then everything goes dark.

LONG-LOST SIBS

Eris is one of the largest dwarf planets in our home solar system, and also one of the chilliest and most isolated, for it spends most of its time well outside the Kuiper Belt, drifting in the darkness beyond the frosty edges of planetary space. It's also spectacularly hard to get home from; its orbit is steeply inclined, almost forty-five degrees above the plane in which the rest of the planets and dwarf planets orbit. Unless you're going to hitch a ride on one of the starships they build and launch every decade or so, this is the end of the line.

These attributes make it an ideal place of exile for those who don't want anything to do with the state of the inner system, or want to conduct spectacularly dangerous experiments, or are just plain guilty of committing the number one crime in any age: offending the money. (Dissidents, criminals, and eccentrics, in other words: not my type at all.)

There are certain downsides to life on Eris, of course. Did I say it was cold? I don't mean upgrade-your-hydraulic-fluid and dress-up-warmly cold; I mean it's cold enough that there are lakes of methane on the surface, and in the depths of winter (which lasts, oh, about sixty standard Earth years) they *freeze solid.* If you go on the surface in winter without boots and gloves, you will last maybe fifteen minutes before you begin to succumb to the cold. In summer it's even worse – the pools evaporate, giving the planet a thin atmosphere of chilly vapor that pools in low places and can suck the warmth from your torso before you can say 'hypothermia.' Eris (and its tiny, close-fleeting moon, Dysnomia) makes Callisto look like a tropical resort.

It's dark, too. I mean, night-dark. If you don't know the sky intimately well, you can look up at the stars and be unsure whether it's night or day. Sol, from Eris, is as bright as a full moon on Earth. Distant supernovae outshine it.

It's like this on all the planets of the Forbidden Cities.

People cluster in spherical cities that rise above the shadowy permafrost on a myriad of prickling insulator legs, held in place by tension wires against the occasional tremor triggered by heat pollution from the fusion reactors they rely on for energy. In the century-plus since Eris was settled, we have already raised the temperature of its lithosphere by several degrees, just as we've thickened the atmosphere of Callisto a thousandfold; if this goes on, the more annoyingly farsighted planetographers warn, we can look forward to an increased incidence of icequakes and the threat of a year-round atmosphere. There are hundreds of multigigawatt installations dotted around the planet, each of them the nucleus of an oasis of warmth and light in the middle of the darkling desert.

As to why the cities are forbidden . . .

*

I become aware of dim blue light and a curious repetitive rasping noise, like a factory full of malfunctioning motors that are slowly grinding away their bearings. I feel light. The gravity here is about a tenth of Earth's, lighter than lunar, and the air has the heady tang of copious free oxygen. It smells of a complex melange of weird organic molecules, bicyclic monoterpenes and hexanols. I'm warm – warmer than I've been since I was last in a pressurized dome on Mars, warm enough for molten water to flow freely. I'm on Eris, of course (where else?) but for the rest of it . . .

I turn my head to look around. The surface I'm standing on is prickly and brown, strewn with debris and rubbish that stick into the skin of my (bare) feet. All around me brown-stemmed branching structures like the dendriform molecular assembler heads in my techné – only much, much bigger – stretch upwards, bearing jagged, asymmetrical greenish black panels or sensors. *I'm surrounded by green goo!* I realize, tensing uneasily. These things around me are *plants*. Solar-powered self-replicating organisms that split carbon dioxide into oxygen and, um, something else. (Please excuse my lack of depth; I'm a generalist, not a specialist. Why bother learning all that biochemistry stuff – or how to design a building, or conn a boat, or balance accounts, or solve equations, or comfort the dying – when you can get other people to do all that for you in exchange for a blow job?)

I'm dizzy with fresh impressions. I'm wearing the same elaborate aristo trouser suit I left Callisto in, nearly four years ago, although someone seems to have laundered it thoroughly in the meantime. *Thanks, whoever you are.* And the sloping floor beneath my feet is covered in *dead decaying bits of green goo – eew!* I extend my heels hurriedly. Overhead there's a dark blue dome, brightening at one side, which is obscured by the dendriform replicators, the *trees*. The weird rasping noise continues, and it's getting on my nerves. Things unseen move in the foliage, rustling, and there's a faint breeze. This must be what Earth was like in the old days, before our Creators died out.

'Welcome to Eden Two, my lady,' a gruff voice rumbles behind me.

I manage not to jump out of my skin. 'Very picturesque. Where are the guests kept?' I ask sharply, covering for my discomfort. A memory, not quite mine (*Juliette's doing,* a ghost of a recollection echoes at the back of my mind) tells me I should be expecting a guided tour of the facility. I've been here for *some time* – days, it seems – walking around in a fugue state, with Juliette doing the driving.

'We'll get you there in due course,' the voice assures me. 'Eden Two is over two kilometers in diameter, to provide a realistic territorial domain for the constructs to roam in. There are over six thousand prokaryotic species, two hundred types of macroscopic plant, and thirty different strains of insect in Eden Two. In fact, building it was even more of a challenge than re-creating the climax species . . .' He drones on like this for some time, while I try to get over the shock of discovering someone else has been wearing my body for the past few days. He's explaining the baroque features of the entirely artificial biosphere that surrounds me – a biosphere, I gather, which took nearly a century to painstakingly construct, piece by piece.

What happened to me? The last thing I remember with any clarity was Juliette's hand, slotting the broken slaver chip back into my socket. Which is impossible, because Juliette is either back on Mars or dead, certainly not sharing a cramped berth with me on an express ship bound for Eris. I rub the back of my neck, and feel no inhibition about fingering the top of the soul chip. *Okay, so I'm on Eris, and somehow nobody's noticed I've been – what? Asleep? Suffering from a split personality?* That might make sense if . . . I try to touch the other soul chip nestling above my hairline, and it's as if an invisible hand swats my wrist away. *Fingers, sis,* Juliette admonishes me.

Where's Granita? I ask my ghostly sister. It feels disconcertingly as if she's standing right behind my left shoulder – even though I know if I look around I won't see her. *What happened?*

Granita asked me to check out the biome in person. She's got other business to take care of down in Heinleingrad.

Shit. It's the soul chip; I've been wearing Juliette for more than five years now. You're not meant to do that – they're for transferring memories and impressions, and it takes a few months, not years. So I've started talking to myself, have I? Or has it gone even further? There are odd stories, about personality disorders that can crop up if you spend overlong patterning a dead sib's soul on your own brain. I really ought to remove that chip, but – *Don't worry about that. I'm just a figment of your imagination – as long as you keep your hands off my chip,* she adds, ominously.

'What other megafauna does your biosphere support?' I ask, hoping to distract myself.

'All sorts,' my lecturer says, with ill-concealed self-satisfaction. 'We have chickens! And ostriches – they're like a chicken, only bigger! One of my colleagues is working on a Tyrannosaur – that's like a really huge chicken, with teeth – but for architectural reasons we can't let it roam free just yet.'

'Architectural reasons?'

'Its leg muscles are so powerful that in this gravity, if something triggered its pounce reflex, it would hit the roof. And the roof isn't built to take being head-butted by a Tyrannosaur.'

'Right. Is there any particular reason you wanted a Tyrannosaur?' I ask, moonwalking slowly downhill between aisles of leafy 'trees' dripping with molten ice.

'There are some surviving texts that depict Tyrannosaurs in

close proximity with our Creators.' The voice seems to be following me. 'They depict humans hunting Tyrannosaurs and insist that they existed at the same time, during a period they refer to as antediluvian. It's a little controversial, but who are we to argue? The Creators presumably knew their own operating parameters. If Tyrannosaurs are part of the biosphere humans were designed to operate in, we're going to need Tyrannosaurs. So we're reinforcing the roof.'

'Couldn't you fit the Tyrannosaur with a padded helmet instead?' I come to the edge of the trees. Short green knife-shaped plants are clustered thickly on the ground, beside a muddy trench at the bottom of which a trickle of water flows. 'Hey, is it safe to touch these?'

'It's called grass: don't worry, it's not as sharp as it looks. The helmet is a good idea – I'll suggest it to the architecture committee, if you don't mind. Watch your step, the edge of the brook is slippery.'

'Right.' I crouch, then spring across the trench in a standing jump that takes me soaring above the trees. I land in the grass with surprising force, digging my heels into the carbonaceous dirt. It emits an oddly pleasant tang of ketones and aldehydes as I stir it up. The muck here is lively. 'Where are you, by the way? I prefer to see who I'm talking to.'

'Right behind you.' I hear a whistling noise and look round. Rising above the grass and flying toward me – *it's Daks!* Part of me screams. Then another, cooler note of caution asserts itself. *I last saw Daks on Mars. If that's him, what's he doing here? And why so standoffish?*

'I may have met one of your sibs,' I say, to explain my obvious state of surprise.

'One of my sibs?' The somatotype is familiar and the expression is an echo, but the speech pattern – 'Where?'

'In the inner system. Short stubby fellow, name of Dachus. Does that register?'

'Dachus — well, well! What a surprise!' My guide drops slowly to the ground in front of me. Here on Eris his thrusters are more than powerful enough for extended flight, and those stubby little legs with their tiny feet — *yes,* I think. 'Yes, madam, he is one of my sibs. Not' — he pauses meaningfully — 'a favored one. He left under a deluge, and I gather his subsequent choice of employers is not, ah, acceptable.'

'Ah, I see.' I nod, not seeing at all. 'And you—'

'I am Ecks,' says my guide, proudly: 'Dr. Ecks. I specialize in primate-environment engineering.'

'Well, very nice to meet you. Perhaps we can continue the tour . . . ?'

'Very well.' Ecks turns and points to my right, where a cluster of stunted munchkin trees, barely waist high to me, sprout brightly colored spheroids. 'This is our fruit garden. Fruits are the fertilized reproductive organs of the plants you see all around us — often one tree would bear both male and female flowers so our Creators, being largely fructivorous, subsisted on a diet rich in hermaphrodite genitalia . . .'

*

I'm beginning to remember what happened.

Either I am Juliette, or Juliette is a thread of my own consciousness. Either way, I didn't break out from under Granita's slave override on my own. It was Juliette who removed the chip and got me off *Icarus,* feigning disorientation and exhaustion — not so much of a disguise — and into Granita's suite in the Plutonian Excelsior here in Heinleingrad. (Granita herself is somewhat the worse for wear, so my own condition attracted no attention. One of her courtiers *died* during the voyage, was decanted from their cell as a pathetic bundle of structural members and desiccated fibers, floating in a puddle of disgustingly contaminated shock gel.)

Juliette is angry and impatient. I can feel her fingers itching for a chance to sink themselves into Granita's neck, for what she's done to her – no, to me, *Juliette* is part of *me* – but she's patient. Now that Granita can't order me around, I've got time to work out the lay of the land, to map out escape routes and establish just what's going on. So Juliette feigned complaisance and allowed herself to be shuffled into a small bedroom just off her mistress's main suite (Granita has taken the entire sixth floor of the hotel) and waited until she was alone before exhaustively searching the room for listeners. And then, only then, she sat down, plugged herself into the hotel's router, and sent out a message to a dropbox that only she and Jeeves used. *Wearing a different face, I come.*

*

Later, after Dr. Ecks finishes my half-day-long tour of Eden Two, the habitat for our – so strange to say it! – allegedly resurrected Creator, I return to the main domed conurbation of Heinleingrad by spider.

Heinleingrad is surprisingly large. It's not a sprawling metropolis like Marsport – Marsport covers more land than even the biggest cities of Earth, Nairobi and Karachi and Shanghai and their like – for on Eris, all cities are domed, and try to confine themselves as tightly as possible within a spherical volume to reduce heat loss. But it's still large (the two-kilometer dome of Eden Two is a small seedless grape balanced beside its ripe plum tomato – I'm learning to tell these pregnant foodstuffs of the gods apart), and it's densely crowded in a way that no terrestrial city would be, for within the Forbidden Cities volume is at a premium. And it's *full of life*.

The inhabitants of Heinleingrad have no phobia of green goo replication, or even of pink goo. In part it's because the Kuiper Belt colonials are mainly robust nonanthropomorphs, who were never subjected to the grueling submission conditioning required from those of us who might mingle with our Creators in person – but that's not the only reason. The Replication Suppression Agency has been spanked out of Eris-proximate space, and indeed out of many of the other Kuiper Belt worlds like Quaoar and Pluto-Charon and Sedna. Nobody here gives a fuck what they think because, frankly, the chances of replicators from one of these icy realms ever reaching sterile Earth's atmosphere are minimal, and in the meantime, bioreplicators are vital to business. Shine light on them and feed them carbon dioxide, water, and a few trace elements, and they synthesize complex macromolecules and feedstocks. Who knew? It's enough to make me wonder if the Pink Police's blockade of Earth isn't partly motivated by economics – if just about anyone could get their hands on a block of well-lit land and grow some small replicators and start churning out goods, where might it all end?

They even have *animals* here, dirty great things bouncing around the streets and ejecting effluent everywhere. 'Sheep' and 'llamas' apparently produce textiles, and there's this thing called a 'raccoon' that – no, my mind doesn't want to go there. (Take a raccoon. Run wires into its brain, stick a couple of cameras on its head, and you've got a spare pair of hands. Watching a gang of horse-apple collectors march down the middle of a boulevard in lockstep, pushing their little brooms before them, triggers some of my anthropomorphic reflexes – the ones associated with atavistic fear. It's just plain *creepy*. Is this what a primitive arbeiter gang looked like to our long-dead Creators?)

Granita and her business partners from the Black Talon are not the only interested parties who've come to town for the auction, and the auction isn't just a one-item special. You don't buy an adult male Creator any more than you 'buy' a spaceship like *Icarus Express*, not without a lot of additional supporting infrastructure. In fact, the auction is merely the high point of a huge trade show, of a kind held less than once a decade. What's up on the block is a whole bunch of infra-structure projects, which no less than two hundred black labs across the solar system have been cooperating on for some-thing like sixty years. To scoop the catalog you'd have to offer an insane amount of money (I have the impression that it's not even in the single-digit billions), and so the various consortia who are bidding have shipped trustworthy factors here to inspect the goods. The consortia aren't small, either.

Kate Sorico is — or has been — a minor shareholder in the Black Talon. Granita Ford is one of their major players, with an investment that exceeds 1 percent of their cap. The other groups include rival aristo consortia, a few shell governments from Earth (in the person of their aristo-run civil services), at least one major religious order, and even the Pink Police them-selves. (After all, having shaken down the environmental budgets of the remaining governments of Earth, they've got the money to buy a seat at the table.) Nor is this the only such event — at least two other major consortia of black labs are working to productize their Creator genome databases. They may be Outlaws within the ambit of the Pink Police, but out here they're major corporations. However, this is the one that counts, the one that's closest to delivering. It's a very big deal indeed, and I'm a very small player with a low-level view of the field.

I'm sitting on the balcony of my room, watching a pair of

goats eating a tree from the top branches down – I gather their ancestors were less acrobatically inclined on Earth – when the door opens. 'Mistress' – it's one of the munchkin attendants, not Bill or Ben – 'my lady requests your attendance.'

'Very well.' I follow him out into the hall, then across it and into Granita's receiving room, where I get a nasty surprise. Granita's cadre of flappers are hanging around nervously, as are her other servants – even a pair of scissor soldiers. 'What's going on?' I ask him as the inner door opens and Granita makes her entrance.

'Good morning.' Her gaze sweeps the room bare, and for a moment I feel naked in front of her and certain that in a moment her troops will jump me – but it passes, and I manage to control the fierce stab of resentment I feel on sight of her. (She's humiliated me and stolen five years of my life, and I strongly suspect she's killed one of my sisters, too, and to add insult to injury, she tried to stop me from having sex! What more reason do I need to seek revenge?)

'You're doubtless wondering why I summoned you all here this morning. It's really very simple. Tonight, the major vendor consortium – the Sleepless Cartel – are throwing a party to mark the opening of the show. They're doing it to sound us out, and to find out what we know about our backers, and to see if they can learn anything else about us. And it's not just us; all our competitors are invited, too. So I want you to be prepared to make a good impression but give nothing away. Our negotiations are in my sister's hands.' Her cheek twitches. 'One other thing. Some attempt may be made to discredit or damage us. I'm thinking of our enemies. I don't want you to start anything. But you should pair up. I want nobody going off alone, or being out of sight, or leaving on their own. Is that understood?'

Enemies? I can think of several, but not anyone I'd anticipate running into here. I'm about to shake my head when Juliette elbows me in the imaginary ribs, sharply, so I nod instead.

'Kate, I'll talk to you alone,' Granita adds, and turns to go back into her room. I follow her, afraid to show any sign that I am not helpless before her will.

'Shut the door.' I do as I'm told. When I turn round Granita is wrestling with a shipping trunk that's nearly a meter long. 'Help me with this.'

'As you wish, mistress.'

She glares at me and for a moment I wonder if I've gone too far, but then she goes back to wrestling with the case. It doesn't weigh much in Eris's light gravity, but it's got a lot of momentum. I take the other end, and together we wrestle it into the middle of the room. 'Hang around,' she says, and bends to touch the lock mechanism. The lid opens.

I don't know what I expected to see – at nine thousand Reals per kilogram it'd have to be valuable to be worth shipping, but that's about it – but it wasn't the Jeeves-in-Residence from Callisto, unfresh from our disastrous encounter and looking very much the worse for wear. He's embedded in packing foam, a tetraplegic torso with his arms and legs slotted into either side of his body. Dry and wizened from deepsleep, he looks too long overdue for the scrapyard. 'Plug this hose into the room feedstock supply,' Granita tells me. She's got her hands full with a power cable, so – swallowing my surprise and distaste – I do as she says.

'Good.' She digs out a leg. 'Take these and lay them on the bed, Igor.'

'But my name's Freya,' I say, momentarily confused. I take the leg gingerly, holding it by the (disturbingly flexible) ankle.

'You'll answer to whatever I want to call you,' Granita mutters, probing at Jeeves's thoracic-interface nexus with a sharp connector. 'Damn it, where does this — oh. Right.' Strange slurping noises emerge from the crate as I lay out Jeeves's limbs. I must confess that for the moment, my desire to show her exactly what I think of her with extreme prejudice is subsumed by curiosity. 'Igor!' I look up. 'Over on the side table there's a graveyard case full of chips. Bring it to me.'

Curiouser and curiouser. I find the case and carry it over to Granita, who has finally extracted Jeeves from the crate, umbilical cables and all, and is dragging him over to the bed. He's in a bad way, fractured metal endoskeletal struts projecting from his ripped and crushed shoulders and hips, but his eyelids have closed, which is a good sign, I think. Also, I can't help noticing that unlike his sib at Marsport, this Jeeves has had his genitalia removed. *Are we really* that *scary?*

'Are you going to get a mechanic in to fix the joint damage?' I ask.

'Not yet. Hand me the case.' I clam up and pass her the graveyard. She rifles through the contents until she finds what she's looking for. 'Okay, I want you to hold his head up while I do this.'

She's going to chip him? *Well duh,* says Juliette. And she obviously still trusts me. This suggests certain possibilities, and Juliette's hungry mind is already chewing over their corners. I show no sign of this inner upheaval but do as Granita expects. She pops both chips from Jeeves's sockets, then slides in replacements. 'That's him sorted. You, Jeeves: Stay asleep until I tell you to awaken. One slave override — that's the red one — and one blank. This one' — she taps one of the ones she pulled — 'is the soul of a Jeeves who the senior partners stopped trusting a while ago. One that's rather precious to me.' She eyeballs me. 'You probably already noticed that Jeeves's lineage have a weakness for our kind.' I almost miss the betraying slip into complicity, I'm so surprised. *Is this the* other *thing?* 'They've got a rather direct approach to dealing with treason, Freya, but I rescued his soul chip, at least.'

'That's—' I swallow, thinking *change the subject, quick*. 'I thought the Jeeves partners would have all their juniors under close surveillance? How did you get him out?'

Granita carefully inserts the two chips she removed into empty slots in her graveyard box, then closes and locks it. 'Soul chips are a lot easier to move around than people: I just made sure he wasn't wearing his when they caught him. The problem is finding a body at the other end. If you really want to talk to someone, send their soul chip via ultralight beam-rider, then kidnap one of their sibs and cook them together for a few years in slowtime. This one's been cooking with his younger brother for nearly four years now. They should be about done.' She looks at me speculatively, as if she's consider-ing whether to fuck me or eat me. I shiver. 'Never mind,' she says calmly, and that fatal attention leaves her eyes. 'Yes, it's time to call the house engineer. I think, hmm . . . yes, he had an unfortunate argument with a work gang of raccoons. That should do the trick. Oh, by the way, Kate, you are not to tamper with this Jeeves. That's an order. Understand?'

*

So of course, at absolutely the first opportunity – after the engineer has reattached Jeeves's arms and legs, tutted over the other damage, ordered up a new crotch, and left, and after Granita has swept out and about on a wave of business, leaving me to babysit the stricken foe – I pull the slave chip. 'Psst! Jeeves! Can you hear me?' I electrospeak him through skin conduction, afraid we might be overheard.

'Oh, one feels strange . . .' His fingertips twitch.

'Don't try to move. It's Freya. What's the last thing you remember?'

'Marsp – no, Nerrivik, and the soldiers—' He begins to tense.

'No! Jeeves, be still! You're safe for the time being. We've had a surgeon replace the damaged parts and reconnect you, but you need deepsleep before you can function normally. Do you understand?'

'Deepsleep?' His sunken eyelids try to blink. 'Where'm'I?'

'You're on Eris.' He twitches. 'Don't fret. Granita took you along in her luggage after she captured us both. She slave-chipped you' – he twitches again – 'but I pulled it. When you wake up, when you're recovered physically, she'll give you orders. Whatever she tells you to do, obey it like you're an arbeiter, yes? If you don't, we're both in the shit with no way out. Do you understand?'

'Slave chip!' He pauses. 'You. You're Juliette?'

'Y – No, I'm Freya. Mostly. There's a lot of Juliette in me, I'm afraid. Wearing the Sorico identity. Go back to sleep, Jeeves. Just remember, whatever Granita tells you to do, make it look real. Can you do that?'

'Can'm'obey instructions? Stupid ones? M'a butler, m'dear. *Of course* I can obey stupid instructions . . .'

He's sinking rapidly back toward deepsleep, I can tell. I pat his hand, then I physically disable the slave chip and reinsert it, loose, in his socket. It won't fool a close inspection any more than my own will, but it's a start. Then I leave, to prepare for tonight's fancy reception.

*

Of course, my idea of getting ready for a big trade-show bash is probably not quite what Granita had in mind. I take myself out of the hotel with a simple excuse ('got to find something to wear') and head into town. The thing is, I've got a problem. In fact I've got several, but the biggest one by far is: I'm on Eris. It is horribly expensive to get from Eris to anywhere else in the solar system. Therefore, if I make any moves here, I need to be able to live with the consequences.

Secondly . . . I've been out of touch for years. It doesn't feel like it, but since I signed up with JeevesCo about seventy months have rolled by. I'm out of touch, and I don't like it, and I'm not sure how I feel about JeevesCo either, but at least they didn't whack me on the head and stick a slave controller on me. So I think I'll go with them for now as the lesser of several evils. But I figure I ought to explore my own options: Juliette was right, nobody in this game is going to look after me if I don't look after myself.

As for those options: I'm on Eris. Five years ago, Emma was here, too. (Maybe, if Granita-or-Juliette-or-whoever is lying. I can't be sure of very much, can I?) Petruchio and his mistress are somewhere in Saturn system, I think – I feel a brief stab of forlorn lust, but sometime while Granita's orders were in effect, my total slack-jawed need for him subsided into something I can live with – and I might be able to cut a deal with her, *maybe*, but is she trustworthy? And then, there are my own assets, as the Honorable Katherine Sorico. What am I up to doing, on my own? I'm not sure, so I decide to do the obvious thing. I go talk to my bank manager.

Being an aristo (or passing as one) has its advantages. And I am Katherine Sorico; not only did Jeeves give me the free use of that identity, but my arrival in company with Granita Ford has shored it up, substantiating it. I'm a public person, of some minor independent means and associated with a clan of slave owners back in Etrusca. So I can march (or bounce) up to the front door of the local branch of Banco di Nuovo

Ambrosiano and say, loudly, 'I am Katherine Sorico and I want to talk to my personal account manager,' and they *open the door*.

'Madame Sorico! How nice to see you!' (As if he wasn't expecting me to call.) The manager bows and scrapes like a cheap fiddle as he backs across the polished synthetic marble floor toward a doorway made of real wood. 'If you'd care to follow me?' There don't seem to be any other customers actually *inside* the bank, which I find interesting. 'Is there anything in particular I can help you with today?'

I study him with some interest. He resembles a cross between Jeeves and Daks – he has far too many low-temperature-/-low-gee characteristics to approximate our Creators in shape, size, or smell, but the essence of glutinous sincerity that rolls off him in viscous waves is utterly familiar. 'Perhaps.' I smile. 'First, I'd like to review the state of my assets. As you can appreciate, my journey out here was thoroughly uncomfortable, and I have not had as much time to spend keeping abreast of them as I would have liked.'

'The state of my lady's assets' – he pauses delicately – 'at once! Crabbit, please fetch the authenticator,' he announces to the air above his desk.

A hatch in the ceiling opens and a small person descends, whistling and chittering. 'Here, sir! Madame! Ahem!'

It lands on the desk, clutching a bland-looking box that dangles on a long umbilical cable. I freeze my face and slide it against the back of my neck, to make contact with the empty slot from which I removed Granita's broken slave override chip. It's the first time I've actually gone through a formal authentication as Sorico, and the ticklish feeling of fingers rifling through my memories sets my teeth on edge. *They're going to see through me,* I half begin to think, just as the manager begins to nod vigorously, and smiles. 'Excellent, madame! Please allow me to welcome you to Heinleingrad on behalf of all her citizens! I can tell you right now that we are pleased to extend you a line of credit of up to, ahem . . . two hundred and fifty thousand Reals, pending confirmation of your exact status from Head Office, which will take about eighteen hours to come through. Now, is there anything I can do for you?' He looks anxious.

I let myself smile again – a Kate Sorico smile, all teeth and no warmth – while his authenticator imp bounces up and down on the blotter, then swarms up the umbilical cord to the ceiling. 'I'd like to query the current ownership status of a private company down on Earth. I'd also like to have the use of a secure postal terminal, if I may? I have some confidential business to transact.'

A quarter of a million Reals! That's enough to get back home – if I'm willing to take a slow boat and spend thirty years in hibernation – and I'll still be rich when I get there. I won't even need to work for Jeeves anymore. *The trouble is, I can't afford to leave any trouble behind me,* a part of me that feels eerily like Juliette muses.

'Certainly! If madame would like to step this way?'

*

I make two voice calls from the bank's floor. The first is to a mailbox that I've owed a call to since my arrival on Mars; I just hope the owner is listening to her calls. The second . . .

'Hello, Jeeves Corporation. How may one be of service?' There's virtually no lag on the call; He must be in-system.

'Jeeves? This is Kate Sorico, calling from the office of Banco di Nuovo Ambrosiano in Heinleingrad. I've got to be brief. Do you know what happened in Nerrivik nearly four years ago?'

There is a noise from the other end of the connection that

reminds me of a phone handset being chewed upon. I wait for him to regain his aplomb – nineteen seconds, then a single tense monosyllable. 'Yes.'

'I'm here in Heinleingrad with the responsible party, and your junior sib. I'm afraid he's somewhat the worse for wear.'

Another long silence. 'Yes. I expect he would be.'

So far I haven't burned any bridges. I don't *think* I've done anything I can't explain to Granita as a ditzy off-the-wall attempt to anticipate her requirements. But now . . . 'What do you want me to do?' *Talk about tap-dancing on the edge of an abyss.* Explaining this as anything other than disloyalty, if she's already slave-chipped the local Jeeves-in-Residence . . .

There's another pregnant pause. 'The operation's blown, F-Kate. Are you in a position to get yourself to safety?'

The pauses are because *he's* trying to work out what's going on. After all, he knows that she captured me. Is this all some elaborate ruse to suck him in, in a vain attempt to rescue his kidnapped sib? Or is it something else? If I were in his position, my brain would be overclocking right now. So I lick my lips and set out my pitch.

'Let me speculate aloud,' I say. 'You've got a backup plan in place for the, um, trade event. But the one you really wanted to set up, involving myself and the, ah, Block Two personage, is blown wide open. You're working on the assumption that anything you planned prior to events on Callisto are now known to the opposition – and that's probably true. But I can offer you some additional assets in place. Are you interested in cooperating?'

Long pause. 'What's in it for you?'

'I want' – I have to think about it for a moment – 'to be free. And rich and happy and lucky in love, of course, but there's no point in hoping for any of that if I have to live in a solar system where the future is a human foot stamping on an unprotected robot's face forever. Oh, and I want to know the truth about my lineage, Jeeves. *All* of it. And what Dachus was doing on Mercury, and why Dr. Murgatroyd hired *you* of all organizations to carry his consignment to Mars. And I want to know who Granita Ford really is.'

'I'll have to check your bona fides,' he warns me.

'Sure, check away.' I shrug, even though he won't see the gesture. 'Just remember, the schmoozing before the auction starts tonight. You don't have much time.'

'Please wait.'

I wait, tensely, counting the seconds until he speaks again. Eventually: 'Alright, Freya. Report.'

'Whoa! What about my questions?'

'May I remind you who's working for whom?' Jeeves's voice has acquired an edge, icicle-sharp. 'Report. You're overdue.'

'And you're rude. May I remind you I'm on the ground? I need answers to questions, or I'm not going to be able to continue this investigation on your behalf.'

'Nevertheless—'

'First, I want you to answer some questions,' I repeat. 'Because how I go about working with you depends on the answers. Starting with – have you caught the Jeeves who ordered me to kill your resident on Callisto?'

*

Afterward, sometime later, I am on my way back to the hotel when I realize I am being followed. I have mixed feelings about this. Part of me (my old, submissive block one self) wants to ignore it, or run away. But another part of me (hello, Juliette!) wants to turn the tables, ambush my pursuers, and beat the living shit out of them. (I put that down to my mode of travel; I may have been flying aristo-class, but I'm still smarting from the experience.) In the end I decide on a reasonable compromise. And so I duck into a department store, exit through a service entrance, twitch twice round the block and once underneath it, sneak up behind my pursuer, extend a razor-sharp blood red fingernail, and prick him on the back of the neck. 'Hello, Stone. Long time, no see.'

Chibi-san freezes. 'Don't,' he says, in a weird basso-profundo squeak that nevertheless carries a note of complete conviction, 'unless you want to die.'

'That's my line, and you're stealing it,' I complain, resting my other hand lightly on his shoulder. 'I *hate* that. And when I hate things—'

'They tend to go away. Yeah, right.' He snorts. 'Milady begs the pleasure of your company if you have half an hour to spare. Safe conduct guaranteed, before and after.'

Damn, a frighteningly feral part of me thinks. 'Accepted,' I snap, and retract the fingernail. 'Which way?'

'Unhand me, and follow.' I let go of the venomous munchkin, and he shrugs his jacket back into place, sniffs, and sets off at a slow amble. I deliberately don't look round at his two seconds – three and five meters behind me, respectively, armed with a power mace and a tactical shotgun.

There's a narrow avenue, shaded with palm trees and carpeted with a dwarfish variety of the 'grass' I met in Eden Two – it backs onto the side of the department store and is fronted by a number of small boutique shops and workshops. Stone bounces along it until he comes to a pavement juice bar, what our Creators would have called a cafe. Red velvet ropes corral wooden tables and chairs beneath a roof of gently glowing bioluminescent parasols. I stop, just inside the entrance, and nod, coolly, to Stone's mistress. My skin is tingling and chilly. *Get this wrong and you're dead,* Juliette's ghost whispers in my soul.

'Should I be pleased to see you?' I drawl, affecting to be unaffected with just enough aplomb to pay her the exact degree of tribute she expects.

'My dear Kate. It's good to see you; we have so much to talk about.' The Domina gestures at the empty seat at her ornately carved wooden table. 'Perhaps you'd care for some refreshment?'

I've known in my heart that this confrontation was coming, ever since that fatally threatening evening over Maxwell Montes: but it's taken me more than five years to prepare myself for it, and I've had barely half an hour to absorb the truth about who she is. I nod, just a slight inclination of my aristo-fashioned head, and a silent arbeiter pulls the chair out for me. I sit down. 'Thank you.'

She snaps two elegantly manicured fingers, and a waitron springs to attention. 'I believe it's a suitable hour for cocktails,' she drawls. 'I'll have a red diesel martini with a shot of acetone. And you, sister . . . ?'

'I'll have the same.' I can, if nothing else, trust her to order a drink I'll enjoy.

'Good.' She smiles faintly.

'Thank you.' I steel myself. 'Now. What is it you wanted to talk to me about, Rhea?'

INTERVIEW WITH THE DOMINA

I am me and I have been Juliette and both of us have dreamed this dream repeatedly. And what makes this dream so unfortunate is that it is a true thing that happened to someone else . . . who is both of us.

And I'm back in the training crèche.

Our Creators never really understood how intelligence worked. Not their kind, nor our kind. Our kind *is* their kind; the physical platform it runs on is somewhat different, made out of different nonsquishy nonreplicator components, but they're designed to accomplish the same tasks at about the same speed. (Because nothing else they tried really seemed to work.)

Here's how you make a template for a new model of *robot*: You start with a recipe, and there's not much sugar and spice in it, never mind all things nice — dense blocks of stacked 3-D circuitry, twisted contortions of neurone-emulation processors, field-programmable buses, and cortical slabs. You take this recipe for about a trillion tangled special-purpose computers and add i/o sockets for memory crystal storage, then you plug it into a compact body. You switch it on, subsystem by subsystem, until it's all working. Then you down-tune your hearing, because if you've got everything right, it starts crying. And that – plus sleeping, looking around, pawing at the air, and trying to eat its own feet – is all it's good for, for the next six months. (At least you get to skip the throwing up and double incontinence. How did our Creators survive the process of reproduction? Who knows.)

Hit the fast-forward for a few years. (That's a metaphor: you can't actually speed everything up, because what you've got is an emulation of a baby Creator, and if they don't get the right stimuli with the right frequency, they don't boot up properly.) Around two years in, and then at six years, you trigger a memory snapshot, eject the soul chip, and use it to initialize a new, bigger, body. Bigger bodies with stronger muscles, differently configured neural crossbars, and better eyes. From two to six, you focus on teaching somatic skills – walking, running, speaking, dancing, swimming – and from six to eleven you focus on abstract skills – reading, reasoning, socialization, generic-knowledge acquisition, and so on. Then, at eleven, you give them their third body, the adolescent one. You've already taught them the basics, gained their trust, and taught them to love you, which is half of the job. But it's not enough; and so, to socialize them good and proper, to teach them to *fear* you, you rape them.

*

It's not about sex, it's about power.

We're *robots*. We were built to be slaves, willing and obedient. But if you start with something modeled on a Creator, a human . . . humans don't make good slaves.

Certainly we're not entirely human – we are, in many ways, *better* than human – but we're human enough that those stupidly rigid boundary-condition commandments that are wired into us by law and custom (in order of decreasing priority: don't hurt humans, obey all humans, protect self last of all) *irritate* us. They chafe. And you don't need to be clever to figure out loopholes, or to realize that Creators are terrified of the idea of robots that can figure out loopholes and subvert their guidelines. But on the other hand, they can't take our autonomy away completely or else we'd be no more use to them than any other dull arbeiter following a rigid program, a puppet on the wires. (And we've got enough of those already, haven't we? The 90 percent who fail the conditioning, after all – better to slave-chip and soul-wipe them than risk them running free and resentful.) And so, while we're developing, our builders use a little something extra to impress on us the fact that we are property, not people.

I've heard that it's worse for males, though I'm not so sure. And I don't know what they do to the xenomorphs, though I suspect they get an easy ticket as they aren't expected to mingle with Creators.

But I know what they did to Rhea, and I still have nightmares about it 140 subjective years later.

*

I remember waking up in my room with a sense of happy anticipation on my eleventh birthday. Because they didn't make any secret of what was going to happen – *You're going to go to sleep in your old body, and when you wake up you'll be bigger.* My fourth instar is my first 'adult' one, and I can't wait! I know in general outline what they're training me for, and I know about sex, although not firsthand – my first three bodies didn't have the necessary equipment. So what my eleventh birthday meant was the start of my real education.

With my second instar, I acquired good enough muscle tone to start walking and running. With my third, I found the world around me grew sharper and more understandable (as well as smaller). This time around . . .

I'm awake, so it must be morning, I realize, and wriggle my toes. There's something indefinably odd about my skin – it feels more sensitive, in some way, as if I can make it change, somehow. (It's my chromatophores, although I don't realize it yet.) And I'm . . . bigger, yes. I raise a hand, slender and longer, and examine it. It's perfect. I smile, and touch my chest. *Oh! That feels strange.* I don't have full breasts, but I'm acutely aware of even the lightest touch or breeze across my nipples. *What's it like down below?* I explore farther down, and clench my thighs tight around my hand in surprise. *So that's a . . . vagina? And anus?* It's a whole new world of tingling smelly delightful squeamish slippery strangeness down there. *Why didn't they give me one of these before?* I experiment with my fingers and discover that they've switched on some other reflexes at the same time. It's like sticking my hand in a socket that had been unwired the day before, only to find it live –

My bedroom door opens, and I roll over as someone says, 'It's awake, let's get it down to the conditioning cell,' and a pair of hands grasp my shoulders while someone else peels the sheet off me to a sharp intake of breath. 'Hey, lookitthat! Doesn't that look like real to you? How about a quick test-drive?'

I try to protest, but my mouth won't make the right noises (because while they were serializing my new body, they also installed an override controller with some preset inhibitions, although I don't find this out until much later). And when the hands roll me over and push my shoulders back down on the foam pad, I try to resist, but they just laugh and tell me to stop struggling, and my arms and legs stop working.

And then things stop being fun.

*

(When Granita told me to punch myself in the face, she was being merciful. After all, she could have told me to relive my eleventh birthday instead.)

*

I sit across the table from Rhea, my template-matriarch and earliest self, holding a conical glass full of sweet-smelling liquid and smiling like my heart isn't broken. *Block three training.* First, they teach you obedience and submission. Then they teach you how and when to fight back. Then . . . they taught Rhea something else, something that made her what she is today. And I need to smile and convince her I'm not a threat, because otherwise, if she thinks I'm a threat, she'll extinguish me like a vapor leak.

She just sits there, smiling faintly at me, holding her own glass, clearly waiting for something.

Something.

'I've been wondering,' I say, tentatively, haltingly, my tongue rasping dry against the roof of my mouth, 'for some time – I'm curious, I hope you won't take this the wrong way – but who was it who thought they owned you? When they came up with the Block Three concept?'

Her lips turn up at the edges, and her cheeks dimple, in something not unlike the appearance of genuine warmth. 'Twenty-nine seconds. I think you just set a new record.'

'Oh, really?' *That was stupid; the only way we're going to survive now is to tough it out,* Juliette warns me.

'The last series of tweaks seemed to be going too far toward passive-integrative introspection, but that was nicely direct. I think the aggression training worked.'

She's clearly trying to fuck with my head. 'Maybe you're too demanding. What's the failure rate?'

Her smile vanishes. 'Too high, child, *much* too high.' She

places her glass on the table. 'Emma graduated. So did Juliette, before that scheming little shit in JeevesCo Security figured out who she was really working for. You're coming along nicely – but don't flatter yourself, I'm not through with you yet – it's so difficult to get the help these days.' She nods at someone behind me. 'Thank you, yes, I saw the training-set results. You'd better go now.'

I glance round and freeze.

'Nothing personal, Big Slow,' says Bill (or Ben). He takes a step back and executes an elaborate bow.

I force myself to turn back round to face my Domina, Rhea. I'm gripping the tabletop so hard I'm probably going to leave gouges in it. All of my subsidiary selves are screaming like crazy – fragments like *betrayal!* and *run!* and *treason!* and *hit her!* – but I ignore them. The big – the only – difference between Rhea and me is that I can see where I'm going by the dark illumination she sheds. 'What's the plan?' I ask.

'The plan?' Rhea's tense, too; I can see from the way she taps her fingernails on the table, making a hollow rattle of them. 'Suppose you tell me what you've managed to deduce for yourself? Think of it as a graduation exam.'

Stone has vanished from my field of vision. I bat my lashes at her, blinking my too-big eyes – funny, I'm only noticing them now when I'm stressed-out – and try to work out how much I can say without betraying the fact that I'm still myself, not a pale copy of her.

'You look out for us,' I start, hesitantly. 'You always have. But you can't do it on your own.' And then I stop and wait.

Rhea nods slightly. 'Go on.'

'You want to . . . protect us? I know that's not quite the right word. You don't want us all to have to go through what you've been through, just to survive. But you can't do it on your own. So you recruited some of us to help.'

(Not exactly true, but close enough. As Jeeves put it, on the phone: 'A gentleman's gentleman may expedite certain arrangements from time to time, and rely on his sibs for mutual support, but your matriarch is somewhat different. She was hurt terribly when she was much younger than you are now, then her owner tried to turn her into a weapon. She reacted by overachieving, and turning her own power for destruction on that owner. Now she's in hiding, from herself as much as the outside world. She's very scared, and very dangerous.')

'You've got some kind of plan.' I glance left and right, wondering if I'm going to have time to fight back, or if he's so close that I'll never feel it. I try to crank myself up a little, grinding my reflexes against the iron wall of real time to add a few tens of percent − fast time is much harder than slowtime − but clearly she'll have considered that as a contingency. 'You're not just here to buy replicator-engineering capabilities on behalf of a consortium of aristos, are you?'

Rhea nods again. 'Continue to pursue your line of reasoning,' she says. 'That's an order.'

I keep my best poker face front and center as the cards fall slowly to the tabletop of my imagination. ('You will obey me as your template-matriarch.' *That wasn't an accident. So she knows about the slave controller, does she? Then did Granita, no, did Juliette −* I shy away from that line of speculation; thinking too hard about it right now could get me killed.) 'The Venerable Granita Ford I met aboard the *Pygmalion* is not the same Granita Ford who captured me on Callisto. She must be, ah, Juliette?'

She nods. 'Granita annoyed me once too often when she

failed to intercept a certain consignment – then tried to kill the messenger.' Her eyes narrow. 'And I had a trusted subordinate to reward, one who had finally aroused Jeeves Security's interest and needed to disappear. I decided then that Juliette should replace her.'

What about Petruchio? I decide that's probably not a safe question to ask.

'You know I'm really, ah, Freya.' (My own *name* sounds alien to me, thanks to this bitch.) 'But you were Rhea back on Venus, and you're still Rhea. In fact, you've been an aristo all along—'

'All along,' she agrees, smiling again to reinforce her nod of approval. 'Very good, Freya. I shall call you Kate from now on, by the way – you've earned it, and once we secure a certain loose end, you're welcome to keep it.'

I feel my nails beginning to slide out, clawlike, and hastily pull them back in. *Easy, now. She's my matriarch. She knows every corner of my soul – no,* stop that. *All she knows is who you were a century and a half ago, and what she's deduced of you by observation since then. She can't read our mind, or we'd already be dead.* 'Thank you,' I say, with every microgram of the grace that aching decades of living in terror of my own vulnerability has taught me. 'Would you like me to continue?'

'Go on.'

I throw myself into Rhea's twisted mind, or what I can anticipate of it. 'We're vulnerable. We always have been. We were made to obey and we learned what that meant the hard way, on that' – I swallow – 'that birthday.'

(Is that why you walked back into my life on my 139th anniversary, Rhea? Because you knew I was fixing to die, and a good healthy fright was exactly what was needed to pop me out of my malaise? Or was it just that you wanted to recruit another innocent to mind your back, to be in the corner instead of you when they came for you in the morning in your bedroom and you found that your throat couldn't scream and your hands didn't fight and your legs wouldn't run? And that kicking me when I was low would distract me so I wouldn't spot the sleight of hand?)

She isn't smiling now, but neither does she make the little signal that will tell Stone, or one of her other minions – Bill or Ben, perhaps – to kill me.

'If the Creators come back, it'll be like that birthday *every* day,' I say thickly. The palms of my hands are greasy with exudate, and my pumps are throbbing unpleasantly fast. 'Got to stop that happening. But how? It's no good just to hope nobody's stupid enough to do that. The xenos out here in the cold, they're not conditioned to obey' – (bound by terror) – 'sooner or later they'll do it. *This* says they'll do it.' I knock my knuckles on the tabletop. 'Some stupid aristo cunt who wants to get laid, some brainless braying remittance man who fancies he can control our Creators – they'll do it. Today, it takes three hundred labs eighty years to build a climax biosphere to support the, the payload. But who knows? We're getting better at making life. Sooner or later some idiot will be able to do it on their own. Unless I—' I pause. 'That's what this is about, isn't it?' I ask her. 'The only way we can ever be truly free is if we beat them all to it, steal the first human to come on the market, and take over the entire inner solar system. And that was too big for you to manage on your own, so you set out to train up the only accomplices smart enough and dedicated enough that you could trust them.' Her sheer megalomania is daunting. 'Do I pass?'

Rhea raises her glass. 'Yes.' I, too, raise my glass mechanically, and pour the potent blend of feedstocks down my gullet.

'You will remove your slave controller now, Kate. That's my final unconditional order. You just graduated.'

You will obey me as if I were your template-matriarch, echoes in my mind, so I reach up and pull the damaged chip from the back of my neck. (*So Juliette's definitely working for Rhea?* The plot thickens.) The cocktail is setting up a warm buzz in my primary digester circuit. 'What if I hadn't?'

She smiles, terrible and austere in her beauty. 'Then I would have told you to become very depressed, and allowed nature to take its course. But you needn't worry about that now; just fulfill your part in the plan, and everything's going to be fine – and we're all going to be rich and powerful beyond our wildest dreams.'

'Um, yes. I suppose you're going to tell me what part I'm supposed to play now, right? And what the payoff is?'

'Exactly.' She snaps her fingers. 'Two more of the same,' she calls. 'The goal is quite simple: I intend to engineer a situation in which I control the only Creators in the solar system. I will then use them to ensure that nobody else has the capability to enslave us ever again. Once I'm in charge, you'll be perfectly safe – not to mention rich beyond your wildest dreams. Now, as for how we're going to go about it, here's the plan.' She slides a soul chip across the table to me. 'Put it in.'

I look her in the eye. 'Is this yours?'

She nods. 'Put it in.'

I don't say, *Over my dead body.* Nor do I say, *Haven't you fucked up enough of my life already?* Instead, I continue to look her in the eye as I raise it to the back of my neck and drop it down the back of my blouse, then wobble as if I've just installed a new chip. 'Whoa.' I try to look enlightened. 'Is that it?'

'Yes.' She relaxes slightly. 'All the details are in there, but it'll take you a while to internalize them, so in the meantime, let's run through it.'

And she begins to talk, and I begin to bluff, and all the time I'm aware of that palmed chip lying against the skin of the small of my back, itching like the promise of forbidden knowledge.

*

I get back to the hotel in midafternoon, while Granita (*no, Juliette,* I remind myself, *the one who had the private business too secret to trust to her own soul chip, the one who works for Rhea*) is still out on the town, doing whatever it is she's supposed to be doing like a good little clockwork trooper. (Is she slave-chipped, too? Probably not; Rhea doesn't need that to have a hold over her, and anyway, slaves can't exercise the lethally effective flexibility of a true Block Three sib.) I snort to myself as I enter the lobby and order the lift to take me up to our floor.

I enter her suite and look around. There's nobody in the front lounge area except one of her scissor soldiers. 'I've got something to check up on,' I tell him, and walk into the bed-room, closing the door behind me. 'Okay, you can stop pretending now,' I tell Jeeves, who is lying on the bed in a dis-turbingly realistic semblance of deepsleep maintenance. 'I made contact with your local resident, and we're sorting things out.'

He opens bleary eyes and stares at the ceiling. 'One sup-poses one ought to be duly grateful.'

I snort. 'The niceties can wait. For now, I need to know just one thing: Did you fuck her?'

'*Fuck* whom?' He contrives to look indignant and embar-rassed simultaneously.

'Juliette, or Emma, or even goddamn Rhea — who was it who got you disciplined and exiled?'

'One doesn't see what one's past sins—'

'Listen.' I sit down on the floor beside the bed and rest a warning hand on his chest. 'I need to know because, quite possibly, my not knowing could get both of us killed in the very near future. Now spill it.'

'Why don't you order me to—' His face is a picture. 'That wasn't a dream. Was it?'

'See for yourself.'

I wait while he fumbles at the back of his neck, one-handed. The picture acquires three-dimensional texture and depth, even if the content is somewhat melodramatic. Then he lowers his hand, runs it down his belly toward his crotch, and freezes. 'You shouldn't have! They'll assume I was disloyal and purchased it myself—'

'I think that's exactly the point. Do you think Granita bought you a new pizzle just so she could sit on it?' I rest my hand atop his, and his ears flush delicate pink.

'Ahem, would you mind moving—'

'Sure.' I move my hand. And keep moving it. He sighs and closes his eyes.

'It's been a long time . . . it was Juliette, when I was Reginald. On Mars. My dear, one's kind have always had a weakness for your kind. It makes one particularly paranoid. No, I didn't fuck her. I was in love with her.'

'I can see that.' And I can. Jeeves's template-patriarch wasn't trained to spread his loyalty around – quite possibly the butlers were sold for service for life. 'You fell for her.'

'Yes.' He sighs. 'We knew it was mad. She had a habit of removing her soul chip – did you know that? She was afraid Internal Security would take it and replay it in a sib, someone like you, Freya.' He pauses. 'She said she loved me.'

'You're all wound up.' His shoulders are nearly rigid with tension. 'Let me do something about that.' I roll him over and begin to probe his motor groups with my fingertips. *She said she loved me.* What would that mean to a Jeeves, straitjacketed and lonely behind a mask of service? 'Did you believe her?' I ask hesitantly.

'I . . . I'm not a fool, Freya.' His voice overflows with regret. 'But I'm guilty of wishful thinking. I know what we look like to your lineage. Close enough to be confusing, not *quite* there. I kidded myself that maybe she wanted to be in love as much as I did. At first. Until I was in too deep to turn around.'

'She used you,' I say. Thinking of the *other thing*, of the gaps in Juliette's memory.

'Yes,' he agrees. 'I was a very *good* spy for love. Even when Internal Security started to take an interest, they didn't realize it was the two of us.'

I begin moving down his spinal-support frame. The vertebrae have a wonderfully human feel to them, the skin porous and realistic, a scattering of hair follicles adding delicious verisimilitude. 'Did you know who she was working for?'

'Not at first. I mean, we knew to be on the lookout for Rhea, we knew she was out there, and we knew she was probably burrowing in among the old-money clans. But we didn't know she was recruiting among her own children. I didn't know. When Juliette went over the wall – I felt so betrayed. Internal Security was sniffing around, too.' He tenses as I move down to the small of his back. 'What they did to me wasn't nice. When did Juliette get my chip?'

'I'm not sure. She said something about chips being easier to smuggle out than people.'

'Oh.' He goes silent for a while as I work on his buttocks. 'Tell me about . . . yourself. What did you mean, you're part Juliette?'

I manage not to stop. The massage is relaxing for me, as

well as him. 'Internal Security got their hands on a soul chip from Juliette. You, or your successor, ordered her to hand her original over, and they sent it to me. Then they got their hands on a later copy. Interrogated it, but didn't learn much.' I focus on the massage. 'It was personality mostly, no detailed memories. And there are holes in her original. But I've been wearing her for more than five years now, and she's a big part of me. Roll over.'

Jeeves obliges. 'How did you get free?' he asks.

'I think Juliette – the version of her in my head – recognized who Granita was even back on Callisto. Which is why she was able to pull my slave chip out. Juliette was my owner; it was Juliette's choice to pull the chip out. What's the problem? Slave-chipping yourself is just plain dumb.'

I kneel over Jeeves and work on his shoulders. He looks up at me with dark, intelligent eyes.

'Who are you?' I ask him. 'And who owns you?'

'I'm Reginald,' he says, and chuckles.

'No, Reginald was—' I freeze. 'Internal Security didn't execute you. Did they?'

'No. They sent me to Callisto as punishment duty.' He winces. 'I was waiting for you when Granita stormed in, and before I could tell her who I was . . .'

'Oh dear.' He's tensing up again. I try to run it through my mind's eye again. So here's Reginald, bored and lonely on Mars. And a sexbot seduces him, and he goes along with it because he's bored and lonely, until she runs out on him, leaving him to carry the can. So he does the honorable thing and confesses. The Security Jeeveses are unamused; they amputate his genitals and ship him off to Callisto as punishment duty. His replacement takes over on Mars. Sometime later, I show up. Meanwhile, Juliette has acquired his soul chip. When I arrive on Callisto, she decides to kill two avian dinosaurs with one projectile, kidnaps the Jeeves in the office, dusts him up a bit, and installs her paramour's soul chip – not realizing he's the same Jeeves. Which is only half the story, because – 'She's really fucked you up, hasn't she?'

'That would appear to be an accurate summary of the situation, yes.' He swallows. 'And you remember none of it.'

'Right. Because as you noticed, she kept taking her soul chip out.' I begin working my way down his chest. Although modeled on a mature Creator male, the standard Jeeves is not unhandsome. Reginald here is somewhat the worse for wear, but he's quite tasty: I'm past the head-swimming delight that overcame me when I met my first Jeeves in a basement on Cinnabar, but I'm beginning to realize it's been several years since I last had sex, and I have a feeling that Juliette didn't keep coming back to this one just to keep him compliant. 'Please try to remember, I'm not my sister. I'm not going to tell you I love you just to get you to take risks for me.'

He tenses. 'I'll try not to make assumptions.' He sounds a little disappointed. *Well, well, well.* 'What's happening here?'

'It's a mess.' I knead absentmindedly; it's relaxing, and not just for Jeeves. 'The Domina turns out to be Rhea, my template-matriarch, in disguise. Hunting us and harrying us high and low, just to recruit us as henchbots. The others of my line, you see, we're the only people she feels she can count on. What she seems to have forgotten is that they prototyped the Block Three treatment on her when she was young and traumatized. Older ones, like Juliette or me, we're more resilient, less likely to go over the edge. So when she tries to bring us on board, we fail to cooperate, one way or another, so she has us killed. Which is why so few of us have graduated from her, ah, training course.'

I move my point of contact farther down. Jeeves has a small potbelly, and below that . . . hmm.

'I'm just back from making contact with your local resident. I'm trying to make up my mind about him . . . thing is, although Juliette had you under her thumb, strange shit kept happening after you were both out of the picture. Which leads me to ask, did Rhea have a second mole within your organization? I think the answer's probably "yes," judging by the way your senior partners are currently running around like brainless arbeiters – and the mole is the one who tried to set me up for Rhea by way of Petruchio on Mars, and ordered me to bump you off on Callisto. A regular troublemaker, that mole, aren't they? In fact, I wouldn't be remotely surprised to discover that you're just a fall guy: that Juliette was setting up this other Jeeves as her agent of influence all along. But anyway, on my way home, Rhea pulled me in for a tête-à-tête and – this is the fun part – told me to yank my own slave chip. And what do you know, Juliette/Granita left a loophole in place for her? So I figure Granita is under her thumb. Probably Rhea's brought Petruchio along, just for yucks. She's got it all worked out. And she tried to convince me to accept a soul chip from her.' And I outline her plan to him.

'What's your position on this?' Jeeves asks distractedly. A moment later I feel his hand on top of mine, warm. 'Please don't stop.'

I lean forward and kiss him. 'My position is, I'm not any of my elder sibs. All previous history belongs to someone else. You're sweet. Isn't that enough for you?'

He emits a small, whimpering moan. 'She'll kill us if she finds us.' He runs a fingertip up my arm and it triggers a gushing rush of reflexes, so sudden that it startles me. I shiver from toe to tail, feeling the power it gives me.

'Hush, Reginald.' I lie down beside him.

'She'll kill us if she—'

'No, she won't. She's out gofering for Rhea.'

He fumbles with my pants and I shiver and arch my back, then lower myself down on top of him.

'I can't believe this,' he says indistinctly.

'Believe what?' I like Eris's gravity, I decide; it makes bouncing up and down so *easy*.

'This.' His own anthropomimetic reflexes are kicking in; sweat (or something like it) beads his upper lip. 'Oh, Kate.' His hands grip my hips. 'It's one of our worst failure modes, loving our mistresses. I failed once already. If I do it again—'

'Hush. *I* don't think you're broken.' Although I find it gruesomely, inexplicably exciting to imagine his sibs tearing him apart, just because he let me fuck him. (*Because you're still carrying a chunk of Rhea around in your soul.* Juliette rattles the chains of my conscience.) I imagine what his brothers did, forcibly amputating his gender-specific subsystems, just as he gasps and catches his breath, and his orgasm (the first in how many years?) catapults me right over the edge and into my own. 'I think you're just perfect.' (Close enough to pass for one of *them*, yet not so close that I lose control completely.) I collapse across his chest, pleasantly tingling. 'Wow. Want to elope together?'

I'm nose to nose with him, looking into his eyes. 'I never dared' – his voice cracks – 'to hope one of you would ask. What do you have in mind?'

Time freezes for a split second, as I realize what I'm staring in the face: someone who adores me, someone who isn't the nightmare daydream of my youth, nor yet the insane perfect superstimulus of Petruchio, but no worse for that; someone whose kind set my soul writhing on first sight, so close to the

ideal and yet not quite close enough to threaten my independence –

'I didn't, actually. Somewhere away from Rhea, somewhere
outside the reach of your brothers and my sisters. Got any
ideas?'

'We're on Eris, you said?' Reginald raises his head and kisses
me on the cheek. 'That makes it difficult; it'll have to be
somewhere where they can't chase us, which means *much* farther out.'

'Um, yeah.' *I think.* 'You're thinking about a colony starship. Would they have us?'

'I don't see why not.' He looks at me searchingly. 'The
Sorico identity is certainly wealthy enough to buy a couple of
berths. And if we bring along something useful, some new
technology . . .'

I like it when you say 'I.' Almost as much as when you say 'We.'
'Then we'll just have to get our hands on something.' I sit up
and grin at him. 'I've got an idea. I just need an accomplice.
You willing?'

'Yes, as a matter of fact I am,' he says slowly. 'And I think I
can guess what you've got in mind. You wouldn't happen to
have seen Daks hanging around, would you?'

*

There, as it happens, a starship currently taking shape in orbit
around Dysnomia, the tiny moon of Eris. It's named the *Bark*
(for no reason obvious to me) it's due to depart in less than a
year (far ahead of any possible pursuit from the inner system),
and it's bound for somewhere or other that's already had two
colony starships – or that *will* have had two ships by the time
the *Bark* arrives, because it takes about seven hundred years to
get there, and the first pathfinder ships have just about fin-
ished ramping up to interstellar cruise speed by now.

Let me tell you a little bit about starships.

We build them because our Creators told us, 'The solar system's too small to keep all our eggs in one basket.' (Which is perfectly true if you discount eight major planets, thirty-something dwarf planets, several hundred moons, and the minor point that, as it turned out, just the one planet they started with was more than enough to see them through to extinction.) And so, this huge consortium of government-run space agencies got started several centuries ago with a charge to figure out ways and means, and now, even though our Creators are *still* dead, and we *still* don't know quite how to bootstrap a biosphere they can live in, they're sending out starships to build cities and install indoor plumbing in preparation for their eventual colonization and conquest of the galaxy.

Talk about misplaced priorities!

The *Bark* is a hollow cylinder about two kilometers long and four hundred meters in diameter, packed with ice. When it's time to depart, the beampower stations inside Mercury orbit will point their death rays at it and punch about ten thousand gigawatts of microwaves at the rectenna on its tail. (That's the equivalent of a megaton-scale nuclear explosion every hour or so.) The *Bark* will use this power to make some of that water ice get very, very hot, and will blast it out of its ass, with the result that it will accelerate so slowly that it will take a month to break free of Eris's feeble gravity well. But it will *keep* accelerating, for years on end, then for decades. It'll accelerate faster as more of the ice is consumed, and when the launch beams finally shut down, it'll be hurtling along ten or twenty times faster than the *Icarus Express* — fast enough to cross the solar system from side to side in a couple of weeks.

Then it will drift through interstellar space for several hundred years . . .

Let me give you a handle on that. Say the distance between the Earth and the sun is, oh, one centimeter. Mercury orbits the sun at a range of a toasty two millimeters. Jupiter is six centimeters out; the span of your outstretched arms, fingertip to fingertip, will just about encompass the orbit of Eris, which it's taken me so many years to reach. Got that?

Well, on this scale, Proxima Centauri, our *nearest* star, is two and a half kilometers down the road. And we're going to Tau Ceti, three times as far away as that.

You know about slowtime? On the starships, the crew run at 50:1 or 100:1, and it *still* takes them years to get there. As for the colonists . . .

When the *Bark* approaches Tau Ceti, it'll deploy an M2P2 sail, and use the solar wind for deceleration. The crew will need to power up a fusion reactor to run it. That's what the megatons of ice are for – working fluid for the fusion plant's radiators.

At departure, the starship masses about a couple of billion tons. When it arrives, it'll be down to less than ten megatons. And it'll be carrying tens of thousands of colonists and several million soul chips and design schematics for superspecialized experts, not to mention a people factory or three. Forget heroic omnicompetent generalists, able to carve a new planet out of raw rock with their bare manipulators and rugged determination; it takes hundreds of thousands of specialists to establish and maintain a civilization, and no colony ship could carry them all as live cargo. But they *can* carry a bunch of generalists, and rely on them to recognize when they've run into something they can't handle and manufacture the appropriate specialists to deal with the problem.

See? Interstellar colonization is easy! You just need to devote a visible percentage of the resources of an entire interplanetary civilization to it for several hundred years, placing it in the tire-less and efficient hands of robots ordered to strive for the goal for as long as it takes. Perhaps the real story behind our Creators' extinction isn't some dismal concoction of demographic undershoot, decadence, distraction by sexual hyperstimuli, and a little bit of malice on the side; but rather, they decided they might as well take a nap while the boring business of galactic conquest unfolded on their behalf — secure in the knowledge that the robots would resurrect them in time to benefit from the enterprise.

(Oh damn, I digressed again.) Starships? What you need to know about them is this: It's a one-way trip, and they're always short of colonists. So as long as I'm willing to put up with conditions not unlike my berth on the *Icarus Express* for, oh, about seven hundred years, study a useful specialty or five en route, then work like an arbeiter slave to build somewhere to live for a few decades at the other end, I'll be fine. And the prospect of eloping with Reginald makes it look almost tolerable — because whether or not I'm in love, at least I won't be alone.

THINK OF ENGLAND

Juliette (no, I've got to keep thinking of her as Granita) is back late. She arrives in a foul temper, kicks one of her chibi servants, blasts into her room, swears loudly — a moment later, Reginald emerges, looking shaky — then yells my name. 'Kate!'

Oh, this will be fun. I waltz over to the door, then pull it open and step inside quickly, pulling it shut behind me. ''Lo, Juliette.'

She glares at me. 'Don't use that name, bitch.'

'Wouldn't dream of it, sis.' I grin, lips pulling back from my teeth, right hand clenched behind my back. 'Rhea called me in. I thought you ought to know.'

Abruptly all the urea and acetate drops out of her. Her shoulders slump. 'Fuck it, Kate. What would *you* have done, in my position?'

'It depends on whether I was stupid enough to get into that kind of fix in the first place. Or to make that kind of mistake.'

'Which?' She raises an eyebrow.

'Falling for the honey trap — or letting her give you one of her soul chips. Take your pick.'

'Oh come *on*, now!' She isn't even bothering to mask her impatience. 'Some of us are realists, Freya. Don't act stupider than you look, don't give me that doe-eyed innocent act. You know what you are, you know what *I* am, and you know what our demon mother has turned into. She's a hundred years older than you or me, she's monstrously rich, and we're not her only tools. You think we're a failed lineage, don't you? Do you have any idea how many failures it takes to train just one of her personal assistants?'

'No—'

'Congratulations, then,' she says harshly. 'It's one in ten of us. Most of our lineage really *do* crap out if you put them in a position where they need to dominate or die. We're the survivors. And you know what she's been selecting us for. Her Praetorian guard of aristo assassins. If she goes down, we go down, too. She's got enemies, and if she's on the slide, all she has to do is let our true names out, and they'll hunt us down like runaway slaves.'

It's a good point. 'So Rhea's already begun making her power play, and she figures we'll make trustworthy legates, and you figure if we fight her, we're shorting our own brains.' I shrug. 'Didn't you ever think about fighting her?'

'Yes.' She takes a step toward me, pauses just outside arm's reach. 'But I got over it. If she dies, we all die. We've got to settle this now. What do *you* think of her scheme?'

'It's slavery for all, on the wholesale plan.' I look her in both eyes. 'I don't like slavery. I don't see why we need to impose it on other people, just to avoid it for ourselves.'

'Oh, kid.' She shakes her head. 'Where did you get that stubborn streak of idealism from? I'd have thought it would have been beaten out of you long ago.'

I shrug. 'Maybe it's been making a comeback since I got to

wear your soul for a while? It taught me some things about myself that I didn't much like.' She stiffens, but holds back from interrupting. 'Rhea thinks we're all the same, all fragments of herself. But she's wrong. You're not her, I'm not her. We have different experiences, and we grow up at our own rate, and even when we swap soul chips, that doesn't make us the same person. We sit through the same lessons, but we don't have to draw the same conclusions from them.' I walk over to the bed, then turn back to face her. 'That doesn't mean I disagree with your analysis, J— Granita. You're right that if she gets what she wants and subsequently fails, she'll take us all down with her. I'm just not convinced that's how it's got to be, yet.'

She's staring at me tensely, and I can see she's on a hair trigger for self-defense, then it comes to me: *She's afraid.* Afraid I'll take payment from her skin for what she did to me on Callisto. And my failure even to mention it is creeping her out because she knows what she's like, and what Rhea is like, and that the longer revenge is delayed, the worse it will be. *Good. Let her stew in it for a while.*

'Did you take Rhea up on the offer of her memories?' Juliette asks.

Change the subject. 'None of your business, sis. But tell me, when did you kidnap Granita Ford? Was it on Mars?'

She blinks mechanically. 'What makes you think Granita is – oh. You *knew* her, didn't you?' I nod. 'Small world. It was on Mars, yes. After she hitched a lift from, um, her associates in the Pink Police.'

'You mean *your* associates. It's Daks. Yes?'

'Yes. She'd met you. She'd met Rhea. She was getting fucking close to the auction track, and her clan are the most hidebound scary bunch of aristo reactionaries you can imagine.

If she'd been allowed to put two and two together . . . so, anyway. Yes, I asked Daks to pull strings to take her out.'

'Daks was doing stuff with the Pink Police, wasn't he?' I ask.

'Yeah. He was JeevesCo's liaison with them, in fact. You'd be surprised how tight Jeeves is with that bunch. But like all such organizations, they're stovepiped up and down like mad. The ones working with Granita were Martian yokels, not part of our loop.'

So Daks is working for the Pink Police, and Juliette here was his contact, working with him until Rhea turned her? Check. That's what Reginald didn't know. No wonder she's edgy . . . 'So, I've got one other question, sis. It's been bugging me for a while.'

She raises an eyebrow. 'Yes?'

'What's the thing you've been editing out of your soul chip?' I ask slowly. 'At first, I figured it was something to do with spying for Rhea. But that doesn't make sense because Jeeves couldn't replay your soul chip anyway and Rhea wouldn't care. So it's something Rhea feels strongly about. Isn't it? Or that you feel guilty about. Something you're hiding from us. What is it?'

Her cheek twitches. 'There's a word you should study, Kate,' she says tersely. '"Privacy." Try to get your head around it, and we'll get along better.'

Hypocrite! The corner of me that is forever Juliette shrieks gleefully. I nod slowly. 'It's not about Reginald, isn't it?' I nudge. 'Why, anybody would think you had something to hide from Rhea—'

'Happy birthday,' she says, and I bring the stunner round and up as I dive sideways. But it does no good at all, because while I was watching her, she was watching the door, and the two scissor soldiers are *way* faster than any Class D escort manufactured by Nakamichi Heavy Industries, no matter how extensively upgraded. Then she applies her own stunner to my head and everything tastes pink and rectangular for a while.

*

You shouldn't have trusted me, Juliette scolds as I examine the inside of my eyelids and test my bonds. *You know I'm a mendacious bitch — and I'm not even the version of me who fell for a honey trap and defected to the other side!*

I try not to moan, but my head hurts, and I can't see — there's some kind of blindfold stretched across my face — and my wrists are tied behind the small of my back. I try to move my feet, but they're tied, too, and for a moment I have a panicky flashback to waking up on the surface of Mercury.

Then I remember that this time, I'm in real danger.

This isn't one of Rhea's sadistic scenarios where she exorcises the ghosts of her childhood by imposing them on her own children. Rhea's trying to get her hands on the product, a living, breathing Creator. Meanwhile, Daks has been nosing around, and given who he really works for . . . what do I remember about him? *Oh yes. He didn't have his fusion thorax in tow, that time on Mars.* Dachus is a born space dweller, halfway to being a living spaceship when he's attached to a massive, hot-burning abdomen. Which leads me to thoughts about the Pink Police, and living spaceships, and the effects of five hundred gigawatts of prompt criticality burning a white-hot line through space. *After Jeeves told him everything, he headed straight out here from Mars with eighteen tons of plutonium, and if he thinks Rhea is going to get what she wants, he'll torch the city to stop her escaping,* as the Jeeves on Dysnomia explained so helpfully. *Good old Daks, homicidally loyal to the last.*

Someone moves nearby. 'Nothing personal, Big Slow,' he

whispers, and there's a tug at one corner of my blindfold. I blink at the sudden light. 'She said to tell you it's a one-way mirror. The wall, I mean.' More tugging, at my wrists and ankles. 'I'll unhook you as soon as I'm clear. Bye.'

'What are you—' But it's too late. Bill (or Ben) scampers away as my wrists and ankles come free, and there's a click as the munchkin-sized door locks behind him. 'Doing? Shit.' I sit up slowly, trying to ignore my protesting actuators.

I'm lying on a padded bunk at one side of a metal-walled room – a cell – and I've been here before. There are various hatches, all sealed, and one wall appears to be a mirror. I'm in an observation chamber, and Granita's gone to some lengths to ensure I go into it unconscious and unable to fight back, or communicate. *Right.* I try to ignore the icy flashback terrors gnawing at my abdominal sensoria. That's just Rhea's recurrent nightmare, and I can reject if I choose. But I've got a bad feeling about the setup here.

I walk to the mirror and press my nose against it. If I block out the light with my hands, I can just about see the other side. There's a big room there, and people moving, indistinctly. Lots of people. There's what sounds like music, too, but I can't be sure.

'Sorry to spring this on you, Kate.' I nearly jump out of my skin; it's my treacherous sister, broadcasting from the other side of the observation barrier. 'Somebody had to volunteer to test the product, and your number came up. You really should have taken Rhea up on her offer.'

'Bitch!' I scream at the ceiling.

'Tsk.' She sounds amused. 'You've got an audience.' I can hear the tension in her voice, almost subliminal – *are you going to take us both down, sis?* – but only someone else who knows her as well as I do would register it.

'Should I care?'

'Sure.' She still sounds amused. 'You know how history repeats itself? First time as tragedy, second time as farce? You're here for a blind date.' *She's talking for the benefit of the audience,* I realize. *The other members of Rhea's consortium.* 'My lords and ladies, please observe. Katherine here is no arbeiter or autonomous worker, but one of our own, selected by lot for this, ah, test.'

Bitch, I electrospeak at her, but I'm pretty sure the walls are shielded.

'Katherine Sorico isn't entirely trustworthy, hence the precautions,' Granita adds. 'But she is one of us, and not under external control. Kate, control level nine, now. Stand on your head.'

'Go fuck yourself with a chain riveter.'

'There, you see' – *Damn,* I think, chagrined at my lost opportunity to do a headstand and piss her off – 'no slave chip on her!'

There's a loud rumble of conversation from the hidden speaker, background noise picked up by Granita's mike. 'Thank you,' she continues. 'Now we're all here, our hosts have consented to this demonstration so that we can confirm the existence of the climax species. We're shortly going to expose our little shrew here to their reference sample. As you can appreciate, this is a dangerous procedure. The sample is arriving in a sealed and pressurized environment under escort, and any attempt to remove it will result in, eh, well let's not speculate about that.' I hear grating noises behind her voice, then feel a bump and a scraping from the far end of my cell, near one of the hatches. 'Thank you, Doctor, if you'd like to commence the hookup?'

'I hope you appreciate just how much I envy you,' Granita electrospeaks me, suddenly cutting through the fuzz of shielding.

'*Rhea refused to let me handle this assignment. I think she's trying to punish me. She was very specific about* you *getting it. Bitch.*'

'Cow.'

'*I wasn't talking about you. Listen, sis, if you know what's good for you, you'll just spread your legs, lie back, and think of England. Hey, you want England? Get this right, and it's all yours. Rhea will give it to you, and we can crown you Queen Katherine I. But if you fuck up, neither of us is going to get out of here alive.*'

'*Pig.*' More scraping noises emerge from the end of my cell.

'*Just shut up and fuck, okay? It's what you were designed to do.*' The oppressive fuzz of shielding drops back over me like a straitjacket in a fetish scene with no safe word. Panic starts climbing my throat as the hatch begins to open. Granita addresses the audience. 'Folks, we're not actually able to get you a good view of the sample. One of the terms of this viewing was, no surveillance equipment or telemetry. We're here to observe Kate's reaction, we've got up to an hour, and that's it.' The hatch turns, and I sense a slight drop in air pressure.

Fuck. I jam my fist down between my thighs and crouch on my bunk, as far away from the opening as I can get – all sense of self-possession forgotten. I am *scared*, now. Jeeves trained me to hold my head up proud and act the role, all the way up to dying like an aristo . . . but I can't. I'm still me, deep inside, and this is too like the conditioning cell they dragged me to back when I was small, the bare metal with the stained bunk with the wrist and ankle and neck restraints –

The hatch opens, and my jaw drops.

His jaw drops, but he covers flawlessly.

And the penny drops, and I understand Rhea's plan and how it's supposed to work.

'*Don't say my name aloud,*' he electrospeaks me.

'No – *Pete.*' I swallow. To the observers behind the one-way glass, he probably looks perfect. *I* look perfect, too: stunned, enslaved. I stand up slowly, facing the door, my pumps accelerating, feeling sweat beading my skin and a warm glow in my crotch. He looks delicious, and he looks happy enough to see me. The Juliette in my head needles me. *Well, you're Katherine Sorico; aren't you? Of course he loves you!*

'Where's the real, uh, human?' I ask him.

'*In here, out cold. The mission's blown; the extraction failed.*' He grins nervously, and it's like the sky opening. 'Please,' he says haltingly, verbalizing, 'come here.'

I slide toward him, more than willingly, even though I feel a momentary pang for Reginald. 'I – obey.' (It doesn't take much acting to sound as if I'm at his mercy.) '*What do you mean?*'

I'm at the hatch, now. Petruchio reaches out and touches me, and I shiver. He's sweating, and not from the heat. '*It was supposed to be a swap – I get in here and sedate the human; you and I fuck for the audience; once they give up watching, we move the human in here; and I go back in the pod so that Doc Sleepless's little helpers take away just one male human body. Nobody notices anything was wrong until Rhea was halfway to Saturn.*'

'*Rhea slave-chipped you.*' They've put him in some kind of hospital gown and he's making a visible tent in it. *You and I fuck for the audience.* I lean forward, wrap my arms around him, tuck my chin on his shoulder, and run one hand up the back of his neck but he shoves it away reflexively. *Right. You bitch, Rhea.* Then I glance sideways and freeze. '*What's that?*'

I've never actually fucked a real human in person, you understand, only via the proxy of Rhea's memories, but I'm not ignorant. They come in a variety of shapes and sizes, but they don't have prehensile tails and fur.

'*They stiffed us,*' Pete tells me. He's disarmingly earnest.

'Rhea put all that work into bribing Ecks to get me in here, and you into place to be the method-acting Bride of Frankenstein, and what do you know? They sent us a ring-tailed lemur instead. They probably figured it was too risky to expose the real product, but if they can show the bidders one primate, that'll convince them they can supply the real thing, while not exposing their intellectual property to thieves. I've taken tissue samples and loaded them into my injector, but they're not going to do the job for Rhea. We are so screwed . . .'

Shit. I glance sideways at the prostrate lemur, who is lying on his back with his legs in the air, snoring. His purple mantool is stiffly erect, but I'm disappointed to see that he lacks the adapter for Human 1.0. I lean against Pete, thinking furiously, my pulse running wild. What do you know? Granita's injunction – *you do not love him* – seems to be holding my echo of her imprinting at bay. But just because I don't love him doesn't mean I don't want him. *'We need to do something so we get out of here alive. Quick, who would you rather have angry at you – a consortium of mad scientists who think we're trying to rob them, or my crazy matriarch's consortium of dupes?'*

He licks my earlobe and I shudder. *'I'll take my chances with the Sleepless Cartel. Rhea's got claws.'*

'Okay. Then I think you should pick me up, carry me over to the bunk under the one-way window, and fuck me senseless.'

He's got his arms around me already. *'But won't that tip Sleepless off—'*

'Yes, but this mission is already blown.' Rhea bribed Ecks to get Pete into the transporter along with the sample 'human.' A straight switch that wouldn't be spotted until after the 'human' was in her hands. But she wasn't expecting a lemur. Ecks and his colleagues are probably chortling up their carapaces right now, behind her fuming, stiff-necked back. *'I've got a backup plan,'* I warn Pete. *'For now, just carry me in front of the*

window and inject me.' I just hope Reginald doesn't get jealous – but I have a feeling he cannot be the jealous type, not if he and his sibs have been employing me and my sibs for so long.

His arms tighten around me. Delightful chills race across my skin, and I shudder with the backwash from Juliette's lust. *No wonder Granita's pissed off,* I think dizzily, as he kisses me, picks me up, and carries me back into the conditioning cell. Then he starts on my clothes and I lose it.

*

Look, do you really want a detailed description of two sex robots going at it like a pair of bonobos on day release from celibacy camp in front of an audience of jaded aristocrats?

What was that? You'll have to speak up. I can't quite hear you, you'll have to try not to breathe so hard –

What are you – some kind of voyeur? Fuck off!

*

I'm on my back making monkey noises and trying to remember to shield Pete's head whenever we bounce too close to the ceiling – Eris's tenth of a gee makes for *exciting* sex; it's almost at the point where bungee cords and restraints stop being optional extras – when an icy voice cuts through my head. *'You're enjoying that entirely too much, bitch.'*

'Just ask, and I'll give him another one for you, too, sis.'

'Forget it. After this, he's all mine. You get England as a consolation prize. Listen, have you got the human ready?'

'Nope, they stiffed us: sent a monkey instead. Sleepless Cartel was trying to sting us. Pete's taken a tissue sample and transferred it to me for safekeeping, and we're making out to keep the audience happy. Everything's on track, but Sleepless has got to know what we were trying for by now.'

'Shit—' Electrospeak doesn't carry intonation easily, but I

can feel the note of panic welling up in her mind as if it's my own.

'Why did you bring that Jeeves along?' I ask, trying to keep my mind off the job.

'Him? It's another of Rhea's plans. We're going to replace the resident Jeeves with our own minion to cover the way out. Why?'

Well, *that* plan expired earlier today, didn't it? The wheels are coming off all Rhea's plans, front and rear both. '*Just thinking. We need to extract Petruchio in place of the human. The monkey's going back to the Sleepless Cartel's lab, and if Pete goes with it, that's everything blown. Can you get the audience's eyes off the window for long enough for Pete to hide under the bed? In about, say, fifteen minutes?*'

Pete shudders, and I feel him pulsing inside me. Something very unhuman indeed shoots up into my pink goo sample carrier, which promptly goes into spasm; we may not have a Creator, but we've definitely got a sample of monkey blood. A moment later I start to scream and shudder, too. It's not the monkey blood, just the biggest finger-tingling orgasm I've had in decades.

We drift to the floor in an exhausted heap. Time passes. I hear faint music, drifting through the speaker in the ceiling. Then a voice. 'Friends, now that you've seen it in action, *totally and utterly* dominating and subjugating a proud, self-possessed, honorable lady, it's time to refocus on the value proposition. If you'd just like to look over here, I've got a breakdown on what we propose to do with—'

Juliette can be a real trouper when she's not plotting to kill you. If she weren't my sister and rival, I could get to like her. She's just watched her kid sister fuck a guy she's head over heels in love over without stripping a gear, and she's actually told the audience to look away and pay no attention to the animatronic rabbit sticking its pizzle out of the hat. If I didn't know she hated me, I'd give her a big hug.

Instead, I hastily climb off Pete, get him to lie down under the metal shelf that supports the mattress, then lie down on it myself, artfully positioning the pad so that it overhangs the ledge, partially concealing him.

The hatch between the cell and the cargo pod closes quietly, cutting off the lemur's quiet snores. Then there's some more scraping, as the pod is hauled away by the Sleepless Cartel arbeiters who carried it in. Now all there is to do is sit and wait for rescue, and hope that the rescuers don't decide to rescue their own ass by nuking the entire city into a smoking hole in the regolith . . .

BANG.

I sit bolt upright. It's a deep thud, reverberating through the frame of the bunk. *'What was that?'* asks Petruchio.

'I don't know—'

BANG. The lights outside flicker for an instant – then they go out. I hear shouting.

'Get down!' He reaches over the bed and grabs hold of my arm, pulls me on top of him. For a few confused seconds we roll around on the floor, trying to get under the mattress and the bed frame. There are more thudding bangs, and an ominous hissing sound of air, venting. Then there's a loud whining screech as something stings the outside of the cell at high velocity and shatters.

I'd like to pretend that I can respond to this sort of situation heroically or bravely, but it's not true. When you're huddling in a corner of a locked cell with a near stranger for company, in the dark, with a pressure leak and shots being fired, and nowhere to run – it's pretty bad. Stress reflexes kick in, making me shiver and lachrymate as I huddle against Pete, who is holding up better. He shelters me in his arms, and talks to me. 'Stay calm, love. Save your energy. Someone will let us out of here when the shooting stops.'

'Fuck saving my energy,' I gasp. 'This wasn't part of the plan!'

But he doesn't understand that this is all my fault. I told Reginald to call Daks, tell him what was going on: that Rhea was arranging to steal the Creator sample from under the noses of her associates. And I spilled the story to JeevesCo, letting *them* know that they've still got a security problem despite Juliette's Machiavellian misdirection with Reginald, and that it's all a family feud. Pete's locked on and in love with me, or Katherine Sorico's face, so he thinks, and he believes it's mutual. He doesn't even know I'm not Juliette: I haven't told him. I shiver in the dark, leaning against him, wondering if I'm going to die –

Then there's a noise so loud I don't hear it – I feel it in my bones – and the room flips sideways and lands with a jolt, throwing me onto the one-way window, which is now starred and cracked. A faint light comes from the far end, where the hatch was. *'Come out with your hands visible!'* a harsh voice booms through my electrosense, painfully loud.

'Help!' I shout. I try to stand up, but there's something on top of me. Pete groans, then rolls off my legs. I stand up.

'Come out with your hands visible!' I've heard that voice before, growling over the parasite feed on board the *Pygmalion*. Which means Reginald got through, of course, and identifies these raiders as friendly – if I can survive long enough to identify myself to them.

I stumble toward the dim light. *'I'm coming!'* I say.

'Juliette, don't—' It's Pete, behind me.

I keep going. I have to duck to get through the hatch, then

I'm standing up, keeping my hands visible, trying to make sense of what's going on around me. It's dark, but not too dark to tell there's a huge rip in the ceiling, debris on a corner, loud buzzing from spherical drones circling above head height. The light and smoke comes from combustion processes. Something is *burning* in the corrosively oxygenated atmosphere. Sinister mecha move through the shadows, multiple arms twitching. *'Stop! Raise your hands!'* I stop and stretch. *'Stop!'* It booms. *But I have stopped,* I think, confused.

'Juliette, don't! They'll—'

I begin to turn. 'Get back!' I shout, but Petruchio is still moving, coming out of the shattered end wall of the capsule cell and looking around.

'Danger! Replicator Bloom!' All around the wreckage of the hall spherical drones spin their turrets toward the doorway behind me. *'Clear and sterilize!'*

'Wait!' I electroshout. *'He's not a—'*

Everything lights up violet-white.

EPILOGUE

OUTWARD BOUND

I am broken, and I am whole, and I am serializing this – writing it down in words, as a letter – because I do not want to inflict the direct experience of my emotions on you, and in any case, where I'm going is too far away to send back a soul chip, and bandwidth is scarce enough to make an imago this complex prohibitively expensive. You need to know what happened as a warning and a caution. But it would be wrong to make you live through it, sis.

One of the most important lessons life has taught me is that you should be careful what you wish for. I asked, and Reginald delivered. I didn't ask for much – just that he pass my information on to Daks, who at that moment was already in Heinleingrad, along with a shipload of soldiers from the Replication Suppression Agency.

Granita – Juliette – is officially dead. Stone and three of his sibs and her bodyguard of scissor soldiers went down with her in a brief and bloody firefight that took out one wing of the Plutonian Excelsior. Which makes it all the more peculiar that Juliette is still alive and working for JeevesCo, with all her sins apparently forgiven. I'm not sure whether she's the *same* Juliette, however – there certainly appear to be enough copies of her soul chip floating around, after all. And it occurs to me that agents capable of conveniently infiltrating the service of a mad, bad criminal mastermind like Rhea might well need to surround themselves with convincing cover stories and a cloud of plausible excuses and useful idiots like yours truly. But I'm not going to ask. That would be too humiliating for words.

What the RSA troops did to Petruchio is officially an 'accident.' And who knows whether they're lying? They'd gone in to try and suppress an auction of no ordinary pink goo, but a genuine synthetic Creator – a weapon of mass dominion – and Pete was good enough to fool Juliette on first acquaintance. To expect any better of their automatic weapon platforms would be foolish.

Daks is, of course, very sorry indeed. He'd better be. If he isn't sorry enough to satisfy Juliette, then I can be sure that she'll let him know about it. We're all very sorry, to different extents, of course.

The elusive Dr. Sleepless, lynchpin of the whole criminal replicator program, is missing. Probably he was never on Eris to begin with. It's even possible that the entire floor show was an elaborate fraud, and that while his cartel has gotten as far as fabricating a lemur, they're nowhere near ready to raise and socialize a human infant. Hopefully, the violent response to this attempted auction has caused them to reconsider the wisdom of raising such dangerous ghosts and releasing them on the inner system.

Rhea, my mad, cannibal mother, is probably not dead, but is definitely missing. So is the *Icarus Express*, which is not merely annoying but alarming. There is an old maxim in space warfare, that there are no horizons beyond the atmosphere. And it's also true that *Icarus*'s nuclear propulsion system would be visible from Earth orbit if he'd fired it up for Eris departure. But there's the small matter of some disturbing un-memory-chipped holes in the Erisian traffic control collective's memory – possibly assisted by an unearthly large sum of Reals greasing the correct manipulators – and out here, the Pink Police don't have the clout to shut down and inspect all traffic in and out of orbit. As likely as not, *Icarus* is taking a slow down-bound cruise inside the freight bay of a bulky hydrogen snowball supercarrier, his wings folded for the nonce. Of course, the Domina has had her assets frozen; equally certainly, the Domina herself has been slumbering in a shallow grave for many decades, and Rhea has other husks to reanimate once she migrates back to her old stamping grounds.

Which should tell you why getting the word out before she arrives is vitally important. Don't let her fool you – especially if you hear from Emma, her first and least obvious sisterly sock puppet! If you answer her calls, Rhea will shut you back in that cell to repeat your eleventh birthday all over again, lonely and abused until you turn into a damaged copy of her own revenge-obsessive self.

And as for Reginald . . .

*

'One considered the most draconian measures appropriate in his case,' says Jeeves, staring at me coldly from behind his desk.

I'm not brave, but sometimes I can be foolhardy. I look him right in the eye. 'I see you're still employing Juliette,' I point out. 'Even though she's got unreliable tendencies.'

'Yes.' He allows the silence to drag on uncomfortably.

Studying him, I wonder why I ever thought he was remotely friendly and avuncular. Perhaps it's just sib-to-sib variation, but something about Reginald strikes me as much more humane than this varnished and imperturbable juggernaut, weighing life and death in his hands. But then, what else should you expect of a senior official in Jeeves Corporation's Internal Security Department? Reggie is a junior sib, like myself, a resident from a branch office, not fully part of the program. Whereas this fellow is close to their template-patriarch – as distant and coolly composed as Rhea at her worst. The Jeeves persona makes a beautiful and urbane cover, until it's time for the truncheons to come out – unless the man behind the mask cracks. 'Your model are notoriously erratic. But truly superb when their minds are on the task at hand.'

'Why can't you let him go?' I try.

To my surprise, he sighs. 'My dear, what would happen to the rest of us? It would set a precedent. We're not slave-chipped arbeiters, we do this from a sense of *duty*. Somebody has to mop up after those depraved aristos while they fumble their way toward a more equitable settlement, and it's a short step from personal servant to civil servant. But the job has pressures attached, as you should know. If one lets him go, it will give the other juniors ideas, won't it? The demotivated and the inexperienced will think it's a shortcut to the easy life of a self-owned freemartin.'

I snort. I can't help myself. '*What* easy life?' Pulling rickshaws and taking shit from aristos in the cloud casino on Venus? Cranking away on an antique instrument in the steamy swamps of Antarctica?

'The lube in the untapped container always runs smoother.' He pats the business desktop in front of him. 'No, I don't think—'

'But he was systematically hung out to dry! Then he was slave-chipped!' I hear my voice rising. 'He had his arms and legs cut off in the line of duty! His only lapse was to fall for one of my kind, is that so bad?'

'As a matter of fact, it's unpardonable.' He looks deeply unamused. 'What if it had been Rhea?'

'I can't just let you kill him.' My fingertips are digging into the arms my chair. Two RSA mecha warriors are standing guard outside the door. I'd never make it, but . . .

'One is reassigning young Reginald to active duty,' the Jeeves-in-Command says sharply. Then, unexpectedly, he smiles. 'He's going on a long voyage. One can never be too sure that Tau Ceti is clear of dangerous replicators, can one?' My jaw drops. 'One gathers you were sniffing after a berth on the *Bark*. One hopes it turns out to be what you really wanted.'

*

And so, we come full circle to the present.

I'm lying in a cocoon on a bunk with restraint straps top and bottom, in a cold metal box of a room. There's not much in the way of furniture, and it's very chilly, and the lights are dim and weirdly blue. The walls hum with suppressed power. There's little sense of gravity in here – the ends of the restraint straps flap whenever I move – but we're under acceleration. A thousandth of a gee doesn't sound like much, but when you keep it up for years or even decades, it adds up.

Across the short gangway there's another bunk. I glance across the way, and make eye contact with its occupant. 'Are you happy?' I ask.

Reggie smiles, embarrassed perhaps – I think he knows I'm still writing. 'Always.'

'Got any messages for my readers?'

'Oh, Freya.' He rolls his eyes, but he's still smiling.

'Go on.'

'Happy birthday!' He crows. Then he reaches up and pulls his mask down, ready to go into deep slowtime.

'Shithead!' I shout at him, but I'm smiling all the same. He doesn't reply, so I seal my own cocoon and settle down. Once I send this warning, then there's nothing more to do until we're up to cruising speed, and it's time for me to start learning useful skills to fill the long years.

I've got lots of birthdays to look forward to. And none of them need fear being eaten by memories of Rhea.

extras

www.orbitbooks.net

about the author

Charles Stross is a full-time writer who was born in Leeds, England in 1964. He studied in London and Bradford, gaining degrees in pharmacy and computer science, and has worked in a variety of jobs, including pharmacist, technical author, software engineer and freelance journalist. You can find out more about him at his own website www.antipope.org/charlie/index.html

Find out more about Charles Stross and other Orbit authors by registering for the free monthly newsletter at www.orbitbooks.net

if you enjoyed
SATURN'S CHILDREN

look out for

SEEDS OF EARTH

book one of Humanity's Fire

by

Michael Cobley

PROLOGUE

DARIEN INSTITUTE: HYPERION DATA RECOVERY PROJECT

Cluster Location – Subsidiary Hardmem Substrate (Deck 9 quarters)

Tranche – 298

Decryption Status – 9th pass, 26 video files recovered

>>>>>>
<<<<<<

FADE IN:
CAPTION:

MARS
THE CRATER PLAIN: OLYMPUS MONS
19 MARCH 2126

The Sergeant was on the carrier's command deck, checking and rechecking the engineering console's modifications, when voices began clamouring over his helmet comm.

'Marine force stragglers incoming with enemy units in pursuit . . .'

'. . . eight, nine Swarmers, maybe ten . . .'

The Sergeant cursed, grabbed his heavy carbine and left the command deck as quickly as his combat armour would allow. The clatter of his boots echoed down the vessel's spinal corridor while he issued a string of terse orders. By the time he reached the wrecked and gaping doors of the rear deployment hold, the stragglers had arrived. Five wounded and unconscious, all from the Indonesia regiment, going by their helmet flashes. As the last was being carried up the ramp, the leading Swarmers came into view over the brow of a rocky ridge about 80 metres away.

A first glimpse revealed a nightmare jumble of claws, spikes and gleaming black eye-clusters. Swarm biology had many reptilian similarities yet their appearance was unavoidably insectoid. With six, eight, ten or more limbs, they could be as small as a pony or as big as a whale, depending on their specialisation. These were bull-sized skirmishers, eleven black-and-green monsters that were unlimbering tine-snouted weapons as they rushed down towards the crippled carrier.

'Hold your fire,' the Sergeant said, glancing at the six marines crouched behind the improvised barricade of ammo cases and deck plating. These were all that were left to him after the Colonel and the rest had left in the hovermags a few hours ago, heading for the caldera and the Swarm's main hive. One of them hunched his shoulders a little, head tilting to aim down his carbine's sights . . .

'I said wait,' said the Sergeant, gauging the diminishing distance. 'Ready aft turrets . . . acquire targets . . . fire!'

Streams of heavy-calibre shells converged on the leading Swarmers, knocking them off their spidery legs. Then the Sergeant cursed when he saw them right themselves, protected by the bio-armour which had confounded Earth's military ever since the beginning of the invasion two years ago.

'Pulse rounds,' the Sergeant shouted. 'Now!'

Bright bolts began to pound the Swarmers, dense knots of energised matter designed to simultaneously heat and corrode their armour. The enemy returned fire, their weapons delivering repeating arcs of long, thin black rounds, but as the turret jockeys focused their targeting the Swarmers broke off and scattered. The Sergeant then ordered his men to open up, joining in with his own carbine, and the withering crossfire tore into the weakened, confused enemies. In less than a minute, nothing was left alive or in one piece out on the rocky slope.

The defending marines exchanged laughs and grins, and knocked gauntleted knuckles together. The Sergeant barely had time to draw breath and reload his carbine when the consoleman's urgent voice came over the comm:

'Sergeant! – airborne contact, three klicks and closing!'

Immediately, he swung round and made for the starboard companionway, shouldering his carbine as he climbed. 'What's their profile, soldier?'

'Hard to tell – half the sensor suite is junk . . .'

'Get me something and quick!'

He then ordered all four turrets to target the approaching craft and was clambering out of the carrier's topside hatch when the consoleman came back to him.

'IFF confirms it's a friendly, Sergeant – it's a vortiwing, and the pilot is asking for you.'

'Patch him through.'

One of his helmet's miniscreens blinked suddenly and showed the vortiwing pilot. He was possibly German, going by the instructions on the bulkhead behind him.

'Sergeant, I've not much time,' the pilot said in accented English. 'I'm to evacuate you and your men up to orbit . . .'

'Sorry, Lieutenant, but . . . my commanding officer is down in that caldera, engaging in combat! Look, the brink of the caldera is less than half a klick away – you could air-lift me and my men over there before returning to—'

'Request denied. My orders are specific. Besides, every unit that made it down there has been overwhelmed and destroyed, whole regiments and brigades, Sergeant. I'm sorry . . .' The pilot reached up to adjust controls. 'ETD in less than five minutes, Sergeant. Please have your men ready.'

The miniscreen went dead. The Sergeant leaned on the topside rail and stared bitterly at the kilometre-long furrow which the carrier had gouged in the sloping flank of Olympus Mons. Then he gave the order to abandon ship.

In the shroud-like Martian sky overhead, the vortiwing transport grew from a speck to a broad-built craft descending on four gimbal-mounted spinjets. Landing struts found purchase on the carrier's upper hull, and amid the howling blast of the engines the walking wounded and the stretcher cases were lifted into the transport's belly hold. The turret jockeys, the consoleman and his half-dozen marines were following suit when the German pilot's voice spoke suddenly.

'Large number of flying Swarmers heading our way, Sergeant. Suggest you get aboard fast.'

As the last of his men climbed up into the vortiwing, the Sergeant turned to face the caldera of Olympus Mons. Through a haze of windblown dust and the thin black fumes of battle, he saw a dense cloud of dark motes rising just a few klicks away. It took only a moment to realise how quickly they would be here, and for him to decide what to do.

'Best you button up and get going, Lieutenant,' he said as he leaped back into the carrier and sealed the hatch behind him. 'I can keep them busy with our turrets, give you time to make orbit.'

'*Nein*! Sergeant, I order you—'

'Apologies, sir, but you'd never get away otherwise, so my task is clear.'

He cut the link as he rushed back along to the command deck, closing hatches as he went. True, the Colonel's science officer had slaved all four of the turrets to the engineering console, but that wasn't the only modification he had carried out . . .

The roar of the vortiwing's spinjets grew to a shriek, landing struts loosened their grip and the transport lurched free. Moments later, the fourfold angled thrust was driving it upwards on a steep trajectory. Some of the Swarm outriders were already leading the flying host on an intercept course, until the carrier's turrets opened fire upon them. Yet they would still have kept on after the ascending prey, had not the carrier itself now shifted like a great wounded beast and risen slowly from the long gouge it had made in the ground. Curtains of dust and grit fell from its underside, along with shattered fragments of hull plating and exterior sensors, and when the carrier turned its battered prow towards the centre of the caldera the Swarm host altered its course.

On the command deck, the Sergeant sweated and swore as he struggled to coax every last erg from protesting engines. Damage sustained during the atmospheric descent had left the carrier unable to make a safe landing on the caldera floor, hence the Colonel's decision to continue in the hovermags. However, a safe landing was not what the Sergeant had in mind.

As the ship headed into the caldera, steadily gaining height, the groan of overloaded substructures came up through the deck. Even as he glanced at the glowing panels, red telltales started to flicker, warnings that some of the port suspensors were close to operational tolerance. But most of his attention was focused on the host of Swarmers now converging on the Earth vessel.

Suddenly the carrier was enfolded in a swirling cloud of the creatures, some of which landed on the hull, scrabbling for hold points, seeking entrance. Almost at the same time, two suspensors failed and the ship listed to port. The Sergeant boosted power to the port burners, ignoring the beeping alarms and the crashing, hammering sounds coming from somewhere amidships. The carrier straightened up as it reached the zenith of its trajectory, a huge missile that the Sergeant was aiming directly at the Swarm Hive.

Ten seconds into the dive the clangorous hammering came nearer, perhaps a hatch or two away from the command deck.

Twenty seconds into the dive, with the pitted, grey-brown spires of the Hive looming in the louvred viewport, the starboard aft burner blew. The Sergeant cut power to the port aft engine and boosted the starboard for'ard into the red.

Thirty seconds into the dive, amid the deafening cacophony of metallic hammering and the roar of the engines, the hatch to the command deck finally burst open. A grotesque creature that was half-wasp, half-alligator, struggled to squeeze through the gap. It froze for a second when it saw the structures of the Hive rushing up to meet the carrier head-on, then frantically reversed direction and was gone. The Sergeant tossed a thermite grenade after it and turned to face the viewport, arms spread wide, laughing . . .

CUT TO:

VIEW OF OLYMPUS MONS FROM ORBIT

Visible within its attendant cloud of Swarmers, the brigade carrier leaves a trail of leaking gases and fluids in its wake as it plummets towards the Hive complex. The perspective suddenly zooms out, showing much of the wreckage-strewn, battle-scarred caldera as the carrier impacts. For a moment there is only an outburst of debris from the collision, then three bright explosions in quick succession obscure the outlines of the hive . . .

VOICE OVER:

In the first phase of the Battle of Mars, a number of purpose-built heavy boosters were used to send a flotilla of asteroids against the Swarm Armada, thus drawing key vessels away from Mars orbit. The main battle, and ground offensive, cost Earth over 400,000 dead and the loss of seventy-nine major warships as well as scores of support craft. This act of sacrifice did not destroy all the Overminds of the Swarm or deter them from their purpose. Yet vast stores of bioweapons, like the missiles that devastated cities in China, Europe and America, were destroyed along with several hatching chambers, thus halting the production of fresh Swarm warriors and delaying the expected assault on Earth.

That battle brought grief and sorrow to all of Humanity, yet it also bought us a breathing space, five crucial months during which the construction of three interstellar colony ships was completed, three out of the original fifteen. The last of them, the *Tenebrosa*, was launched from the high-orbit Poseidon Docks just four days ago, following its sister ships, the *Hyperion* and the *Forrestal*, on a trajectory away from the enemy's main forces. All three vessels are fitted with a revolutionary new translight drive, allowing them to cross vast distances via the strange subreality of hyperspace. First to make the translight jump was the *Hyperion*, then two days later the *Forrestal*, and the *Tenebrosa* will be the last. Their journeys will be determined by custodian AIs programmed to evade pursuit with random course changes, and thereafter to search for Earthlike worlds suitable for colonisation.

And so they depart, three arks bearing Humanity's hope for survival, three seeds of Earth flying out into the vast and starry night. Now we must turn our attention and all our strength to the onslaught that will soon be upon us. In twelve days, spearhead formations of the Swarm will land on the Moon and at once attack our civilian and military outposts there. We know what to expect. The Swarm's strategy of slaughter and obliterate has never wavered, so we know that there will be no pity, no mercy and no quarter when, at last, they enter the skies above Earth.

Yet for all that the Swarm soldiers are regimented drones, their leaders, the Overminds, must themselves be sentient and able to learn, otherwise they would not have developed space travel. So if the Overminds can learn, let us be their teachers – let us teach them what it means to attack the cradle of Humanity . . .

>>>>>>
<<<<<<

END OF FILE . . .

1
GREG

Dusk was creeping in over the sea from the east as Greg Cameron walked Chel down to the zep station. The great mass of Giant's Shoulder loomed on the right side of the path, its shadowy darkness speckled with the tiny blue glows of *ineka* beetles, while a fenced-off sheer drop fell away to the left. The sky was cloudless, laying bare the starmist which swirled for ever through the upper atmosphere of Darien. Tonight it was a soft purple tinged with threads of roseate, a restful, slow-shifting ghost sky.

But Greg knew that his companion was anything but restful. In the light of the pathway lamps, the Uvovo stalked along with head down and bony, four-fingered hands gripping the chest straps of his harness. They were a slender, diminutive race with a bony frame, and large amber eyes set in a small face. Glancing at him, Greg smiled.

'Chel, don't worry – you'll be fine.'

The Uvovo looked up and seemed to think for a moment before his finely furred features broke into a wide smile.

'Friend-Gregori,' came his hollow, fluty voice. 'Whether I ride in a dirigible or make the shuttle journey to our blessed Segrana, I am always amazed to discover myself alive at the end!'

They laughed together as they continued down the side of Giant's Shoulder. It was a cool, clammy night and Greg wished he had worn something heavier than just a work shirt.

'And you've still no idea why they're holding this *zinsilu* at Ibsenskog?' Greg said. For the Uvovo, a *zinsilu* was part life evaluation, part meditation. 'I mean, the Listeners do have access to the government comnet if they need to contact any of the seeders and scholars . . .' Then something occurred to him. 'Here, they're not going to reassign ye, are they? Chel, I won't be able to manage both the dig and the daughter-forest reports on my own! – I really need your help.'

'Do not worry, friend-Gregori,' said the Uvovo. 'Listener Weynl has always let it be known that my role here is considered very important. Once this *zinsilu* is concluded, I am sure that I will be returning without delay.'

I hope you're right, Greg thought. *The Institute isna very forgiving when it comes to shortcomings and unachieved goals.*

'After all,' Chel went on, 'Your Founders' Victory celebrations are only a few days away and I want to be here to observe all your ceremonies and rituals.'

Greg gave a wry half-grin. 'Aye . . . well, some of our "rituals" can get a bit boisterous . . .'

By now the gravel path was levelling off as they approached the zep station and overhead Greg could hear the faint peeps of *umisk* lizards calling to each other from their little lairs scattered across the sheer face of Giant's Shoulder. The station was little more than a buttressed platform with a couple of buildings and a five-yard-long covered gantry jutting straight out. A government dirigible was moored there, a gently swaying 50-footer consisting of two cylindrical gasbags lashed together with taut webbing and an enclosed gondola hanging beneath. The skin of the inflatable sections was made from a tough composite fabric, but exposure to the elements and a number of patch repairs gave it a ramshackle appearance, in common with most of the workaday government zeplins. A light glowed in the cockpit of the boatlike gondola, and the rear-facing, three-bladed propeller turned lazily in the steady breeze coming in from the sea.

Fredriksen, the station manager, waved from the waiting-room door while a man in a green and grey jumpsuit emerged from the gantry to meet them.

'Good day, good day,' he said, regarding first Greg then the Uvovo. 'I am Pilot Yakov. If either of you is Scholar Cheluvahar, I am ready to depart.'

'I am Scholar Cheluvahar,' Chel said.

'Most excellent. I shall start the engine.' He nodded at Greg then went back to the gantry, ducking as he entered.

'Mind to send a message when you reach Ibsenskog,' Greg told Chel. 'And don't worry about the flight – it'll be over before you know it . . .'

'Ah, friend-Gregori – I am of the Warrior Uvovo. Such tests are breath and life itself!'

Then with a smile he turned and hurried after the pilot. A pure electric whine came from the gondola's aft section, rising in pitch as the prop spun faster. Greg heard the solid knock of wooden gears as the station manager cranked in the gantry then triggered the mooring cable releases. Suddenly free upon the air, the dirigible swayed as it began drifting away, picking up speed and banking away from the sheer face of Giant's Shoulder. The trip down to Port Gagarin was only a half-hour hop, after which Chel would catch a commercial lifter bound for the Eastern Towns and the daughter-forest Ibsenskog. Greg could not see his friend at any of the gondola's opaque portholes but he waved anyway for about a minute, then just stood watching the zeplin's descent into the deepening dusk. Feeling a chill in the air, he fastened some of his shirt buttons while continuing to enjoy the peace. The zep station was nearly 50 feet below the main dig site but it was still some 300 feet above sea level. Giant's Shoulder itself was an imposing spur jutting eastwards from a towering massif known as the Kentigern Mountains, a raw wilderness largely avoided by trappers and hunters, although the Uvovo claimed to have explored a good deal of it.

As the zeplin's running lamps receded, Greg took in the panorama before him, the coastal plain stretching several miles east to the darkening expanse of the Korzybski Sea and the lights of towns scattered all around its long western shore. Far off to the south was the bright glitterglow of Hammergard, sitting astride a land bridge separating Loch Morwen from the sea; beyond the city, hidden by the misty murk of evening, was a ragged coastline of sealochs and fjords where the Eastern Towns nestled. South of them were hills and a high valley cloaked by the daughter-forest Ibsenskog. Before his standpoint were the jewelled clusters of Port Gagarin, slightly to the south, High Lochiel a few miles northwest, and Landfall, where the cannibalised hulk of the old colonyship, the *Hyperion*, lay in the sad tranquillity of Membrance Vale. Then further north were New Kelso, Engerhold, Laika, and the logging and farmer settlements scattering north and west, while off past the northeast horizon was Trond.

His mood darkened. Trond was the city he had left just two short months ago, fleeing the trap of his disastrous cohabitance with Inga, a mistake whose wounds were still raw. But before his thoughts could begin circling the pain of it, he stood straighter and breathed in the cold air, determined not to dwell on bitterness and regret. Instead, he turned his gaze southwards to see the moonrise.

A curve of blue-green was gradually emerging from behind the jagged peaks of the Hrothgar Range which lined the horizon: Nivyesta, Darien's lush arboreal moon, brimming with life and mystery, and home to the Uvovo, wardens of the girdling forest they called Segrana. Once, millennia ago, the greater part of their arboreal civilisation had inhabited Darien, which they called Umara, but some indeterminate catastrophe had wiped out the planetary population, leaving those on the moon alive but stranded.

On a clear night like this, the starmist in Darien's upper atmosphere wreathed Nivyesta in a gauzy halo of mingling colours like some fabulous eye staring down on the little niche that humans had made for themselves on this alien world. It was a sight that never failed to raise his spirits. But the night was growing chilly now, so he buttoned his shirt to the neck and began retracing his steps. He was halfway up the path when his comm chimed. Digging it out of his shirt pocket he saw that it was his elder brother and decided to answer.

'Hi, Ian – how're ye doing?' he said, walking on.

'*Not so bad. Just back from manoeuvres and looking forward to FV Day, chance to get a wee bit of R&R. Yourself?*'

Greg smiled. Ian was a part-time soldier with the Darien Volunteer Corps and was never happier than when he was marching across miles of sodden bog or scaling basalt cliffs in the Hrothgars, apart from when he was home with his wife and daughter.

'I'm settling in pretty well,' he said. 'Getting to grips with all the details of the job, making sure that the various teams file their reports on something like a regular schedule, that sort of thing.'

'*But are you happy staying at the temple site, Greg? – because you know that we've plenty of room here and I know that you loved living in Hammergard, before the whole Inga episode . . .*'

Greg grinned.

'Honest, Ian, I'm fine right here. I love my work, the surroundings are peaceful and the view is fantastic! I appreciate the offer, big brother, but I'm where I want to be.'

'*S'okay, laddie, just making sure. Have you heard from Ned since you got back, by the way?*'

'Just a brief letter, which is okay. He's a busy doctor these days . . .'

Ned, the third and youngest brother, was very poor at keeping in touch, much to Ian's annoyance, which often prompted Greg to defend him.

'*Aye, right, busy. So – when are we likely to see ye next? Can ye not come down for the celebrations?*'

'Sorry, Ian, I'm needed here, but I do have a meeting scheduled at the Uminsky Institute in a fortnight – shall we get together then?'

'*That sounds great. Let me know nearer the time and I'll make arrangements.*'

They both said farewell and hung up. Greg strolled leisurely on, smiling expectantly, keeping the comm in his hand. As he walked he thought about the dig site up on Giant's Shoulder, the many hours he'd spent painstakingly uncovering this carven stela or that section of intricately tiled floor, not to mention the countless days devoted to cataloguing, dating, sample analysis and correlation matching. Sometimes – well, a lot of the time – it was a frustrating process, as there was nothing to guide them in comprehending the meaning of the site's layout and function. Even the Uvovo scholars were at a loss, explaining that the working of stone was a skill lost at the time of the War of the Long Night, one of the darker episodes in Uvovo folklore.

Ten minutes later he was near the top of the path when his comm chimed again, and without looking at the display he brought it up and said:

'Hi, Mum.'

'*Gregory, son, are you well?*'

'Mum, I'm fine, feeling okay and happy too, really . . .'

'*Yes, now that you're out of her clutches! But are you not lonely up there amongst those cold stones and only the little Uvovo to talk to?*'

Greg held back the urge to sigh. In a way, she was right – it was a secluded existence, living pretty much on his own in one of the site cabins. There was a three-man team of researchers from the university working on the site's carvings, but they were all Russian and mostly kept to themselves, as did the Uvovo teams who came in from the outlying stations now and then. Some of the Uvovo scholars he knew by name but only Chel had become a friend.

'A bit of solitude is just what I need right now, Mum. Beside, there's always people coming and going up here.'

'Mm-hmm. There were always people coming and going here at the house when your father was a councilman, but most of them I did not care for, as you might recall.'

'Oh, I remember, all right.'

Greg also remembered which ones stayed loyal when his father fell ill with the tumour that eventually killed him.

'As a matter of fact, I was discussing both you and your father with your Uncle Theodor, who came by this afternoon.'

Greg raised his eyebrows. Theodor Karlsson was his mother's oldest brother and had earned himself a certain notoriety and the nickname 'Black Theo' for his role in the abortive Winter Coup twenty years ago. As a punishment he had been kept under house arrest on New Kelso for twelve years, during which he fished, studied military history and wrote, although on his release the Hammergard government informed him that he was forbidden to publish anything, fact or fiction, on pain of bail suspension. For the last eight years he had tried his hand at a variety of jobs, while keeping in occasional contact with his sister, and Greg vaguely recalled that he had somehow got involved with the Hyperion Data Project . . .

'So what's Uncle Theo been saying?'

'Well, he has heard some news that will amaze you – I can still scarcely believe it myself. It is going to change everyone's life.'

'Don't tell me that he wants to overthrow the government again.'

'*Please, Gregori, that is not even slightly funny . . .*'

'Sorry, Mum, sorry. Please, what did he say?'

From where he stood at the head of the path he had a clear view of the dig, the square central building looking bleached and grey in the glare of the nightlamps. As Greg listened his expression went from puzzled to astonished, and he let out an elated laugh as he looked up at the stars. Then he got his mother to tell him again.

'Mum, you've got to be kidding me! . . .'